Nicolas Mathieu

Nicolas Mathieu was born in 1978 in Épinal, a small town in north-eastern France. After studying history and cinema, he moved to Paris, where he worked variously as a scriptwriter, a news editor, a private tutor, and a temp at City Hall. His first novel, *Of Fangs and Talons*, won the Erckmann-Chatrian prize, the Transfuge prize and the Prix Mystère de la Critique. His second novel, *And Their Children After Them*, was published to universal acclaim in 2018 and won various prizes including the most coveted prize in France, the Prix Goncourt. He lives in Nancy.

OF
FANGS
AND
TALONS

NICOLAS MATHIEU

Translated from the French by
Sam Taylor

SCEPTRE

Originally published in French in 2014 by Actes Sud,
Arles, France, as *Aux animaux la guerre*
First published in Great Britain in 2021 by Sceptre
An imprint of Hodder & Stoughton
An Hachette UK company

This paperback edition published in 2022

1

This book is supported by the Institut Français
(Royaume-Uni) as part of the Burgess programme.

A CIP catalogue record for this title is available from the British Library

Paperback ISBN 9781529331608
eBook ISBN 9781529331592

Printed and bound in Great Britain by Clays Ltd, Elcograf S.p.A.

Hodder & Stoughton policy is to use papers that are natural, renewable
and recyclable products and made from wood grown in sustainable
forests. The logging and manufacturing processes are expected to
conform to the environmental regulations of the country of origin.

Hodder & Stoughton Ltd
Carmelite House
50 Victoria Embankment
London EC4Y 0DZ

www.sceptrebooks.co.uk

INSTITUT
FRANÇAIS
ROYAUME-UNI

For Véronique

Algeria, 1961

That autumn, people were killed in broad daylight. In the streets. In good faith.

The centre of Oran was daubed with slogans. Three capital letters – FLN – stood out on the yellowed walls, spreading hope or fear, depending which side you were on. As if the war were an advertising campaign.

The smell of burned wood hung constantly in the air. The young women no longer strolled along boulevards, arm in arm, alluringly innocent. The handsome, dark-haired men in loafers had put away their smiles. They looked cross as they read newspapers on café terraces.

In the European neighbourhoods people slept badly, and not because of the heat. Anxious fathers hid pre-war revolvers under their pillows. Even grandmothers, wild-eyed and venomous, were ready to kill or to die. Oran was a monstrous wedding cake, an imbroglio of bombastic monuments and narrow streets where fear and hate flowed like wadis in spring.

As evening fell, people would still linger in public squares, in the shade of fig trees, to play cards or chat over anisette. But already there was a lack of belief in this sweet old way of life. The men had lost their rhythm. They spoke in low voices and their gestures were more careful. They wearily wiped sweat from the backs of their necks with hot handkerchiefs. Sheets, shirts and skirts all looked perpetually unclean. The sky, once eggshell blue, was now gunmetal grey. And that summer, on the beaches, the nervous, all-enveloping excitement that rose within the teenage girls, the desire that so frightened their mothers, was less intense than usual.

As October stretched out endlessly before them, Pierre Duruy and Louis Scagna drove through a busy boulevard in a Simca Vedette. Pierre was at the wheel. A cool breeze rushed through the open windows, whipping their shirt tails. They both wore ties and Scagna had on sunglasses. They had just finished work and now they were off to do their duty.

The day before, explosives had been left in the sewers of the Algerian neighbourhoods. Nobody knew exactly where. The Organisation Armée Secrète was made up of many cells, each unaware of the others' existence. That afternoon, five people were killed in a deafening blast. The black village shook, but they were used to it there. Twelve-year-old Ahmed was a shoeshine boy, and since the start of the hostilities business had been slow. His mother called him a lazy little good-for-nothing, which was unfair, but it made him laugh because obviously this whole thing couldn't be too serious and soon life would go back to normal.

Ahmed never found out how the story ended. Because about five o'clock, shards of metal from a blown-up manhole tore through his chest, leaving fist-sized holes behind.

Pierre Duruy was from Oran, like Ahmed. He was a good man who had his reasons, and when people mentioned little Ahmed to him, he thought about little Francine. Each man had his martyrs; each found ways to justify his crimes.

Pierre did not plant the bomb that killed the little shoeshine boy, but he could have done, and he wouldn't have felt guilty about it.

'So now you know everything!'

Pierre was annoyed by Dr Fabregas's enthusiasm. He and Scagna came to the doctor's office every morning at seven precisely before going to work. It was a calm place. An opulent silence filled the room, and the walls were decorated with eighteenth-century anatomical engravings. The doctor sat behind his desk on a worn leather chair that bore a permanent stain from his pomaded hair. Together, the three discussed ongoing actions, and Dr Fabregas provided them with information about police operations and army movements. Most importantly, he gave them their orders.

At that time of day the doctor, who lived just upstairs, was elegantly dressed and as pink-cheeked as a newborn baby. As usual, he hadn't skimped on cologne. His nickname in the movement was Coco.

Ever since childhood, Fabregas had dreamed of being a leader. After all, he had always excelled. He'd been top of his Latin class and had taken his baccalaureate a year early before going to university in Paris. In school the other kids had never taken him very seriously. But since then, after marrying a ship-owner's daughter, he had made his way in life. He'd even stood for election. He had granted favours, greased palms, saved a few people's skins. Now he was the leader.

That morning, he had greeted them looking like a dutiful hero. Pierre, annoyed, had gritted his teeth.

'We now hold Oran, or at least the city centre. And they're starting to get the message in Paris. But we have to make examples of people. And I'm not talking about the National Liberation Front. You know what's worse than the enemy? The fence-sitters! The ones who can't decide which side they're on. We've had so much trouble already this summer, preventing people from going on holiday. They have to understand: ordinary life can't just go on.'

It was true: in July, almost as soon as the school year was over, the *pieds-noirs* had tried to flee the destruction, crossing the sea to Spain and visiting friends and family in France. So they'd had to make examples of them. Pierre had taken part in these educational operations. He remembered a pharmacist, shot down in the street as he was loading his suitcases into the boot of his Mercedes. The man had died in Bermuda shorts, with a fishing net under his arm. Pierre tried not to dwell on such bitter memories.

3

'We have to show them the cost of their fence-sitting. The Organisation has given us a list of targets. People whose jobs put them in contact with both communities, who might be passing on information. This week, we'll take care of the concierges. Next week, it'll be the postmen and the telegraph operators. Then the doctors.'

Fabregas laughed nervously at the mention of his colleagues. Pierre did not. Deep down, Fabregas envied him. Of course, Pierre didn't have the doctor's contacts, his social skills, his qualifications; but people listened to him, and they admired his sangfroid, the discreet detachment he showed amid all the petty game-playing. And, unlike Fabregas, he had fought in the war.

Behind his desk, the fat man appeared to stifle a burp, grimacing before pointing to a pair of names.

'This couple. We're almost sure that they're working with the FLN. They look after a building that's mostly occupied by civil servants. They're always on the lookout, collecting information, taking notice of when people come and go. I need you to go there tonight and eliminate them both. Shouldn't take long.'

And so, that pleasant evening, Pierre and Scagna entered the Saint-Eugène neighbourhood in a stolen car. Their destination was a concrete building that mimicked Moorish architecture, meticulously managed by its concierges, Latifa and Kamel Biraoui, twenty-seven and twenty-three years old respectively.

Pierre was relaxed. For several months now, these moments of action had been his only form of recreation. The rest of the time, he was worried sick about his family, his country, the future. How long had it been since he last slept more than three hours in a row? Often, as he examined columns of figures all day long at the harbour master's office, his vision would blur. Or his chest would feel so tight that he had to excuse himself for a moment and go to the bathroom to splash water on his face, loosen his tie, get his breath back. At least during operations things were clear. He followed the narrow path that led to his objective. His mind grew gloriously sharp. Usually, before going in, he would drive back home to

4

shave, change his shirt, wash his face, comb his hair. He liked these moments of precision and simplicity, when reality would finally bend to his will. Then he became more dangerous than a machine, relentlessly focused, inhumanly efficient.

Beside him in the car, Scagna was sweating. He was hungry and nervous and anxious to get the whole thing over with. He worked at the customs office, a strategic position for the OAS. Before, his job had been tranquil and privileged. From time to time, a crate of whisky or a shipment of cheese would find its way to his office. Nowadays he had to ensure that arms sent from Egypt or Russia did not reach the hands of the enemy, and that the arms his friends had ordered did not get lost on the way. Since the start of the hostilities, he had put on nearly twelve kilos in weight. He felt nostalgic for the cushy, influential old days. The quiet drudgery of bureaucracy had given way to the hassles of history and that made him sad.

They arrived at their destination, but Pierre couldn't find a parking space. It was a residential neighbourhood lined with spotless saloon cars and four-metre-high palm trees. An odour of salt and gunpowder mingled with the smell of the succulents. Oran hesitated on the edge of darkness. Patient and heavy, the night seemed to rise from the ground in breaths. Birds continued to chirp happily.

At last, the two men left the car double-parked. From the boot, they took the two Astra F automatic pistols they'd been given the day before. They were modelled on the famous German Mausers and some said they were even superior. The Astra F was the preferred weapon of the Guardia Civil, and some Spanish friends had sent them two crates. In perfect sync, Pierre and Scagna pulled back on the breech and a bullet entered the chamber of each gun. They smiled at each other, like children handed a new toy.

It was still hot, so they went in shirtsleeves, weapon in one hand, apparently casual. What did they have to fear, anyway? The OAS had control of Oran. When it ordered people to flout the curfew, the boulevards were filled with thousands of men, women and children. The ice-cream vendors made a fortune on evenings like this.

Three strides and they were across the street. Scagna used a pass to open the building's gate. The interior courtyard had a neglected look, only a few cacti surviving in the flowerbeds. Youssef, the gardener, no longer came to work. No water spurted from the small fountain covered with fragments of glazed tile. A tortoise shell lay in a corner. Momentarily distracted by the peacefulness of the place, Scagna looked at Pierre. He was staring up at the sky. Scagna barely had time to catch sight of a woman hanging out her washing on the second floor before she rushed back inside. Nobody wanted to know.

The Biraouis lived on the ground floor. There was only one entrance. Scagna used the pass again and the two men slipped into the concierges' lodge, a silent, gloomy one-bedroom flat with a low ceiling. As soon as the door fell shut behind them, they moved forward, guns at the ready. Scagna was breathing heavily, and with an impatient gesture Pierre ordered him to hang back. As they advanced, the smell of cooking grew stronger. They heard the clatter of pans. Madame Biraoui was making dinner.

They entered the living room. It was clean, the furniture cheap. On a shelf were some torn, dusty, well-thumbed books. An old wireless stood on a copper tray. Kamel Biraoui was sitting at the table, pencil in hand, the newspaper unfolded in front of him. A cigarette was smouldering in an ashtray, the smoke rising slowly through the still air. He looked up. Pierre tensed his arm. A gunshot, and the concierge's forehead fell to the table. The detonation echoed between the walls. Slightly stunned, the two intruders needed a few seconds before they were ready to go on. Was that the sound of broken crockery? Maybe not. Pierre waved his gun hand at Scagna, urging him past. In the kitchen, they found Latifa waiting for them. She was holding a knife, the blade pointed towards them. She wasn't crying. She wasn't thinking. Her mouth remained shut. She was praying. Not that she had much faith left; for some time now, she had preferred dialectics to the surahs of the Qur'an. Scagna aimed his pistol at her. He hesitated.

'Go on,' said Pierre.

Some eggs were boiling in a saucepan on the gas cooker. Their shells kept knocking against the pan's metal sides, *thunk-thunk-thunk*. Suddenly, a child's cry rang out. The sound came from another room, at the back of the apartment. So Latifa's prayers had been in vain.

Pierre cursed before firing a bullet into her mouth.

She seemed to deflate, her whole body collapsing onto the floor in a single motion, making only the faintest rustling noise. The two men looked at her. An impressive quantity of blood was pouring from her obliterated mouth. Fragments of smashed teeth had flown across the room. But most surprising of all were her dark, beautiful, wide-open eyes, which, for a second or two, continued to stare with the anxiety that had entered them just before she died.

Pierre quickly found the only bedroom. He scanned its contents. Dim light from the courtyard outside filtered through the shutters and stretched across a mattress on the floor. A few toiletry items were arranged on a chest of drawers. Two damp bath towels hung on the back of a child's chair. And, in the corner, there was a cot, where a little kid, barely two years old and newly orphaned, stood screaming its head off. Its face was round, its eyes big with fear, and teardrops sparkled in its long black lashes. When Pierre moved closer, the child screamed even louder. It was calling for its mother.

Irritated by the noise, Pierre held out his pistol again. The barrel, still warm, was only a few inches from the little brown head. Less than the width of a football away. Amused by this idea, Pierre thought that what he had to do really wasn't so difficult after all.

But he sensed a presence behind him and, almost immediately, felt something unpleasant touching the back of his neck.

'Do it and I'll blow your head off.'

Scagna was a sentimental man. That was obvious not only from the decision he'd just made, but from the quaver in his voice and the trembling of his hand.

Pierre lowered his weapon and the child fell silent for a second, curious about the change that had taken place in the room. The two men bolted. As they ran away, the child started yelling again behind them.

Out in the courtyard, the laundry hung across the balconies snapped in the evening breeze. It was a cooler wind now, blowing from the port, scented with iodine and petrol. The inhabitants who'd heard the gunshots had shut themselves into their apartments. In a few minutes, they would call the police and swear they hadn't seen anything. Scagna went first and Pierre was tempted to shoot him in the back. His heart was spluttering like an old car engine. Strange images flashed through his mind. He recognised this feeling. It came to him every time. During the war, he'd been part of a detachment of soldiers who'd attacked a small farm in the Vosges where a handful of exhausted Germans had taken refuge. There, for the first time, he had felt this almost annoying surge of extra energy, which was always accompanied by a strange taste in his mouth, as if he'd bitten a silver fork. They'd taken no prisoners that day, more out of fear than cruelty. They'd been kids, though, the Krauts: seventeen or younger, the Wehrmacht's last recruits, Boy Scouts tossed into battle like a few matches onto a bonfire. Pierre had seen the last one shit himself. War had revealed to him his own nature. That strange, metallic taste in his mouth.

They soon reached the street and Scagna jumped behind the steering wheel, started the engine, shifted into first, and was about to set off when he noticed Pierre standing in the road, next to the driver's-side door. Waiting.

'I'm driving.'

'Don't be an idiot. We're pushing our luck already.'

'Fucking hurry up, then!'

Scagna obeyed, lifting his fat arse over the gearstick before slumping into the passenger seat. 'You're out of your mind. What the fuck were you playing at with that kid?'

'Shut your mouth. I don't want to hear another word.'

Pierre said this without looking at him. Before driving away, he slid the Astra F under his seat. Scagna did the same. Then he set off towards the port. The air was mild and Pierre drove quickly, one hand on the wheel, the other leaning out of the open window. After loosening his tie, he said: 'Give me a cigarette.'

'We need to get rid of these guns,' said Scagna.

'What did I tell you? Shut your fucking mouth.'

The sun was setting. Scagna rolled up his window. He was a bit cold now and he needed to piss. Not only that, but he'd lost his sunglasses. He wished he was with his wife and kid. They were having sausages tonight. Monique would probably tell him off for being late. He would just smile and whistle, then take off his shirt and his belt, unbutton his trousers, and eat in his vest, a napkin on his shoulder. God, he felt so thirsty, suddenly. And where the hell was Pierre going?

'If you're just trying to check that we're not being followed . . .'

'Don't make me tell you again,' Pierre hissed, turning towards him. His lips were so thin, they looked like a scar.

The Simca wound through the city for a long time. The light drained quickly from the buildings' façades, as it does every evening by the sea. Pierre smoked three cigarettes without uttering a word. The wind blew against his face as against a locked door. What fury lay behind that closed expression?

'This is it,' he said at last, before slowing down.

A Coca-Cola delivery truck was parked outside the terrace of the Meteor Café, where a few young men were drinking aperitifs. Legs sprawling, heads thrown backward, they all wore open-necked shirts. Two were in uniform. They had that chilled-out, seen-it-all look that girls are supposed to adore.

Pierre parked the Simca next to the lorry and pulled the pistol out from under his seat before getting out of the car. Scagna wanted to yell.

It was at this exact moment that the lorry driver emerged from the café to pick up another crate of soda. He was a Muslim, in his forties, his forehead lined with deep furrows. He wore blue canvas trousers held up by a hemp cord and a vest that exposed his hairy, angular shoulders. His eyes were tired but alert. When he saw the weapon in Pierre's hand, his forehead grew even more corrugated and his Adam's apple slid quickly up and down. His lips opened a little, revealing very white teeth and almost black gums. He was about to say something. Pierre didn't give him time: he put a bullet into the man's forehead, as if he were an animal in an abattoir. The man collapsed. On the terrace, nobody batted an eyelid. Partly out of habit, partly out of fear. And, well, it was only an Arab.

Pierre was already back in the car. Scagna kept his mouth shut and Pierre drove away, horrifyingly calm, checking his mirrors before turning onto the road. Behind them, the café owner was asking his regulars to give him a hand unloading the rest of his order. One of the young soldiers, some kid from Montargis, stood up to call the police. His fingers were shaking so violently that it took him three attempts to dial the number properly.

PART ONE

God is good, but the devil isn't bad either.

Fernando Pessoa,
The Book of Disquiet

France, 2008

MARTEL

Martel had always been a bad son. And for as long as he could remember, he'd never had enough money.

When he was a little kid, his father would beat him for spending all his Christmas and birthday money at once, without a second thought. 'You think you're an American?' the old man would ask. 'You need to get this into your head: the harder you work for something, the more it's worth.'

Martel realised this later – in the army, at the factory – but he kept splashing his cash with no thought for tomorrow, buying himself expensive clothes that he never wore, buying rounds for friends, once even buying a car just so he could drive around a suburb of Abidjan.

His mother had had him late in life and she'd mollycoddled him, which had done him no favours in the end. Particularly as his father had compensated for this by being even stricter. When Martel came back from school covered with bruises, his clothes torn, his mother would cover for him: she'd keep quiet about the broken windows, the Fs in his school report. She used to lie like that almost every day, so his father wouldn't find out. God knew what he'd have done to the kid if he'd known about him beating up the boy next door or slashing his history teacher's tyres. Once, she even told the headmaster that her husband was dead, just to keep her darling son out of trouble.

Martel had a way with the ladies. He had pretty eyes and he knew how to appear gentle, cruel, complimentary. He could ask them for anything, but he always spent his money on them anyway, so they were no worse off. He would spoil his women.

He remembered his first girlfriend, Laurence, whom he'd met at school. She used to love *Pause-Café*, a soap opera starring Véronique Jannot, and all things Asian. After her father lost his job, she didn't go to school for several days. It was rare back then, and shameful, especially if you were out of work for a long time. Martel and Laurence didn't go out together for long – he never even slept with her – but it was with her that he had his first real deep conversations. About the future, society, work, family. Normally Martel was in such a rush, but he took the time to sit with her in a bar not far from where she lived, slowly sipping his lemonade as they talked. He still remembered that feeling of intimacy and seriousness. Laurence was crazy about him, and she cried her eyes out when he broke up with her. It was funny, thinking about it now, that he'd dumped Laurence for a girl whose name he couldn't even recall.

Martel had got into a lot of trouble as a kid. Sometimes pretty big trouble. Just before he ended up in prison – and also to get away from his father – he'd signed up early for the army. They'd known how to put his particular talents to good use. They'd trained him up, then kicked him out. Through other failures, he'd toughened up even more. At times, he'd made quite a lot of money. Not that it lasted him long, of course. When his father died, he'd gone back to the Vosges and picked up the threads of his old life, basking in his mother's inordinate love for him.

When that poor old woman started losing her marbles, Martel decided to move back into the house so he could look after her. A dozen times a day, she would ask him if he'd fed the cat. A dozen times a day, he would help her search for her handbag, her teeth, the TV remote, and the medicine she'd been prescribed for her stomach problems, which he could never be sure she'd remembered to take.

And so the bad son had got a job at the factory and he'd taken care of his mother, helping her use the toilet, driving her to the adult day-care centre, keeping his mouth shut when she was in a bad state.

And then one day she'd called him a fucking bastard. That had made him laugh.

After that, the insults came more often, and so did the indignities. It became a lot less funny then.

One Sunday afternoon, while they were watching a wildlife documentary on television, something terrible had happened. As usual, his mother was asking him questions about who did what and why, and Martel was patiently answering her, using bland, simple phrases, like someone talking to a child. But gradually, an unpleasant smell of shit had spread through the small living room. Martel couldn't believe it. He took refuge in the kitchen and started opening cupboards, turning on taps, anything to take his mind off what was happening. Surely they hadn't reached that point. In the end, though, he'd had to face the reality of his situation. He'd had to undress his mother and clean the shit off her aged body. This time, he knew, things were not going to get better.

After that, his mother's condition had gradually worsened. It took various forms, sometimes funny, sometimes scary, but always surprising. Once, for example, she told him over breakfast that she'd always hated sucking men's things but that you couldn't always do what you wanted in life. Martel learned lots of things that would never even have crossed his mind before. His mother had a body, and she had used it in various ways. For her son, this was a deeply unpleasant discovery.

So, finally, he'd put his mother in an old people's home. It was one of the best in the region, of course: the staff were very nice and the toilets were cleaned twice a day.

After that, every six months Martel would receive a bill for 12,576 euros and 15 cents. He wasn't such a bad son after all. He'd done what was best for his mother. Martel earned 1,612 euros and 13 cents per month. He worked at the Velocia factory.

RITA

Rita hadn't eaten breakfast and she was in a rush as usual. So, in spite of the icy patches on the tarmac, she drove fast along B-roads, empty fields flashing past her windows. It had rained and then frozen, so the country-side was covered with a fine layer of frost. In their remote cottages, their farms, and their housing estates, the elderly could feel the cold creeping up their bodies. In the Vosges, the winters were long. And, after a certain age, you knew there was no guarantee that you would make it through to the spring.

In the mountains, the construction workers were on furlough and the schools had closed temporarily because of the snow. They were like ghost ships, hollow and echoing. Their pipes moaned in the cold and snow-drifts hung from their roofs.

Rita, though, was having hot flushes. She'd even opened her window. It happened like that sometimes, these sudden spells of heat or impa-tience, when nothing seemed right and irritation crawled under her skin, like ants. Staring at the road ahead, muscles tensed, she was anxious for something, though she couldn't say what. She thought back to the conversation she'd had with Duflot three days before, which was perhaps at the root of her annoyance.

'Well, I just read your email but I don't have a clue what you're talking about. Did you do the inspection or not?'

'It's complicated,' Duflot had whined.

'What happened?'

'The butcher, that Colignon . . . well, he wasn't very cooperative.'

'He didn't let you work?'

'He did. It's not that . . .'

'Ugh, stop beating around the bush! Did he threaten you or what?'

'Not really, boss. It's more just the way he is.'

'He was intimidating you?'

'Let's just say that the conditions for the inspection were not ideal.'

'And what about the letter? Did you tell him?'

'No. I just thought it'd be better to wait for a more suitable moment.'

'Your email was really confusing, Duflot. I didn't understand what you were trying to say. Are you telling me that nothing's changed at all?'

'Well, I was still pretty emotional when I wrote it.'

'Okay, look, I'll pay a visit to this Colignon on Monday morning. I'll be in the area anyway. But you need to grow up a bit, Duflot. I can't always be there to hold your hand, you know.'

'I know, boss, I know . . .'

'All right, I've got to go. Have a good weekend.'

'You too.'

Rita's job had been increasingly complicated of late. The economic crisis was used to justify everything. Politicians, judges, bosses, even staff representatives, they all agreed: work had become such a rare commodity that nobody was in a position to sniff at whatever they were offered. In the end, the employees had convinced themselves of this too. And the labour code was now less a shield than a millstone, dragging down the forces of productivity. Everyone seemed to agree on this: you had to cut them some slack, be cooperative. Look at the Germans: they knew how to tighten their belts! And the Chinese, hundreds of millions of them, helping their economy to grow like crazy without moaning about holidays or bonuses or lunch hours or overtime.

Rita was a labour inspector. Some said she was in cahoots with the unions. She'd read bits of Marx when she was at university, enough to make her believe that economics was at the root of everything. Her college friends had all changed sides since then. The only revolution accomplished by her generation was the mass migration from flats in the city centre to second homes in the countryside every weekend. Rita wouldn't have minded getting her share of the cake either. She took no pleasure in being holier-than-thou. She didn't hate money. But – and this was her big problem – all this stuff still made her angry. At her age, she still found herself raging against the state of the world.

She'd felt that rage just the previous Friday. At the moment when she received Duflot's message, she'd been at an industrial tribunal. Ten workers from a local paper mill were claiming back-payment of several years' overtime. The tribunal found in favour of the mill's owners, on the basis that they were going through terrible financial difficulties. 'You must be kidding,' said Rita. 'Mrs Kleber, please! What difficulties?' The factory was run by a holding company that had siphoned off more than 650,000 euros in dividends at the end of the previous fiscal year. Yes, but since then, with the market in crisis and unemployment rising . . . Well, you understand.

This kind of thing would happen more and more. She'd kept her cool, she hadn't raised her voice, but . . . My God, how hot is it in this damn car?

Rita noticed that the speedometer needle was edging past 60 m.p.h. and she took her foot off the accelerator. Dying in an accident would hardly constitute revenge on the Zeitgeist.

She turned on the radio – RFM, as usual – and music filled the inside of the car: a sentimental old song about falling in love in a lift. She caught sight of her reflection in the rear-view mirror and, without even thinking, tried to smooth out the crow's feet around her eyes. Ageing was just one more problem, and not the most pressing. The fact that she wanted a beer at eight thirty in the morning was more worrying, for example.

Swept along by the music, she began observing the landscape. A layer of mist hung over the fields, soft and billowing as a belly dancer's midriff. The dark spires of pine trees rose into the low white sky. It was beautiful. It gave her a faint desire to shoot herself, but it was beautiful nonetheless. And her Saab 900 was tracing harmonious curves through that unending beauty.

It was a tiny little village located somewhere between Bruyère, Corcieux and Saint-Dié: just a single street with houses lined up on either side. Rita knew this area well. Not only did she live around here, but she'd recently devoted a lot of time to a wave of redundancies at a local factory. She'd met the union representatives and the factory managers. It wasn't going well, although the Works Council secretary was definitely worth the trip. When she thought about him, she felt something pleasant stir inside her, the kind of vague excitement you get when you're organising your holidays. She still hadn't called him, though. She felt hesitant.

She parked on a kerb, not too close, and slammed the Saab door. She shivered. At this altitude, the cold was more biting, and she never wore gloves or a scarf. The village, with its closed shutters and empty geranium pots, was not exactly a hive of activity. The silence was occasionally broken by the throb of a distant car engine, rising slightly before fading into silence. The church bells rang every hour, and from time to time an elderly person would shuffle across the street. Above the Grandemange garage, a sign for Bibendum Michelin swung creaking in the east wind. On a wall, an old Cinzano ad was slowly fading to invisibility.

She sniffed before heading towards the bar that faced the church. The Café de la Poste was empty, apart from one young, skinny guy leafing through a magazine behind the counter. He was smoking a cigarette despite all the No Smoking signs. When the door opened, a little bell rang and he looked up expressionlessly from his magazine.

Rita sat at the bar, where two Suze ashtrays flanked a revolving stand of hard-boiled eggs. In one corner, there was a pinball machine and a dilapidated table football table. The bulbs hanging from the low ceiling were lit, despite all the daylight flooding through the window.

'I thought you couldn't do that any more . . . Smoking in public places?'

The young man smiled broadly before stubbing out his cigarette under the counter.

'It's too late now. You've given me the urge.'

He was still smiling, unsure what to say. He wished he could think of something witty. He knew this woman – she'd come here before to have a drink. And there was something about her, despite her worn-out boots and her shapeless parka. She was never going to win Miss France, even if she were twenty years younger, but there was definitely something about her.

'What can I get you?'

'Twenty Winstons,' sighed the inspector, throwing away two months of abstinence. 'And a lottery ticket.'

The man put these items on the bar in front of her. 'Seven twenty.'

'God, it gets worse every time I start smoking again!'

'Gauloises are cheaper.'

'I don't want to actually *become* my mother.'

The young man's smile reappeared. Instinctively, to reassure himself, he felt with his foot for the case containing his new pool cue. It was a Parris, more than five hundred euros, with an ebony butt and an ash shaft. From time to time, he liked to screw the two parts together and slide the smooth wood between his fingers. It was so perfect, he felt almost embarrassed, as though such an object couldn't possibly belong to him. Ever since he'd bought the cue, he hadn't let it out of his sight, bringing it to work with him and taking it home again in the evenings.

His name was Jonathan. The previous Saturday, he had reached the final of a pool tournament in Gérardmer. He'd lost, of course: a real shame, since the first prize had been a Yamaha moped. He'd easily have found a buyer for it, with all those kids coming to the bar to play table football. He'd been saving up for some time so he could buy a car, a second-hand Seat Léon, which he believed was the only way he'd ever get a girlfriend. All his mates drove amazing cars – Toyota Supra, Golf GT, a souped-up Peugeot 106 that could do 140 m.p.h. on the motorway to Nancy. Some of them used to work, or still worked, at Velocia, the nearby car-parts factory. He'd have liked to do that too, work in a factory. The money was pretty good when there was plenty of business. And they all had those flash cars, and girlfriends . . . well, most of them. They all took the piss out of him for it – shy kids are always the butt of their friends' jokes – but nothing nasty. Jonathan was a good guy, after all. And Rita thought so too. This was maybe the third or fourth time she'd made a detour to the Café de la Poste and this young man's systematic smiles, overlarge signet ring and patchy little moustache were starting to become familiar to her.

'Could you tell me how to get to the Colignon butcher's shop?'

'It's about fifty yards up the street, on your right,' he replied. 'You can't miss it.'

Before leaving, she hesitated. She was thirsty.

'Anything else?' the young man asked.

She shook her head and went out. Jonathan watched her walk away, then went back to his magazine, where dubious news stories were enlivened by pictures of naked women.

MARTEL

'Hi!'

'Hi,' replied Martel, stamping the wrist of a teenage girl in boots, miniskirt and too much make-up.

The girl, who was maybe sixteen, maybe a little younger, smiled idiotically at him. She was probably stoned; most of these kids were. She wasn't the prettiest one there, but she wasn't the ugliest either. She was wearing tartan braces over her almost non-existent breasts. Martel smiled back, then pushed her through the door; there were other teenagers, dressed more or less the same, waiting in line behind her. Inside, the first band was on stage, making a lot of noise and surprisingly few mistakes. Generally, the opening acts weren't that tight. Two weeks before, Martel had found himself wondering if the band Romano Saint-Tropez had ever played their instruments before.

'Cool tatt,' said a young blonde, wearing a miniskirt over her jeans. Despite the late hour, she was still in sunglasses.

'You too,' said Martel, stamping her bare shoulder.

She laughed at this, and her boyfriend – a big guy with a beard in a Motörhead T-shirt – looked pissed off.

Ever since Bruce the temp had collared him at the factory to offer him this extra work, Martel had felt like he'd been transported back in time. For years, he'd hidden his forearms under long-sleeved shirts, but now he was like a kid again, enjoying the feel of a skin-tight Fred Perry polo shirt and rediscovering the effect that his faded, twenty-year-old tattoos could still have on girls. He hadn't even thought about those drawings for years. Some of them – the least respectable ones – were still hidden on his back and along his ribs. Martel had really made the most of his youth, as his skin could testify.

Bruce the temp – 'the Duruy kid', as the people around there called him – was on the other side of the entrance. He, too, was employed as a doorman. In the artificial light reflected from the walls, his muscles rolled like gears. You could see them shifting and sliding under his skin, coiled like thick rope, bunched in massive knots. Apparently Bruce couldn't quite believe his luck at being so muscle-bound. He made a meal of every movement, tensing as if he were about to rip a tree out of the ground or strangle an elephant with his bare hands. Given the choice, he would have worked the door topless. When he realised that Martel was watching, Bruce winked at him.

Martel was sick of being a bouncer at these gigs full of yokels. The money was pathetic – 150 euros max – and it wasn't even that easy. After filtering out the undesirables at the door, he had to keep things under control inside the club. The kids were bored shitless, so they drank as much as they could and there would always be at least five or ten morons who'd end up getting into a fight – anything to escape their boredom and help them forget that sexy Cynthia had, yet again, turned them down.

But the most dangerous one was Bruce. Not long before, that dick had beaten someone up for spilling his beer and the poor victim had almost lost an eye. Bruce was a volatile mix of steroids and stupidity. So Martel watched his co-worker more vigilantly than any of the punters. He didn't want Bruce to end up dead or in prison. He was a grade-A prick, but it was only thanks to him that Martel could pay his bills every month.

Once most of the customers were inside, Bruce took over on the front door, keeping an eye on the comings and goings, preventing people jumping the queue, and barring entry to anyone who'd just puked outside. Martel, who was taller, surveyed the inside of the club. He walked around, leaned on the bar, and waited for it to happen. The bands were pretty mediocre, but they were loud and energetic and they had lots of flashing lights. Martel was now over forty, and he was still stuck with this for entertainment. He chewed a matchstick, because you weren't even allowed to smoke here, and counted the songs, constantly hoping that the next one would be the last.

Time generally passed pretty slowly.

'You want a beer?'

The girl had very dark eyes, a broken nose, and an impressive cleavage. Martel looked her up and down, then nodded. After that, she tried to have a conversation with him, despite the deafening music and the earplugs he wore to protect his hearing. The girl had a strategy, though: she stood very close to him and loudly complained about everything under the sun. The more she talked, the more obvious it became that everything in the world was shit except her and maybe Martel, if he agreed to screw her. A few yards away, two of the girl's friends were watching them and giggling hysterically. It was all pretty ridiculous but not entirely unpleasant.

On stage, the Rageux, a hardcore band from Brest, were thrashing happily away. They could barely play and their songs were hardly original – stuff about girls, corrupt politicians, getting smashed on tequila, mates who get killed on motorbikes – but they were all in their early twenties and you could tell. As the concert neared its end, the crowd became increasingly excited. The Rageux had a song in the charts, 'Super Bad Cop', and they were obviously going to play it at some point. Every time a song ended, people yelled out for it.

From the bar, Martel could see the scattered stars of cigarette ends glowing in the darkness. One day, for a laugh, he'd counted all the No

Smoking signs in the club. He'd found twenty-eight. The dark-eyed girl had her arm around his waist now. He hadn't asked her how old she was. Probably better not to.

Just then, the singer came out on the stage riding a Peugeot 103 SP moped, a kepi on his head, holding a truncheon instead of a microphone. He revved the engine and petrol fumes spread through the concert hall. That was the signal. The crowd lost it. ' "You hunt by day, you hunt by night, you lose your gun, your woman's gone, Super Bad Coooop . . ." ' The bassline, thought Martel, really made you want to get your head kicked in. But he didn't have time to pursue this line of thought, because someone was tugging at his sleeve.

'Oi, what do you think I'm paying you for?'

'What?' said Martel. He couldn't even hear his own voice.

'The toilet floor's inch-deep in puke. How do you explain that?'

'Young people drinking too much, I imagine.'

'No shit, Sherlock! Now stop lazing around and do your fucking job: kick those little bastards out.'

'Chill, Thierry,' said Martel. 'And try not to talk to me in that tone of voice, if you don't mind.'

'I don't know why the fuck I ever hired you.'

'All right, calm down, I'll sort it out now.'

He nodded to the dark-eyed girl and set off in the direction of the toilets.

Thierry was the fly in his ointment. A sour-tempered man in loafers and a denim jacket, he was a town councillor as well as a concert promoter, the king of village halls for miles around, and Martel had known him since secondary school. Back then, Thierry would never have dared talk to him like that. Every time he handed him his wages – always in cash, crisp new bills – Thierry would slap him on the shoulder. Unfortunately, Martel needed the money.

In the toilets, he found two girls slumped on the floor, half-conscious and covered with sweat. One of them, a blonde, had puke in her hair and her bra had vanished. The other one was cute and was wearing a Ralph Lauren polo shirt. She must have got the wrong club night. He gently woke her up and advised her to get the hell out of there. He shook the other one, but she didn't stir. He'd take care of her later.

The men's room was Party Central. Five or six guys were smoking joints, chatting and nodding. They barely even blinked when they saw him come in.

'Hey, man.'

'I'm going to count to one,' Martel announced.

'It's cool, man.'

'No problem.'

'Stay calm, dude.'

'Hey, we're leaving, okay?'

They left, their joints badly hidden in the palms of their hands. Seeing them move out in single file like that, shoulders slumped and faces slack, they looked oddly like a caravan of camels.

After that, Martel checked all the cubicles, kicking open the doors and recoiling each time at the mess inside. He sighed and went back to check on the braless girl. He took her outside and she instantly looked more alive: spots of colour appeared on her cheeks and her eyelids flickered. Martel had cleaned her hair with toilet paper and water.

'Will you be okay?'

'What?' asked the girl, covering her bare chest with her hands.

'You'll be okay.'

Sometime later, the crowd was pouring slowly through the exit into the cold, damp, silent night. Martel spotted Bruce a little way off in the car park. He was offering a complicated handshake to two men in tracksuits who had clearly not been at the concert. As Martel walked over, the two men cleared off.

'So?'

'A good night's work,' said Bruce.

'What did they want?'

'Same as everyone else.'

'So it's okay?'

'Perfect,' said Bruce, patting his jeans pocket. 'I haven't counted, but it looks like enough for more than two hundred bags.'

'What do you mean you haven't counted?'

'Well, I haven't added it all up yet, you know.'

'You blow my fucking mind sometimes. I told you to count it as you got it.'

'Don't worry, everything's cool,' said Bruce.

'All right, let's wrap things up.' Martel sighed. 'I'll meet you inside for a beer in a minute.'

Martel and Bruce sat at the bar and waited for the roadies to finish up on stage. The men carried away the band's equipment without a word, fags in mouths. They were almost all dressed the same: black T-shirts, steel-toe boots, jeans halfway down their arses. Martel watched them; Bruce didn't. Just then, Thierry turned up. He was holding a huge glass of whisky and Coke on the rocks, sipping it through a straw.

'Lads,' he said. 'I'm disappointed.'

Martel was standing between them, so Bruce clung to the bar and leaned backwards to get a better view, his arms tensed like cables.

'To be honest, it looks to me like you don't really give a shit.'

'What are you talking about, Thierry?'

'Go look in the toilets. And the car park. There are still at least fifty kids out there smoking joints and pissing around while you two are in here drinking your free beers.'

Martel exhaled deeply and stared at a point straight ahead of him – in this case, a flyer pinned to the wall that showed Sarkozy leading a zombie army in pursuit of three motorcyclists. One of the bikers was wearing high heels and fishnet stockings. Martel glanced at his watch. It was nearly eleven thirty and he was on morning shift tomorrow. Consequently, he needed to get his money as soon as possible and go home.

'Just spit it out, Thierry, we're knackered.'

'Yeah, we're fucking dead here,' agreed Bruce. 'What's your point?'

'Maybe there's been a misunderstanding. Here's my point: you're here to work. And I'm only supposed to pay you for what you do.'

Martel's bank account was about eight thousand euros in the red. His bank manager called him every week and talked to him as if he were a half-wit. In his wallet was a Sofinco card, which he was using to try to pay off all his debts. He felt like he'd been holding his breath for months now. And now Thierry Molina, standing there in his loafers with a look of mild disgust on his face, was trying to short-change him.

'Listen for yourselves,' Thierry said, pointing at the ceiling.

'What?' asked Bruce, lighting a cigarette. 'I don't hear anything.'

Martel could hear the muffled sounds of car horns, shouts and whistles. But in his opinion the car park, unlike the toilets, did not come within his jurisdiction.

'It's unacceptable, lads,' Thierry declared in a pompous voice.

Martel tried to stay calm. Focus on Sarkozy and the zombies. Don't lose your temper. He had pins and needles in his hands. He always feared that someone was going to push him too far.

Thierry sucked up another mouthful of whisky and Coke before shaking the ice in his glass. 'I'm sorry, lads. I'm going to have to take this out of your wages.'

Martel turned his head a few degrees. 'You what?'

'You haven't done your job, lads, simple as that.'

Outside, the din grew louder.

'Listen to those little fuckers.'

'I think you've got us mixed up with the cleaners, Thierry. Our job is to keep them in order while they're here. Full stop.'

Behind him, Bruce nodded angrily.

'I'm sorry, but you've left me no choice. I've deducted fifty euros each. Next time, maybe you'll do a better job.'

He handed them their envelopes. Martel counted eighty euros in his.

'Are you taking the piss, Thierry?'

'My hands are tied. That's management, lads. Next time, if you do everything you're supposed to do, I'll slip you a bit extra.'

Bruce stood up and was about to grab his boss by the lapel when they heard a huge roar and turned to look. It was coming from close by, just behind the doors. And it was getting louder, with some weird noises, laughter, the clash of metal and a sound like cows mooing. They could hear people yelling encouragement too. Then more mooing.

'What the fuck is that?' demanded Thierry, heading towards the doors.

'That little shit,' hissed Bruce, watching him walk away.

Martel remembered that Thierry used to smoke quite a lot of weed when they were in school together. He had a heart murmur and always skipped PE. His parents had a mansion in the hills above Épinal. On weekends, Thierry would often invite his friends to go and party there. For a long time, he went out with a girl who was very pretty, if a bit over-weight . . . What was her name? And now he thought he was some big shot, just because he'd produced a couple of records and presented a rock show on the local radio station. He knew a few presenters from the RTL9 television channel too, and during the NJP jazz festival, you could often see him drinking with the stars on the Place Stan' in Nancy. So maybe he was a success in his own field. He made money and apparently he was friends with the band Cookie Dingler. More to the point, though, he had just ripped them off.

'What are we going to do?'

'I need money,' Martel replied simply.

'Well, here you go.'

Bruce took a wad of crumpled bills out of his pocket and began to count them.

Martel watched him, trying to count along because Bruce was not wholly trustworthy in terms of his mental-arithmetic skills. They were interrupted by yelling from outside. Thierry had started shrieking like a madman. There was a weird sort of bellowing noise too. A heartrending, bestial sound.

'What the fuck is that?' asked Martel.

'Thierry going mental.'

'I dunno . . . it sounds like an animal to me.'

'Here you go, one thousand six hundred. Not quite as much as I thought . . .'

'I told you to count it as you got it. I'm sure some of those guys are scamming you.'

'No way. Impossible.'

Bruce was a dealer. He sold hash, ecstasy and a decent amount of coke on the door at concerts. Martel didn't want to know where he got it from or how much he sold or anything at all that could implicate him in the business. He just took the cash. When Bruce had got him to work at the concert hall, he'd told Martel: we're partners now. Since then, he handed him his share of the proceeds – half, more or less. Martel didn't really understand why. In exchange, he let Bruce hang around him. In the factory, the bodybuilding temp was always there, whenever he turned his head, and now, when someone wanted to talk to Martel, they had to go through Bruce. That made him important. Martel was the secretary of the Works Council, after all. Having said that, he really couldn't tell if Bruce was following a cunning strategy or if he was just completely stupid.

The doors swung open to reveal Thierry: his hair was dishevelled, he'd lost his denim jacket, and his trousers were mud-stained.

'Get out here, for God's sake!'

'Why? What's up?' asked Bruce.

'I said get out here! And fucking hurry up!'

'I don't think so,' said Martel, going behind the bar to get himself another beer.

'Me neither,' agreed Bruce, handing his glass to Martel.

'Lads, I promise you,' Thierry begged.

'Having problems with some little yobbos, Thierry?'

'Two hundred euros each, right now!'

He tried to reach into his jacket pocket before realising that he was no longer wearing a jacket.

'Two hundred and fifty tomorrow. You have to go out there, lads, seriously.'

Behind the doors, the wailing was growing louder and more plaintive, and each time one of the men in the car park honked his horn or revved his turbo-charged engine, the wailing intensified. The sound sent shivers down their spines.

Intrigued, Martel went to the exit. 'Problem is, Thierry, we can't trust you any more.'

'Sorry, Thierry,' added Bruce, mockingly raising his glass.

'Lads, listen. Three hundred and fifty tomorrow, but you have to stop this bullshit now.'

Martel pushed the door open with his foot. 'Oh, shit,' he said.

A cow was trapped inside the metal fences used to funnel customers into the club. It had to weigh at least forty stone and it was struggling and mooing desperately. Its head was lowered, its horns stuck in the barriers, eyes bulging with terror. The more it bucked and battled, the more enmeshed it became in its steel straitjacket. It was bleeding from a deep wound in the back of its neck and its hoofs were stained red too. It was hard to tell if the blood on the hoofs was the cow's or if it came from the men who'd shoved it into that trap.

'You'd better call the cops,' said Martel.

'Forget it – I've got enough shit on my plate without adding this. You need to get rid of it. I'll pay you. You have my word.'

'I don't think your word is worth much any more, Thierry.'

Martel spoke calmly and tried to avoid looking at his boss because he was afraid he would lose his cool. The pins and needles were numbing his hands.

He moved closer to the cow and the animal charged, wounding itself even more. In the car park, there was another chorus of car horns.

'Go round the back way, Bruce, and get rid of those morons.'

'Cool,' breathed Thierry, wiping the sweat from his brow. 'See, if you'd done your job properly . . .'

'That remark is going to cost you another hundred euros.'

'Oh, come on, we're not at school any more.'

Martel turned around. Thierry was standing there. Martel grabbed him by his collar and spoke in a voice so low that it almost sounded like he was talking to himself: 'You're going to pay us five hundred euros,

Thierry. Five hundred each. In fact, you're going to get the money right now.'

Martel was a very big man. And Thierry didn't like the smell of his breath, or the sound of it so close to his face. He felt like he was in conversation with a time bomb. He freed himself and headed towards the emergency exit. 'All right, I'll get it. I'll be back in a minute.'

Martel watched him running away on his little legs. He felt the strength surging through his arms and shoulders. Christ, he'd almost torn the little bastard to pieces.

He and Bruce waited until everybody had left: the roadies, the wait-resses, the last customers, who kept enraging the poor beast with their car horns. The cow was motionless now, moaning softly, its hide covered with cuts, one sad round eye staring at the two men.

'What do you reckon it's thinking?' Bruce asked.

The ground and the barriers were splattered with blood. The animal was exhausted, its tongue lolling. Steam rose from the thick, wide tongue, which hung nearly six inches from its mouth, next to the eye that kept staring at them. The cow's breathing was hoarse and jerky.

'I think it's dying.'

'It's suffocating,' Martel agreed.

'He'll never pay us five hundred.'

'Let's just deal with it. Has everybody gone?'

'I think so,' said Bruce.

'We need to finish it off. We'll never get it out of there alive anyway.'

A brief chorus of moos came from a neighbouring field, and the cow made one last effort to free itself.

'Shit,' said Martel, his throat tightening.

Bruce stepped closer to the animal and stroked its head. He spoke to it in a calm, humming voice. Then he moved his hand to the cow's back. In the darkness, Martel couldn't really tell what he was doing. The panting died down; it was almost over. Then he saw Bruce put the barrel of a Colt .45 to the animal's eye. He could have sworn that the eye closed.

'Fuck!' Martel gasped.

The gunshot rang out, the cow's skull exploded, and its body suddenly relaxed with a heavy sigh and a creak of metal. The barriers collapsed under its weight.

Bruce turned around, gun in hand, looking pleased with himself. 'I reckon we can get it out now.'

'Shall we burn it too, while we're at it?' Martel shook his head. 'I can't believe you used a fucking gun! If the cops turn up, you're in deep shit.'

'You think?'

'Find the cartridge. Quickly. We've got work tomorrow morning, remember.'

Bruce, put out, got down on his knees and began searching.

RITA

'What can I get you?' asked the butcher, even before the bell above the door had stopped ringing.

Behind him, strings of *saucissons* and sausages decorated the white-tiled walls. The glass-fronted refrigerators were filled with every imaginable cut of meat. Rita was a little surprised to find such a well-stocked shop in a godforsaken hole like this. There were even a capon and two guinea fowl in the front window, displayed against a backdrop of dry ice and a Christmas tree, leftovers from the holiday that had ended a few weeks before.

The butcher stood waiting in his tight white apron. He wiped his hands on a clean towel. His face was unlined, but it was hard to tell how old he was. His lopsided mouth curled into something resembling a smile. Rita said nothing. Silence was a strategy that often produced interesting results.

In the back room, something metal clattered to the floor and they both shivered, but the butcher acted as if he hadn't heard anything. All the same, his odd little smile disappeared and he put his hands flat on the countertop.

'Madame?'

Jacques Colignon had been feeling under the weather lately. Marie-Jeanne had gone off to a spa, as she did every year after the Christmas holiday. He hadn't heard from her for two days now, and he still hadn't dared call the hotel. It was probably just some problem with her mobile phone. Maybe she'd forgotten the charger. She was pretty scatterbrained, Still, he didn't like not knowing how she was.

'I don't have all day, madame.'

Rita handed him her card. The butcher read it and came around the counter to usher her out of the door. His body language was that of a man who was going to deal with this problem quickly.

'Your colleague's already been round. I explained the situation to him.'

'Ah? And how did that go?'

'Madame, I have work to do . . .'

Upstairs, something else crashed to the floor and the butcher's face froze. 'Listen, you'll have to come back another time. My wife isn't home and I've got my hands full here.'

He had already opened the door and was waiting for Rita to leave. The cold air blew in from outside and shook the bell above the door.

'Next time, call before you drop by. My wife will look after you. She's the one who deals with all that stuff.'

'According to your social-security declarations, your wife only works part-time.'

'So?' This time, there was a glimmer of curiosity in his eyes.

'We sent you several letters. Haven't you read them?'

The man shrugged and opened the door even wider, ignoring the icy draught. Rita stepped further back inside and looked around with an approving expression. 'You've got a nice place here. I bet you have customers coming from all over.'

The butcher's hands were beginning to go numb in the cold. He sighed and closed the door. 'What's your point?'

3 6

'What's your annual revenue? Four hundred thousand? Four hundred and fifty?'

This estimate seemed to amuse the butcher: his strange little lopsided smile reappeared. Then he quickly controlled himself. 'I'm not stealing from anyone. I do my job, that's all.'

And nobody could deny that he did it well. If only everyone else was as hard-working as him! At least Marie-Jeanne would know how to deal with the situation. He'd call her as soon as he'd got rid of this woman.

'Except that, in my opinion, you'd need staff to keep a shop like this going. I find it hard to believe that you do all the work on your own.'

'I can assure you that we pay all the tax we're supposed to.'

'That's not really my problem. You see, quite often in places like this, the spouse's full workload isn't declared. That way, you can save a bit of money for holidays and so on . . .'

The butcher no longer seemed quite so eager for her to leave.

'The only problem is that, one day, your wife will be retired. And she won't be eligible for a full pension. Because she declared herself part-time.'

'That's our business, not yours.'

'For you, monsieur, it's an ideal situation. I see that, of course. You pay less social security and there's no chance of your wife ever leaving you. Because, if she did, she'd basically be on the street . . . In fact, if you think about it, it's practically slavery.'

'For God's sake,' groaned the butcher, grabbing Rita by the arm and shoving her towards the exit.

Making no attempt to resist him, the inspector continued speaking in a composed voice: 'And what about your apprentice?'

'All right, I've heard enough. You'll have to talk to my wife about this. I can't help you.'

'Yes, I could call your wife. Explain her rights to her. That would only be fair.'

'Listen, madame, what do you want, exactly?'

'I'm just the same as you, Monsieur Colignon. I want to be allowed to do my job.'

37

After a brief hesitation, the butcher flipped the sign on the door around and asked Rita to give him five minutes to tidy up a bit.

'As you like,' said Rita.

The butcher went upstairs and the inspector heard a brief fracas somewhere above.

When he came back down again, she thought she heard other, more distant sounds . . . the sound of footsteps quickly fading to silence.

'All right, let's go. I'm warning you, though, this'd better be quick.'

Rita made sure it was a lightning visit. Wearing a cloth hygiene cap, she asked a few questions, glanced around the butchery, checked the order books. The place was certainly clean. The cold room was cold, the electrics were up to standard, and Monsieur Colignon actually seemed quite pleased to be able to show off his equipment: it wasn't state-of-the-art, but it was well-made and German and it did the job. During their tour of the premises, Rita congratulated him several times and Colignon began to relax a little. She was filling out a form when she mentioned that she wouldn't be against the idea of a quick drink before she left.

The butcher checked his watch. He was still tormented by what she'd said about his wife's pension. He wanted only the best for Marie-Jeanne, and now he wondered if what he was doing was right. The shop's assets belonged to both of them. All the same, he couldn't help feeling a little awkward. Not long before, Marie-Jeanne had wanted to open a bank account in her own name. She'd asked for a rise too. He'd refused, of course: it made no sense at all.

Rita sat at the small table where the butcher usually ate his morning snack and watched him as he rummaged through the contents of the fridge. It was warm here and the windows were misted, rendering the landscape outside almost invisible; she could make out nothing but a dark mass, the nearby hills, an expanse of pine trees.

'What can I get you to drink?'

'A beer would be good.'

'It's ten fifteen in the morning.'

'Uh-huh.'

'All right.'

The butcher opened a can of beer for her and poured himself a glass of Coke. Then he put a salami and a few pickles on the table. Rita watched him: the simplicity of his movements, the dexterity of his short fingers, their chewed nails. She poured her beer into a glass and took two long gulps. This was always the best moment.

'So?' asked the butcher, sardonically.

'So, everything's in order,' Rita admitted.

'What a lot of fuss over nothing. You cost me half a day of work.'

'I didn't come here by chance, Monsieur Colignon.'

He waited, his hands joined on the table. He was still thinking about Marie-Jeanne. Something unpleasant seemed to cling to all his thoughts, like those spider webs that stuck to his face when he climbed the steps out of the cellar.

'If it was only up to me, I would never have paid you this visit,' she said. 'Neither would my colleague.' She paused, then added: 'You know, a lot of the time, we go on information provided by outside sources. Complaints.'

The butcher shrugged. That was people for you.

'And the apprentice?'

Nothing. No reaction at all. He sniffed, but not out of embarrassment.

'You do have an apprentice?'

'He's declared.'

'Where is he?'

'He's not here.'

'His school contacted us.'

'I was the apprentice before him. I know what to do with the kid.'

'I understand that.' Rita took her time finishing her beer and the butcher stood up, arms crossed, waiting for her to leave. 'I heard him upstairs earlier. I know he's here.'

'I think you'd better go now.'

'You work that boy too hard. He doesn't even go home every night. His father called us too. It's undeclared work, Monsieur Colignon. I'm afraid you're going to have to give me a bit more of your time.'

'You've been drinking. Get out of here now.'

'We received a complaint,' said Rita, sounding almost affectionate.

At this, the man stepped towards her, placed his large hands on the table and articulated very clearly: 'I want you to go, madame.'

Rita could smell it. He gave off a faint odour of bleach and the skin of his face was perfectly smooth. Like fish skin, she thought.

Colignon added: 'Talk to my lawyer. I don't have to listen to this in my own home.'

His lips looked like a charcoal sketch, flecked with a few raindrops.

'Your wife wrote to us. She wants you to rectify the situation. She's going to leave.'

'What are you talking about?'

'She's not going to work here any more. We sent you letters. Just read them. You'll see.'

The butcher's face fell, like a house of cards. His eyes began to dance around, seeking something to cling to.

'I'm sorry,' breathed Rita.

He couldn't look at her. His fists were balled, the knuckles white. 'I want you to leave now. I have work to do.'

'I'm going to take the apprentice with me, Monsieur Colignon. Everything will be all right.'

He checked his watch before going back into the shop. He'd lost a lot of time.

Allain was wearing black combat boots and a Slayer T-shirt two sizes too big for him. Rita had found him in the attic, in a little nook furnished with a camp bed, a bedside lamp and a stool. A few heavy-metal magazines were strewn across the floor. He slipped them into his backpack before leaving.

'Colignon has my console.'

'Your what?'

'My Nintendo. He took it off me because I was playing too late at night.'

'Don't worry, we'll pick it up another time.'

'How is he?'

'Everything will be all right,' Rita promised, pulling him towards the exit.

They went out the back way, avoiding the shop, from where they could hear the regular thwack of meat cleaver against wood. Before leaving, Rita also called the police. The butcher looked like a man at the end of his tether. Better send someone to check on him.

They'd been driving for several minutes and the kid wouldn't stop wriggling in his seat.

'What's wrong?'

'What will happen now?'

'We'll find you another boss. Another butcher. Someone more relaxed.'

'Oh, right.'

And then the kid asked if she could change the radio station. 'This music is crap. Don't you want to listen to something else?'

'I like Goldman.'

'And where are we going?'

'You'll see.'

The Saab snaked along the mountainside, as if suspended above the ravine. In this landscape, the music sounded different, darker. The verticality of the panorama, the void below, the spikiness of the forest, the shadow on the road, all of this induced a rising nausea.

'Urrgh, I hate nature,' the kid spat.

Rita smiled and turned up the volume. When she lit a Winston, the boy cadged one off her.

They were silent for a while. Then Rita's mobile buzzed. A text. It was that Works Council secretary, the one at the factory where they were

41

laying people off. The Saab was now moving through a flatter landscape, with meadows and large buildings, sawmills and half-abandoned farms. He wanted to see her again. He was thinking about her. The message was perfectly simple and direct. Rita shook her head. Beside her, the kid was methodically chewing his fingernails as he stared at the road.

Suddenly Rita's eye was caught by a movement up ahead. Thinking it must be an animal, she lifted her foot from the accelerator.

To her left, someone came hurtling out of the undergrowth. A young woman, maybe a teenage girl. It was hard to say. She was running frantically, throwing desperate glances back over her shoulder, her limbs threatening to pop from their joints with each stride. Obviously, she wasn't out for a morning jog. Everything about her screamed panic. Particularly the fact that she was running around in the middle of nowhere, dressed in nothing but her knickers.

Rita couldn't believe what she was seeing. She slowed down and honked the horn. When the boy beside her spotted the girl, her body covered with mud, he started muttering, 'Oh, my God, what the fuck?' while continuing to bite his nails. The girl started waving her arms. Even from a distance, Rita could see her wide, frightened eyes. She stepped on the brake and the wheels halted. The back of the car skidded out slightly and Rita coolly steered the other way, placing one hand on the boy's chest out of fear that he might be sent hurtling through the windscreen. The car went into a spin then, veering towards the ditch. Rita tried to regain control by accelerating, but it was too late. As they slid forward, she heard the kid chanting, 'Fuck fuck fuck fuck fuck.' Then there was a massive crunch and the rear windscreen shattered. This all happened very fast. The Saab was stuck in the ditch, motionless. Bathed in sweat, Rita turned off the engine. The silence was absolute. A thread of smoke rose from a chimney. The entire countryside seemed dumbstruck.

'You okay?'

'Yeah.'

'Don't move, all right? Stay here.'

*   *   *

42

Despite the pain in his joints, Pierre Duruy had managed to follow the girl through the woods. He'd hurried, always finding the shortest way, just like he used to do, cutting through enemy lines or the labyrinthine streets of Oran. In his position overlooking the road, he watched through binoculars as the woman in the khaki parka struggled out of the damaged car. It was an unusual, angular-looking car, a foreign make.

Once she'd got out of the ditch, the woman in the parka immediately ran over to the girl and wrapped her in her jacket. She rubbed her back and held her tight. Despite the distance, Pierre Duruy could hear the girl's sobs.

The old man wondered if he'd done the right thing. He was more than seventy years old now: did it really make sense to get involved in all this stuff? How much did the girl know? How much did she understand? When he'd found her locked in the caravan, outside the Farm, it hadn't even struck him as strange. It was only thinking about it later that it had started to gnaw at him. For some time now, he'd been trying to do the right thing.

Well, the shit was about to hit the fan, that was for sure. The idea amused him. Given his own situation.

He moved the binoculars so he could read the car's registration number. 2031 RK88.

Well, what would be would be.

Puffing and panting, he turned back to the Farm. Curiously, he hoped that the woman in the parka would take good care of the girl.

THE FARM

They all called it 'The Farm' yet no one had ever seen any animals there, and nothing much grew there either. The garden was tiny and overrun with weeds. In truth, it looked more like a rubbish dump, with rubble all around and that hovel in the middle.

Nevertheless, 'The Farm' was what everyone had always called it.

It was an old south-facing building, two floors plus the attic, full of cold draughts, whining floorboards, involuntary judders and two chimneys. Several times over the years, it had been practically destroyed. But each time, it had somehow survived, been rebuilt. And, like a bone that had healed after a serious fracture, it had grown horribly sturdy. Even so, there was something rickety and crippled about its physiognomy.

Originally it had been a hunting lodge. A place where high-born revellers would get smashed together after riding through the woods, shooting anything that moved. Money from the cotton mills had ensured its prosperity before a combination of winters, deaths and the indifference of younger generations had brought an end to the building's golden age. The farmers around had pillaged it then for stones and wooden beams. Imperceptibly, the forest had retaken its lost ground.

Around the mid-1930s, a family from the village of Rambervillers had moved in. A down-at-heel, shady bunch, the Humberts sold rabbit pelts, sharpened knives, and pushed around wobbly carts filled with all sorts of useless, half-broken crap that they would sell for a pittance. But mostly what they did was distil mirabelle plums into a foul-tasting eau-de-vie that caused fights all over the region.

The Farm had been more or less renovated during the reign of the Humberts. But when their sons had found no one to marry in the region, they left, abandoning the Farm to the forest and their sisters to the natives.

During the war, its isolation had made it useful once more. Food was stored there, along with fugitives from Poland and Romania. After the Liberation, it was forgotten again.

And then, one morning, Pierre Duruy had arrived, with his wife and daughter. They were tired and dirty. They'd just driven more than six hundred miles in a Peugeot 203. The infernal noise of the engine had kept little Liliane awake throughout almost the entire journey. The Duruys had left Toulon, bringing two suitcases with them. On the way, they'd bought some winter clothes – to keep them warm and, above all, to cheer them up. It was early autumn and they were heading north. Pierre had chosen a pea jacket, while Jeanne had consoled herself with a coat made from weasel fur that was supposedly hard-wearing. Liliane had insisted on wearing her new anorak inside the car until the heat turned her bright red and half mad. Her constant whining had caused arguments and delays.

For four months now, the family had been moving from hotel to rented room, drinking instant coffee, cooking tasteless food, keeping a low profile. Liliane had stopped going to school. Pierre paced around like a caged lion, smoking too much and losing his temper for the slightest of reasons. Their life was the sort of nomadic, dangerous existence that teenage boys in boarding-school dorms dream about. But the Duruys had no desire to be pirates or highwaymen, and for them it was more like a foretaste of Hell.

That morning in 1962, Jeanne Duruy had regretted not wearing stockings as soon as she got out of the car. 'It's cold,' she complained, as the wind blew under her skirt.

'It'll be all right,' Pierre promised, holding her by the shoulders.

During the journey, the couple had exchanged some hard words. There had been times when Jeanne really hated her husband. It was all because of Pierre and his stubbornness that they were living like fugitives. Particularly since he'd never bothered to ask her what she thought about anything. How long had it been since she'd had any influence over her own life? Her father had been killed like a dog as he was coming out of the town hall. They'd shot him in the face and she'd never even been able to see his body. Only a figure covered by a grey sheet with his best pair of shoes sticking out at the end. After that, she'd got pregnant at the worst possible time. And, despite Pierre's promises, they'd had to leave Algeria. She hadn't chosen or wanted any of that. Sometimes she felt as if she were living a stranger's life, desperately trying to muddle through as best she could while she waited to be given back the happiness she'd known before: all those endless summers and those beautiful white flat-roofed houses.

Jeanne was weary. She wasn't even forty but she felt old. And, instinctively, she cursed the sight of that shack in the middle of the woods.

A few weeks before this, in Toulon, the neighbour had come to knock at their door. He was a big guy with a cyclist's face, in a vest and slippers.

'There's a call for you,' he said, as soon as they opened the door.

No hello, no how-are-you. And he turned on his heels and headed straight back to his one-bedroom flat, where his wife was breastfeeding her youngest child.

Pierre had given the Nadals' number to a handful of friends and family, in case of emergency. But the Nadals were not exactly enthusiastic about doing their neighbours a favour. Their attitude, and the attitude of the French nation generally, seemed to be: these people leaving Algeria, expecting us to pander to their every whim, they need to learn that the high life is over!

Swallowing his pride, Pierre followed Nadal into his apartment and picked up the receiver, which was dangling against the wall. Nadal and his wife stayed close by. After all, it was their home. Pierre stuck his finger into his ear and closed his eyes before speaking.

'Hello?'

'It's Fabregas. We need to meet.'

'Why?'

'We have things to discuss. You need to come over here.'

'Over where?'

'Alicante, of course!'

'No way.'

'What's up? You afraid of getting sunstroke?' Fabregas laughed. The doctor always saw the funny side. And after two minutes of discussion, during which Pierre made clear his mistrust, Fabregas agreed to make the trip himself. They arranged to meet for dinner the following Wednesday. Fabregas promised to come alone, and to be discreet.

As he left, Pierre said, 'Thanks! Thanks a lot!'

Nadal, the neighbour with the cyclist's face, muttered: 'Yeah, yeah.'

Back at home, Pierre started to wonder what exactly Fabregas wanted. He was one of Pierre's oldest friends. But what did that mean now? Since April, the OAS had been settling scores. Pascal Remila had been killed the previous week, coming out of a café in Perpignan. Jo Sanchez had been grassed up. The cops had arrested him in Paris after a brief chase through the fourth arrondissement. His way had been blocked by civilians. French Algeria had fallen out of favour. Four men armed with MAT-49s had been deployed to eliminate Gaspard Tassopoulos. The time of oaths had gone and now they were living in an age of suspicions and betrayals. Hierarchies were growing vague, organisation charts falling to pieces as people absconded or were arrested. Under pressure, the OAS was dissolving into small cells where the old order grappled with new terrors. Comrade betrayed comrade to see his boss supplant a rival. Brothers in arms wallowed in endless remorse. Men of honour were transformed into fanatical executioners. Blood was spilled, as usual, but in 1962 it was spilled over nothing.

Pierre, too, had been determined to stay, not to leave his mother's grave in the hands of the Arabs. He'd wanted to live and die in Oran, like his father and grandfather before him. But once the die had been cast, there was no point in messing around. The port of Oran was in flames, clouds of black smoke erupting into the sky, people burning anything they couldn't take with them. They set up camp by the dock, waiting for a ship to Marseille. They had, in the end, given up.

When Pierre finally resolved to get out of there, some of his comrades had refused to let him go. A few hardliners had even recommended blowing up planes as a way of dissuading those who wanted to leave. A million people, ruined and desperate, had packed their bags and left, Pierre among them.

On the day in question, he made a few preparations to welcome Fabregas. On his orders, Jeanne bought a soup tureen. On the dining-room dresser, Pierre arranged a place mat, a fruit basket, and that enamelled tureen in the shape of a pumpkin. Inside it, he hid his Modèle 1935 automatic pistol and a spare magazine. Just in case.

Their guest was very personable, as usual. He was a successful man, at ease in every situation, with a loud voice and a pot belly, holding their child above his head, a kind word for everyone. He made up some stories about problems on his train journey there, and everyone laughed. The doctor had been covered with sweat when he arrived, his camel-hair coat folded under his arm. With every movement he made, the smell of his cologne filled the air. It was his signature.

Pierre had hugged him when he came in. This was not Pierre's style, and the doctor had immediately understood. He'd laughed and done a twirl as he took off his jacket, to show that he'd come unarmed.

After that, the dinner went well, despite Liliane's tantrums. No matter how many times Pierre punished her, she didn't stop. She'd been that way ever since they'd left Oran.

Jeanne had made *sobrasada* pastries and a salad of marinated peppers. After this starter, they ate a macaroni-and-meatball gratin. For dessert, they had dates bought fresh that morning at the market. The doctor devoured everything, punctuating each mouthful with excessive compliments. The two bottles of Chiroubles wine barely lasted until dessert. Throughout, they chatted enthusiastically, swapping news about various people and talking about the future with a forced optimism that was like a form of politeness for these people who had no idea what they would be doing twenty-four hours later. Night filtered through the shutters, bringing the sea smells, hydrocarbon vapours and high-pitched voices of women from the working-class neighbourhoods of Toulon. When it was time for coffee, Jeanne put Liliane to bed before retreating to the kitchen to wash the dishes. Despite the water flowing from the tap, she recognised the sound of the doctor's gold lighter. Then a cigar smell spread through the apartment. Anxiously, she put her ear to the door, the rubber gloves scrunched up in her fist.

'You can't go on living like this,' the doctor said. 'There's nothing for you here in France. And we need you with us in Spain.'

'I can't ask that of Jeanne.'

'Things have changed. We have support now.'

'Yeah, right. They're trying to extradite you.'

'Not at all. That's just for the gallery. We can rely on our friends. Franco's nephew is on our side.' And then, sententiously, Fabregas added: 'We will never go back. That's over, my friend.'

'We'll see.'

'Think about your safety, at least.'

'Oh, yeah? And who am I supposed to fear, exactly?' Pierre said, irritated.

'Everyone. The police, the commandos who don't want to retire, the secret service, the FLN . . . everyone.'

'That doesn't change a thing. We're not going to leave. I'm French. At least they can't take that from me.'

An awkward silence followed and Jeanne feared that the men were about to catch her spying on them. But, after clearing his throat, Fabregas said, in a light-hearted voice: 'Very well. But you'll need to hide for as long as it lasts. Things will settle down in the end.'

'Not after what we did.'

'Oh, they will, they will. You'll see. De Gaulle is a politician, not a man of principle. That's what they don't understand. He'll wipe the slate clean eventually. Just like he did with the collaborators after the war.'

'That's a strange comparison.'

'What do you expect? The only just causes are victorious causes.'

'You're a politician too.'

'Ha!'

A chair scraped across the floor, then the dresser drawer groaned open. Pierre was serving his guest a glass of eau-de-vie.

'Cheers.'

'Cheers.'

The doctor slammed his empty glass down on the table and looked amused. 'Actually,' he said, 'I think we can play a clever political trick. And, at the same time, get you out.'

Pierre let him talk.

'You'll take the money. Or part of the money. And I'll tell the others that you left with all the loot.'

'I thought Gorel was the treasurer.'

'Oh, Gorel! I've talked to Gorel. We've come to an arrangement.'

'You have the money?'

'Not all of it. Just some.'

'How much?'

'Doesn't matter. The point is, some of them imagine that I've got millions. Gold ingots!' The doctor laughed again. 'Right now, though, it's more of a pain in the arse than anything else. All these cunning little bastards are trying to squeeze me for money. If I can get rid of the cash, it'll be one less reason for us to kill each other. Anyway, most of the guys trust you.'

'That's not the impression I got.'

'It's true. And if you go away, it'll create an optical illusion. A mirage. I'll have put the treasure in a safe place, you see. I'll have the upper hand again.'

'We begin as soldiers and we end up as bandits.'

The two men fell silent. Pierre poured them some more eau-de-vie.

'To your good health!' the doctor said. 'I'll get you some of the cash and new identity papers. After that, you'll travel east. My sister has the keys to a house in the Vosges. A safe place, in the middle of a forest. Her husband's from that region. She offered the house to me as a hideout. And you already know the area.'

'I passed through during the war. Jeanne won't like it, though. It's freezing cold up there.'

'It's pretty, though. And the air is pure. It'll be perfect for your kid's allergies. And at least it'll be home: you won't have to keep moving all the time. Just settle down there. The locals won't bother you. After that, time heals all wounds, as they say.'

'You reckon?' Pierre said sarcastically.

The doctor burst out laughing again. An incorrigible theorist, Fabregas had a weakness for improbable combinations and convoluted plots. In the eyes of many people, this made him a brilliant strategist. Pierre did not share that opinion. What he took from this plan was that he was being given a house in a remote location and a nest-egg to start again. He couldn't turn his nose up at that.

'Are you sure?' Jeanne had asked again, fearfully eyeing the half-destroyed yet somehow indestructible shack.

The little girl hung from her hand, sweaty and exhausted, saying things that no one could understand in her whiny voice.

Without bothering to reply, Pierre shoved a Gitanes between his lips and headed to the door. He hadn't been expecting a miracle, but this place was a ruin! The hairs on his forearms stood erect in the cold east wind.

This was where their new life would begin, Pierre decided. But the damp had welded the door to its frame, and the key that Fabregas's sister had given them was no use at all. He shouldered the door open and instantly the smell hit him in the back of his throat: a bitter mix of ammonia and undergrowth. He lit his cigarette to mask the stink and give himself courage.

In the kitchen he found a fireplace big enough for a man to stand inside, several chairs in a decent condition, a cracked stove, some open cupboards, and a dresser. On the table were a dozen empty beer cans and an enamelled steel coffee pot. He picked it up. It was full. Full of old piss. His teeth sank into the Gitanes' filter.

He made a quick tour of the house. Four rooms on the ground floor, including a bathroom. The floorboards were covered with constellations of cigarette burns. There were no doors. Scraps of wallpaper hung from the walls, on which were scrawled insults, lyrics from 1960s pop songs, anti-Gaullist slogans.

To get upstairs, he had to climb a ladder that he found in the garage. In the bedrooms, mattresses lay, like corpses, surrounded by clouds of cigarette stubs. From this, Pierre deduced that the local boys must bring their not-too-fussy girlfriends here to screw. And, once the sex was over, they went downstairs for a well-earned piss in the kitchen.

At least the roof wasn't too bad.

When he went back downstairs, he heard sneezing. Jeanne must have caught a cold already.

A month after sneezing, Jeanne started coughing. She never wore the ferret-fur coat that her husband had given her. One night, some time after his wife's death, Pierre Duruy went down to the cellar and inserted the barrel of a Ruby automatic pistol into his mouth. In the end, though, he had more difficulty giving up on life than on his illusions.

After that, he led a shrunken existence, taking care of his daughter – badly – and expecting very little from life. In 1968 he was pardoned for being a member of a terrorist organisation and given back his name, but he remained on the margins. He didn't get involved in politics any more, or in anything at all really. He was content to make money, coldly and unscrupulously.

MARTEL

Before hitting the sack, Martel had gone over the figures again. He was in trouble, even deeper in the red. The next day it would be over. He might even be in prison – he couldn't rule out the possibility. He'd thought about giving a speech to his friends, to explain. Maybe he'd have to call Cofidis and beg for a loan. Or rob a corner shop. But there was nothing open at this time of night anyway. He was truly fucked this time.

Especially as his cousin had come over for a coffee. He hadn't seen her in years. She was one of those proletarian beauties: glorious at sixteen, faded at twenty, spending the rest of their lives dyeing their hair and sipping Mazagran while their kids wailed around them. Now forty, she was a single mother, leading a sour life of loneliness, TV and crosswords. To start with she'd found it hard to talk about, but . . . well, the fact was her mother was in a bad state. She was losing her marbles, like Martel's mother had. They needed to put her in a home, but that was so expensive . . . Martel explained that he wasn't in a great position himself. The economic crisis and all that. The factory was sometimes closed several days a week. His cousin knew this, of course: she watched the news. She nodded gravely, dropping another sugar cube into her coffee. She didn't leave before being given an envelope, though. There wasn't much inside, but that's how bad habits start.

Martel got out of bed and went to the living room. When they'd sold the house, he and his mother had come to live here. It was a decent place, not too expensive, with a lift. It had been his idea and he'd chosen the apartment. Now he lived here alone, but he hadn't changed much. The plastic tablecloth decorated with pictures of fruit bowls was still there, the doilies and net curtains too. He'd thrown out the velvet sofa but kept the Stressless armchair with matching footrests. Every time he brought someone home, especially a girl, he had to explain the décor. Not that he'd brought many girls back recently. When Bruce went to the red-light district in Strasbourg, he'd asked Martel if he wanted to tag along. Martel had shaken his head virtuously, but the reality was that he couldn't even afford a hand-job at the moment.

He lit a cigarette and looked around the empty car park, then checked the time on the DVD player: 2 a.m. already, and he was working in the morning. In other words, his night was screwed. He turned on the TV and flicked mindlessly through the channels, cut his toenails on the coffee-table. He wished he could talk to someone about all this.

The hour of reckoning was close at hand.

Trade unionism was not a vocation for Martel. Until the army, he'd never wanted to join anything. And then in the army he'd done as he was told. After that, at Velocia, he'd just tried to get by and somehow found himself getting elected as secretary to the Works Council. His first four-year term had passed in a daze, but he'd gradually got used to it.

He still remembered his first Works Council meeting. Shyly, file in hand, he'd had to introduce himself to the managers. You never saw the bigwigs down on the factory floor. He'd practically blushed as he said hello. Mrs Meyer, the head of HR, had gone around warmly shaking everyone's hand, her pretty smile turned on and off by remote control. The craftiest ones had stood in the corners, talking among themselves, laughing loudly, playing the role of vulgar plebs.

As soon as the meeting began, old Cunin started griping. According to him, the head of HR wasn't fit to preside over the Works Council. They needed the managing director or someone. And, since that was how things stood, the meeting was suspended.

Martel had been startled to see the others weighing in like that, ordinary blokes who didn't look like much. They might whinge a bit on the factory floor, but no more than most. In all honesty, he'd had a blast. It had felt like a sort of vengeance. And then there was the vocabulary of the meetings – obscure, legalistic, delivered in a vindictive tone, close to outright disrespect – and the trench warfare, the theatre. Each side played its role. Management was pragmatic, the unions were divided: there was the conciliatory CFDT, the struggling FO, and the hawkish, extreme CGT. As for the executives' representative, the chair was left empty. Too much work, apparently. It was pure entertainment.

The factory was just like all the others: no matter how hard they tried, there really wasn't much they could do to turn back the tide. And there they were in the middle of it all, a focal point, a space where war was possible. An unequal battle, admittedly, but even so this was where the resistance was organised, where the bosses could be threatened, criticised, bullied. And then there was this new weapon, abstract and brutal and unimaginably powerful: the law. If you knew how to use it, the law was a shield that could break every enemy assault. Martel learned how to tip the balance of power. With two articles in the labour code, they could build an impregnable fortress. It was magnificent.

Later, Martel moved to a different union, took classes at the Confederation. He became an important man at Velocia, forging a reputation in line with his personality as someone who knew how to pick his battles, only sticking his neck out when it really mattered. His word, carefully timed and fully informed, carried weight. The first battle he won, he saved a guy who deserved the sack. Martel understood, then, how it worked: it wasn't a question of justice or truth, but of defending your mates' interests.

When their time in office came to an end, the old Works Council veterans left with stuffed envelopes, thanks to an early retirement plan.

They also left seats to fill. At the next election, Martel became the Works Council secretary. It was essentially an administrative post, but Martel enjoyed its perks, particularly the chance to speak to management as equals, as if the disparity in their payslips no longer mattered.

It was an old factory, struggling in a competitive market. More and more often, constructors went elsewhere. So, one fine day, two consultants from Paris came to downsize the staff. They made only one appearance on the factory floor. Both men were young and wore pointy shoes. They walked through Hall Two without looking up, without shaking a single hand. They were given carte blanche to stick their noses anywhere they wanted, to open every file. The girls in the administration department giggled among themselves. One of the consultants was cute, the other less so, but they'd come down from the capital in a Peugeot 607 and they were polite and witty. The girls liked seeing them about the place. It made a change.

In the end, they handed in their report and all the temps were dismissed. All these people who worked year-round suddenly vanished, with their debts, their pay-offs, all the skills they'd learned. After that, they put an end to overtime: too expensive, the consultants explained. Some of the administration positions were merged; two executives were fired. Their duties were reallocated to other colleagues, who had to pick up the slack without working overtime, of course, because that was now prohibited. In other words, they did the work for free. They were executives, so they were paid a flat fee, not an hourly rate, and they were content with the status conferred on them by their impressive job titles, even though those job titles no longer meant very much. At last, the managing director became hard-nosed. The night-shift guys, who had organised their lives around their jobs for years, and were paid extra in compensation, were put on day shift and replaced by younger, cheaper, less annoying workers who weren't union members.

The tension at the factory rose a little higher. The time had come.

One morning, very early, Martel arrived carrying his file binder, which he was rarely without these days. He was wearing overalls, as always. He gathered the union reps plus a few of the older, more outspoken guys whom everyone listened to. The atmosphere was tense, conspiratorial. He made them an offer. The Works Council, which had always been well-run, had amassed quite a lot of money. About thirty thousand euros in all.

'I've got a proposal for you,' said Martel. 'If you follow me, we'll double your holiday vouchers.'

The disappointment in the ranks was almost palpable. Holiday vouchers? What the fuck? They were at least expecting to go on strike or beat up a foreman . . . *something*. What was this bullshit about holiday vouchers?

Martel leaned across his desk and all the men moved closer to hear what he was going to say. What it means, Martel explained, is that you'll be able to buy holiday vouchers worth 150 euros for fifteen euros. With those vouchers, you can do your shopping, eat at restaurants, rent a hotel room for your holiday, whatever you want.

The thicker ones were happy: it sounded like a great deal. The others wondered what he wanted in exchange. But still nobody really understood. Martel played his trump card. What he wanted in exchange was a strike. Not a loud-mouthed, futile strike, where they fried sausages on the picket lines and watched their jobs disappear. He wanted a subtle, undeclared strike: sabotage, lowered productivity, extended lunch hours. He wanted the factory to sink slowly into a hole. He wanted the foremen hauled over the coals, the boss summoned to Headquarters. What he wanted was a giant, meticulously organised fuck-up, discreet in its operation but implacable in its effects. The men would be paid to mess around, basically, until the management gave in to their demands. And if they were fined, who cared? They'd be compensated with holiday vouchers.

To approve this expense, the Works Council had to vote. Martel summoned an extraordinary meeting and – to the surprise of the head of HR – all the unions agreed to squander a budget carefully accumulated over fifteen years. And yet the only reason that sum even existed was that the unions had never been able to agree on how it should be spent.

After that, the 150-euro vouchers sold like hot cakes and the factory was plunged into disarray. Raw materials went missing; productivity slumped in spite of threats and fines; deliveries no longer reached their destinations; the machines went on the blink; and the number of accidents rose dramatically, even prompting the visit of a labour inspector.

Her name was Rita, and she and Martel quickly came to an understanding.

'I'm going to send a report to the regional office,' she told him. 'I've never seen figures like this before. A twenty-five per cent increase of accidents in two months! Your factory is turning into a slaughterhouse.'

Martel smiled at her.

'You don't agree?' she asked, surprised.

'Oh, I do. Absolutely,' Martel answered, his mind elsewhere.

She smiled back at him.

Later, the inspector met with the head of HR, since the managing director was absent, having been summoned by the board of the PSA Group, who were furious about all the bungled orders.

'It makes very little difference whether it's your fault or your employees' fault,' Rita explained. 'Legally, you will be held responsible. By you, I mean the management. You have to do something because, at this rate, there will soon be a serious accident and that will cost you dearly.'

'But we can't personally monitor every employee,' the head of HR countered.

'I understand. But perhaps this is a management problem. Why don't you see what you can do in terms of employee relations?'

'No, but listen, these people are doing it deliberately! They're playing politics. They're trying to bring the factory down so they'll get what they want.'

'Ah, you see. You even say it yourself. It's a political problem. Maybe you need to meet them halfway . . .'

'I'm sorry,' the head of HR said sanctimoniously, 'but a business exists above all for its customers. We're not in the school playground. If they keep on like this, we'll lose our last contracts and then what will happen? They won't have jobs any more.'

Arms crossed, Martel stood listening.

The inspector calmly replied: 'I know that. But in the meantime, your customers don't seem entirely satisfied with the situation. In my opinion, you need to find a way to balance everyone's interests.'

Now, in his living room, thinking back to that meeting, Martel couldn't help smiling again. He liked the woman's style, the back of her neck, the way she wasn't easily taken in.

'Anyway,' she'd concluded, 'I'll stay in touch with you and with the Works Council secretary. I'll need to attend the next health and safety meeting. Until then, we just have to hope that nothing serious happens. Oh, and check your accounts. I'm not sure that you're economising in the right areas.'

Martel had accompanied the inspector to her car. She drove an old Saab. Like her, it was nice-looking even if it had quite a few miles on the clock.

'I think we'll be seeing each other again,' the inspector said, before putting on her sunglasses and reversing out of the car park.

But the next time, it had been her colleague who'd come in her place.

In the end, the management had given the night-shift guys their old jobs back and rehired a few temps. This concession was quickly followed by a rise in productivity. Then a Romanian factory had gone on strike for pay rises. After they, in turn, had been labelled uncompetitive, part of the factory's output had been relocated.

Be that as it may, and even if the Works Council's finances had taken a hit, Martel had clearly emerged as the victor in this battle.

After that, he'd eased up a bit at work. He started spending more time in the managers' offices, gossiping, networking, checking which way the wind was blowing. On the factory floor, he would buy coffee for everyone. He walked around the building in overalls and espadrilles, openly flouting the safety procedures, his binder full of documents under one arm. During meetings, he spoke as little as he had before, but people listened more carefully to him now. Even within the hallowed corridors of the Confederation, his future had become a subject of conversation. And he was handsome too: he'd look good on television.

He grew so confident that he almost forgot about his financial worries. The bank manager, unaware of his meteoric rise, was quick to remind him. So when Bruce had suggested his idea of rock concerts, Martel had agreed and become Thierry Molina's personal slave. Unfortunately, it was still far from enough.

Sometimes, when he went to visit his mother, she was lucid enough to recognise him and she would thank him repeatedly for her individual room, the wonderful staff, the delicious Paris-Brest she'd been given for dessert. All the same, she did worry about how much it was all costing him. 'It's fine, Mum,' Martel would reassure her, his large hand imprisoned in her little ones.

From then on, Martel had granted himself a few credit facilities. He'd kept a few holiday vouchers without paying for them. No one was going to pick a fight with him over a hundred euros missing from the till.

Next, he'd paid for some training programmes to be developed. They were expensive but absolutely necessary (and also completely fake). A friend of his forged the invoices, pocketing 10 per cent for his troubles. Martel siphoned off just over ten thousand euros in this way.

And the next day – in a few hours' time, in fact – Martel was supposed to present the Works Council accounts to his fellow union representatives and the factory management. They were almost thirteen thousand euros short. He should never have let things go this far. Now he was fucked.

He lit another cigarette. And that inspector, Rita . . . Fucking hell, what would she think of him?

RITA

'I won't be coming to the office today, Duflot.'

'Really?' the young inspector asked, in mock-surprise.

It was five o'clock in the afternoon. Duflot had undoubtedly packed his bag already and was counting the seconds until the bell rang.

'Less cheek from you, young man,' said Rita, who had a guilty soft spot for the little prat with his college degrees and his dead-end future. 'I was in an accident. My car's a write-off. And I'm a bit shaken.'

'Nothing serious, I hope,' Duflot said, at last showing some concern.

'No, just bruises. The back half of the car's a mess, but I'm okay. Oh, and I saw your butcher too. Problem solved.'

'Yeah? Didn't he remind you of someone?'

'What do you mean?'

'I don't know . . . Michel Fourniret, Fred West, someone like that . . .'

'Anything else new at work?'

'Not really. Oh . . . yes! The newbie's here.'

'Ah yes, little Saraoui. I'd completely forgotten her. So how is she?'

'Well, I think I might be in love.'

'Again?'

'She even persuaded me to do some work.'

'Surely you're exaggerating, Duflot . . .'

'The fraudsters will soon learn to know and fear her. She's passionate about the labour code. And super-hot too!'

'Don't forget who you're talking to!'

'Oh, yeah. Well, anyway, we went to visit a café in Dompaire.'

'And?'

'The owners couldn't be bothered to find their Licence IV. I don't even know if it existed when that place opened. So I quoted it directly, to impress her.'

'Did it work?'

'Kind of.'

'Well, you're a *kind-of* kind of guy. See you tomorrow, Duflot. We should know the extent of the damage by then.'

'Take care of yourself, boss.'

'You too.'

Before hanging up, Rita wiped the water from her drenched hair off the receiver. Then she went to the bathroom to take another look at the mark from her seatbelt on her left shoulder. The bruise was rainbow-coloured and not altogether unpleasant-looking.

She took a tube of aspirin from her medicine cabinet and chewed one while she put on a sturdy, comfortable old pair of Dr Martens and took one last look at the girl, who was now sleeping silently in her bed, face down and mouth half open.

Meanwhile, Laurent was waiting by the bookcase in the living room below. He'd designed that bookcase himself, ten years earlier. The oak planks, loaded with records and books, were supported by short piles of bricks. The idea was to distribute the weight in the most balanced way possible. Each extra kilo made the whole thing more solid, without the need for any screws or wall plugs. The bookcase was virtually indestructible . . . unless you took out all the books and records, of course.

'I'm thinking of getting rid of it,' said Rita, as she came downstairs.

Laurent turned to smile at her, despite this low blow. 'May I know why?'

'I dunno . . . Just to change things. It takes up so much space too. There's too much clutter in my life.'

Laurent didn't rise to the bait. 'How's the girl?'

'She's calmed down. Or, rather, the Lexomil knocked her out. Thanks for coming round, anyway.'

They were the same height and more or less the same age. Standing side by side, they both felt younger. The two of them looked like old school friends, or maybe a brother and sister.

'I don't think you'd have had any trouble finding someone to help you, with a naked girl in your car.'

Rita headed towards the kitchen and Laurent followed her. There was a large oak table in the middle, although still plenty of space for the oven, the gas hob, the brand-new Fagor fridge and the countertops. In one corner, an old mastiff was snoring. His name was Baccala, and he, too, had come into Rita's life by running naked through the woods, abandoned and starving.

The inspector opened the oven that she used as a bar and took out a half-empty bottle of Bushmills. She grabbed two glasses from the sink and began to pour, but Laurent put a hand over his glass.

'You're wrong,' said Rita, before taking her first mouthful.

'I'll have a Perrier or a glass of orange juice if you have any.'

Rita found some mineral water in the fridge. 'That fridge of yours is incredible,' she said, kicking it closed. 'Everything I put in it freezes in about five minutes.'

'It was a bargain. I thought it'd make you happy.'

'Good thing you're there to take care of me.'

She drank his good health before pouring herself a second glass.

'That's quite a thirst you have.'

'It's been quite a day. Anyway, you can talk . . .'

Laurent nodded. 'We might have got along better if we'd both got drunk at the same time.'

'Or both stayed sober.'

Laurent's back was reflected in the French windows behind him and Rita was touched to see the beginnings of a bald spot at the crown of his head. 'Well, I'm glad you're here,' she admitted.

Laurent looked pleased, but quickly changed the subject.

'I can't help thinking that we made a mistake with this kitchen.'

'What do you mean?' Rita was grateful for this diversion. Declarations were not really her thing, especially after she'd been drinking.

'It's like the whole house has been swallowed by the kitchen.'

'That was how I wanted it.'

'And that's how I designed it.'

'So what's the problem?'

'Well, I never saw you cooking anything.'

'Exactly. But I thought your house was supposed to serve as your office.'

'I can see where you're going with this . . .'

'And I don't remember seeing you do much work recently.'

Laurent put his hands in the air, apologetically. 'My fault. I shouldn't have started.' He showed his regret in a few grimaces, then continued; 'So how will you get to work now the Saab's all smashed up?'

Rita thought about this while she filled her glass again.

'Insurance should cover it. In the meantime . . . I don't know. I could ask Duflot to come and pick me up.'

'He'd like that. He lives right at the other end of town.'

'Yeah. Plus I imagine he's already offered his services to the new girl.'

'You've got a new girl?'

'Careful! Duflot's already marked out his territory. No, I suppose I'll have to rent a car. A 206 or something small like that.'

'I could lend you mine.'

'Yeah, right. A labour inspector in a Mercedes.'

'Seriously, though, when are you planning to inform the cops?'

'I'm not.'

'She's not a dog, Rita. You don't know anything about this girl. Where she came from, what she was doing there . . .'

'If you want my opinion, she's been through quite a lot.'

'All the more reason to tell the cops.'
'We'll see.'

Laurent knew her better than anyone. They'd lived together for five years. He couldn't remember the details: a sleepless night in Dublin, holidays on the Île de Sein, a conversation over seafood about one day having children together, the pink nail varnish she used to wear in the late 1980s. When he met her, in 1988, he'd just signed a contract with a major distribution outlet. He rode a Norton Commando, often without a helmet but always in a pair of Ray-Bans. He was a show-off and a hopeless romantic, who loved B-roads and drunken weekends with friends. His hair was still quite long then, his father had just died, and out of respect he'd decided not to get a tattoo. He began designing massive supermarkets. In Berlin, a wall fell and he was among the first people to sense the new opportunities there. In those countries still recovering from a Communist hangover, he would build transparent towers, design shopping centres, trace a future of vegetable aisles, promotional sales and strip lights. Now he liked well-run firms, working lunches, all-expenses-paid holidays. Since he was earning quite a lot of money, he got his hair cut, sold his motorbike, and took off his sunglasses. Since he worked too hard, he started drinking. Since he was always absent, he forgot Rita. And when they saw each other, they would get drunk, argue and fuck like crazy. One day, Rita remembered she was free and decided to leave him. And so Laurent Debef, who'd always been a nice boy, if a little slow on the uptake, had understood. He started drinking more, leaving the management of his company to younger, more ambitious colleagues. Despite all the money he spent on her, Rita didn't come back. She refused most of his gifts and slept with him occasionally, because it felt good and it was nobody else's business. One day, he built a house next door to hers and Rita was angry with him for more than a year. They will never completely leave each other: they're neighbours now. All the same, Laurent missed the boat. And Rita will never have children.

*   *   *

66

They talked about various things. Laurent was a little hungry, so Rita made him some soup. She just ate an apple. She continued drinking obstinately, unhurriedly. She thought about her new lodger. It was all very enjoyable. And then Laurent stood up. It was ten o'clock already.

'All right, I'll see you later,' he said, kissing her cheek. 'You know where to find me if you need me.'

'Okay.'

'I do wonder where she came from, though, that girl . . .'

'We'll see.'

'You don't seem too worried. You don't think it's a bit weird? A teenage girl running around in her knickers in the middle of February? She must have been escaping from *something* – it's just obvious.'

'Don't start having a go at me, Laurent.' Rita sighed. 'Not tonight.'

Laurent dropped the subject and she slammed the door behind him. Her head felt heavy. Fuck it.

She lit one last Winston and put the empty glasses into the sink. As she closed the ground-floor curtains, she saw a light on in Laurent's house, on the other side of the hedge. She stood there for a moment, watching. Then she remembered the girl asleep upstairs. She felt happy. Often, after work, she would quickly eat something and have a couple of drinks in front of the TV. From time to time, she'd try to be good, try to think what else she could do, but in the end she always had a drink. It was nice to have company for a change.

Upstairs, the girl was still sleeping, on her back now, her face strangely serene. Her black hair was all tangled. Without thinking, Rita moved a strand away from her face, stroked her cheek, her shoulder. She had round shoulders, like a child's. She looked a bit like that actress, the girl in *Last Tango in Paris*: a sweet little face, slightly chubby, with full lips and rings around her eyes that gave her a serious look. And the curly black hair, of course, wild against the white sheets. She was cute.

Rita examined her, giving free rein to her curiosity. After a while, she even lifted up the sheet and looked underneath. The girl had very pale skin and you could see the bluish veins beneath it. She had a round belly, small breasts, long legs and narrow feet. Her toenails were grimy. She looked seventeen or eighteen. Rita's fingers smoothed a circle around the girl's belly button. She was still sleeping peacefully, thanks to the Lexomil. Then Rita touched her wide nipples. It was strange having someone at her mercy like that. She realised what she'd been doing and it made her laugh.

After brushing her teeth, for once, she put on an oversized T-shirt. Droopy's sad face covered her chest. Then she went to her bedroom, turned off the bedside lamp and tried to find a bit of space next to the girl.

She stayed like that for a long time, daydreaming. The passing minutes shone red from the display of her Sanyo radio alarm clock. When she accidentally pulled at the blanket, the girl moaned and muttered some incomprehensible words. She looked as if she were defending herself against something. She started twitching and Rita pressed herself against the girl's body, whispered soothing words into her ear.

Soon, the inspector realised that she was hungry.

She went back down to the kitchen and made herself a cheese sandwich. Baccala watched her, wet-eyed, tongue lolling. She tossed him a bit of bread covered with Bovril – his favourite snack. Then the dog followed her to the sofa, where she wrapped herself in a blanket before eating her sandwich in front of the TV. She felt good, weary but calm. In the end she fell asleep in front of the late-night news. Australia was on fire. Outside, the temperature was close to minus ten.

MARTEL

He parked the Volvo in its usual spot, pulled his sleeves down over his tattoos, and stubbed out his cigarette in the overflowing ashtray. Before leaving the car, he forced himself to breathe more slowly, then jumped at a knock on the window. It was Locatelli and Léon Michel, both looking haggard. Oh, shit, thought Martel, opening the window. They know.

'At least let me get out of the car.'

The two men obeyed, then immediately began talking over each other.

'You have to see this.'

'I've never seen anything like it.'

'It's unbelievable.'

'They took away a machine.'

'The stamper for the WX9. It's gone!'

'We were supposed to have it until 2010.'

'Fucking hell, those bastards!'

'They deserve to be shot.'

Léon Michel used to be an activist and tended to regard violence as the solution to every problem, even if it was a just a coffee machine that didn't work or someone trying to explain to him how social-security contributions worked.

'Who? What?' Martel demanded, interrupting this flow of words. 'What machine? What the hell are you talking about?'

They explained it to him. A machine had been moved out during the night. It had been dismantled by the recently hired temps and the engineers who were supposed to repair it. The morning shift had found a big open space in Hall One when they got to work that day. Nothing remained but the shape of it on the ground, a clean spot amid all the dirt, like the pale rectangle left behind when you take a painting off a wall.

'They're moving the production.'

'And the night shift didn't notice anything?'

'They weren't working. It was the weekend of November the eleventh and, since the order books are practically empty, they decided to give the guys a rest.'

'They should have told the Works Council, don't you think?'

Locatelli blinked so fast he looked as if he was trying to send signals in Morse code.

'Of course,' said Martel, before the other two could answer.

In Hall One, there were a few clusters of anxious faces, but most people were still working.

'What a bunch of bastards!'

'We won't let them get away with it.'

'What can we do?'

'We need to get hold of those temps for a start . . .'

'They were just following orders.'

'You think that's a reason?'

'I'm telling you, we need to get them.'

'They've left anyway.'

'No, I saw one of them this morning. That big Arab.'

'Bastard.'

You could see the bitterness in their expressions and gestures, in the way they moved from one group to another, talking and talking.

The foreman, Serge Claudel, called to Martel: 'Hey! What the hell's going on here? Tell your friends to get back to work.'

'Don't worry, Serge,' Martel told him soothingly. He was feeling way more relaxed now. This mess was his big opportunity.

He went to all the machines and told his friends to start work again. The Works Council meeting would take place at ten, as planned. Then they'd find out what was going on. Behind Martel, the foreman was running around, saying: 'Yeah, good, about time too.'

Just then, Locatelli – who had vanished some time before – reappeared. He was beside himself. 'There's a problem with Denis.'

'Where?' the foreman asked.

'At the coffee machine.'

Martel and the other two rushed over there. Denis Demange was perhaps the most stupid, surly man in the factory, and that was saying something. He got through two packs of Pall Mall and a dozen cups of coffee every day, and once he got started on the Arabs, or the French football team, or the way the bosses calculated overtime, it was impossible to shut him up.

Martel was the first to reach the common area in Hall One. Denis Demange was there all right. He was holding Hamid the temp by his throat and apparently trying to ram him inside the coffee machine. Behind him, on a cork noticeboard, there were paparazzi photos of female TV personalities bare-breasted on the beach. There was also a list of car-sharers and the obituary of a colleague who'd been crushed by a mechanical press five years earlier.

'What's going on here?'

'Mind your own business, Martel. I've got a bone to pick with this cunt.'

Hamid, for his part, looked oddly detached, as if all this were no more than a minor inconvenience.

'Come on, Denis,' Martel said, putting a hand on his shoulder. 'Just calm down.'

'Don't you fucking touch me! Those temp bastards nicked our machine.'

'Don't be ridiculous. You know that's not what happened.'

For a while now, the temps had been the target of constant abuse. They were hated because they were better-paid, because they were in the bosses' pockets, because they divided the workers, because they didn't do the work properly.

Martel grabbed Denis by the collar and pulled him backwards. 'Come on, Denis, we can sort this out.'

'Oh, so now you're defending them?'

'I defend all the workers here. Including you, Denis. Now, come with me.'

Through the hall, amid the repeated sighing of the machines, the pneumatic hum of the presses, Martel accompanied Denis to his post, one hand on his shoulder, as if they were best mates out for a walk together. Denis struggled to keep up with Martel's long stride. He also struggled to free himself from Martel's strong grip, but in vain.

'Denis, just give it a fucking rest, will you?'

'I know what I'm doing. Nobody gets to tell me . . .'

Martel grabbed the back of his neck and squeezed. From a distance it looked like an affectionate gesture, but Denis knew it was nothing of the kind.

'No need to get all riled up like this, Denis. I'm going to take care of it.'

It took Denis a minute or so before he felt able to start work. With Martel's huge hand on his neck, he'd felt something strange: a sort of panic, like the time when his laces had got caught in the blades of a lawnmower. He promised himself he would have his revenge.

The Works Council meeting began and Martel quickly showed his hand. 'Before we get started, I'd like to remind management of its obligations. The Works Council must be kept informed of all changes to working conditions. Instead of which, you had the WX9 moved without telling us.'

'That's true,' the head of HR admitted. 'Let me explain why—'

'Another time. For now, you need to listen to me. You didn't inform us even though you were obliged to do so. Consequently, I've called the labour inspector.'

'That really wasn't necessary,' said Mrs Meyer, smiling prettily as she fiddled with her silver Dinh Van ring.

'Interrupt me one more time . . .' said Martel.

His tone was unpleasantly neutral. It was hard to tell if his sentence was a threat, a question or an order.

He looked Mrs Meyer straight in the eyes. She smiled nervously. The other union reps hid their embarrassment as best they could, pretending to read documents, playing with their phones, cleaning their fingernails with a Bic biro lid.

Martel let the silence hang. 'The meeting is suspended,' he said at last.

'You don't have the authority to make that decision on your own,' the head of HR protested.

'Do you have a better suggestion?'

She hesitated. She analysed the situation. She suspected that Martel was eager to avoid presenting the Works Council accounts. This would be an opportunity to put him in a difficult position. Then again, if she lost Martel, who would management have to deal with next? She decided to throw in the towel. 'The meeting is suspended.'

The representatives all stood up and left. Martel was the last one out.

In the factory, his name was on everyone's lips. The excitement was almost palpable.

As soon as he got the chance, Martel went out to the car park and locked himself into his car. Droplets of mist covered the Volvo's windows. Once inside, he felt cocooned. That was a close shave, he thought, as he called Bruce. 'I'm going to need you.'

'Oh, yeah?'

'Your friends, the Ben-somethings.'

'The Benbareks?'

'I need to see them.'

'For money?'

'Get me a meeting.'

'You sure? The Benbareks don't mess around, you know . . .'

'Just do it. And call me when it's sorted.'

Martel started to think. That story with the machine had really saved his skin. It was a miracle. But now he had to act fast. Even if it meant relying on Bruce and his hare-brained plans. It probably wasn't the most prudent decision, but what choice did he have?

Seconds passed. How much would he need? Fifteen, twenty thousand euros?

And then after, to keep going?

Well, he could think about that later.

Martel and the inspector walked through the factory. Fluorescent lighting had replaced daylight. They walked at a leisurely pace, taking their time.

'They broke the rules, no doubt about it. But ultimately the employer owns the means of production, so there's not much we can do.'

'I understand,' said Martel.

'You can take them to court for not informing the Works Council, but I don't see any way for you to get the machine back. The judge might well find in your favour, but it could take months.'

'I'm glad you came.'

They kept walking, both of them staring straight ahead. Outside, the cold November wind embraced them. The inspector slid her hands under her armpits.

'It's over there,' said Martel, pointing out the car park.

'I know.'

They were walking almost in slow motion now.

'Do you see this kind of thing often?'

'No.'

After a pause, she added: 'Usually, with this kind of case, the person sends me a letter. And I reply with a letter.'

'It's good of you to come, then.'

They were there now. She opened the Saab's door.

'Nice car,' Martel observed.

'It's getting old.'

'I still like it.'

She held out her hand and he grasped it in his.

'Your hands are freezing.'

The inspector got into the car and Martel stuck his cigarette between his lips before shoving his hands into the pockets of his jeans. He wasn't wearing overalls, for once. The cigarette end glowed red in the cold evening wind. The car wouldn't start. The inspector kept trying, but nothing happened. Martel decided to knock on her window.

'It's the damp weather. Your battery must be flat.'

'Probably.'

'I can take you. My car's just over here.'

'No need.'

'Please, I insist.'

She followed him to his car and he drove her home. Neither spoke. They stared at the dotted line in the middle of the road. They didn't have the radio on. They didn't know what to say. All the same, the time passed too quickly. Martel dropped her outside her house, which backed onto the forest.

'Well,' said the inspector, opening her door. 'Thanks for the lift.'

'My pleasure.'

'I'll send a tow truck to get the Saab.'

She appeared to hesitate. Then she got out of the car and walked to her house. A nice place, Martel thought, shifting into first. He'd been dreading today, but it hadn't turned out too badly at all.

RITA

In the end, Rita spent the night on the sofa. When she woke, it was already light outside and she had to protect her eyes from the sun as she looked out of the bay windows. She was surprised by an agreeable sensation of familiarity. The smell of warm coffee, toast. The sound of Laurent's voice, close by. He wouldn't normally just come into her house like that, though, without calling ahead, even if he had a set of keys. Rita thought he was probably here to see the girl, and she didn't like that idea.

She checked her watch. It was gone ten already. She was supposed to be at a building site near Remiremont right now. She'd discovered a shady contractor there, who systematically used substandard materials. It was a small-scale scam, but the houses he'd built all over the region were starting to crack. Eventually, one would collapse completely. It seemed better to prosecute the contractor now than to wait until they needed a team of rescue dogs to find some poor family under a pile of rubble.

She clambered off the sofa, stretched, and noticed that she was still in the Droopy T-shirt. She couldn't let the kid see her dressed like that. She had to keep up appearances. So, without a sound, she slipped into the utility room next to the garage. She found some dirty clothes in the laundry basket there and put them on, and she was about to join Laurent and the girl when she suddenly shivered. Laurent had come in without her even realising it. Now she thought about it, anyone could have done the same. She had to be more careful, with the girl there. She had to protect her from the bastards who had stripped her naked in the first place.

So the inspector began rummaging around the garage. The empty space left by the Saab only emphasised the surrounding disorder, and it took her a good five minutes to find what she was looking for. It was hidden in a corner, inside its cover: a rifle that had once belonged to Laurent, a souvenir of his fleeting passion for clay-pigeon shooting. Rita didn't really like weapons, not even a leisure item like this one, but Laurent had insisted that she keep it. If she didn't, he'd said, he would install an alarm system while she wasn't there. After two weeks of arguments, she'd agreed to keep the gun, and she hadn't touched it since. But things were different now. She took it to the living room and slid it under the sofa. She could find a better place for it later.

'I see you're making yourself at home,' said the inspector, as she went into the kitchen.

Laurent stood up, looking sheepish, and Baccala imitated him before trotting over to sniff his mistress.

'I found her in the garden. I think she was trying to slip away.'

'Really?'

The girl was sitting at the table, holding a piece of toast, a bowl of coffee in front of her. Apparently she'd been through Rita's wardrobe and, if she had been planning to slip away unnoticed, she'd really chosen the wrong clothing. She was wearing skin-tight white underwear and a sleeveless Complice T-shirt that offered a generous view of her bra. She also appeared to have applied her make-up that morning with a trowel.

'Why's she dressed like that?'

'Well, I didn't choose her clothes,' Laurent promised. 'Like I said, she was about to escape. I caught her just in time.'

'You could hardly miss her, in that outfit!'

'She was wearing your old bomber jacket too. If you look beyond her sartorial tastes, though, the girl does have something.'

Rita, teeth still gritted, poured herself some coffee, tore off a piece of baguette and joined them at the table.

The girl looked less like a kid in all that make-up: twenty, twenty-two, maybe even older. It was hard to tell. Rita reached out hesitantly towards her, without making contact. Then she knocked on the table to get her attention.

'What's your name?' No answer. She tried again in English.

'Don't waste your time. She won't talk. She hasn't said a single word to me, anyway.'

'I heard her talking last night. In her sleep. I don't know what language it was, though.'

'Eastern European, maybe?'

Rita shrugged.

'I suppose there's no point in me bringing up the idea of calling the cops again?'

'I'll deal with this in my own way.'

'Fine.'

Laurent recognised the bitter smile on Rita's face. Bad memories. He was about to leave, but Rita held him back. 'Come on, don't sulk. Just give me a few days. Enough time to make her better. After that, I'll do what needs to be done, you know I will.'

'As you like.'

'I'm going to need your car too.'

'Why?'

'To buy her some new clothes.'

'Ah, so you're adopting her . . .'

Laurent didn't press the point. He just gave her that condescending look, the 'I know you' look that Rita found incredibly irritating. He knew, by now, that he was a permanent part of her life. Maybe he imagined he had certain rights over her, a sort of permit enabling him to meddle in her affairs. Usually that attitude put her into a rage. Right now, she found it reassuring.

'Okay, so now it's just the two of us. I'm going to put the TV on to start with because I need to make some calls.'

This time, Rita put her hand on the girl's wrist. Looking up at her, the girl's dark eyes immediately misted over. Her lips were very pale. Her dirty black hair fell in graceless curls around her face. She was trying not to cry.

'Don't worry, my lovely. Everything's going to be all right now. We're going to buy you some clothes. That'll make you feel better.'

The girl didn't seem particularly reassured by this.

'All right. Well . . .'

Rita went into the living room and turned on the television, as she'd promised. She found an episode of *The Pink Panther* and turned up the volume. Then she came back to the kitchen and opened the French windows.

'Do what you want, okay? If you want to run off, you can. I'm not going to keep you prisoner.' She let a few seconds pass. 'You understand?'

The girl nodded. But she didn't dare finish her toast until Rita had left the room.

'Hello?'

'Oh, are you the new girl?'

'Yes. Is this Mrs Kleber?'

'Exactly. So how's it going?'

'It's going well. I'm settling in. I went to Eschlinger this morning, the DIY shop. It was terrible. Those people don't give a shit about us. They weren't in compliance with a single safety rule. I wrote up an official report.'

'Okay. Halima? That's your name, right?'

'Yes.'

'Listen, don't overdo it. You can scare them into making the important changes. After that, just leave it.'

'But it's the law.'

'I know that. Just go easy. It's not our job to close every shop we inspect. Ask Duflot to go with you – he can explain how things work.'

'I don't think that will be necessary.'

'I disagree. You'll see. Would you pass him to me now, please?'

'As you wish.'

There was a silence. Then she heard Duflot's voice.

'Hello, boss! Everything okay?'

'I won't make it into the office today. How are things going?'

'Not great. She refused to eat lunch with me at the Chinese place today. I'm a broken man.'

'Well, cheer up. I told her she has to go with you on your inspections. She seems like a good person. But please explain to her that there are limits to what we can do. She'll start a war if we're not careful. I'm relying on you to show her the ropes.'

'I'm your man, boss. Enjoy your break. I'll take care of everything.'

'Stop calling me "boss", Duflot. I'm not a TV detective.'

'All right, sorry.'

'And for your information, I'm not on holiday. Something came up, that's all. I'll be there tomorrow. And you'd better have everything in order when I get back . . .'

'*Jawohl.*'

'And try not to act like a prick, for a change.'

'Hello?'

'Yes, hello. This is Mrs Kleber. I'm calling about the Saab. The accident yesterday. Any news?'

'Yeah, and it's not good. The steering column's been knocked out of shape. And for an old model like that, the bodywork alone is going to cost you at least five thousand euros. You'll have to talk to your insurance company.'

'Have you done an estimate?'

'Um . . . Hang on. Yeah. Seven thousand eight hundred. That's the best we can do.'

'Four thousand and you'd better agree with the expert or I'll take care of your garage. Understood?'

'What are you talking about?'

'You've been warned. I'm the labour inspector. You tried to rip me off. That's how these things go, I get it. But if you don't make an effort, I'll pay you a little visit and I think you'll be surprised by how difficult it is to meet the requirements of the labour code.'

'You're crazy! I can't go down to four thousand. That wouldn't even cover the parts.'

'As far as I'm concerned, it's already sorted.'

'I'll sort this with your husband.'

Rita made the sound of a buzzer on a quiz show when the contestant chooses the wrong answer. 'Sorry, there is no husband. Just sort it with the insurance company. Goodbye now.'

Next, Rita called her insurance agent, who seemed optimistic. Then her brother: not that she had anything much to say to him, but she'd promised to keep an eye on him. After that, she called her mother and promised to drop by soon.

'The next time you see me, it'll probably be at the funeral parlour.'

'Mum, that isn't funny.'

'Well, you'd need a dark sense of humour, too, if your son had been acting like a moody teenager for the past fifteen years and your daughter lived next door to the love of her life and didn't even realise it!'

'Ugh, give me a break. Actually, I just talked to Gregory. Apparently he's got a new band. He's talking about auditioning for the next series of *Pop Idol*.'

'Your brother is an artist, darling. He explained that to me again last week.'

'And how much did it cost you?'

'Only twenty-five euros. But I had to listen to his latest compositions.'

'How were they?'

'Not too bad, actually, although I'm pretty sure he stole the melody from Julien Clerc and half the words from Barbara.'

'Hmm.'

'Listen, why don't you come to dinner this weekend with Laurent?'

'I can't believe you're still trying to get us back together! You're an incorrigible old busybody, you know.'

'You should make the most of it while I'm still alive.'

'I'll talk to you soon.'

'I hope so.'

Rita also briefly considered calling the big guy who'd sent her a message just before the accident. He wanted to see her again. She'd liked his message: simple, direct, and it made her feel good. But, well, if he really wanted to see her again, he could call her.

In the living room, the girl had fallen asleep in front of *The Bold and the Beautiful*. Nestled under Rita's blanket, her feet resting on the coffee-table, she was breathing regularly, her mouth half open. Mascara was running down her cheeks in little streams. Rita watched her for a moment. She felt surprisingly good, all things considered. She was knackered, but her heart was full. She went to the bathroom, took a quick shower, then put on a clean pair of Levi's, her boots, a linen shirt and a navy-blue sweater. When she went back downstairs, she found her lodger washing the dishes. Rita told her not to bother, but the girl insisted. There already seemed to be an instinctive intimacy between them, as though they'd been having these banal conversations for years. They sat facing each other and drank another coffee in a relaxed silence, before Rita decided it was time to get going. First, though, she had to convince the girl to take off her make-up and put on a sweater.

They drove to Nancy together to do some shopping at H&M and Printemps, dressing the girl from head to toe. She seemed thrilled by this experience. Later, they went to a café, where Rita had a beer and the girl a Coke. Rita's new lodger was not exactly talkative, but she smiled constantly and said, 'Thank you,' a lot. At least she understood French anyway. She made no attempt to dissuade Rita from giving her so many presents; in fact, she actively encouraged her to buy more. Once she was dressed properly, the girl looked genuinely pretty in a slightly odd way: she had a fortune-teller's face, expressive, childlike eyes, and that thick dark curly hair. In the street, she tried to attract the attention of boys but withdrew into shyness as soon as they glanced at her. Rita was fascinated.

They walked around for a while after nightfall, to let Cinderella show off her new outfit. She'd chosen an enormous wool scarf, which she coiled around her neck and face until she almost disappeared beneath it. Wrapped up nice and warm, she stared at passers-by and greedily window-shopped. Whenever people looked at her curiously, though, she would shy away from them. Once, she stopped in front of a jewellery-store window, but Rita made it clear that she'd spent enough that day. A little later, the inspector felt a hand gently grip her arm and after that they went to buy some waffles.

Back in Laurent's Mercedes, the girl turned up the sound on the stereo and played a few CDs that she found in the glove compartment. She and Rita began to chat in hesitant English. The inspector's gifts and patience were finally having an effect. The girl answered a few bland questions. Her name was Victoria and she was eighteen years old. That was what she claimed, anyway, and Rita pretended to believe her. On the other hand, she refused to reveal her nationality or what had brought her to France.

When they started driving along narrower, unlit streets, Victoria's expression darkened. She stared obstinately at the road markings, as if they might suddenly vanish or lead them over the edge of a cliff. Rita put her hand on the girl's arm and sensed the tension, the hostility, as if the Victoria of a few moments before had gone into hiding. When they got home, Rita suggested they have a drink, but Victoria was exhausted. She preferred to go straight to bed and she fell asleep quickly, having first folded away all her new clothes.

After indulging all her whims, Rita felt better than she had in a long time.

The next day, to thank her for that extraordinary afternoon, Victoria gave back some of the money she'd stolen from her before.

PIERRE DURUY

Lydie Duruy frowned and took a drag on the rubbery joint, while Didier Deslicovic rummaged frantically around under her T-shirt.

'Hey, Didier,' said Lydie, 'if you can't get hold of better shit than this, I reckon you'll have to find yourself a new girlfriend.'

'What the hell are you talking about?' said the dealer, pouting. He pulled the joint from Lydie's fingers and took an expert drag.

'Forget it. I need to go anyway.'

'You've gotta be fucking kidding me. I'm letting you smoke this stuff for free and you're criticising me?'

'So?'

'You're taking the piss, seriously. I drive you everywhere in my car, I introduce you to everyone, I get you smokes and all that, and now you're being a fucking diva.'

'Yeah, thanks for showing me the high life! See ya . . .'

'Hey!'

But the door of his souped-up Clio had already banged shut, leaving him alone with his high-end car radio and the petrochemical smoke from

85

the bad shit that he dealt in every low-rent housing estate between Épinal and Remiremont.

Before driving off, Didier honked his horn aggressively several times: his way of saying, *Who the fuck does this bitch think she is?* Ignoring him, Lydie walked through the decaying woods that surrounded the Farm. She hoped that her grandfather hadn't heard anything. Before reaching the house, she took a sweater from her Eastpak backpack and put it on. It was better if Gramps didn't see what she was wearing underneath.

Sitting at the kitchen table, Pierre Duruy had heard everything. He sipped his coffee and made a mental note to deal with the situation later. That girl was going to be trouble if he didn't do something about it.

'I'd have preferred it if my grandson had come to see me on his own,' the old man muttered, after putting his cup on the table.

'I understand, Mr Duruy,' said Martel.

In fact, though, he wasn't sure he had understood. His hearing was still playing up, and the old man spoke so quietly.

The kitchen was dark and overheated. The light, falling from the counterweight ceiling lamp, made an almost perfect white circle on the table between them. Martel sat facing the old man, who waited, hands joined in front of his cup. The stove purred contentedly nearby. Beneath the table, a kitten silently rubbed itself against the men's legs, cautiously affectionate.

'Was this your idea?'

'Partly.'

'Why did you bring that girl here?'

Sitting on a stool a little further away, Bruce placidly followed the conversation. From time to time he would show his discomfort by touching a spit-covered finger to a recently exploded zit.

'You shouldn't have brought her here.'

Martel nodded. Pierre Duruy was not the sort of man it paid to disagree with.

Then again, if Bruce was to be believed, the old man was a shadow of his former self, these days. When he walked, there was something uncertain about his figure, as if he were seen through a heat haze. Dark red blood vessels were visible through his paper-thin skin. His eyelids drooped, giving him a melancholic air that bore no relation to his temperament. His mouth, on the other hand, was still very much in character: a line carved in flint.

Martel rested his elbows on the table and leaned forward. His shadow covered the two cups and the sugar bowl. 'You're absolutely right. And I know who you are. I don't want to lecture you in your own home.'

'How kind,' the old man replied sarcastically.

However, Pierre Duruy did wonder how this tall, intelligent-seeming guy had ended up going into business with his grandson. Bruce had a screw loose. Now that he was old, coming towards the end, the past had been smoothed out in Pierre's memory. He leaned over it, as if the past were a map and he could see all its faults, all its greatness. He could spot the places where he'd gone off the rails; he could remember all his unforgivable rages, his ill-fated journeys. Too often, he hadn't been there for his family. Bruce's existence was a constant reminder of that. He had to watch over him now, protect him while he was still alive.

'Who was that girl?' he asked then, even if he could guess the answer.

'A whore,' Martel replied coldly.

'What did you want with her?'

'Nothing. It's complicated.'

The old man shrugged.

Sometimes the house creaked or sighed as the wind hammered against the windows. Pierre Duruy picked up the kitten by the scruff of its neck and placed it in his lap. He began stroking it, a little too hard. His gaze returned to Martel.

'For money.'

'I have to find her, Mr Duruy.'

'You shouldn't have brought her here. Not without asking me, anyway.'

'I understand,' Martel repeated. 'I totally understand.' His head swayed from side to side. He was growing impatient.

Ever since the girl had vanished, the others had been pressuring him. Two days before, he'd received a call in the evening, from a hidden number. He hadn't answered, but later he'd discovered the Benbareks' truck parked outside his apartment building. It had stayed there all night, a huge, impenetrable presence in the almost-empty car park. Unable to sleep, Martel had got out of bed on several occasions. Each time, the truck had still been there. Next night, same thing. Now, whenever his phone rang, Martel got stomach cramps. The Benbareks were after him. They blamed him for the money. He had to get hold of that girl: it was the only solution.

Martel went through all this in his head, then said: 'I don't want them to push me too far, Mr Duruy.'

'No one wants that,' said the old man, before turning to his grandson. Martel turned too.

Bruce had nothing to add to the conversation. He swayed on his stool. In truth, he didn't really understand what all the fuss was about. Ten or fifteen thousand euros . . . a whore . . . what was the big deal? The Benbareks could wait. They made threats, they made promises; he was used to it. In the end, everyone counted their money and it all started again. To him, this hand-wringing seemed pointlessly dramatic. Not to mention boring.

He stood up and looked out of the window. The land around the house was cluttered with junk: an old car, a few empty wire spools, some scrap metal, a shopping trolley. Two or three years ago, he used to push his sister around in that trolley – she loved that. And over on the left, there was a caravan and a dismantled bulldozer, looking like some prehistoric creature. This whole mess seemed to sum up forty years of petty crime, unambitious and inglorious. Bruce hated this place. He hated his family's reputation as scrap merchants. By teaming up with people like the Benbareks, he'd been hoping to find a way out of this shithole. Drugs and girls: they were the way forward. They made money, they didn't tire you out, and at least you got to meet people. It was just a shame that his grandfather had felt the need to stick his nose in.

He could see the caravan door flapping in the wind. His grandfather had cut the padlock and the girl had run off.

'I think I'm going to turn in,' he said finally.

'Good,' said his grandfather.

He and Martel watched as the giant cleared the table, wiped it with a sponge, and disappeared into the dark corridor.

'You shouldn't have got him mixed up in this kind of thing.'

'I misjudged him,' Martel admitted.

The old man walked over to a cupboard and took out a Perrier bottle with no label.

'Let's have a drink.'

'I don't want to bother you.'

'It's a bit late for that.'

At the end of the corridor, Bruce crouched down. Arms circling his knees, he listened. He knew his grandfather would never have got out the eau-de-vie in his presence. The two men were talking calmly now. Talking about him. Always the same crap: most of the stories were ancient history, but he couldn't shake them off. He balled his fists and pressed them against his eyes until he saw stars.

Lydie went through the garage so she wouldn't bump into her grandfather. She was pretty stoned and if he noticed he would yell at her until she cried her eyes out, as always. Sometimes the old man seemed completely senile, but at others he was like an ogre that could sniff you from miles off and never let you out of its grip.

When she got upstairs, she went straight to the back bedroom to see her mother. And there it was: that unique smell. Obviously she wasn't used to it yet. Then again, it was very recent.

Other than the unmade bed, the room contained a heater, a clothes rack, a portrait of a sad clown by Bernard Buffet, some cat photos pinned to the wall around the pale rectangle left by a mirror.

'Mum?'

The fat woman was dozing in the chair they'd lent her at the hospital. Lydie opened the window to let some air in. The cold woke Liliane, who tried to sit up.

'Don't move, Mum. I'm going to change your bandages.'

The fat woman smiled as Lydie took care of her, making the bed and opening the door so the air would circulate.

'How was school?'

'Great.'

'I'm happy to see you, sweetie. I was just thinking about you, in fact.'

Lydie recognised the whining, sentimental tone. Her mum had been drinking again.

Lydie moved a lamp closer so she could see what she was doing. After that, she undid her mother's dressing-gown and nightdress. The smell intensified. From under the bed she took the first-aid kit.

Two weeks earlier, her mother had been badly burned. No one really knew what had happened. Pierre had found her passed out next to the cooker, her synthetic dress half melted and stuck to her skin. Her face had been burned too and she'd been lucky not to lose an eye. They'd had to shave her head.

When Lydie came home from school that day, the ambulance was still parked outside the house. She remembered the looks on the paramedics' faces. They'd seen the way the Duruy family lived. Since then, Liliane had been confined to her chair, playing the role she was born for: Medea convalescent. She talked constantly about how unlucky she had been, about what a bitch life was. And she warned her daughter about men, of course.

When she'd finished changing the bandages, Lydie held her breath and kissed her mother's unburned cheek. Liliane grabbed hold of her and stroked her hair, her cheek. She cried a bit.

'You're so pretty, my darling.'

'Mum, please . . .'

'You don't know how lucky you are. Make the most of it, darling.'

Liliane cuddled her for a while, and Lydie put up with this in silence.

'You know what would make Mum happy, my sweet?'

Lydie freed herself and went to fetch a bottle of sparkling wine from the cellar. She moved quickly, fearful of the darkness and the echoes produced by the concrete walls. She ignored the gun rack where her grandfather's weapons were kept under lock and key, and the table with its mouldering papers and old Olivetti typewriter. From time to time, the old man would think about writing his memoirs, telling his side of the story, before coming to his senses again. She also paid no attention to the tin trunk that had always been padlocked but, curiously, no longer was. Lydie hurried back to her mother's room, then abandoned the patient to her bottle and took sanctuary in her own bedroom.

It was her haven, a chaotic treasure trove, its walls covered with photographs of film stars, unsmiling models, singers showing off their abs. Lydie turned on the TV and muted it so she could listen to NRJ radio. In this scented cocoon piled high with clothes, cuddly toys, magazines, half-empty bottles, coloured candles and a million other things that sheltered her from the reality of the Farm, Lydie rolled a joint and smoked it while she did her make-up.

Meanwhile, Bruce had swallowed a few pills – one creatine monohydrate and two L-glutamines. Then he took his top off, checked that his Calvin Klein boxer shorts were visible, and started pumping iron in front of the wardrobe mirror. He worked his shoulders first, then his biceps, and then did fifty pull-ups. In the background, his stereo played Skid Row, Rage Against the Machine, Audioslave. Martel had left a while ago, not even bothering to say goodbye to Bruce. Before he went to sleep, Bruce played with the Colt .45 he'd found in the tin trunk, down in the cellar. Swaggering around with twenty-two-inch shoulders was already pretty cool but carrying this gun around too was just crazy. Fucking hell, he was definitely going to find that bitch. He slipped the Colt under his pillow and was asleep within seconds.

Downstairs, Pierre Duruy was smoking in the kitchen, staring into space, one hand resting on his right knee. All alone, he brooded vaguely over the meaning of life.

JORDAN LOCATELLI

Lydie didn't like school much. She'd had to retake a couple of years. Or maybe just one. Oh, who cared? Anyway, she was one of the few girls at the vocational school in Bruyères, and by some way the one with the biggest breasts. In other words, she was the number-one object of desire for the male pupils. There was practically a riot every Wednesday, when her class had swimming.

The PE teacher had asked her not to wear her Union Jack bikini any more, the one that was two sizes too small and had white straps that turned transparent when they got wet. But apparently Lydie hadn't been listening when he'd said that and he didn't seem too eager to press the point.

When she came out of the water, the teacher made a strange movement, as though he was shooing a fly away from his nose. Then he clapped his hands to distract the line of boys, who were all greedily ogling Lydie. All except Jordan Locatelli, who simultaneously wanted to die and to kill everyone else in his class.

Until then, Jordan had not shown much interest in girls. All things considered, he preferred mechanics. What he liked most of all was fixing things with his dad. For the past few years, the two of them had been trying to renovate an old Renault R8 Gordini. They would spend whole weekends looking for spare parts, changing the brake discs, straightening a dented wing, or doing up the dilapidated mill where they still kept the old wreck they'd bought for peanuts. Jordan's father could easily have used an old Clio engine or something, but he was a nostalgic, meticulous baby boomer, and the elixir of youth would be provided only by the legendary Sierra engine awkwardly positioned at the back of the car. The R8's famous lack of comfort and traction were the prices he had to pay for this obsession.

When father and son had done a hard day's work, when their hands were black as ink and their fingers sore from twisting metal, they liked nothing better than sinking a can of beer together. They would each drink in silence while contemplating the bright blue bodywork with its glorious double white stripe.

And one day, it would run again. Jordan felt sure of that, in spite of what his father's factory workmates might say.

But for the past few months, Jordan had taken no pleasure from all that. His heart had filled with an inexhaustible well of hate and boredom. Sometimes he would just feel depressed or uncomfortable or violent for no obvious reason.

He and his friends spent their time hanging around doing nothing, shoulders slouched. Occasionally they'd play video games at Lucas's house, smoke a joint in the woods, go on bike rides. On Saturday nights they would drink beer until they puked, behind the Bruyères train station, or in the fields, or near the Saint-Dié church ... it depended. They would talk about football, motorbikes, the girls they wanted to screw. But Riton was the only one of them who'd actually done it. Everyone knew that.

All in all, apart from Jordan's strange moods, they had a laugh together, the five of them. Riton was the eldest. He looked a bit like Belmondo, which explained the two bones he'd broken doing stunts on his moped. Lucas was known for liking other people's girlfriends and for his perfectly blue eyes, which were nonetheless not quite enough to make up for his bow-legs and weak chin. Samir, a.k.a. the Cramp, spent his life squeezing his blackheads and waiting to lose his virginity. Boris tried to make people respect him despite his fat belly and the fact that he was always there even though no one had invited him along. Jordan was the youngest of the group and was willing to do pretty much anything to make the others forget that fact. Like daily death-defying rides on his old Yamaha even though he had no licence and wasn't old enough to ride one yet.

The previous Saturday, they'd all gone for a ride on the motocross track. After a few laps, they'd smoked cigarettes under the awning of a concrete refreshment stall that was closed for the winter. Jordan had made sure everyone knew he was in a bad mood.

'Oh, stop being such a miserable cunt!' Riton said.

The others had noticed too. He'd been sulking for weeks. What the hell was his problem?

Jordan didn't say anything, just continued looking sullen, although he was flattered that they were taking some interest in his mental state. Normally he didn't smoke, but he was so grateful that he cadged a fag off Boris, who complained half-heartedly. But Riton smirked.

'I know what's up with Locatelli,' he boasted.

'Oh, yeah?'

'Go on, then, spit it out!'

Riton took a drag on his Chesterfield, narrowing his eyes to look shrewd. 'The Duruy girl's broken another heart, lads.'

The others laughed and whistled. Jordan denied it, but it made no difference. God, life was shit. His best mate, the only one he told all his secrets, had just betrayed his trust purely out of boredom, because the winter was too long and there was fuck-all else to do.

'I promise you, lads.' Riton grinned. 'He told me himself. Didn't you, fatty?'

Jordan spat contemptuously on the ground.

'I know the Duruy girl,' Riton continued pitilessly. 'She goes dancing every Saturday night at the Sphinx, that whore. You'd know that too if you could get into the Sphinx.'

Jordan picked up his helmet and started to walk away.

'Let him go, lads. He wants to be alone so he can cry.'

'Yeah, right, course I do,' Jordan replied, with his usual razor-sharp wit.

Thankfully, his 125 started first time and he sped off, front wheel barely touching the ground, without even bothering to put his helmet on. The wind blew hard into his face, but that wasn't what brought tears to his eyes.

Ever since this betrayal, Jordan had stayed away from his friends. On Saturday evening, he'd gone for a ride on his moped alone, feeling like an idiot. He rode aimlessly and had found himself at a remote bar full of laughing drunkards.

He had several beers with them and exchanged some sick insults. Because he barely knew them, he felt able to tell them everything about his miserable life. Then he drove off, weaving along unlit B-roads with his ear buds in. By some miracle he made it back home, but just as he was riding slowly into the garage he lost his balance, ripping his jeans and making a huge racket. After that, he didn't remember anything. He slept restlessly, for a long time. In the morning his father was waiting for him, along with the biggest hangover of his short life.

'You got home late last night,' his father said. He was wearing a red, white and blue ski hat and smoking a roll-up.

Jordan groaned as he searched through the cupboard for a packet of Pepito biscuits. The kitchen tiles were freezing under his bare feet. The cold seemed to penetrate his entire body.

'Do you know how long I've been hanging around waiting for you? We were supposed to go to the scrapyard today, remember.'

'I know, I know . . .'

His father had left the coffee machine on, with the best of intentions. But having been heated since eight o'clock that morning, the coffee had taken on the colour of engine oil and the unpleasant taste of burned nutshells. All the same, Jordan poured it into his Snoopy bowl, then wedged the pack of biscuits under his arm before heading for the living room so he could watch TV as he had breakfast.

His father took off his hat and rubbed his scalp. What would his wife do if she were still there? She'd always been quick to dish out a good slap. Maybe he ought to yell at the boy, but he didn't dare. The thing was, six months before, they'd been getting along really well. What the hell was happening to his son? The comforting hum of the television interrupted these dark thoughts.

'I'm going out for a while,' he said, putting his hat back on.

In the garage, he stroked the bodywork of his beloved R8 without noticing the damage Jordan had caused the night before.

'Hey, boys, has one of you got a ciggy?'

Lydie had gone into the boys' changing room without knocking, her hair still wet, her low-rise jeans showing off a flash of hips and the top of her underwear. Her hair was blonde with dark roots. She would some-times wear fake freckles on her nose. That day, she'd put on lip gloss. Her mouth was as appetising as strawberry chewing gum.

As soon as she walked in, the changing room descended into chaos. The boys, who were getting dressed, started shoving each other to the floor, giving wedgies, whipping arses with wet towels. A pair of trunks had even flown through the air and splatted against the door. Lydie didn't blink. 'Hurry up! I need a fag before we leave.'

Riton got there first. He was already dressed, his bag hanging over his shoulder, a pack of Chesterfields held out towards her. Jordan tried to speed up, but apparently his Adidas trainers had shrunk two sizes while he was in the pool. So Riton and Lydie disappeared amid lewd taunts and jeers. Through the half-open door, Jordan just had time to see his former friend giving him the finger.

Behind the pool, several flights of steps led down to a housing estate where every building looked identical. It was a quiet place, perfect for smoking, drinking and snogging. Jordan rushed down there. When Riton saw him coming, he laughed. 'Hey, check out this loser!'

Jordan stood in front of them, out of breath and looking embarrassed. 'We're leaving in five minutes. The bus driver's already honked his horn twice.'

'So fucking what?' said Riton, slipping his arm behind Lydie's back.

She handed the cigarette to Jordan. 'Here . . .'

Jordan put the stub between his lips and it was like a kiss.

'Oi, you three! You're for it now!' The PE teacher was running down the steps, pointing imperiously at them.

'Fuck, fuck, fuck,' they muttered. While Lydie and Riton stuffed gum into their mouths, Jordan took the time to have one last drag, savouring the thin film of lip gloss that covered the hot filter.

'What the hell are you doing? We're late thanks to you! I'm sending you straight to the headmaster's office when we get back.'

'So? Who was it?'

Behind his desk, the headmaster was dipping a teabag into a mug bearing the FBI logo. With his white shirt, the sleeves rolled up, his striped tie, and his twitching bulldog face, he wouldn't have looked out of place on an American TV show about an alcoholic detective in New York or Baltimore, with friendly whores and weirdos on acid. Except that the cops on TV would never have worn a Black & Decker T-shirt under their shirt. That little detail ruined all Francis Lebourois's attempts at stylishness. The headmaster of the Jeanne d'Arc vocational school was fifty-two and divorced, with three daughters, one of whom had followed him into the teaching profession.

'You'll tell me in the end,' he said, concentrating on his tea. 'Mr Ladurte, remind me: when was the last time you had a passing mark in any of your classes?' Riton opened his mouth to reply, but the headmaster beat him to it: 'Except for sport, obviously.'

Smirking, Riton kept his mouth shut.

'You have never passed a single class! Not once in all the time you've been here. You're a moron, Ladurte. And I don't care if you tell your parents or the schools inspector or the local newspaper what I said, because it's true. You're a moron, and here's the proof. Your school record.' He picked up a thick brown folder from his desk and threw it at Riton, who caught it.

'Go on, take a look. I don't think you'll ever get a job, Ladurte. It's not that you're more stupid or unpleasant than most of your classmates. But still, it's true: you're unemployable.'

Riton leafed through the sheaf of his school reports and psychological test results until he came to the comments written by his primary-school teachers. Won't stop talking. Lazy. Easily distracted. Would clearly rather damage school equipment than concentrate on his maths course.

He looked amused.

'What did I tell you?'

The headmaster's office was located in the basement and its windows looked out on the playground. The bars on the windows were intended to protect him from the malevolence of the school's pupils and, in particular, stray shots from the boys playing football. The bars created an elaborate pattern of shadows that stretched across the floor, up the headmaster's back and down the faces of the accused, providing an atmosphere of incarceration that went well with the tone of their discussion.

Sitting back in his chair, the headmaster began to sip his tea.

'What bothers me, Ladurte, is that so many others imitate you.'

'But, sir—'

'I know, Ladurte,' the headmaster interrupted. 'I know it's not your fault. You're a victim of the system, I know that. But you know the school rules where smoking is concerned. For God's sake' – his voice suddenly rose – 'I even gave up smoking myself just to set a good example! So I'm not going to let you get away with a crafty fag behind the swimming pool.'

Riton, Lydie and Jordan waited calmly, in silence. They knew Lebourois. All they had to do was wait for the storm to pass. Glaring at them, he took another repulsively loud sip of his tea.

Like Lebourois's ex-wife, Jordan found the noise hard to bear. He had recently acquired a romantic view of human existence and it was ill-equipped to deal with trivialities of this kind, like when his father farted during breakfast or left the toilet door open while he was taking a shit. He glanced at Lydie to check that she wasn't too disgusted by this vileness and was surprised to find her on the verge of hysterical laughter. He wanted her so badly and yet she seemed so unattainable. One look at her breasts bouncing under her sweatshirt and he wanted to die on the spot . . .

'It was me, sir,' he stammered, turning his face away.

'What?' the headmaster asked.

'The cigarettes, sir.'

'Oh, really?'

'Yes, sir.'

'Are you trying to be a hero, Locatelli?'

'No, sir.'

'You don't smoke, boy. Stop trying to pull the wool over my eyes.'

'I'm telling the truth, sir. It was me. They had nothing to do with it.'

Jordan stood up straight and stared defiantly into the teacher's eyes.

Lebourois stood up and grabbed the pack of cigarettes that had been taken from Riton.

'All right, then, show me. Go on, Locatelli. Show me how you smoke.'

Jordan did as he was told, holding the cigarette between his thumb and index finger and grimacing as he swallowed the smoke. His feet tapped against the ground.

'Perfect!' the headmaster said, with heavy sarcasm. 'I feel like I'm watching Bambi imitating Marlon Brando, but naturally I believe you. What are you, a thirty-a-day man, Locatelli?'

Riton and Lydie burst out laughing.

'Get out, both of you. Three hours of detention each. Go on, out!'

Jordan got a glimpse of Lydie's belly button as she stood up, a silky little notch in her sweetly rounded abdomen. His throat tightened.

The headmaster was staring at him meaningfully. 'So tell me, Locatelli, why are you sacrificing yourself for those two?'

'I'm not, sir.'

'You're normally pretty intelligent, Locatelli. Maybe not the hardest-working kid I've ever seen, but nothing like that moron. At least you chose to be here. And your teachers are generally pleased with you. So why try to shoot yourself in the foot?'

'I don't understand what you mean, sir.'

Jordan stared stubbornly down at his trainers, his neck stiff and his feet continuing to beat time.

'All right ... Well, I can't force you to tell the truth. But I know what's going on. I was young once, you know.'

Jordan didn't believe this for a minute. Suddenly he felt an unbounded disgust for his life, for this school where he was supposed to spend the next two years, for this prick who thought he understood him and was trying to be nice.

'And I know it's not been easy, with your mum and everything . . .'

The boy glared at Lebourois.

'Listen, I think you need some help,' the headmaster insisted. 'I'm going to arrange a meeting for you with the school counsellor. We're going to get you through this.'

'No, thanks.'

'You're making a mistake. Anyway, I can't be accused of having double standards. One more cock-up like this and I'll have to expel you. So try to stay on the straight and narrow, all right?'

The headmaster had known dozens of pig-headed kids like this one, thin-skinned teenagers capable of ruining their lives over a six-month sulk. Eventually they had to find a way out of it themselves. Some started smoking hash, others spent their nights wanking over images on the Internet, or their weekends getting smashed out of their skulls. He'd met so many good kids who'd gone bad in that way. There was nothing anyone could do. Even so, it was heartbreaking to watch it happen.

'All right, off you go. Go back to your class and try not to get into any more trouble. And, for God's sake, stop looking like some lovesick puppy. No girl wants that.'

Jordan rolled his eyes and stomped out of the room, his schoolbag on his back.

Outside, night had already fallen and Jordan waited in the bike shed, hands in pockets, one foot leaning against the wall. He'd taken off his scarf and gloves and he was shivering in the darkness. At last, Lydie appeared. He recognised her instantly from the sway of her hips, her breathtaking figure perched on too-high heels. He took a step, shivering even more violently. She strode quickly forward and he was about to break into a run to meet her when the car park lit up. Lydie ran over to the Clio Williams that had just turned on its headlights. The driver manoeuvred slowly and methodically towards the exit, the gravel crunching under the tyres, the engine throbbing as it ticked over. After it had left the car park, Jordan spent a long time listening to the sixteen-valve engine rumbling through the icy air before fading into the distance.

Then, pissed off, he straddled his bike and took off. No matter how much he thought about it, he didn't see how he could possibly turn up to school in his father's Gordini.

THE BENBAREKS

Martel picked up two frozen pizzas and dropped them into his trolley. It was late and the supermarket was almost deserted. There were gaps in the aisles and the floor was marked by the day's comings and goings. A song by Calogero played through hidden speakers, reminding the shop's customers that it was about to close for the night. Martel kept his phone glued to his ear as he did his shopping.

'Pretty strange place to meet.'

'I know,' said Bruce, embarrassed. 'There was nothing I could do. I reckon they're just taking precautions. They're wary.'

'Of who? Me or the cops?'

'Dunno, really. These guys aren't stupid. They know what they're doing.'

'And the money?'

'Ah . . . well, that's not really the problem. They've got all the dough they need.'

'The problem is figuring out whether they'll give us any,' said Martel, picking up a pack of water bottles. The floor was so grimy, he felt like he was walking on sticky tape.

'Anyway, I've made a commitment,' Bruce added.

'So?'

'No, nothing.'

'All right. Tell them I'll be there.'

'Okay, cool.'

As he looked for toothpaste, Martel added, without thinking, as if talking to himself: 'You think this is a good idea?'

Bruce didn't know what to say. It was the kind of question you just didn't ask. Uneasily, he asked: 'Well, what's the worst that could happen?'

Martel hung up. He was alone in his aisle. Several rows of strip lights went out, one after another: textiles, electrical appliances, toiletries. He hurried towards the exit.

The motorway to Nancy was bordered by desolate waterlogged fields and tall black pine trees. The November sky pressed down, low and grey. The tyres of passing cars glided over the tarmac without any resistance, making a wet, sticky sound as they went. Martel had parked his Volvo estate on the hard shoulder. He drummed on the steering wheel as he waited, glancing at his watch every couple of minutes. A few heavy raindrops fell onto his windscreen, and within seconds a hundred others had followed. Soon it was pelting down, to the total indifference of the surrounding landscape and the cars that kept speeding past at 80 m.p.h. Occasionally, one would come too close and the Volvo would sway from side to side.

Martel had stopped just after the Bayon exit and he scanned the two lanes that came in the opposite direction, on the other side of the metal guardrail. The downpour intensified and now the passing headlights struggled to pierce the curtain of rain.

At the top of the hill facing him, a BMW appeared and flashed its headlights twice before parking on the other side of the road. Martel wiped away the condensation so he could see better. The BMW had tinted windows and it sat there like a block of granite, dark and glossy. Its hazard warning lights came on and Martel's phone rang. A hidden number.

'Hey,' said a voice.

Martel stared at the BMW across the road. He could just make out the presence of the man at the other end of the line. 'Hey,' he answered.

'Fucking shitty weather, right?'

'We could have met up somewhere nicer.'

'Well, we're here,' said the voice.

They waited, the two of them, in a tense silence. At last, Martel swallowed and said: 'So . . .?'

'Your mate told us about you.'

'Do you have something for me?'

The hazard lights kept flashing imperturbably. A lorry rumbled past, shaking the Volvo and concealing the BMW as the voice answered: 'He didn't tell us everything, though, your friend. We found out all sorts of stuff on our own.'

Martel's stomach tensed. 'That's old news.'

'All the same . . . It's impressive.'

'Good, then.'

'We want to see you.'

'Where?'

'We want to see you right now. See what you look like.'

'I don't understand.'

'Get out of your car.'

'You're kidding.'

The rain was falling so hard on the car's roof that Martel could hardly hear what the other man was saying.

'We want to take a look at you.'

Martel thought he could hear laughter in the background. He wondered how many of them there were in the BMW. He wiped the condensation off the window again and stared up at the sky. It was lashing down outside.

'Martel,' said the voice, 'sometimes in life, you just have to get wet.'

The fucking Benbareks . . .

'I need fifteen thousand,' said Martel.

'So we hear.'

Nothing happened.

'Make up your mind, man.'

Shit, thought Martel, before opening the door. His jacket was soaked the second he stepped out of the car, and very soon afterwards so were his jeans and his feet. The water streamed over his face. He did his best to protect his phone. 'Happy now?'

'So far so good. How tall are you?'

'What the fuck is this?'

But the voice didn't say anything, so Martel answered: 'Six-four.'

'Not bad. And you look pretty fit.'

A white Golf swerved past, splashing him from head to foot.

'I need money.'

'Yeah, yeah, we get it. We have something for you. And we think you may have something for us. It's not every day we find guys like you around here.'

'What did you hear about me?'

'Nothing special. You left a trail of good memories behind you. And some less good ones too . . .'

The guy on the phone laughed softly.

Martel wasn't cold, despite the rain. He was burning up, in fact.

'We'll call you,' said the man, before hanging up.

The BMW's headlights came on and the flashers went off.

'Bastards,' Martel grunted, slipping his phone into a pocket. He ran across the road, hands shielding his face so he could see a few feet ahead. In three strides, he reached the central guardrail. Cars sped past, flashing their headlights and honking their horns. On the other side, a green Twingo almost knocked him over. Martel got to the BMW before it had had time to move away. He stood in front of it, dripping, and stared at the opaque windscreen. Then he hammered on the bonnet a few times and the driver's window slid down, revealing a small, yellow-skinned man with curly hair.

He was grinning. His eyes gleamed curiously.

Martel went over to the window.

'You've got a nerve, man,' said the small guy.

'Damn right,' said a voice behind him.

Martel leaned down to get a better look. Beside the small guy was another small guy, identical, dressed in the same shiny, expensive Hugo Boss suit. The guy in the passenger seat had a very neat three-day beard. He was staring at his phone screen, tapping away frenetically. Martel looked back at the driver, whose face was grimacing with disgust.

'Don't get too close, man. You'll mess up the car.'

Martel obeyed. 'I need money. What do you want?'

'We'll let Bruce know about that.'

Martel couldn't believe it. How could someone so small be so sure of himself? When he saw the gun in his right hand, he suddenly understood. The man sniffed.

'Don't worry, it's no big deal.'

Just before the driver disappeared behind the tinted glass, he winked at Martel. His pupils were like lead shot: same size, same metallic density, same cold, dull appearance. The BMW moved off slowly and Martel was left standing there. It was a pain in the arse, getting back to his car.

And it rained all day long.

The next morning, Bruce turned up at the factory's union office with the money. He looked very pleased with himself as he tossed the envelope onto Martel's desk. Martel grabbed it and slipped it into a drawer.

'Five thousand,' said Bruce. 'I took my share.'

'Your share?' asked Martel.

'Well, yeah.'

Martel sneezed, then blew his nose loudly. 'What share?'

Bruce shrugged. 'My share. I give you your share for the concerts, don't I? That's just how it works.'

'And how much was your share?'

'Two thousand, I think.'

'You think?'

'Well, yeah,' Bruce said, swaying from foot to foot.

'I get it,' said Martel, and sneezed again. 'You're trying it on. It's human nature. How much did you take?'

'Five thousand,' admitted the bodybuilder.

'Put it in the drawer with the rest. I'll keep it all. This isn't your concern.'

'I'll bring it on Friday.'

Martel nodded as he contemplated his fingernails, then began to bite them. 'So what do they want, the Benbareks?'

'They gave me the name of a street in Strasbourg. Red-light district. They want us to nab a girl.'

Martel sat up as though he'd been slapped. 'What the fuck? Why?' He spat the bit of nail from the tip of his tongue.

'No idea. It's not exactly rocket science, though. You go there, you grab a girl, and that's it.'

'But . . . fucking hell. Why that particular street?'

'They want one of these two.'

Bruce took two photographs from his wallet. A sad-looking brunette, and a girl with Asian features, who looked like she'd had a tough life. The pictures had been taken on the street: they were wrapped up warmly, but in miniskirts. The photographs couldn't have been more than a few days old. Bruce had folded them in half to fit them into his wallet.

Martel examined them for a few seconds. 'No way,' he said finally.

'What?'

'Kidnapping girls? Are you crazy? I wouldn't even do it for fifty thousand.'

'But what about the money?'

'Give me your share and I'll hand it all back to them.'

'That won't be easy,' said Bruce, lowering his head.

Martel sneezed yet again and cursed. 'Fuck, what did you do with that money?'

'I invested it. Don't worry – I'll have doubled it by the end of the week.'

Martel got up and stood very close to him. Bruce had the feeling that Martel was sniffing him. Maybe it was just because he had a cold.

'Honestly, it's no big deal,' Bruce reassured him. 'There's no risk. We nab one of the girls, we keep her for a bit until the Benbareks are happy, then we get the rest of the money.'

'Oh, they want us to keep her as well? Are we supposed to take turns raping her while we're at it?'

'We have all the space we need at the Farm. You don't have to worry about a thing. There's a caravan, and nobody ever comes there. Honestly, it'll be fine. I've thought of everything.'

'You've thought of everything? You think that's reassuring? Give me a fucking break. What about your grandfather? What will you tell him? That you've opened a childcare centre?'

'Calm down, it'll be fine, I'm telling you. It's a rock-solid plan. You're just not used to it any more.'

Martel stared incredulously at Bruce as if he were the spitting image of Adolf Hitler or something. He wasn't even angry now. It was worse than that.

'I ask you to get me a meeting with two little pussies in suits and we end up mixed up in a kidnapping! The whole point of this was to get out of the shit, not deeper into it.'

'I know, I know, but it's fine. I swear.'

Martel went back behind his desk and slumped onto his orange velvet chair, a relic from the 1970s. He rocked back and forth for a while.

'You need to give me that money. I don't care how you do it, but I want the cash tomorrow. Understood?'

'All right, all right.'

Martel took his time blowing his nose, then asked: 'Have you ever heard me making threats? Physical threats, I mean?'

'No.'

'Have you ever heard me acting like a big shot, saying I was going to smash someone's face in or whatever?'

'No, no . . . Why, what's up?'

'Do you think I'm a compulsive liar? That I make stuff up?'

Bruce shook his head.

'Good. Then listen carefully. If you don't give me that money tomorrow, I will break all your fingers with a hammer. You got it?'

The telephone rang then and Bruce took that as his signal to leave.

Martel answered. It was a woman from the administration department. She sounded very emotional. She'd just posted invitations to an extraordinary Works Council meeting on Friday. This time, it was really happening. There were going to be redundancies at the factory.

Martel sat for a moment, watching his friends at work in Hall Two. He felt suddenly very alone in his little goldfish bowl.

PATRICK LOCATELLI

Martel would know what to do.

That was what Patrick Locatelli had been telling himself for the past two days, ever since the union representatives had been summoned by management to an extraordinary Works Council meeting. Given the current situation – the machine taken away in the middle of the night in November, the state of the order books and stocks – everyone at the factory assumed the worst.

Martel would know what to do. That was Patrick Locatelli's mantra as he had his breakfast – the same every morning: a bowl of *café au lait*, two slices of buttered toast, and some orange juice – in his tatty old dressing-gown.

That week, he was on mornings. So, as always, he'd woken up at 4.30 a.m., two minutes before his alarm clock went off. He liked being up before everyone else, showering and getting ready while Jordan was still in bed – and his wife, when she was still alive. He enjoyed the silence, the freedom of movement, the singular colour that the sky turns as night fades, the energising feeling of being one step ahead of the rest of the world.

But for now, sitting in the kitchen, looking out at the profuse dark forest on the hills behind his house, he was worried sick. Most of the time, Patrick Locatelli was fairly content with his lot: after all, he had a job, and his kid, and his R8. And he would get the engine to work again one day, no matter what his friends at the factory said.

True, Christine was dead and that had driven him mad with grief, left him with a pain so intense he felt like he was going to die too. But, as ugly as it sounded, time did heal. Even if he would never have admitted it, for example, he had started looking at other women in the street. He'd started imagining things.

At work, when the female temp in charge of quality control came to the factory floor to buy sweets from the vending machine, the men liked to mess around. Her name was Muriel and she was a local girl, cheeky and hot-blooded and ridiculously tall. The lads called her the Giraffe. She was young, and jokes and whispers followed her around. But when Patrick was there, even if he was in a cheerful mood, nobody dared. They kept silent out of respect. Patrick had always appreciated this consideration. But then, last week, he'd found himself checking out Muriel's legs. And, in all honesty, it had got on his nerves.

For a long time, he had imagined that Christine could see him, that she was watching over him, that she was still there, not far away, looking down on him, and this had consoled him. Then it had become an embarrassing idea. For several months, he had avoided giving himself certain intimate satisfactions.

In the end, however – even though he remembered her face perfectly, and even though the memory of it always produced a rush of tenderness in him, as well as a feeling of sadness and irrevocable loss – he'd started masturbating again.

All the same, his colleagues had been really nice. For a while, their wives had cooked for him and Jordan. Every evening, they would bring a Tupperware box of something delicious, often their speciality: roast potatoes with bacon, homemade lasagne, *gratin dauphinois*, *tête de veau* in vinaigrette. They'd taken turns to visit, making sure he was all right, never outstaying their welcome. And then at work, Denis – who wasn't exactly known for his generosity – had covered for him when he started screwing up. The foreman, too, had turned a blind eye to his waning productivity: after all, it was hardly surprising if he found it hard to care about meeting those targets any more. And Martel had organised a kitty, to help him out. Everyone had contributed to it. Friends mattered.

That was what the factory was: a world of pain and comfort, and a world that kept shrinking – going from more than 250 men to only forty now. Patrick preferred not to think about what would become of him if the factory closed. People he'd known since childhood, practically. Some of the men's fathers had worked there, and some had passed on the torch to their sons. In the old days, the factory bosses would hire you outside the school gates, after you'd graduated, and sometimes you'd stay there until you retired. The factory had devoured entire generations, surviving strikes, feeding families, splitting up couples, breaking bodies and spirits, swallowing the dreams of the young, the anger of the old, the energy of a community that in the end didn't imagine any other fate for itself.

Naturally there were old reheated hatreds, jealousies, things that could never be admitted. Like 'Arabs go home' scrawled in indelible marker on the lockers of two Moroccans who'd lived in the area for years. But all in all the men loved the ambience there and tried to do their jobs as well as they could. They grumbled about the bosses, of course, but without any real conviction, and they all drove cars fitted out by Velocia. Anchored by the factory, their lives remained bearable; the lives of men.

Patrick didn't finish his second slice of toast. He took his bowl to the sink even though it was still half-full.

Washed and shaved, he put on a pair of jeans, a Vittel T-shirt and his Décathlon fleece. Before leaving, he went to check on Jordan. He'd started doing this when Christine died. He and the kid had grown closer. They'd had some pretty deep talks, or as deep as they could manage. They'd reminisced about holidays by the sea, picnics, slaps his mother had given Jordan, cuddles he'd refused because he was too old; they'd recalled the afternoon snacks she used to make him – bread and butter with a mug of hot chocolate – back when Jordan was still in primary school. Together, they'd looked through all the photo albums. They'd had to bury a lot of regrets. Patrick had seen his son suddenly grow up.

One morning, the kid had found his father weeping, just before he had to go to work. Even though he'd promised himself he wouldn't do that. The problem was that it wasn't just the grief, the changes, the emptiness he had to deal with – it was the exhaustion too. In addition to the hours he worked at the factory, Jordan's father was now saddled with the responsibility for supervising homework, paying bills, preparing meals, all the things Christine had always done. Not to mention the sleepless nights, when he missed her so much he could hardly breathe, when he feared he wouldn't manage without her. So, that morning, still in his dressing-gown, his receding hair in disarray, feet in his old velvet slippers, he'd weakened. It was dawn and Jordan wasn't supposed to be up yet. Only he was. And as Patrick tried to hide his face in his hands, as his shoulders shook and his smooth white head gleamed under the fluorescent light, his son turned on the radio and made some more coffee. That morning, they had breakfast together.

Things were better now. Tragedy had given way to everyday worries. His son was an awkward age: foul-mouthed, thin-skinned, sometimes listless and sometimes hyper. His father didn't know what to do with him when he was moody like that, when he was being a drama queen. On the whole, though, he sensed that they were heading in the right direction. It was just life – stupid, painful life – and it went on. Jordan was growing. Soon, everything would be fine.

As for the factory, Martel would know what to do.

After putting on the steel-toed boots that he'd left under the radiator the night before, Patrick Locatelli turned off the lights, closed the door behind him, got into his car, and set off towards the factory.

The Opel Kadett stopped at the junction of the roads to Bruyères and Corcieux. As he'd done every morning for weeks, Denis Demange was waiting for Patrick to pick him up. Standing in the cold, his hands shoved into the pockets of his fur-lined leather jacket, he was smoking his fifth Pall Mall of the day. His shaved head was covered with a flat cap, and at his feet was his kitbag, a souvenir of his military service. In a single movement, he tossed his cigarette into the ditch, picked up his bag and opened the passenger door.

'Hey.'

'Hey,' Patrick replied, without even looking at him. He was thinking about other things. Denis didn't mind: he was brooding over the same troubles.

They had to drive about fifteen miles to reach the factory. Soon, the car began to warm up. Denis took off his coat and started glancing at the driver, looking for a way to start the conversation.

'We're really fucked this time,' he said quietly.

Patrick didn't react.

'And your Martel won't be able to do anything about it.'

When the driver still didn't say anything, Denis scowled. Patrick was an awkward bastard. And ever since the accident that had deprived him of his driver's licence, he'd had to share a car with this man every day. They'd arranged with the foreman to work the same hours. When he thought about that extraordinary Works Council meeting, he felt the rage growing inside him. This job was more or less all he had.

'It's the same shit every time,' Denis grumbled, after a few moments' reflection. 'We complain, we go on strike, we lose money and we get fucked.'

Patrick turned on the radio. Dire Straits gave him a brief respite, before Denis started up again.

'You old guys don't give a fuck. You'll be fine if the factory closes, because you've been there so long. It's not the same for us. I've only worked there seven years. How much will I get if they give me the boot?'

Patrick turned the radio dial until he found the news, and Denis shut up. Beneath his cap, Denis felt large beads of sweat pricking his scalp. Rummaging around in his leather jacket, he found his packet of cigarettes. He was tempted to light one in the car just to annoy Patrick. But, well, there was no need to go that far. After all, it was good of Patrick to go out of his way to pick him up every morning. Not to mention his wife had died not that long ago.

As for Patrick, he paid no more attention to the news than he did to his passenger. He was sure of only one thing: Martel would know what to do.

BRUCE

His grandfather hadn't spoken a word during the journey. Just before Bruce got out of the car, he had said simply: 'I'll pick you up at six.' Then, after a second and without looking at him: 'Behave yourself now.'

After that, the Citroën BX rose a few inches with a pneumatic sigh before driving away. On the pavement, Bruce hesitated. Around him were tall buildings, their balconies decorated with flowers. A narrow stretch of sky was visible between the rows of tower blocks. People were coming home from work. It was a sunny day and the city hummed with the sound of relaxation. Bruce didn't like cities. He didn't understand the pleasures of cramped spaces, of packed crowds on café terraces. When he grew up, he would live on a farm just like his grandfather. Intimidated by the street, he hurried over to the doctor's surgery.

This was his first time, so he waited alone for a moment, looking through some magazines without saying anything. The woman on reception finally saw him there, though, and she sounded very kind, if a bit angry. 'Did you come here on your own?'

He nodded.

'Nobody came with you?'

When he didn't reply, the woman made clear her disapproval.

'And how old are you, young man?'

'Twelve,' Bruce lied.

'All right . . . Well, take a seat. The doctor will see you in a minute.'

He remembered to say, 'Thank you.'

Later, someone did come to fetch him. It was a man with long hair, glasses and a moustache. His dark red velvet trousers were worn at the knee and he smelt of sweat.

On the walls of his office, there were posters of children and animals. One showed a boy who looked ill. Apparently that had something to do with the cigarette that someone next to him was smoking. Another poster told Bruce that he shouldn't hesitate to call the 'green number'.

In the middle of the room there was a small table and a child's chair. There were felt-tip pens, crayons, paper, toys in a red plastic box, building blocks on the floor. Once Bruce had sat down, the man came and knelt next to him on the carpet. Bruce understood then why the man's trousers were so worn at the knees. He felt a sort of tightening in his chest at this idea. He had always been afraid of damaging his clothes, but somehow that was always what happened.

Bruce and the man with the moustache began talking. The man asked him how old he was and which class he was in. Bruce didn't like it when people asked him those two questions one after the other, because the answers always made them draw certain conclusions and nod understandingly. The man said that wasn't the case at all. The conversation wasn't unpleasant. The man congratulated him and, while they chatted calmly, they also did a jigsaw puzzle together. It was a very easy puzzle, for little kids, and it showed Lady and the Tramp eating spaghetti. The man never put the right piece in the right places and Bruce had to keep correcting his mistakes. All the same, Bruce didn't mention this to the man in the worn trousers because he didn't know him and feared how he might react. And also because the man seemed nice and Bruce didn't want to hurt his feelings.

'How do you get to school in the mornings?'

'My dad takes me.'

The man hesitated before fitting the last piece of the puzzle into place, and Bruce smiled happily at him.

'Do you want to do another one?' the man asked.

'No, not really.'

'Do you want to play with something?'

Bruce shrugged.

'How about drawing something?'

'If you want.'

So the man gave him a sheet of paper and a few felt-tip pens and asked him to draw his house.

'Do you like school?'

'Depends.'

'School can be annoying.'

'Yeah, sometimes.'

'Do you like it when your daddy takes you?'

'Yes.'

It was especially hard to draw a straight chimney. Bruce had noticed that the kids in his class drew them perpendicular to the roof, which was obviously stupid. But they were just kids. So Bruce concentrated, the tip of his tongue sticking out between his lips. The man's questions got on his nerves now. He really hated it when people said 'your daddy'. It was his dad: he wasn't a little boy any more.

The man asked him an incredible number of questions. About school, what he thought of this or that, what he liked watching on TV and why, and about his mum and his grandfather. Each time, the man murmured approvingly at his answer, without opening his mouth. Mmm-hmm. Mmm-hmm. It ended up sounding like a lullaby. Bruce drew diligently. He'd started with his dad, then his grandfather, then mum and his sister.

'What's that?' the man asked, pointing to a corner of the drawing.

'Our suitcases.'

He had drawn six different suitcases, each one recognisable from its handle.

'Do you want to go somewhere?'

Bruce shrugged. He had to fill the house with something, and suitcases, he'd realised, were particularly easy to draw. He almost always put them in his drawings.

'What job does your daddy do?'

Without thinking, Bruce corrected him: 'My dad.'

'Yes, your dad.'

'I don't know.'

'Was it him who brought you here?'

'No.'

'He wasn't free?'

'I don't know.'

'Would you rather talk about something else?'

'Yes.'

After that, there had been quite a few questions about his mum, which didn't cause too many problems.

At last, the man asked: 'Do you know why you're here?'

Bruce looked up from his drawing. 'It's almost done.' The chimneys pointed straight up at the sky.

'It's good.' The man turned the drawing towards him to take a closer look. 'It's a very good drawing,' he added, smiling at Bruce.

Bruce didn't need anyone else to tell him this. Even so, it was nice to hear.

'Have you noticed the size of the people around you?'

Of course he'd noticed. He'd drawn them.

'Could you explain why this one is so big and you are so small?'

The man kept bugging him like that for a while. If he'd known this was going to happen, he'd have chosen to do a second jigsaw instead. Time started to slow down. His legs itched. He began reading the posters again.

'Do you remember Sandra?'

'Yes.'

'Do you want to tell me about her?'

'Not really.'

'Are you sure?'

'I don't know.'

'What do you think of Sandra?'

'Nothing.'

'Do you think she's kind?'

'Yes.'

'Do you think she's hard-working?'

'Well, yeah.'

'Do you think she's pretty?'

The man with the moustache, still kneeling on the floor, put his hand on the back of the chair. He spoke very softly. Listening to the sound of his voice, you'd have thought that any answer would have been fine. But Bruce wasn't a kid any more.

'Do you sometimes wish you were in her place?'

'No.'

Bruce tried to shuffle his chair away from the man, but the big hand was still resting on the back of the chair and it didn't move. A sharp smell came from the man's armpits. That smell bothered Bruce and the man was bothering him now too.

'Would you like to tell her something?'

'No.'

Bruce stood up and turned his back on the man. He closed his eyes. Time went faster if you closed your eyes. Actually, he didn't know if that was true but he thought it would be good if it could happen now.

'I'd like you to come and sit down again. We were having a nice chat, weren't we? Please come and sit down.'

Bruce shook his head. He needed to piss now too. And it suddenly seemed to him that he'd been there a long time and his grandfather must be waiting for him.

'I'd like us to keep chatting a little bit longer. About what you did to your classmate. I think you'd feel better if we talked about it.'

Bruce walked sideways towards the door, as if he were playing a game.

'Okay, I understand that you've had enough,' the man said reassuringly, as he in turn stood up. 'We've nearly finished.'

'My grandfather's waiting for me.'

'He can wait a little longer.'

'No!' shouted Bruce, now very anxious.

'There's nothing to worry about.'

And the man advanced towards him, one hand reaching out. Bruce turned abruptly, opened the door and ran out.

'Hey, wait!' called the woman at the reception desk, as he rushed towards the exit.

He'd forgotten his jacket in the man's office. But he didn't care about that. He mustn't keep Granddad waiting.

On the way back, his grandfather still wasn't very talkative. The air was warm that evening and the horizon glimmered orange and pink as the sun set.

Bruce began to doze as he was gently rocked by the swaying of the Citroën and reassured by the familiar smell of his grandfather's Gitanes. He felt good.

'I talked to your doctor,' his grandfather announced suddenly, jolting him from his torpor.

Bruce looked at him, puzzled.

His grandfather turned his eagle-like head towards him, smoke pouring in clouds from the cigarette in his mouth. 'The school called him. He told me that the girl's parents are moving her to a different school.'

Bruce leaned his head against the window. The glass was hot and he could feel each rise, each bump, each downward slope in the vibrations against his forehead. It felt good.

'You don't have anything to say?'

Bruce closed his eyes. He was asleep. 'I'm sleeping,' he said.

The old man grabbed roughly him by the hair. The pain made him cry out and his grandfather growled: 'Don't take the piss out of me. What do you have to say for yourself? Why did you do that?' In a lower voice, he added: 'How could anyone do something like that?'

Bruce felt the tears rise up his throat. It was hard to keep them in. His eyes were burning. He didn't understand and he couldn't find anything to cling to. He wanted to hold his sorrow inside.

'Silence won't help you. Just wait till we get home.'

The long grey car hugged the road's winding curves. At every moment, it felt as if the Citroën was about to leave the ground, but its narrow tyres remained fixed to the tarmac while the car's body swayed and listed lazily. It moved fast, bringing with it all the sorrow and the violence.

MARTEL

For once, Bruce was there early. He was drinking coffee with two other temps in a corner of Hall Two. This was, despite its name, the oldest part of the factory. The brick walls and metal girders rose to more than sixty feet high. Halfway up the walls, narrow windows ran along the side of the building, letting in daylight dimmed by two decades of dust, but at that moment, it was still night-time. The other halls had been designed using more modern materials and their machines were more efficient, as well as more expensive. Yet the workers had a soft spot for Hall Two. Their predecessors had fought and slaved there. Men had died. Occasionally, even now, a serious accident would remind them of the dangers of the old days. But, most importantly, Hall Two was home to a brand-new coffee machine and the union office. In Hall Two, they felt freer of their bosses than they did elsewhere in the factory.

'For all the good it ever did us,' said Hamid, whose life had taught him fatalism.

'Yeah, I wasn't planning on spending my whole life here either,' Martial agreed. 'I mean, all the old guys here look like total fucking idiots.'

'Shut up, will you?' grumbled Bruce, who was trying to see Martel in the union office.

The two others fell silent and looked in the same direction, eager to work out what was going on in there.

The office had been built twenty years before. The union had spent a long time fighting for any kind of office at all, and at the last minute the management had found a way to piss off their opponent by giving them a sort of transparent cubicle, all glass and plastic, fifteen feet by twenty-five, surrounded by vending machines. All right, lads, here you go, this is your office. Have fun with it! They had quickly put up blinds and posters, but after a while the transparency of the place had become part of the landscape. They'd got used to having secret meetings in a goldfish bowl, surrounded by spectators.

Now Velocia's last three temporary workers stood in front of the coffee machine, watching the meeting of the factory's permanent staff, to which they had not been invited. They could see men sitting on chairs and cardboard boxes, with Martel standing behind his metal desk. For now, the Works Council secretary was listening, not speaking. From time to time, one of the men would start yelling and they could hear the muffled echoes of his rage. Everybody got his turn to speak, and waves seemed to pass through the assembled workers. A hand was raised, several mouths opened. They saw Léon Michel get to his feet: he'd been there thirty years, so of course he would have plenty to say about it. They saw Pierrot Cunin, who'd been a delegate back in the seventies, the kind of man who knows everything and understands nothing, bellowing in his thick accent that going on strike was the only solution. The temps tried to work out who was saying what, but their view was blocked by the electoral posters that covered the glass walls. Standing together with the CGT. The CFDT is here to protect you. The FO is on your side.

It was seven in the morning and the machines had been silent and motionless for the past two hours. As soon as the men had

124

abandoned their posts, the foremen and supervisors had wisely retreated to their offices. They'd received instructions. So Hall Two was deserted, as hollow and sonorous as a cave. Amid that vast emptiness, the union office looked like a space capsule drifting through darkness.

'What the hell are they even doing in there?' groaned Martial, as he rolled himself a cigarette.

'Talking.'

'You don't say.'

'Our contracts are up at the end of the week anyway. And there's fuck-all chance of them being extended. You're going to have to make some new friends, Mars.'

'Shit, that's true,' said Martial.

'I thought you couldn't stand anyone here.'

'Even so . . .'

Their contracts had been systematically renewed every month for the past two years. Thanks to the Works Council, Hamid had been able to take his two kids to Disneyland Paris. Martial had even managed to save a bit of money for the first time in his life. That was how he'd bought his Lancia, a flashy car that was as fragile as an egg. Martial had a wife too, and two young daughters, but that was another story. As for Bruce, he'd found Martel here. So, all in all, the three temps didn't feel like laughing.

'Check that out, lads,' said Hamid, who'd turned the other way.

The other two did the same. In the car park, a big Audi had just pulled up.

'That's Mrs Meyer.'

'With Subodka.'

'They're up early for once.'

Two figures emerged from the silver estate car, shoulders slumped by the weight of their briefcases. Sonia Meyer came first, scarf pressed to her mouth. The managing director hadn't put his coat on that morning: surprised by the raw cold, he hurried to catch up with the head of HR.

'Vultures,' said Martial, watching the managers head towards the administrative buildings, which glowed with a warm yellow light.

'All the same, I'd do her.' Hamid had emphasised his desire with an obscene gesture that he immediately regretted. With that kind of woman, it wasn't a good idea to show them any disrespect. Because if you did, you'd just be proving them right in the low opinion they already had of you. Besides, Sonia Meyer hadn't always been a bitch. A worker had been found drunk and she hadn't punished him the way she should have done; one old guy who'd missed a few months of contributions had still been given his full pension when he retired. A blind eye, a helping hand . . . people remembered things like that.

'Did you know the managing director was coming?' Bruce asked.

'Nah, I thought it'd just be the factory boss,' replied Martial, crushing his roll-up stub under his heel.

'That's not a good sign,' Hamid said. He took a box of Tic-Tacs from his overalls pocket, popped one into his mouth, and offered the box to the other two, who both shook their heads. In the upstairs offices, shadows moved. Something was astir in high places.

Meanwhile, in the union office, it was Martel's turn to speak. They had all vented their fury, and now he could conclude proceedings. Bruce's heart started to pound.

Bruce had been in love with Martel for almost a year now. He'd found work at Velocia without actually wanting to, after his grandfather had cut him off. Not that he really needed more money. The drug-dealing made him three or four thousand euros a month easy. But he had to do something, or his grandfather would be all over him again. So that was how he ended up signing with a temp agency. Unfortunately those idiots had managed to find him a job.

At first, Bruce had so obviously not given a fuck that he'd turned everyone against him. But what did he care? It's not like he was planning to stick around in that factory anyway. And then Martel had brought him in for a face-to-face talk and everything had changed. Ever since then, Bruce had done all he could think of to keep the older man's attention. So, when Martel had agreed to work as a bouncer alongside him,

Bruce had believed that they were now best friends. That they were going to do fantastic things together.

Inside the goldfish bowl, Martel explained to the men what he was planning to do and what they could expect to happen. Before he'd finished, Subodka and Meyer showed up in Hall Two. With a wave of his hand, Martel asked them to wait. They obeyed, too afraid even to look at each other. Sombre-faced, they listened to the silence of the machines, observed the absence of men at their posts.

Then the workers came out of the office. Martel was last. He closed the door behind him. Subodka and the head of HR went around shaking hands and saying hello. None of the men refused their handshakes, even though fifteen minutes earlier some of them had been calling for the machines to be dismantled, the factory set on fire. When it came down to it, they were all embarrassed. The little game of mutual loathing, power battles and negotiated compromises was coming to an end. Someone asked where Mr Caron, the CEO, was. He would be here soon, they were told. All right, then. Mrs Meyer, all smiles and looking pretty in her low heels, promised that she would talk to them later, after the Works Council meeting. She sounded like a nurse. The men understood. Martel and the delegates went off for their meeting with management.

'So now you know everything.'

Mr Subodka had shown them a PowerPoint display full of edifying graphs. The company's cash flow, the market, profit margins, turnover: all of those curves were nosediving. The only exception was costs, which were rising at alarming, exponential rates. Velocia was like a beached whale. This time, they had no option. They would have to close the factory.

'Not that I'm telling you anything new,' said the managing director. 'This factory has been making a loss for at least five years. Every time we turn the electricity on here, we lose money.'

Old Cunin, who had been shaking his head incredulously since the beginning, finally spoke up: 'It's not our fault if the market's in decline, though.'

'We never said it was, Mr Cunin,' said the head of HR, appeasingly.

'So why should we have to pay for the choices you've made?'

'You're not the only ones suffering. We're going to have to cut seventy-one jobs at Headquarters.'

'So you say. I know how that works. This is the third wave of redundancies we've had here. It's the same thing every time.'

'We have no choice. As the management of this firm, we are responsible for ensuring its future health.'

The executives' representative, who rarely came to meetings, spoke up too: 'Your entire presentation is based on supposition. We've been through economic crises before. It's no reason to close the factory.'

'The rising costs represent structural elements,' the managing director retorted. 'This factory is inherently unprofitable. Your equipment is too old, salaries are too high, the transport costs are enormous . . . I could go on.'

'You think we're paid too much?!' Léon Michel yelled. 'I've been here thirty years and I make five thousand euros a month net. And you think that's too much?'

'That's not what we were saying,' the head of HR assured him. 'We simply meant that the salaries here are not in line with salaries elsewhere. Particularly in this factory, where the unions have been able to negotiate certain advantages. And that's not a judgement, just an observation.'

The men smiled at this warm memory of the old days, when the influx of work was so high that they'd had to work crazy hours. At the height of its productivity, the factory had employed almost four hundred workers. Ten- and twelve-hour shifts had been topped up with overtime. They were well-paid in those days; there'd been more accidents, but at least the workers' families had reaped the benefits. Léon Michel and Pierrot Cunin were the only ones left who had experienced that golden age. According to them, there had been a genuine camaraderie back then between workers and bosses, both sets of employees fighting side by side as the work rained down and the revolution seemed at hand. They gloried in their ability to produce 10,000 parts every day. They forgot for which masters they had accomplished these Stakhanovite records.

Back then, strikes were fairly common. At certain moments, for reasons that weren't clear, the factory would go into a sort of convulsion. Exhaustion, stolen hours, shortened lunch breaks, all these minor indignities would suddenly combust in a surge of unanimous anger. Certain men distinguished themselves on the front line of this battle, and people still talked about them thirty or forty years later. Bernard Schmitt, René Humbert, Dédé Scoppa . . . those men had secured the meal allowance, 200 per cent overtime rates, the guaranteed end-of-year bonus. When they died, funeral processions of two thousand people followed their coffins to the cemetery: the family first, then the union representatives, with the local politicians bringing up the rear.

But they had been mythologised for so long that the old men had forgotten the realities of the time. Lives burdened by overwork, bodies broken and deformed, life expectancies shortened, horizons narrowed.

In a cheerful voice, Mrs Meyer announced that a letter would be sent to every employee. Support terms would be agreed in consultation with staff representatives. They would have to talk money, of course, and she was prepared to negotiate; they would devote the necessary time to this process. Unfortunately, Velocia was in a desperate situation. Millions in debts and losses; shareholders having to shell out their own money yet again . . . So those made redundant would have to be reasonable.

'Reasonable?' squawked old Cunin.

'You think it's reasonable to fire us with no compensation?' said someone else.

'How many of us do you think will be able to find another job around here? All the factories are closing. We're one of the last.'

Sonia Meyer sat down, joined her hands, and leaned forward. Behind her was a black-and-white photograph of a forest, vertical and labyrinthine. 'I can promise you that we will do all we can to make sure that nobody is left stranded. You can count on us to provide you with all the support you need.'

Then she picked out a pink folder from her Mandarina Duck briefcase. She handed out photocopies. As each man looked at the sheet of paper in his hand, his eyes widened and he let out a curse. The room was filled with the sound of chair legs being scraped over the hideous sandstone mosaic that covered the floor.

'You're not serious?'

Mrs Meyer's pretty smile tensed a little. 'This schedule is in line with standard legal provisions.'

'You could give us a bit more time!'

'Wait!' Martel shouted.

This was his first intervention. Everyone turned to him with a feeling of relief. Subodka thought: Here we go at last. The head of HR made an effort to appear focused, determined, humane.

'If I understand this correctly,' said Martel, 'the employees will receive notification that they are being made redundant next week. Two days after that – on the sixteenth – you have our first meeting. On the eighteenth, we are informed about your support procedures. The notice period begins on the twenty-second. It ends on the twenty-eighth. And the factory will close for good on the ninth of March.' He smiled sweetly. 'Is that correct?'

He had modulated his husky smoker's voice to sound mild-mannered, but his calmness fooled nobody. Tapping his index finger against the schedule, Martel raised his voice slightly as he articulated the words slowly: 'Am I understanding this correctly?'

Mrs Meyer pretended to understand that he was questioning the specific dates on the document. 'In fact, this is a provisional schedule.'

'Please,' Martel said, with a friendly smile, 'could you confirm that everything will be settled by the twenty-eighth and that the factory will close on the ninth of March?'

'That is our plan. It's a basis for discussion. Obviously, arrangements can be made. The associates . . .'

Abruptly standing up, Martel knocked his chair over. The metal seatback crashed noisily against the tiled floor. He picked up his mobile phone and dialled a number from memory. Aware of the impression that the Works Council secretary was having upon his colleagues, Subodka attempted a countermove.

'There's no need for this sort of behaviour. We're all adults here, Mr Martel. You know the factory's situation. We're here to negotiate.'

As before, when the managing director and the head of HR had approached the union office, Martel raised his hand, ordering them to be silent. And he waited, phone to his ear, head tilted sideways, chin almost touching his chest. Nobody said a word. An icy silence fell upon the room. So everyone heard the ringing, then the click when his call was answered.

'Hello,' said Martel. 'I'd like to speak to Mrs Kleber. Yes, that's right, the labour inspector.'

The management representatives shook their heads regretfully. They'd understood what was going on. The secretary was going to play for time. The head of HR thought about her schedule for the coming weeks. A succession of meetings at which she would repeat the same things and get shouted down as if she alone were the embodiment of capitalism.

So, a meeting was arranged with the labour inspector, then they yelled at each other a little bit before agreeing to meet again on 16 February.

'In the meantime, Mr Martel,' the head of HR reminded him, 'we need to reschedule that meeting to examine the Works Council accounts.'

'Of course,' Martel said.

'The inspector can come along to that too, if you like. She might find it amusing.'

'What exactly are you insinuating?'

'Oh, nothing, nothing. You're always very critical of our management. I'm interested in taking a closer look at yours.'

Voices were raised again, a few insults thrown. Subodka calmed everyone down. In a way, Mrs Meyer was tougher than he was.

Outside, forty men stood waiting. Encouraged by all the shouting they'd heard during the meeting, they jeered the management representatives as they came out of the office. There were also a few women with them: employees from the administration department who'd come to offer their support. They wore the same anxious expressions that mothers and girlfriends used to wear back in the days of mass conscription. They'd try to soothe the men's anger, believing that it would do them no good to let their emotions spiral out of control. Besides, most of the women would find work again after the factory closed.

The managing director and the head of HR were not intimidated. After all, they knew what they were doing; they understood how the process worked. They knew that the secretary's ploy was a red herring, that a strike was impossible, that the labour inspector no longer possessed any power. In other words, they knew the law.

Martel was immediately bombarded with questions. He was asked if this would go all the way, if there was any hope, maybe, if they were willing to compromise, oh, and what had she meant about the Works Council accounts . . .?

'Later,' he said, freeing himself from their arms. 'We'll deal with that later.'

He was looking for Bruce and, when he finally saw him, he headed straight over there and drew him apart. Martel had had time to think during the meeting. He knew there was no other way out.

'It's worse than we thought,' he said. 'The factory's fucked.'

'What do you mean?'

'We're going to do it.'

'Do what?' Bruce stammered.

'The Benbareks. We're going to do what they want. But only one girl, okay?'

And just to be sure that he'd understood, Martel grabbed him by the arm. Bruce hurriedly nodded.

'I'll take care of it. I promise. It'll be fine.'

'And you'd better not fuck up this time.'

Curiously, Martel looked rejuvenated, although he also seemed far less reassuring.

That evening, Bruce spent a long time rubbing Synthol into his arm. But it took more than a week before the bruises left by Martel's grip began to fade.

PART TWO

But in the end, I know you'll be the one standing.

Rocky IV

RITA

They parked next to each other in the car park of the Manhattan, a small, remote bar located at the edge of Saint-Dié. It was dark and the first snowflakes were falling, heralds of a big storm forecast for the next day. The green neon sign spelling out 'MANHATTAN' was reflected on the damp tarmac. A bar, five streetlights, and twenty parking spots. It was a sinister-looking place and Rita briefly wondered what she was doing there.

When Martel had asked her to meet him for a drink, she had made a token attempt to play hard to get. The truth was, though, that she'd been waiting quite a while for this. They'd spent a lot of time together over the past few weeks. That was at least one good thing that had come out of the redundancies at the Velocia factory.

When he asked her, he leaned his face very close to hers. It was a strange habit of his: invading your private space when he wanted to speak to you. At first, Rita had wondered what he was doing.

'I had lots of ear infections when I was a kid. I had an operation, but I'm half deaf on one side now.'

'I can speak louder if you want.'

'Don't worry, it's fine like this.'

She hadn't pulled back. And then he'd asked her out, just like that. And now here they were.

Rita got out of her rented 206 and zipped her parka up to her nose. She felt excited, and vaguely annoyed too. The next day she had to take the girl to the police station and she couldn't stop thinking about it. Well, what choice did she have? Victoria had no identity papers. She couldn't go out on her own, enrol in a school or take driving lessons, never mind find a job. It was time to stop acting like her nanny and show a bit of toughness.

Martel joined her and immediately apologised. 'I know it's not a great place, but at least we won't bump into anyone from the factory here.'

'It's fine with me, don't worry.'

They headed towards the entrance. Their shoulders were almost touching and they both stared straight ahead.

Almost as soon as they got inside, the bar owner asked them to close the door behind them. With his nineteen-stone body, thick moustache and honest gaze, he looked a bit like a sea lion. A Budweiser sign shone on his head, giving him a sickly look. Close to the entrance, a guy in a track-suit and trainers was playing darts with an electronic dartboard. Other than him, the only customers were a badly dressed woman sipping banana-flavoured lemonade at the bar and two teenagers playing pool at the back of the room. Martel suggested to Rita that they sit at the bar and the owner turned down the radio so he could take their order. Rita hesitated.

'I'll have a Picon,' said Martel.

'All right. Me too.'

Martel sat on a stool as the sea lion poured two draught beers.

Martel was wearing a brand-new leather jacket and a denim shirt. Rita had never seen him dressed like this before. He reminded her of that guy from *Reservoir Dogs*, the handsome dark-haired one with slightly slumped shoulders, pale blue eyes and a furrowed brow. What was his name? She'd google it when she got home.

They clinked glasses and drank in silence.

'Anyway, I wanted to thank you for what you did.'

Rita shrugged. She hadn't done anything special. In fact, she'd simply reminded the head of HR of the terms of the labour code. Mrs Meyer knew the labour code as well as she did, but there was something a bit too self-assured about her that had got on Rita's nerves. Eventually she'd had to spell it out.

'Given what happened with the machine that vanished during the night, I would advise you to show some good will.'

'We didn't break any laws.'

'I know that, but imagine how it would look in the papers. If I were you, I'd back off a bit on the schedule. You could also discuss the criteria for the redundancy order.'

'We didn't do anything wrong,' the head of HR insisted. She didn't look quite so cute with her lips pursed like that.

'Listen, we know all that. The factory belongs to you, so you can do what you want with it. And I am perfectly within my rights to open an investigation. Or two. The only thing is, I don't have enough staff. With so many people being made redundant around here, it might take a while to finish the investigation. But if everyone does their bit . . .'

In the end, the head of HR had backed down. The factory's closure had been postponed by a month. She'd bought them some time.

'It'd be a good idea to hire a chartered accountant,' said Rita, after finishing her drink.

Martel signalled to the bar owner, who began pouring more beers. Rita took off her parka and asked for a pen and paper so she could write down the contact details of an accountant she knew.

'Call him. He's good. You shouldn't expect miracles, but he's done this kind of thing before. He'll do what needs to be done.'

'What do you mean, I shouldn't expect miracles?'

She shrugged. 'I mean, you can't fight this. The factory is going to close.'

Martel was left in suspense, waiting for her to add something positive or encouraging. It didn't happen. They started drinking again. Martel thought about his friends. When the schedule had been changed, the men had got worked up. If management backed down on that, maybe there was still hope. They could get the media on their side, put pressure on the mayor. And yet the inspector had never given him any illusions. Already Martel was imagining the local kids throwing stones at the windows of the abandoned factory. Two winters from now, nothing would remain of it but ruins.

The sea lion gave them a bowl of olives with their third round.

'Maybe we should find a table at the back. It'd be easier to have a conversation there.'

She followed him. On the way there, Martel nodded at one of the boys playing pool.

'How's your dad?'

'He's all right,' the boy replied, blushing.

'I haven't seen him for a while.'

'He's on mornings, I think.'

Martel didn't react. Patrick Locatelli hadn't set foot in the factory for more than a week. There were a few like that, who practically didn't even bother getting out of bed any more.

'Well, tell him I said hello.'

'Okay.'

Martel and Rita sat in a booth near the toilets. They both smiled when they saw the painting on the wall: some dogs playing poker.

'You seem to know everyone round here,' she said.

'And I chose this place so we wouldn't bump into anyone! Yeah, it's a small town – it's hard to avoid seeing people you know.'

'Not that it makes any difference.'

'Well, we wouldn't want your husband to see us,' said Martel, in an ironic voice.

'No danger of that.'

'You're not married?'

'Not really, not any more.'

They were slightly drunk now and speaking more freely. After a while, the darts player managed a triple twenty and the electronic board started flashing and beeping like crazy.

The bar owner laughed. 'What is that racket?'

'Only the best arrow I've ever thrown, Bruno!'

'Maybe you should buy everyone a drink,' suggested the woman with the banana lemonade.

The sea lion laughed, thumbs in the pockets of his leather jacket. But in the end he did offer free drinks to all the customers – a beer or a *kir* on the house.

It was seven o'clock and the atmosphere was starting to warm up. The radio played an old Billy Joel hit. Soon, two more customers entered the bar. They looked like soldiers: shaved back and sides, with a little tuft at the front. They wore identical bomber jackets and workmen's boots. They ordered pints and stood just behind the guy in the tracksuit, who suddenly lost his ability to throw a dart straight.

For a while, Rita and Martel talked about their lives. They felt tired, ready to open up. The words came easily and they wanted to tell each other the kind of things that they might generally keep to themselves. Old stories about their families, their sex lives, the fears that you try to hide and that define you more than anything else.

'I only became secretary of the Works Council by accident, really. I mean, I like it but I've never actually thought I was up to the job. You act like you know what you're doing, but it's a bit like being at school. You can get away with it for a while, but then something happens . . . like these redundancies. Or like when my mum got sick. It was almost too real to be believable.'

Rita listened, a half-smile playing on her lips.

'Do you have children?' Martel asked, without really thinking.

'No.'

He hesitated a second. 'Would you like to?'

'Probably. Well, to be honest, I'm not sure any more . . .'

They were torn from their intimacy by raised voices. The soldiers were making fun of the darts player, who was now bright red and refusing to budge, even though he obviously wanted to run away.

Martel had twisted round in his chair. He was trying to understand the conversation, but his bad ear made it difficult. 'What are they saying?'

'Nothing. They're just pricks.' He made as if to stand up, but Rita put her hand on his arm. 'Let it go. What do we care?'

Martel had a feeling of relief, of simplicity, as when you finally manage to untangle a knot in your laces. 'Do you want to get something to eat?'

She didn't say no. The bar owner's daughter, who had just started her shift, chose that exact moment to come over and clear their table. 'Are you finished with your glasses?'

'I don't know,' said Martel, raising his eyebrows.

'As you like,' Rita replied.

'Then yeah.'

Beneath the table, their knees touched. Rita looked at her watch and stood up. 'I forgot. There's something I have to do. I have to go.'

'You couldn't put it off?'

'No.'

She pulled herself together, patting her pockets until she found her car keys. Then she looked at her watch again.

'I'm really sorry. I arranged to have dinner with my mother. I absolutely have to go.'

'Of course,' said Martel, smiling understandingly.

'I'm going to the Ladies, and then I'll be off.'

As he watched her walk away, he couldn't help imagining her in her underwear, her long bare legs, the black cotton taut against the soft white flesh of her bum. He wanted to encircle her hips with his arms and press his face between her legs. She would put her hands on his shoulders . . . he'd breathe in the smell of her pussy . . . she'd run her hands through his hair. The idea intimidated him because it might well happen eventually. He stood up and paid for all their drinks before returning to the table.

'Are you going to cook?' he asked her.

'That was the idea. Although, given how late it is, I don't know how I'll manage.'

'I know a nice little restaurant near where you live.'

She seemed to freeze.

'I drove you home once. When your car wouldn't start, remember?'

Rita really wanted to leave now, but Martel was writing something on a scrap of paper he'd taken from his wallet.

'This is the address. It's a pizzeria in the valley, the Capri. It's nothing amazing, but I like it. No background music, check tablecloths – you know the sort of place.'

Rita had already put on her parka. She glanced at the piece of paper that Martel had given her. 'I already have your number.'

'I know,' said Martel. 'For work. I'm giving it to you so you can ask me out to dinner next time.'

Rita played with her zip for a few seconds before making up her mind. 'All right. Well, I'll see you.'

'Till soon . . .'

There was a moment of clumsy hesitation: her advancing, him standing. In the end they shook hands. She left without turning back. He watched her until the door closed behind her, hoping she would grant him one backward glance.

Outside, a fine dusting of fresh snow covered the cars, the ground and everything around her. The occasional car moved fast through the darkness. The radio presenter was advising people to drive carefully. The storm was almost here.

BRUCE

Back to the wall, Colt .45 in his hand, Bruce hurtled down the staircase of Tower Nine. He was breathing fast and he could feel his heart banging against his ribcage. He'd been overdoing the coke ever since he'd lost his job at the factory. Not to mention the steroids he was getting from a friend at the gym. He was like this all the time now: tense, irritable, incapable of concentrating.

He'd almost reached the cellar when the light in the stairwell went out. Somewhere above him, a man started complaining in Arabic. Bruce heard a dog barking in one of the apartments. Then the light came back on. He descended the final flight.

The cellar had a low ceiling and contained about fifteen stalls. It smelt of earth, moped oil and old crates. Daylight filtered dimly through some basement windows. Bruce advanced sideways, still tightly gripping his gun. He passed the Miclots' stall and saw an old Conforama sofa-bed, a few jars of damson plums, and an exercise bike that had never been used. Then he skirted around the Ladjimi kid's scooter, covered with padlocks. In the distance he recognised the security door protecting the Lamberts' stall. Mr Lambert would sleep there sometimes, when it became impossible in his apartment.

At last he reached the stall belonging to old Kemali, the road-mender who'd fallen in his bathtub the previous summer and been taken to a hospice against his will, even as he'd begged the paramedics to let him die at home. Since then, his children had been arguing about what they should do with the old man's apartment, a tiny one-bedroom flat that had cost their father twenty years of minimum-wage earnings. Yet his stall was still there, unused. Bruce froze. His sweat-drenched T-shirt was cold against his back. He licked his lips nervously, as he did every few seconds – another side-effect of the cocaine. Fuck, his feet hurt. He desperately wanted to run. He opened his mouth and tried to suck in air.

It was precisely at this moment that he heard laughter behind the stall door. Without thinking he threw himself forward and shouldered it open. Inside, the stall was tiny and dark and filled with shouted insults coming from every direction. A fluorescent ceiling light came on, flooding the space with brightness, dazzling Bruce. For a second he was disoriented. In his panic he held the Colt in front of him and squeezed the trigger ten times. Bodies fell to the floor and the fucking Colt kept biting at emptiness: click click click click.

'Fuck you, motherfuckers!' Bruce yelled, his eyes wide as saucers.

In front of him, two kids were rolling on the ground, dying in agony like people do on TV.

'Go fuck yourself,' shouted a third kid, Nonosse, who threw a large lead ball at his face.

Bruce dodged it easily. He was so hyped up he could have evaded heavy machine-gun fire, like that guy in *The Matrix*.

'You missed, motherfucker. Now you're gonna get it.'

He tried to grab the kid by his neck, but Nonosse was well-trained in the art of escaping fists and he stole away. Bruce's momentum sent him flying into a metal shelf: an ice skate crashed down and hit Younes in the head. The pain was so intense that Younes immediately stopped moaning and writhing on the floor. A mark appeared on his forehead. A few red drops shone bright against his skin and then the blood really began to flow and Younes started wailing, 'Mummy, Mummy, Mummy!'

'Come on, shut your mouth,' Bruce begged, trying to gag the boy with his free hand.

'Our mum's going to kill us,' said Mounir, leaning on an elbow.

Bruce swore and attempted to grab Younes's arm and lift him up, but the kid struggled and howled even louder.

'Please shut up! If you shut up, I'll lend you my gun.'

He handed the Colt to the kid, who stared at it. His shoulders were still shaking, but his tears had already dried up. He grabbed the gun and his big brother wiped the snot from his nose with his sleeve. The little kid didn't even notice. In his head, this was as good as Christmas.

'That's a crappy gun,' said Nonosse, vaguely jealous.

'And you'll give us some bullets?' asked Mounir, as he inspected Younes's forehead.

'Yeah, course.'

Younes nodded and gave several little sniffs. In his tiny hands, the Colt was breathtakingly beautiful.

Bruce rushed to get back to the apartment before the kids. Before that, he had retrieved his gun and told Mounir to go to the pharmacy for some plasters to cover his brother's wound. He'd also warned them not to go home straight away because they needed to give the bleeding time to stop. When Marie-Rose saw him run along the corridor while she was pouring tea for her neighbour, she went after him.

'Hey! Where are the children?'

Bruce kept going without a word, then locked himself into his room. In the kitchen the two women began talking indignantly. And not without reason.

Bruce had been living at Hamid's place for two weeks now. They'd both been temps at Velocia, and when Bruce had asked him if he could crash there for a night or two, Hamid had sounded unenthusiastic. Hardly surprising: their three-bedroom apartment was on the small side, and his wife wasn't exactly easy-going. But Bruce had laid down a 500-euro note. It wasn't much, considering that he planned on staying there for at least two months, but a 500-euro note was something you didn't see every day. It was mauve, perfectly crisp, and featured a picture of a cable-stayed bridge. So in the end they came to an arrangement.

Mounir, the eldest, had moved out of his room and he and his brother had found themselves with a sort of strange new cousin, weirdly nervous and not very bright, but a really nice guy all the same. Bruce showed them loads of things, like how to roll a joint or steal a CD by covering the anti-theft device with a two-euro coin. Not only that, but he bought them an Xbox and some games. Marie-Rose had to impose a curfew after catching the three idiots playing video games at two in the morning. You should have seen the kids' faces when they had to go to school the next morning.

'But you can't let him just get away with it like that!' her neighbour exclaimed.

'I know!'

Bruce listened to them discuss his fate while he wondered what to do. Another 500-euro note would not be enough this time. He wouldn't go back to the Farm, though. When his grandfather had noticed his Colt was missing, he'd gone completely mental. For the first time in years, he'd got out the old truncheon and had started hitting Bruce. It was a horrible thing to see, an old man like that busting a gut trying to hurt him. Bruce decided to get the hell out of there. Particularly since the old man had threatened to call the police on him.

Yeah, Bruce had had it up to here with being told what he could do and who he could see. He was sick to death of that old bastard. He wasn't stupid enough to tell him that to his face, though.

Because his grandfather wasn't just some random old man. Every time Bruce had dealings with the gang leaders in the area, he knew they were only agreeing to see him because of his surname. For many, Pierre Duruy was a legend, a name that carried echoes of his past reputation for violence and impunity. Ever since he'd been a little kid, Bruce had noticed the respect that everyone showed his granddad. Neighbours, local thugs, even the cops. And all this in spite of the way they lived on the Farm, with its junkyard and Bruce's alcoholic mother. Even so, he was sick of the old man.

For a start, when Bruce's father went away, Pierre Duruy said he could never see him again. True, he wasn't the nicest man in the world and he'd cheated on Bruce's mother, but still . . . he *was* his father. As a teenager, Bruce had bumped into him occasionally, at railway-station cafés, in nightclubs and discos. His father wasn't stingy: he always bought Bruce a drink when they met by chance like that. Once, they even got a hotel room together with some girls. He hadn't seen him recently, though. In fact, he didn't have any idea where he lived. But who cared? He wasn't a kid any more. The old man could go fuck himself. Bruce would manage perfectly well on his own now.

Bruce had not been wasting his time since leaving the Farm. He'd gone into partnership with a wholesale dealer from Épinal and now he sold coke and hash pretty much all over the *département*. He'd given up on concerts and was now focused on discos and secondary schools. He'd even got Younes and Mounir selling a few bars of hash for him. Everybody was happy.

Bruce loved the feeling of importance that his business conferred upon him. When he went to the local council estates, the kids acted like he was Tony Montana. At night, he rubbed shoulders with all the night-birds: rich kids, wannabe thugs, pretty girls and lost souls. Blonde beauties who would one day be lawyers or cardiologists kissed him on the cheeks in places where everyone sipped mojitos while listening to the latest Pharrell Williams hits. They held his shoulder and whispered in his ear. Everywhere he went, he carried himself with the cool, arrogant swagger of a man who knows he is the crucial connection between the dingiest dives and chicest mansions. He was happy.

He'd bought himself a car too – an old BMW 5 Series with 80,000 miles on the clock – and he'd joined a newly opened gym in Saint-Dié. With all the products he was taking, he was starting to bulge and flex like a superhero. The only part of his body that wasn't ripped was his legs. In underpants, with his enormous torso, he looked a bit like a crane with its feathers plumped. Still, never mind. He was getting hormone injections in his thighs and spending three hours a week on the bike, so that imbalance would soon be rectified. In the meantime, he walked around in a leather jacket that he wore unzipped to show off the Gold's Gym bodybuilding vest underneath it. His pupils were the size of pinheads as he ground his teeth, looking for fights with anyone who crossed his path.

From time to time, he would pick up Younes and Mounir from school and the three of them would hang out in front of the tower block with the other neighbourhood kids. To impress them, Bruce would strike poses, flexing his lats, his abs, making his triceps ripple up and down his arms. He'd even caught a cold, fooling around like that in the middle of winter. But he was every bit as addicted to those kids' admiring looks as he was to his dietary supplements.

As soon as the neighbour left, Marie-Rose came to his room. 'What the hell is going on?' she shouted, banging on the door. 'Where are the children? You think you can live in our apartment and just do whatever you want?'

It was still early and Bruce didn't plan on going out any time soon. So he put his headphones on, listened to a Meshuggah compilation, stripped off and – after snorting a quick line of coke – started doing press-ups. When he was nice and tense, he posed in front of the mirror. People could piss him off all they wanted. With arms like that, what did he care? He spread them out, palms to the ceiling, and his chest opened, like a strange flower. He held the position for a moment and his phone began to ring. It was Martel. He answered straight away. Behind the door, Marie-Rose was still nagging him.

Two days before this, Martel had come and found him as he was pissing about with a dozen kids outside Tower Nine. It was dark, but Bruce recognised the Volvo at first glance. He could have run off then – that was his initial instinct – but Martel had taken his time walking over, and Bruce thought that seemed like a good sign. So he stood up before telling the kids to clear off.

'Go on, get out of here, I have to see someone.'

'No, man, you fuck off!'

'Exactly.'

'Yeah, no kidding, cuz. Where do you think you are?'

And the kids had started insulting him like you wouldn't believe. The worst ones were two siblings, a little girl with plaits spinning around on rollerblades and her big brother, who held onto her to stop her falling. In the end, Bruce decided to meet Martel halfway, but he curled his lip to show how unfazed he was.

'Hey, man, good to see you. I was just about to call you—'

'Have you found the girl?'

In the darkness, Martel's dark eyes were illuminated by the light from the surrounding tower blocks. It was hard to tell if the emotion Bruce saw in them was anger or gloom.

Bruce began by complimenting his new leather jacket. 'Looks great – where'd you find it?'

Instead of answering him, Martel took him by the arm and led him away. For a chat, presumably. That was how they ended up alone in the park. Martel sat on a swing while Bruce preferred to stand, a few feet away, drawing in the gravel with his shoe.

'I went to see your grandfather.'

'When?'

'A better question would be "why".'

Bruce stiffened. Martel took his time lighting a cigarette. The eleven tower blocks in the estate loomed all around. Most of the windows were illuminated and in almost every apartment you could see the bluish flutter of a TV screen. It was cold. The rumble of traffic on the motorway was audible in the distance.

'If I'd known all that at the start,' Martel said, 'I never would have got involved.'

'What did that old bastard tell you?'

'Doesn't matter any more. It's just, in this kind of situation, you need to trust each other. Instead of which, you leave home, you vanish, you don't answer the phone. What am I supposed to think?'

Bruce hesitated. 'You can trust me.'

'Fucking hell, Bruce . . .' Martel looked seriously weary. He took one last drag then tossed his cigarette at Bruce. 'We can't just forget this shit, Bruce. We need to find the girl. *You* need to find the girl.'

'What? Why me?'

Bruce adopted a strange tone then, like a school dunce who'd just been given a load of extra homework. For him, that whole affair was in the past. The little bitch had disappeared? Good for her. As for the cash, they'd have to see. If the Benbareks insisted on getting it back, he'd figure something out. This was what he told Martel.

'I don't think you really understand. Your little friends are parked outside my apartment building in their truck every fucking night. And I have to deal with the factory closing. So it's up to you to find the girl. I'm not asking for a favour here. I'm telling you what you have to do.'

Martel swung gently back and forth as the conversation went on. Bruce would agree to anything as long as it got Martel out of his hair. After a while, the conversation turned to the factory and Martel told him the latest news. Then Bruce explained about living at Hamid's place, about the kids, about Marie-Rose whining all the time.

'All right, I have to get going,' Martel said.

He stood up and the two men found themselves face to face. Bruce moved closer, all smiles. He felt relieved. They were friends again, so everything was good. He didn't need to hide out any more. They shook hands.

'You're sniffing a lot,' Martel remarked. 'Have you caught a cold or something?'

Bruce just shrugged. Martel smiled, and so did Bruce, and then his hand was burning with unbearable pain and the next thing he knew he was on his knees. Martel was breaking his thumb. No sooner had the grip on his hand loosened than Martel's fingers were wrapped around his throat. Almost immediately, he began seeing stars.

'Listen to me, you fucking half-wit. I don't give a shit if you want to get high or piss around with the ghetto kids or act like some big-shot gangster. That's none of my business. But the Benbareks are dangerous. They're not just play-acting like you – they'll do just about anything to be taken seriously. Do you understand that?'

Bruce nodded and Martel knelt next to him, then whispered into his ear. He spoke a few short sentences, repeating each one until Bruce nodded. Finally, Martel asked him if he understood.

'Yes.'

'What?'

'I'm going to find the girl.'

'Go on.'

'At any fucking cost . . .'

'There you go.'

And to drive the point home, Martel twisted his thumb back, breaking it completely. The pain was so bad that Bruce started writhing around, bellowing like a heifer. Martel let go. And that was when he saw them. They weren't alone in the park.

A dozen figures were standing about ten feet away. Some wore hoods, others were bare-headed. The kids moved closer, feet dragging in the gravel. Each one held up his phone. Martel tried to see their faces, but the feeble halo cast by the screens wasn't enough to light them. They fanned out, fearless and silent. Behind them the tower blocks rose skyward, like back-up. Crawling on his arse, Bruce tried to reach them, to put himself out of harm's way.

'You'd better all go home,' Martel said.

'*You* go home!' said the fat boy holding his rollerblading sister's hand. The kids advanced, phones held up like shields.

'Fuck off, man.'

Martel had been retreating without even realising it.

'The girl, Bruce,' he said one last time, before leaving.

So, when Bruce saw Martel's name on his mobile screen, he answered on the first ring. Martel didn't bother with small-talk.

'So . . . the girl?'

He had a one-track mind now.

'I think it's okay.'

'What does that mean?'

'I'm looking for her. I've got a lead.'

There was a silence, then Martel said: 'There was a message on my machine earlier.'

'Yeah?'

'A really weird message.'

Bruce wondered if this was some sort of test, like those questions his teachers at school would sometimes ask, when it felt like another question was buried under their words. Generally, in situations like that, the best thing was to say nothing. This was what Bruce did now.

Martel went on: 'It sounded . . . like a child moaning . . .'

'But you don't have any kids.'

'Fucking hell, that's not the point. I don't want to get messages like that. I don't want to be mixed up with anyone capable of leaving that kind of bollocks on my answer machine. We need to get out of this shit. Fast.'

'Yeah, I know, don't worry . . .'

'Bruce.'

'Yeah?'

'I'm going to take it out on you.'

MARTEL

When he got home, Martel put the coffee machine on, then took a shower.

He'd left the Manhattan about eight thirty, half drunk and irritated by the two skinheads who'd been bullying the darts player. He'd got home without difficulty in the old Volvo estate. On the other hand, he'd struggled to climb the three flights of steps that led from the garage up to his apartment. The lift had been out of order for months, but Martel had warned the owners' committee that he didn't have any money to pay for crap like that.

Under the jet of hot water, he gradually started to feel better. His shoulders were numb, as if he'd been rope-climbing, and his neck was stiff. Every morning, he woke feeling more exhausted than the day before. He kept going by gulping down endless cups of coffee . . . and quite a lot of alcohol too. He had to think about the redundancies, about Bruce, about that girl. He looked at his hands and felt old. The water streamed over his skin, darkening the ink of his tattoos.

Martel had spent a large part of his existence fleeing commitment. He'd avoided group holidays, football teams, steady girlfriends. Of course he'd been in the army, but in a way that had brought him freedom from responsibility. Other people took the decisions; all he had to do was obey.

He often thought about that film with De Niro and Pacino. He must have seen it a dozen times. In the film, De Niro explains that a good bank robber has to be able to leave behind everything – his car, his apartment, his friends, his wife, his kids – in thirty seconds. Any attachments and you're fucked: the cops have a way to find you. The moral of the story was obvious. If you own something, it owns you. This idea of zero possessions had served Martel well for a time, back when he had nothing to lose.

But since coming out of the army, life had got its claws into him. It had wrapped itself around him, like a straitjacket.

It had all begun when he'd had to take care of his mother. Now he was trapped. He was afraid of frozen pipes, economic crises, flu epidemics, terrified that he would lose his reputation or his car keys. And then there was his debt to the Benbareks. It was late enough now that their truck was probably parked outside. He caught his breath. If only the inspector . . .

He came out of the shower and tied a towel around his waist. He wiped the mist from the bathroom mirror. His eyes still looked lost, his mouth self-satisfied, but the effects of the alcohol were surging back. He put on a pair of jeans and a T-shirt. The comforting smell of freshly brewed coffee spread through the apartment. He poured himself a cup before going into the living room to look down at the car park. The snow was falling heavily, but there was no sign of the Benbareks' truck. He exhaled with relief. So what could he do now? Wait for Bruce to call, like he did every night? Maybe he should go looking for the girl himself. In truth, though, he would rather stay inside in the warm. He could watch a film for a change. An old Clint Eastwood movie, for example. Cup in hand, Martel leafed through his DVDs. A western? *Dirty Harry*? Or maybe that one about the kidnapping, with Kevin Costner?

On the day of the kidnapping, Bruce had come to fetch him, very early in the morning. It was still completely dark outside. They'd headed to Strasbourg. As planned, Bruce had picked up a powerful but inconspicuous car, a burgundy Peugeot 605.

Bruce seemed anxious throughout the journey. He kept sniffing and drove with his eyes aimed at the rear-view mirror. Martel turned on the radio. He wanted to hear the news, but it was still too early so he had to make do with some dreary jazz.

'We have to get there before the sun rises,' Martel said.

Bruce nodded.

The horizon was starting to lighten.

'You're not very chatty.'

Bruce shrugged. 'There's nothing much to say.'

Arms crossed, Martel stared moodily at the road. 'There's one thing that bothers me . . .'

'What?'

'Why that street? Why those two girls? And why do we have to keep them hidden for a week?'

Bruce shrugged again. 'Who knows? They're Arabs, aren't they? Anyway, it's too late now.'

Martel leaned back in his seat and closed his eyes. Bruce was right: it was too late to turn back now.

They drove like that for almost an hour, then Bruce parked the car by the side of the road. Inside the boot there was a plastic box filled with earth and a jerry-can of water. He poured some water into the earth and mixed it up with his hands. Then he began to smear the number plates with this freshly made mud. When he'd finished, Martel helped him wash his hands with water from the jerry-can.

'Fuck, my hands are freezing,' Bruce grumbled.

'Yeah, it must be minus five out here. I'll drive the rest of the way.'

They left the jerry-can by the side of the road. Martel drove fast, in the middle of the road, flashing his headlights as they rounded curves. But they didn't see anyone else.

It was just after six when they arrived at Quai Pasteur. A shroud of mist hovered above the Cours de l'Île. On the other side of the road, a wall was covered with graffiti. The shadows of trees were starting to spread across the pavements.

'There's nobody here,' Martel said.

'I'm not surprised – it's too fucking cold.'

'So what do we do? Where are they?'

The 605 was moving slowly as they had this conversation, and just as Martel asked where the whores were, he found himself almost face to face with a girl in make-up waiting inside a parked car.

'They always stay in the cars when the weather's like this,' Bruce explained.

'So do you know where we can find the two we're looking for?'

'Just over there.'

He pointed at a blue Ford Focus. They kept moving forward at the same speed.

'I saw two of them,' Bruce said, after they'd passed the car.

'Me too.'

'So what do we do?'

'I'll turn around and go past again.'

'We'll have to go to a car wash afterwards,' said Bruce, digging a bit of mud from under his fingernails.

'What?'

'The number plates are a mess.'

'I thought you were supposed to burn them?'

'Oh, yeah . . . shit.'

On the Quai Menachem-Taffel, Martel made a U-turn. Now they looked more closely, the street wasn't as deserted as it had first appeared. In cars parked along the pavements, a figure moved, a ceiling light came on, there was a lighter flame, then cigarette smoke billowing behind a windscreen. Martel felt as if he were visiting a cave: little by little, his eyes became accustomed to the darkness and he started to spot all kinds of things hidden in the corners.

On the other hand, there were no johns here at all. The girls were finishing the night wrapped up in thick sweaters, listening to the radio and smoking fags, eyes shielded by sunglasses. The day rose up from the ground and found them there, limp with tiredness, fighting back a vague desire to weep.

Again, Martel drove past the Focus, then parked the 605 a few yards further on. He adjusted his rear-view mirror to get a better view. On the other side of the road, a face appeared behind the window of a Volkswagen Kombi and a slightly chubby woman stared at them. The Peugeot's engine purred. The woman breathed on the window, drew a heart in the condensation, and waved them over. Martel put both hands on the wheel, as if he were about to take his driving test.

'All right, go. And be quick.'

Bruce cracked his knuckles, then got out of the car, carefully closing the door behind him.

Martel started the stopwatch function on his watch and his hands returned to their position on the steering wheel. The tenths of seconds whirled past, the seconds ticking one after another. In the rear-view mirror, Martel saw Bruce walking along the line of cars. When he reached the Focus, he blew in his hands to warm them up, then tried the handle of the passenger door, but it was locked. So he took a foot-long metal pipe from inside his jacket and smashed the window. Shards of glass went flying. Turning his face away to protect his eyes, he hit the window twice more before shoving his forearm into the car to open the door.

Martel didn't hear a single sound. He breathed in through his nose and out through his mouth. One minute, ten seconds. Bruce opened the door, dropped the metal pipe and dragged the passenger out by her hair. She was an Asian-looking girl in a silver Puffa jacket, fishnet stockings and very high heels. She didn't struggle.

At that moment, Martel spotted a movement in the rear-view mirror. Another girl had got out of a car a little further away. Then the whole dock went into action stations, silently. Doors opened, figures appeared. Martel's eyes flickered from side to side as he gauged distances. He shifted into first and stepped on the accelerator, ready to release the clutch.

'Fuck, what's he doing?'

Bruce had let the girl in the silver jacket run away and dived inside the Focus. The driver's-side door opened and Martel got a glimpse of very dark hair flying in a gust of air. The second girl fled too. A red scarf, black clothes, long legs. Bruce clambered out of the car and ran after her. On the pavement, the other girls stood hesitantly. One of them, an African woman with a shaved head, put a rape whistle to her lips. The shrill sound seemed to split open the sky. Suddenly, it was day.

'Fuuuck!'

Martel shifted into reverse, right arm behind the passenger-seat headrest, and the car squealed backwards. He passed the running girl, then slammed on the brakes and rushed outside. All he had to do was open his arms and he'd caught her. Without thinking, he punched her in the head. The girl went as limp as a rag doll.

'Come on!' he yelled at Bruce, as he got back into the car.

There were now maybe a dozen girls screeching and shouting on the nearby pavements. They all had their phones out. Some were making calls, others taking photos or videos. The African girl was still blowing fiercely into her whistle.

Bruce tossed the girl onto the back seat and jumped into the passenger seat. Around them, they could hear people yelling about the police, shouting insults. Martel put his foot to the floor: first, second, third. He sped along the street at more than 80 m.p.h., going as straight as he could. Several cars coming in the opposite direction were forced to veer sideways. The V6 engine roared in the fresh morning air as a creamy light spread over the city and Bruce, eyes wide open, clung to anything he could find. In the back seat, the girl's body went crashing from one side to the other. They were soon on the motorway. After that, Martel stuck scrupulously to the speed limit.

They took the first exit and followed a complicated route home to make sure they weren't followed. Now Martel was driving along a B-road like an old man. They were only a mile from the Vosges: nearly there. Bruce had climbed into the back of the car and taped the girl's arms and legs together.

'Do you know her?' Martel asked.

Bruce caught Martel's eye in the rear-view mirror and looked away. The countryside around was brown, dirty, the road lined with barbed-wire fences. The overcast sky dominated the landscape.

'I asked you a question.'

'I don't know her.'

'What got into you?'

'What do you mean?'

'Why didn't you nab the first one?'

'I dunno. This one was younger. I thought she'd be less of a pain.'

Martel focused on the road. 'Can't you fucking blow your nose? It's getting on my nerves, hearing you sniff like that all the time.'

A little later, Martel stopped on the hard shoulder.

'What are you doing?'

'I need to piss. Is she awake?'

Bruce peered under the blanket he'd spread over the girl's body.

'Doesn't look like it. You really knocked her out, dude!'

'Shut up. And don't touch her.'

'What?'

The jet of urine hit the ground and white steam rose through the air. Martel was deep in thought. Something had bothered him about this whole affair since the beginning. That envelope from the Benbareks with the photographs of the girls. And then everything had moved so quickly and he'd been so desperate for the cash that he hadn't really thought it through.

The cash had all gone. As soon as he'd decided to do the kidnapping, it had all gone up in smoke. Some of it had gone into the coffers of the Works Council, but he'd allowed himself a few pleasures too. His leather jacket, some CDs by Johnny Cash and Jerry Lee Lewis, a few films and a Browning hunting rifle. A Blu-ray player too. He'd even bought *Platoon* again to watch it on the new format, but he wasn't that impressed. He didn't see much difference between DVD and Blu-ray. He started rummaging around in his pockets, but he'd left his cigarettes in the car. So he went back. Bruce was still messing around with the girl.

'What are you doing?'

'Nothing.'

– 'Leave her alone.'

Martel offered him the packet of cigarettes, then took one for himself. 'Let's put her in the boot and get a coffee,' he said. 'We need to talk.'

'What do you mean?'

'All right, enough playing around. Every time I ask you a question, you pretend you don't understand what I'm on about. This time you're going to answer me.'

'You don't think we should hide the girl at the Farm first? It's not far from here.'

'We're going to put her in the boot. I want to deal with this now.'

He lit Bruce's cigarette and then his own.

A woman with unkempt grey hair served them before returning to the dishwasher that she was frantically trying to fix. From time to time she would mutter, 'Oh, for God's sake!' and sigh as if her life were over.

They were alone in the café and Martel was speaking quietly, almost in a murmur. Their cups sat on the red Formica table, alongside Martel's hands. Bruce's remained in his pockets. He hadn't touched his coffee and his eyes were red.

'Stop looking like that.'

'What?'

'You have to tell me, for God's sake. I knew there was something weird about all this right from the beginning.'

'I've just heard a few rumours, that's all. I don't see what difference it makes.'

'The difference is that we're now caught between the Russkies and the Benbareks.'

'What do you mean?'

'This whole plan to kidnap a girl – it has to be a way of getting revenge on that guy.'

'Tokarev?'

161

'Yeah.'

'So?'

Martel's face froze. He hissed between his teeth: 'So this Tokarev might just kill us to piss off the Benbareks. We're in over our heads here. Getting mixed up with the Arabs was bad enough, but the Russians . . . that's a whole other level.'

'They won't be able to find us anyway. They've never seen me and I don't know those pricks at all.'

'Lower your voice,' Martel muttered, checking that the woman hadn't heard anything. 'Those whores were taking pictures of you this morning, you moron. And you're not exactly inconspicuous, are you?'

Bruce sat up, looking proud. With all the hassle that day, he'd almost forgotten that he had a 48-inch chest.

'You'll have to keep a low profile for a few weeks. We'll hand over the girl. And hope that everything will be okay.'

'Of course everything will be okay.'

'And blow your fucking nose!'

The woman glanced over the counter at them. The bodybuilder was doing what he'd been told while the other went outside. Through the front window she saw him pacing around with his mobile phone glued to his ear. He was very tall, and quite well-built too. Maybe they were brothers or cousins. The bodybuilder had looked meek as a lamb, anyway, when the tall one raised his voice. Two coffees . . . She wasn't going to earn a living if that was all the custom she got in the morning. And if this bloody dishwasher didn't start working, she might as well shut up shop. It was true what the tall one had said, though: it really was annoying listening to the other sniff all the time.

In the end, Martel had started watching *Rocky*. But he hardly took anything in. He couldn't concentrate. Life was unbelievable sometimes . . . The factory had had to close for him to finally meet a woman he liked! He had replayed the conversation with Rita at the Manhattan at least ten times. He couldn't find anything wrong with her. Even next to the head of HR, Rita had nothing to be ashamed of. And Mrs Meyer was an impressive woman.

The doorbell rang and Martel jumped. It was gone ten on a Friday night: way too late for anyone to bother him. He went over to the window. Still no truck in the car park. Barefoot, he put his slippers on before looking through the spyhole in the door. Total darkness. The doorbell rang again.

'Hang on,' said Martel.

He hesitated. Was he going to call, 'Who's there?' like some little old lady? No, fuck it, he hadn't sunk that low. He put the door on the chain and opened it a few inches. Nobody. No light. And yet the doorbell rang for the third time.

BRUCE

Since that phone conversation with Martel, Bruce had actually started his investigation into the girl's whereabouts. This consisted mostly of driving around for hours, staring into space as he listened to Guns N' Roses.

Often, as he rounded a bend beneath the white sky, he had the impression that he'd reached the end of the world. He felt as if a hand were gripping his chest and strange thoughts ran through his head, like trains. He saw Martel, his sister, his grandfather, and – most of all – his mother. And then came sadness, not wholly unpleasant, in which he wallowed while listening to Scorpions or Springsteen ballads. He turned up the sound and thought about his Colt in the glove compartment. He was someone now, wasn't he?

He'd had to give up living with his mate Hamid. When Younes had come home with an egg-sized bump on his forehead, Marie-Rose had not believed the story they'd made up about him falling on the stairs. She'd lost it completely and Bruce had scarpered, stuffing his belongings into

164

his bag and leaving without a word. Since then, he'd spent two nights in a motel. It hadn't been much fun, particularly as he'd spent the whole time fearing that the Benbareks or Martel would turn up at any moment. His paranoia wasn't helped by the vast quantities of coke he sucked up his nose. Now, before starting his BMW, he lifted up the bonnet and checked under the seats. Once, he'd found the car radio tuned to Chérie FM when he never listened to anything but Skyrock or – at a pinch – RTL2. He'd almost pissed himself in shock when he heard Whitney Houston's 'I Will Always Love You' coming out of the speakers.

Finally, Bruce had caught a lucky break. Unless it was just that this part of the world was so small, shrivelled and inbred that it was impossible to lose anything for long. That was how he felt whenever he went to the supermarket. He always seemed to bump into someone he knew there: a former schoolmate, some old woman who knew his mother, whatever. There was no way out of this shithole.

It was a Thursday evening and he'd been driving for at least an hour under a cloudless sky. It was cold and dry and he could smell the snow about to fall, along with a hint of woodsmoke in the air. He thought about nothing as he drove. He didn't feel like going home. He had nowhere in particular to go. So it was that he found himself in a remote village a mile or two from the Farm. There was nothing much there, just a street, twenty houses, a butcher's shop and the Café de la Poste, a seedy bar that attracted a surprisingly big crowd at weekends. The young people of the area all went there to get drunk on Stella Artois, eat *croque-monsieurs* and play table football. Until one in the morning, the music was loud, the atmosphere testosterone-fuelled. If you wanted to get into a fight, this was the perfect place. Come closing time, the last remaining customers would knock back a few glasses of eau-de-vie for the road. Every year, several of them would end up in a ditch, and one or two would not emerge alive from the wreckage. Thankfully, the necessity of supporting small businesses in a rural area still held greater sway than the requirements of road safety.

Bruce didn't go to places like that very often, and when he did he tended to act like a dick, showing off his superiority by taking coke instead of drinking pastis. But that evening, he felt sick and tired and the sign for the Café de la Poste, with its old-fashioned typography, made him feel better, as if he'd been transported back to his childhood. He knew the barman too, a skinny guy with a moustache called Jonathan who'd gone to the same school. So Bruce decided to stop there for a few drinks, parking his Beemer right in front of the café so everyone could get a good look at it.

Since it was a weekday and only 8 p.m., the place was fairly empty. Two red-faced men in their fifties were having one last *rouge lim'* before driving home. The butcher's boy was playing table football with some guy who'd been unemployed forever, the dregs of a shandy going warm on the side. Behind the bar, armed with a box-cutter and some Superglue, the barman was changing the tip of his pool cue. Early the next day, he had a competition in Bains-les-Bains. He was hoping to close soon so he could get a good night's sleep.

'Hey, guys,' said Bruce, as he walked through the door.

The barman smiled, glanced at his watch, then checked the clock on the wall. 'Hey, Bruce. You want something to drink?'

Bruce leaned on the bar and said: 'Yeah, go on, give me a beer.'

He drank fast, watching the others from the corner of his eye. His thighs twitched nervously on his barstool. The radio was playing the commentary of some football match. Bruce was uncomfortably hot but he was reluctant to take off his bomber jacket. All he had on underneath was a bodybuilding vest and his shoulders were covered with acne, thanks to all the hormone injections he'd been getting in his thighs. He ordered another beer. 'And put some music on, man. I fucking hate football.'

Jonathan tried to find another radio station and the two old guys got up and left, nodding to the barman as they went outside. Roberta Flack began singing 'Killing Me Softly'. The butcher's boy and the unemployed guy gave up on the table football and went to the bar.

'You want a drink, lads?' Bruce asked, as his right leg continued to jiggle.

They shrugged and ordered a beer each, muttering a brief thank-you to Bruce.

The bar had a downbeat, resigned atmosphere and Bruce stuck out like a sore thumb there with his muscles, his questions and his pinhead pupils.

'What are you doing in the area?' he asked the strangers. 'I've never seen you here before.'

'I work for Colignon, the butcher in the village,' replied the butcher's boy, wiping the foam off his upper lip. 'Well, I did.'

'What about you?' Bruce asked.

'I do a bit of building work here and there,' said the unemployed guy, looking vaguely embarrassed.

'Oh, right.' And, just to make sure, Bruce added: 'You haven't seen anything strange going on recently, have you?'

The other three looked incredulously at him, wondering if he was taking the piss or what.

'No.'

'What sort of strange?'

'Nah, doesn't matter. I was just curious.'

Jonathan wiped down the bar, picked up the unemployed guy's already empty glass and put it into the sink.

'Whoa, not so quick!' said Bruce. 'We're not done yet, amigo. Give my friend another beer.'

The unemployed guy nodded his thanks and immediately downed half of his next glass.

'Serve yourself a drink too,' Bruce ordered the barman. 'On me.'

Jonathan poured himself a Coca-Cola and the others made fun of him. What was wrong with him anyway? He never drank, didn't have a girlfriend, and he rode a bloody moped. This went on for another fifteen minutes and the three stooges drank another round of beers. The butcher's boy and the unemployed guy were much friendlier now. They laughed over nothing, asked Bruce about his BMW. Must cost a fortune, a car like that . . . After a while, the bodybuilder took off his jacket and the other two started feeling his muscles.

'Lads, what counts isn't the volume, it's the quality of the muscles.'

'Dead right,' said the butcher's boy, who knew a thing or two about it.

'Some blokes have big muscles but no strength, you know? It's all water. You could wring 'em out like a sponge. You, come over here . . .'

And he beat the unemployed guy in a one-sided arm-wrestling contest.

About ten o'clock, they moved onto whisky and the atmosphere went up a notch. A Pink Floyd song came on the radio and the butcher's boy jumped onto the bar and started playing an air-guitar solo. The barman wanted him to come down, but the other two – who had spent the last half-hour calling him 'Mrs Jonathan' – obligingly advised him to shut his mouth.

After a while, the unemployed guy turned into a philosopher and started talking about women, politics, immigration and the cost of living. The butcher's boy, who didn't know much about all that stuff, told a strange story about the labour inspector who'd come to the shop and the butcher's wife who'd left him. He was going to tell the others about the accident with the Saab, but the jobless guy interrupted him.

'We wouldn't be in this situation if it wasn't for the bloody Chinks stealing all our markets!'

The three drinkers laughed and toasted the health of the barman, who combed his moustache with his lower incisors while waiting for them to drink up and leave.

This went on for quite a long time and they were soon all the best of mates. They ordered coffees to finish up, to clear their heads a bit. In the empty village square, the bar's front window gleamed with a lazy yellow light. From outside, an observer could see three men slumped on the counter, shoulders hunched, gazes vacant. Then the butcher's boy remembered what he'd been about to say earlier before he was interrupted by Jobless.

'Fucking hell, lads, you won't believe this . . .'

For his part, Bruce had no doubts whatsoever about the butcher boy's story of a naked girl running out of the woods. He asked for details, thinking that Martel would be pleased with him. He thought about calling him straight away, but in the end he decided to wait and surprise him.

To celebrate, he poured three lines of coke onto the bar and rolled a 100-euro note that he passed first to the unemployed guy and then to the butcher's boy. After a good snort each, they hugged one another and promised to meet up again soon. Then the butcher's boy threw up on the floor. Sweat dripped from his waxy face and he was shivering. In a panic, the barman started saying over and over that the kid couldn't stay there, so the unemployed guy offered to take him back to his place. Bruce said he'd come along too. Jobless wasn't happy about this, but he didn't say anything. He didn't have much choice, really.

It was already Friday and Bruce was thinking that it was going to be a great day.

RITA

Sitting cross-legged on the sofa, iPod ear buds in her ears, Victoria flicked through the latest *Cosmo* while her foot tapped in time to the music. On the coffee-table, her magazines were neatly stacked. She was cutting photographs out of them with a pair of scissors and sticking the images into a large spiral notebook.

The rings around her eyes had faded now. She'd caught up on her sleep and she'd put on some weight too. She even spoke a bit of French. Rita watched her from the kitchen, glass in hand, the cordless telephone pressed to her ear.

'Mum?'

'Darling?'

'Listen, I've only just got back from work, so I won't be able to cook you anything tonight. How about I invite you to a restaurant for dinner instead?'

'Oh. But I don't have anything to wear.'

'Just put a pair of knickers on and you'll be fine! I'm not taking you to the Ritz, you know.'

'Listen, darling—'

'Mum, I'd really like it if you'd say yes. Anyway, there's someone I'd like you to meet.'

'Oh, really?' her mother said, suddenly perking up.

'Yeah, but relax, it's not what you think.'

'Oh, well, never mind. But your brother is here. And if I'm reading his sign language correctly, he wouldn't mind being taken out for a free hot meal.'

'All right. Tell him to come along too. Actually, pass him to me, will you?'

The girl stood up. She paced aimlessly around the living room like a cat, rubbing herself against the furniture, letting her fingertips graze the spines of the books on the bookcase. Rita could hear the music she was listening to, even from about twenty feet away. Now and then Victoria would close her eyes to listen more closely.

She'd changed a lot recently. The curves of her body had grown more pronounced. She seemed tense, impatient, filled with an energy that served no purpose. She pranced around, struck poses. When Laurent came, she was all over him. The other day she was sitting in his lap before he could even protest. She was always trying to catch his eye. She wanted to go out.

What bothered Rita most of all was her lack of consideration. She acted like a fourteen-year-old kid. She left her clothes lying all over the house, spent hours tarting herself up in the bathroom, cut her toenails at the kitchen table, spilled her nail varnish on the sofa, burst out laughing or into tears for no apparent reason, wore way too much make-up, wanted to live in America, be a singer, fall in love . . . In fact, she already was. With Laurent, naturally. And with Rita too, a bit, even if she hated her at the same time, especially when Rita refused to lend her clothes or dragged her out of bed at noon.

While she waited for her brother to come to the phone, Rita watched Victoria sashay sexily and brainlessly around the living room and thought: What the hell am I going to do with this girl? Introducing her to her brother, she knew, was the worst thing she could possibly do.

'Hello?'

It was him.

'Yeah, Greg?'

'So I hear you're going to introduce us to the new Mr Kleber tonight. I can't wait to meet him!'

'Are you sure you're not too busy writing sad songs and sipping Malibu?'

'There's more to life than rock 'n' roll, sis. There's family too.'

'Yeah, family seems particularly important to you at the end of every month, I've noticed.'

'You're so cynical.'

After a few more jibes of this kind, Rita said: 'All right, listen. I'm coming with Laurent and a girlfriend of his. And you have to promise me that you won't act like an idiot, okay?'

'You're inviting your ex's girlfriends out to dinner now?'

'Mind your own business. Anyway, she's not really his girlfriend. More like an exchange student, I suppose.'

'An exchange student?'

'Exactly.'

'But—'

'I haven't finished. Dinner is on me. You can have a calzone, some profiteroles – you can even drink wine – but spare us your bullshit for once. Don't complain, don't get hammered, don't try to monopolise everyone's attention . . . And, above all, don't you dare try to get off with Laurent's exchange student.'

'Whoa! Take it easy.'

'Shut up. I think I've made myself clear. If you watch your step, I'll owe you a favour. Okay, now pass me back to the queen mother. We're running late as it is.'

Grumbling half-heartedly, Gregory did what his sister had told him.

'Well, I don't know what you told him, but His Majesty doesn't look best pleased.'

'Mum, I'm counting on you. This is important. Let me explain. The person you're going to meet is this poor girl. Laurent and I are looking after her. She's not at her best right now, and I don't want Greg to take advantage of her. You understand?'

'We'll do what we can, darling.'

'All right . . . See you soon, Mum.'

Next, Rita dialled Laurent's number while looking out at her neighbour's lit-up windows. He answered, and almost immediately his figure appeared behind the French windows about fifty feet away. He waved, and Rita responded by raising her empty glass.

'Hello, Kleber. Good day?'

'Not bad. Listen, I have a favour to ask.'

'If you want me to look after Victoria, the answer's no.'

'Oh, calm down. You're not as irresistible as you think. The poor girl hasn't seen a real man in weeks. You might as well make the most of it because it won't last.'

'Okay. And you were calling to ask me for a favour?'

Unthinkingly, Rita lifted her empty glass to her lips, then put it on the table and went upstairs to her bedroom. 'You remember I'm taking Victoria to the police station tomorrow?'

'Yes.'

'But whatever happens, wherever she's from, she won't be going back there.'

'You're planning to adopt her.'

'Maybe, I don't know. Anyway, it's possible that they'll have to hold her there for a while. So I've arranged a little dinner with my mother, to introduce them.'

'Your mother? You want to give Victoria another bad example to follow?'

'Exactly. Two generations of rebellious women – that can't do her any harm. But listen, I'm really late and guess what.'

She looked unenthusiastically through the dresses in her wardrobe, then closed the door and fell onto the bed.

'My brother's going to be there.'

'Shit.'

'Yeah. Can you imagine what he'll be like when he sees her?'

Laurent laughed.

'It's not funny. She's a kid. When I got home earlier, I found the fridge wide open and she was asleep with one of my T-shirts pressed to her nose. And tomorrow . . . Well, I don't know what they'll do with her. I really want this to go well.'

'And you're depending on my manly presence to calm things down.'

'Exactly. Can you do that?'

'Where are you planning to take us?'

Rita rummaged around in her pockets. On the little scrap of paper, Martel's writing was surprisingly legible, almost childlike. 'The Capri. It's a pizzeria in the valley. Nothing fancy. A guy from the Velocia factory recommended it to me.'

'It's not exactly close. And a Friday night too . . . We should probably have booked a table.'

'Come and pick me up in twenty minutes. I'm getting my car back tomorrow, by the way.'

'Before or after taking the girl to the cops?'

'After, I suppose. I'm going to the police station tomorrow morning.'

'All right. I'll be there.'

Rita hung up and tossed the phone onto the duvet beside her. She felt suddenly shattered. She could hear little noises coming from downstairs. The patter of feet, as if a rabbit were running around on the wooden floor. A presence. She lay back and closed her eyes for a second. Her right hand tightened around Martel's note.

JORDAN LOCATELLI

Jordan had ridden back from the Manhattan in slow motion, feet close to the ground, out of fear that he would take a tumble. All the way home, his bike had sprayed snow behind it, so dirty that it looked almost like lemon sorbet. When he got higher up the hill, though, it became white, soft and powdery.

He and his father lived in a small, one-storey house just below the edge of the forest. It always smelt of undergrowth where they lived. When his mother was alive, she used to wear herself out trying to wash the faint stink of mould from the wardrobes. But no matter what they did – insulating the roof, turning up the heating, plugging in fragrance diffusers – the scent of the forest never went away.

The house was a simple, square building with a steeply sloping roof. A driveway led to the garage door, with two windows above it. The front door was actually on the side of the house. Firewood was stacked neatly against the wall. It was an unpretentious place.

As he entered the driveway, Jordan turned off the engine and the headlights and rolled silently up to the garage door. The silence sounded much deeper than usual, as it always did after a snowfall. In the quilted emptiness, nothing could be heard but the quiet hiss of wheels in motion. Jordan braked a few yards from the door, letting the bike slide into the snowdrift before coming to a halt. A shadow emerged from behind a hedge of white thujas.

'Hey, fatty.'

It was Riton. Under his helmet, Jordan smiled. He and Riton had hated each other from a distance for some time now. He never would have imagined it would be Riton taking the first step. He was the older kid, after all, the leader, the one people wanted to be friends with.

Jordan got off his bike and walked over to shake his hand. The snow creaked under his Dr Martens. 'What are you doing here?'

'I was in the area,' said Riton. He spat on the ground and his saliva made a hole in the snow. There were a few cigarette stubs and a cluster of similar craters just behind him, indicating that he'd been standing around there for some time. 'Actually, I've got a present for you,' Riton added, with a wink. And he took a joint from his Yamaha jacket. 'What do you say?'

Jordan pulled a face. He'd been hoping for a relaxing evening with his dad. Some food, some small-talk, maybe a beer or two. They both needed that. But what he said was: 'Cool. Follow me.'

Even in the darkness, Jordan and Riton's footprints were clearly visible, leading through the snow to the neighbour's garden shed. The two teenagers shoved the lawnmower and some bags of fertiliser out of the way to make a space for themselves. Hunched up and shivering, they took turns smoking the spliff, laughing hysterically while trying not to make too much noise, which made them laugh even louder.

'I'm glad you came round,' said Jordan, getting his breath back.

'No problem, bro,' Riton replied, clipping him playfully round the ear. Then he grabbed Jordan's collar and shook him up a bit.

Feeling happy, Jordan pretended to fight back. Riton didn't stop. Laughing, they struggled clumsily with each other, their arms gradually tensing more and more as they grew annoyed. Riton wanted to show his strength so he put Jordan in a headlock. Instantly, the younger boy stiff-ened. He wanted it to stop, right then and there. He grabbed Riton by the hair and braced himself against one of the shed's walls to try to throw his adversary off-balance. There was a huge cracking noise as some metal objects came crashing down from a tool rack. It was so loud that it sounded as if a dozen horses had stampeded into the shed under a torrent of scrap metal. Sobered by this, the two boys let go of each other and listened, hearts pounding, too frightened to look each other in the eye. In that snowy silence, the din they'd made was probably audible on the other side of the world, and the neighbour was a former swimming instructor, a massive guy who had grabbed Jordan by the neck several times before, usually because his bike made too much noise. Jordan had never mentioned these assaults to his father, out of fear that Mr Locatelli would feel obliged to defend his son's honour by fighting that amphibious colossus.

After a minute or so, Riton decided to pick up the joint and stub it out against the shed wall. Myriad glowing little balls fell onto the ground and flickered for a moment in the wind's caress. Jordan was freezing now and he wasn't in the mood for this shit. He started tidying away the fallen tools. Riton watched him.

'I have to go,' said Jordan, after checking that everything was in order.

'Chill out, dude. What's your hurry?' Riton observed him from a distance with bloodshot eyes and a sneering expression. 'You're scared, aren't you? God, you're such a fucking pussy . . .'

'Leave me alone.' Jordan was really torn. He was desperate to get back into the warmth now, even if it meant losing face. Riton had warned him before they'd smoked: this was hardcore Maastricht skunk, strong enough to keep you in stitches all night. Obviously, getting scared out of your skin was not recommended when you'd been smoking that kind of stuff. Jordan felt ashamed and anxious, his body stiff and disjointed. And Riton was savouring his distress: he tilted his head to the side, raised his eyebrows and grinned strangely, as if he'd just learned that Jordan still pissed his bed at night.

'And to think I almost felt sorry for you.'

'What are you on about?'

Jordan desperately needed something to drink. To get that foul taste out of his mouth – a mix of earth and bile – he wanted an ice-cold Coke, on the rocks, maybe even with a slice of lemon. He tried to get past Riton so he could exit the shed. He had to get out of that place, lock himself into his room for the weekend. He could read some old comic books, eat biscuits and drink bottles and bottles of Aldi soda. But Riton grabbed his foot. He had no intention of letting Jordan get away.

'Your girlfriend, the Duruy bitch. We saw her tonight at the Alchimiste, with Lucas and Samir.'

'Oh, yeah? And why am I supposed to care?'

Riton laughed. 'I'm so glad you're taking it like that.'

During the course of that day, Jordan had seen Lydie several times, mostly when she wasn't even there. He invented her like that, wherever he was, seeing her in some stranger's ponytail, in a passing denim jacket, in a girl's neck on a staircase, a pair of swaying hips in a corridor. Lydie was beautiful, soft, round and warm, and his hands could never touch that softness, that roundness, that warmth. Not only that, but other hands touched her all the time, other lips kissed hers, other bodies rubbed against hers, other cocks nestled inside Lydie's soft round warmth. Fucking hell, that girl was driving him crazy.

'Come on, you need to piss off now. My dad must be wondering where I am.'

Thankfully, the skunk had given him the munchies on an epic scale. When he got home, he'd be able to console himself by devouring a mountain of salty, fatty snacks that would smear his lips and fingers and drown his sorrows in grease. Stupidly, he thought about his mother. She had been a brilliant cook. He remembered her lasagnes and her shepherd's pies, her specialities. Her desserts were amazing too. Her pear and chocolate charlotte had cast a magical spell over his entire childhood. All Mum's flavours. She wouldn't be there when he went home and he felt an unexpected childish sorrow at this realisation. His eyes shone. This happened to him occasionally since he'd started wearing contact lenses. Later, he'd put on glasses and it would be better.

'We saw her with that other girl,' Riton continued maliciously. 'The ugly one, I can't remember her name. They were looking for someone who could get them into the Sphinx. You know she's not with that guy any more, right? The one with the Clio Williams. Apparently, that wanker follows her around everywhere.'

'Let me past,' said Jordan angrily. 'I don't give a fuck about your stories.'

'Whoa, whoa, calm down! We need to talk, the two of us. I don't want you to hear this from someone else.'

'For fuck's sake,' growled Jordan, giving Riton a shove. If that bastard really wanted a fight, so be it. Jordan wanted to feel pain right now anyway.

'Hang on, just listen. She talked to me about you.'

His heart leaped.

'She likes you, actually. See, there's no need to get upset, is there? I don't give a shit about that girl. We just go out together a bit, no big deal. We fool around, but that's all.'

'Are you going out tonight?'

'Yeah. With my cousin Mars.'

'Where?'

'Depends. We'll see.'

'Is Mars the one who worked at Velocia?'

'Yeah. He's got a new car, an Alfa. He's fucking crazy. We're going to pick up the girls and go dancing somewhere.'

'I thought your cousin had a Lancia.'

'Exactly.'

'And a wife.'

'Doesn't stop him going out when he feels like it. Anyway, stop being such a miserable sod!' And, leaning towards him fraternally, Riton said: 'Girls come and go, but mates, they're what really matter.'

Outside, the storm was growing stronger. A curtain of white was enveloping the shed, erasing the two boys' footprints.

'You think you could pick me up too?' Jordan asked.

'I'll have to see what my cousin says. I don't know if we'll have enough room. I'll let you know, anyway.'

'Come on, I've bailed you out plenty of times.'

'I'll send you a text if it's happening,' said Riton, opening the door, letting the howling wind into the shed's interior. His eyebrows fluttered meaningfully as he shook Jordan's hand, suggestive of all the fun they'd be having later. Then he closed the door behind him, leaving Jordan to his dark thoughts.

Jordan stuffed a stick of chewing gum into his mouth. The taste of chlorophyll didn't make him feel any better.

VICTORIA

Victoria usually got up at about three in the afternoon. She and her roommate Jade ate breakfast in their dressing-gowns, sharing the latest news from the night before in a hybrid of English, French and expressions borrowed from their respective native languages. Every phrase was accompanied by gestures, mimicry and nods.

Jade was almost ten years older than her. More to the point, she had been doing this job for five years, while Victoria was still a novice. That was really what made Jade seem like an older sister. They lived together in a renovated studio flat on rue de Louvain, with a kitchenette, a bedroom for Jade and a sofa-bed for Victoria. They never brought anyone home. No clients, no colleagues, no friends. Sometimes Jimmy Comore would drop by, but Victor Tokarev – the boss – rarely did. He had a horror of girly interiors: teddy bears, candles, pastel colours, all those ornamental knick-knacks that women like to scatter over the surfaces of a new place as soon as they take possession of it. When he was forced to visit them, he would remain standing in the doorway, looking soaked in his putty-coloured raincoat, bags like puddles under his eyes. Even in summer, when he wore gaudy short-sleeve shirts, he still looked strangely damp. Some of the girls called him Frogman. Though only behind his back, obviously.

It was his usual method to pair new girls with old hands. To set them a good example. The resignation of the more experienced girls, acquired through years of being beaten and let down by false saviours and real bastards, was supposed to subtly influence these kids brought over from the back of beyond to find themselves on the game in a foreign land without any idea of what they were doing or even where they were. The street signs on Quai Pasteur soon taught them that.

Jade was a plump brunette who dyed her first grey hairs and exhibited her breasts in dresses cut in the shape of martini glasses. Her vaguely Asiatic nickname was the result of her almond-shaped eyes. She'd been born in Bulgaria.

When they'd first moved in together, Victoria had clung to Jade like a lifebuoy and Jade – despite a few snide remarks – had helped keep her head above water. She'd introduced Victoria to those little glasses of Coke with rum in them that had felt like such a treat and had made her feel so much better. Nothing really seemed to matter much after that: the clients were easily fooled because she was in the mood for hugs and laughter. There wasn't too much rum in them, just enough to give her back her smile. Victoria adored them.

Victoria's youthfulness and candour had quickly got on her room-mate's nerves, however. The little idiot was amazed by everything, constantly veering between hysterical happiness and sobbing sorrow. She pleaded with them to let her go home, refused to get out of bed, hid her money so she could buy shoes, pigged out on chocolate, fell sick, stole Jade's clothes, had a crush on some TV actor, was immediately best friends with any streetwalker who smiled at her, begged for forgiveness, wanted hugs. Jade felt old just watching her.

Soon Victoria had an admirer. A cop, no less. After two or three tricks, he insisted on taking her out to lunch at a nice restaurant he knew on rue du Vieux-Seigle. First Victoria pretended she didn't understand.

Then she turned him down. When she went to bed, though, she imagined those dates – starter-main-course-dessert, a table in the middle of the room, white wine – like something from a romantic comedy. When the meal was over, they would leave the restaurant together, walking out into the warm night, and perhaps he would take her hand. Some moron would cross their path and disrespect Victoria, and the cop would knock him out with a quick uppercut before walking her home with no strings attached, the perfect gentleman.

For a while, that fable was like a lullaby for Victoria. And because she never accepted any of his invitations, the cop became obsessed. He decided he wanted to rescue her from that world, to make her happy for ever. Victoria thought she was saved and she told Jade about it. She started putting on airs, even when she was working, turning down clients because they were ugly or fat or because she supposedly didn't want to sleep with cripples any more. Jade put up with this, knowing it wouldn't last.

She did end up going to eat lunch on rue du Vieux-Seigle with her cop. Victoria had secretly put some money aside, and with that she'd managed to buy a pair of Diesel jeans, some Prada boots that were on sale, and a Zadig & Voltaire T-shirt that fell down over one shoulder, revealing her bra strap. Victoria and her cop had stared into each other's eyes while devouring a seafood platter, drunk a bottle of Gewürztraminer, and shared a *poire belle Hélène*. Afterwards he'd driven her to the bus stop. In the warmth of his car, they'd kissed and Victoria had felt sad. Resting her head on the cop's shoulder, she'd thought about men's flabby bellies, their stinky penises, their suction-cup kisses and soft lips.

But towards the end of the night, the cop's attitude had changed. He seemed suddenly sad. It was their first real date after all, the first time they'd been together without fucking, and this detail had changed the way the cop thought about the whole thing. Now he started to worry about his professional future. He looked around nervously, in a rush to get rid of her, promising he'd call her, and Victoria had found herself on the pavement before she even had time to put her jacket on. It was a lot colder outside than it had been in the 308.

She'd got back to the apartment around five o'clock, feeling bloated. She had a migraine coming on and she was late for work. But who cared? They could all go to hell. She wasn't going to do that any more. She was in France now, after all: they couldn't force her. The jeans she was wearing cost 150 euros!

Inside the apartment, Victor was waiting for her. No sooner had she opened the door than he grabbed her by the wrists and threw her to the floor. Then he kicked her in the belly twice, like a footballer practising penalties. Victoria started bawling and begging. Sickened, Victor wiped the Rimmel that had run down her face with the sole of his shoe.

He dragged her over to a cupboard in the corridor and grabbed a metal coat hanger. He unfolded it, then bent it in two before twisting the two stems into a sort of long braid. He pushed Victoria down onto the sofa-bed, one knee on the back of her neck, then pulled down her jeans and tore off her underwear. Victoria was so frightened that she pissed herself. Jade watched and heard everything through the half-open door: Victoria's streaming face, her hair sticky with tears and make-up, and the strange animal noise that emerged from her throat. Victor was sweating and the drops fell heavily from his forehead onto Victoria's naked skin. She shivered at each drop and wailed even louder. Then the coat hanger came down on her thighs for the first time and she lost consciousness almost immediately.

The next day, Victoria checked the damage in the bathroom mirror, moaning as she rubbed antiseptic cream onto her gashed thighs, vulva and bottom. The black and purple marks from that terrible evening remained on her skin for a long time. Jade had been kind to her then. During the few nights of convalescence that Victor had been obliged to grant her, Jade brought her herbal teas in bed and massaged her wounds with essential oils to help the healing process. The idea that she might be scarred for life was the hardest thing for her to bear. As if all those clients' dicks would be inside her for ever. Victoria wept herself to sleep and Jade hugged her, made her Nutella pancakes, ran her hot scented baths . . . She even cleaned Victoria's urine off the carpet. Yet Victoria felt certain that this was the bitch who'd grassed on her.

After that, Jade and Victoria went on living side by side, a life filled with friendship, hugs and laughter that barely concealed the vicious hate they bore each other. Their daily existence was repetitive, menacing, prison-like. After breakfast, Jade would use the bathroom while Victoria tidied the kitchen and living room, half listening to the TV as she worked. She'd secretly drink a rum and Coke, sometimes two, then chew chlorophyll gum to mask the smell of the alcohol. After that, it was her turn to take a shower, before putting her make-up on. Coal-black and blood-red were her colours. They brought out the pallor of her skin, through which thin, meandering blue-green veins could be seen. Her clients, her regulars, loved the milky whiteness of her skin. Some of them saw it as a sign of purity. Others imagined a corpse or a little girl. Whatever turned them on.

When she worked, Victoria always felt cold. And yet she appeared better suited to the bad weather than many of the other girls. On the pavements of Strasbourg there were quite a number of Ivorians, Liberians and Ghanaians selling their bodies thousands of miles from home so they could pay back their enormous debts. They got stuck with the worst stuff: animals, excrement, torture . . . They often found themselves at the mercy of former whores, fraudulent old witches who threatened the lives of their parents and cast spells from across the sea. On the Quai Pasteur, the wind cut into these women like a razorblade. Tottering on their high heels, knees knocking, they rubbed their arms and scowled. And, as drips of snot formed at the tips of their noses, they would dream. They dreamed about a man who would take them away from all this. They dreamed of becoming singers, film stars, of opening a fashion boutique, anything. They dreamed of going back to school, starting a family, and they dreamed of the fix waiting for them back at their flat, the bottle of white cooling in the fridge.

Victoria was perhaps the dreamiest of them all. Escapism was second nature to her and had been since she was a little girl. She imagined palm trees, lagoons, big cars and white carpets. And since leaving home to become an au pair and falling into the hands of Victor, she'd got into the habit of escaping in the blink of an eye, drifting for hours on end in cocooning, consoling daydreams as life continued to beat around her, kept at a distance by her lack of belief in its reality. In that way she could ward off the present, forget the recent past. Because behind her invented sunsets and little glasses of rum and Coke were forbidden things: those first few weeks in France, when she was being trained. Her memories were vague. The barking had grown almost silent, the reflections had faded, the neon lights, the pain in her knees and belly, her throat sore from screaming, an endless exhaustion. When she arrived, Victor had handed her over to specialists – some Bulgarians who lived in a big, rundown house. They tamed girls first by beating them with planks on their thighs, arms and bellies. Then they pinched their breasts until they blacked out. After two or three days of this, the girls – more dead than alive – would open their legs without protest, and the procession could begin. Victoria fled those visions, those sensations of something disgusting rubbing itself against her, those sickly-sweet smells, the taste of piss in her mouth. She turned her face away, unable to understand why her throat was suddenly tight, her hands trembling. She filled her ears with music, numbed her brain with television. She thought: It's okay, I'll get my revenge. Now stop thinking about it.

The length of her working nights depended on the number of clients. Once she'd done eight or ten, she would call Jimmy Comore on the mobile they'd given her. Soon he would turn up in a midnight-blue BMW Series 6, tinted windows, 18-inch Replica rims. She'd get in beside him. He was black, very young. He listened to west-coast rap and wore clothes too big for him. At first she'd thought he would be nice to her – the younger girls always confused beauty with happiness and Jimmy was very good-looking. Except that his eyes had no pupils. They were as grey and dull as steel ball bearings. And there was a long scar on his shaved head. He took the money Victoria earned, offered her a drag on his spliff, and pocketed ten euros himself. He'd warned her before that if Victor ever found out about those ten euros, he would slice off her nipples with his knife. Jimmy had shown her the knife and even mimed the action, pinching the imaginary nipple between index finger and thumb, lopping it off with a clean quick cut. Sometimes he'd put on a rubber glove and feel around inside her vagina to make sure she hadn't hidden any cash up there. His face showed no emotion when he did that: no disgust, no excitement. He was just doing his job. Victoria was an object. She didn't cry when it happened – what was the point? She thought about something else.

According to Jade, Jimmy Comore was worse than Victor, worse than anyone. According to her, he was from Sierra Leone, even if his name suggested otherwise.

'I've heard he was a child soldier. That black bastard's killed loads of people. With machetes, with machine-guns, anything. He's an animal.'

Other times, Jade claimed Victor had found him in a brothel. In any case, they would never learn anything about him by looking into his eyes. Or through pillow talk. Jimmy Comore didn't sleep with any of the girls.

Generally, by the time Victoria got home from work, Jade was already there. Victoria gave a silly smile, a hypocritical hello, then quickly got showered, eyes closed. She ate a ready-meal while sipping a rum and Coke in front of the TV, before taking a Tranxene tablet and falling asleep straight away, icy hands wedged between her thighs, curled up in her cotton pyjamas, tennis socks on her feet, earplugs in her ears. Sometimes she thought about her family.

RITA

After driving for more than forty minutes, they finally spotted a neon sign in the colours of the Italian flag. Laurent parked the Mercedes in the Capri's car park. He'd driven carefully, following the tyre tracks of other cars. All the way there, Rita had been gritting her teeth. Victoria, on the other hand, had struggled to contain her excitement. She played with her hair, hummed under her breath, kept turning around to watch the taillights of the cars that had come the other way as they receded into the darkness. From time to time she put her ear to the window to listen to the sound the tyres made as they spun through melted snow.

Now they were there. Rita looked grim. Laurent was already thinking about the return journey.

'Probably better if we don't stay here too long. The snow is starting to settle. It might not be easy getting home.'

'Don't worry, I have no intention of staying long,' Rita said.

'Probably better if you don't drink too much either.'

'Calm down. I know how to behave.'

'Oh, really? Even with your family?'

Rita smiled. 'I can't help it if I don't like Christmas.'

Laurent laughed. The previous Christmas Eve, Rita had poured Grand Marnier on the Christmas cake and put a match to it. The curtains had almost caught fire.

'I want to smoke a fag before we go in.' She opened the car door and the wind howled inside.

Laurent half feared that the Mercedes was about to fly into the air. 'Ugh, what a night!' He groaned, trying to see the sky through the windscreen.

With its sloping roof, its wooden balcony and the Christmas lights still flashing from its windows, the Capri looked more like a Swiss chalet than a trattoria. While Laurent removed the face of his car radio, Rita went over to lean on the guardrail that ran alongside the nearby canal. She spat into the ink-coloured water, just to see what would happen, and watched the ripples form at its surface before vanishing almost immediately. Snowflakes dotted her short hair. Just behind her, Victoria was hopping about and rubbing her arms to keep warm.

Before they'd left, Rita had made a phone call to Jean-Philippe, an old friend who worked as a lawyer in Épinal. He'd once been her lecturer when she was a student in Nancy, but he didn't teach any more; in fact, he spent more time reading *L'Équipe* and eating enormous feasts than he did working on his defence speeches. His nickname at the courthouse was Couscous-Whisky. Rita got in touch to tell him about Victoria. A girl without ID papers whom she'd rescued without telling anyone. What lay in store for her? What would the cops do to her?

'*Oh, la la,*' said the lawyer. He'd been incapable of saying much more than that. 'You know, it's not really my speciality, illegal immigration.'

'I know that, but just give me a rough idea,' Rita had insisted.

Jean-Philippe was a terrible lawyer in court, too sketchy and dishevelled to impress a jury. But he was an eminent scholar in his field. He'd always been a star at the university, with his own coterie of fans. He would smoke cigars in class, undo the top button of his trousers after lunch, and in winter he'd sometimes keep his fur cap on in the lecture hall. These eccentricities had contributed to his aura but they hadn't helped his career. Deep down he didn't really like working and was not unhappy with his fate as a sort of flawed genius, perpetually tipsy. He mostly dealt with minor cases now – neighbourly disputes and other trivial matters – and spent the majority of his time in the Étoile d'Or, a greasy spoon not far from the courthouse, on a backstreet that ran behind the basilica. He had friends there, his own napkin ring. The woman who owned the place forced him to take his pills. Rita could tell from the sound of his breathing – congested, vaguely repulsive – that he wasn't in the best of health.

'Listen, on the face of it, I would say it doesn't look good,' Jean-Philippe had explained. 'Anything related to illegal immigrants is bad news right now. She's not a minor, is she?'

'I don't know.'

'Hmm. Sounds to me like you've got yourself mixed up in a shitty situation. How long have you been holding her?'

'I'm not holding her. I'm just looking after her while she gets her strength back.'

'If I were you, I'd go to the cops as soon as possible.'

'That's the plan. I just wanted to know what might happen to her.'

'They'll probably lock her up somewhere. If she's a minor, she should be all right. If not, she'll probably be taken to a detention centre.'

'That's exactly what I want to avoid.'

'You could always get her a lawyer. I know some good ones.'

'Yeah, I'll do that. Thanks, Jean-Philippe.'

'You're welcome. You should come and eat lunch with me someday soon. It's been too long.'

That was why Rita was in such a bad mood. And Victoria's enthusiasm, her brainless innocence, was making Rita feel even worse. And now, to top it all, her brother was on his way . . .

*   *   *

Within the room's salmon-coloured walls, there were a dozen tables with checked cloths and candles. Most were empty. It was very warm and a pleasant smell of pizza filled the air. Rita's brother and mother were sitting at the back. As soon as he saw them come in, Gregory stood up. The old lady just waved. Rita's brother was wearing his leather trousers: not a good sign. He also had on a skin-tight grey sweatshirt, a black jacket, motorcycle boots and silver rings on practically all his fingers.

'*Heyyy!*' he said, adjusting the sunglasses that he wore as a sort of headband.

Oh, shit, Rita thought. She made the introductions. Her mother hugged Laurent and stared into Victoria's eyes as she took her hand.

'Calm down, Mum. You look like you're about to read her palm.'

'She's beautiful. She reminds me of someone.'

When she kissed her brother's cheek, Rita got a whiff of his familiar smell. She was not unaffected by it. They sat down, Victoria to Rita's left. Gregory swapped seats to be close to the girl. Straight away he began chatting to her, smiling constantly, making all sorts of sound effects and mimicries to help her understand what he was saying. Everyone was listening; he looked ecstatic. And Rita couldn't help feeling some pleasure at seeing him happy like that. Sometimes he couldn't be bothered to put one foot in front of the other, he was never far from the next depression, and he loved it when people felt sorry for him, but when he made an effort to be charming, the effects were often dazzling. Wherever he was became the centre of the world.

Victoria didn't say a word. From the light in her dark eyes, you'd have thought she was an eight-year-old girl at the circus for the first time.

'Would you like an aperitif?'

A stooping waiter handed them menus. They asked for a bottle of Italian wine and, while the waiter was taking their orders, Gregory slid his arm behind Victoria's back.

'Jesus! What did I tell you on the phone?' Rita hissed.

'Calm down, I'm not going to eat her.'

Laurent, alone at the head of the table, looked as though he was keeping score.

The waiter brought their food: two Reine pizzas, one Capri, one Orientale, and a Vosges salad. Rita poured everyone a glass of wine, except her mother, who'd ordered a half-bottle of mineral water. While she was tossing her salad to mix up the croutons and bacon bits, the old lady leaned towards her daughter. 'So?'

'So what?'

'Who is this girl?'

'It's a long story.'

Laurent was asking Gregory a whole series of questions in the hope of turning his attention away from Victoria. Rita took advantage of this respite to give her mother the background to Victoria's story.

'And you didn't inform the police?'

'No.'

'You did the right thing.'

Rita's mother had fled Franco's Spain with her parents when she was still a young girl. As an exile, an immigrant and an activist, she was highly suspicious of men in uniform.

'Although I am planning to take her there tomorrow.'

'Take her where?'

'The police station. Things are getting complicated. She can't do anything without ID papers. I don't even know how old she is.'

'She didn't tell you?'

'She can barely speak two words of English. She's living in her own little world. You could imagine anything . . .'

'But what do you imagine?'

'I'd rather not think about it.'

'I'm still in touch with the association, you know. The girls there could advise you, maybe find you a lawyer.'

'That's an idea. Do you ever go back there?'

'Oh, no, they don't need old bags like me. But I will tell you one thing: they're too soft.'

This idea amused Rita. As far as her mother was concerned, Robespierre was just a sentimental fool and Lenin had lacked conviction.

'It just seems like that to you because your generation did all the hard work when you were their age. Abortion, the pill, and so on.'

'Yeah, I've heard those excuses before. There's still plenty to be done. Wages especially. Women are still paid like maidservants.'

'It's a way of compensating them for their pregnancies,' said Laurent, who had failed to draw Gregory's attention away from Victoria and was now following the two women's conversation.

'What do you mean by that?' Rita demanded.

'Oh, nothing. Just that since men aren't as involved in bringing up their children, they spend more time at work. That means they have more responsibility, and therefore they're better-paid.'

'That's rather simplistic,' said Rita's mother, condescendingly.

'I wasn't saying it was right.'

'That's not how it sounded,' Rita said.

He sighed. 'Never mind. Do you want another drink?'

'Yeah, that's right, change the subject.'

Rita's mother held out her glass.

Soon they ordered a second bottle. Rita noticed that Victoria kept filling her own glass. She was drinking quickly and her cheeks were visibly reddening. Rita also discovered that the girl spoke better French than she'd realised. At the same time, she couldn't help finding Victoria quite beautiful, a wild child with her too-long hair and her tipsy teenager's face. Apparently Gregory was of the same opinion. He and the girl were looking at each other with come-to-bed eyes now. Rita observed her brother as he exercised his charm: the way he put Victoria at ease, the way he touched her without seeming to. She grew more and more irritated, screwing up her packet of Winstons in one hand and – since she couldn't smoke in the restaurant – downing glass after glass of wine. She finished the bottle and got the dregs in her mouth: bitter taste, dry tongue. At last she'd had enough.

'It's good to see you, Greg.'

Interrupted mid-flow, her brother kept smiling but with an air of wariness now. 'It's good to see you too.'

'So, have you been up to anything special recently?'

'What do you mean?'

'I mean in terms of your career. You know, rock 'n' roll glory. Live fast, die young, all that.'

Gregory's smile widened. He pushed back his chair and got to his feet. 'I think I'll get some fresh air.'

'Yeah, right.'

He signalled to Victoria to follow him outside to smoke a cigarette. She jumped up and went after him without hesitation.

'Hey, hang on!' Rita called.

But her mother held her back. 'It's okay. He's not going to hurt her. I think he's probably more infatuated than she is.'

Shrugging off her mother, Rita grabbed her coat and went outside, lighting a cigarette even before she'd reached the door. Disapproving looks appeared on face after face in the restaurant, all of them turning towards Rita's mother and ex. They acted as though they hadn't seen anything.

Outside, the snow was falling even harder. The road, the car park and the entire surrounding landscape were now nothing more than a flat, thick, soft, crunchy whiteness. Only the canal still retained its dark colour, like a blade on a bare belly.

Rita spotted Victoria and her brother talking and smoking at the bottom of the steps, their cigarette ends glowing intermittently and lighting up a bright eye, a flicker of skin, a quick-vanishing pair of lips. To keep warm, they were leaning close together, hands in pockets and shoulders hunched. Victoria's sweet little face was almost entirely swallowed by her red scarf. Gregory pressed himself against her, held her by the waist. They looked like two teenagers in a school corridor. He was about to kiss her when a car turned off the road into the car park. Its round yellow headlights illuminated the couple who, dazzled, instinctively pulled apart.

Rita turned on her heel and went back inside the restaurant. She'd had enough. She wanted to go home now. The idea that they might have an accident on the way back seemed almost welcoming.

*   *   *

'And what do you think about it, Laurent?'

'I don't know. Rita has become very attached, though. It's going to be hard.'

'And the others?'

'What others?'

'Well, I don't think that girl just decided to run through the woods half naked for the sake of it.'

'I haven't really thought about it.'

'Does Rita still have that rifle you gave her?'

Laurent opened his mouth to laugh before quickly realising that the old woman wasn't joking. 'I don't think she's in that much danger. I mean, to the point where she'd need a gun . . .'

Rita's mother thought for a moment, then rested her papery hand on Laurent's. 'You're right. I'm probably imagining things. It can get so boring in winter, you know.'

It's annoying, thought Laurent. With old people, you can never tell if they're going to cry or if their eyes are just watering.

LYDIE

The radio alarm went off at six, as it did every morning, and Lydie listened to the latest Beyoncé single as she stretched between the sheets. She wasn't a morning person, but Friday was a really special day. The first day of the weekend and the best night of the week. Everything suddenly seemed easier, and way more interesting. As the hours passed, her body became a sort of lightning rod and all the electricity in the atmosphere shot through her, from her thighs to her hips, all the way up her spine. Sometimes it took all her self-control not to start running like a lunatic through the school corridors.

And on Friday mornings, she and Nadia had technical drawing together. Lydie curled up like a big cat just at the thought of this. They had a new young teacher that year, Mr Gomez, and he was so cute. The two girls would dream up fantasies about him, fantasies that left them breathless with desire. He wasn't much taller than they were but he was really muscular, with a back to die for and longish brown hair. And his hands were like doctor's hands. It was impossible not to start imagining stuff.

All the way through that class, Nadia and Lydie whispered to each other while they stared longingly at him. Nadia, in particular, crossed the line. She kept raising her hand because she didn't understand and she needed him to explain things to her in person. So Mr Gomez would come over and he'd crouch near them, so near that they could hear him breathe and smell his scent, a mixture of shower gel and long-lasting deodorant. They'd wriggle in their seats, on the verge of hysterical laughter, looking up at him doe-eyed, lashes thick and dark with mascara. They'd even managed to convince themselves that he had a crush on them. Of course he's into us – who wouldn't be?

On the other hand – and here the smirk was wiped off Lydie's face – in the afternoon they had to suffer through three full hours of technology with old Hirsch. His grey hair slicked back with Brylcreem, the old man gave off a stench of stale tobacco and hammered away at you with his lisping, over-articulated instructions. And then there was that little froth of spit that always appeared at the corners of his mouth. God, he was disgusting.

But Friday was a special day. Lydie threw back the sheets, put on a pair of tracksuit bottoms and her slippers and went to the bathroom, toiletry bag under one arm. Her grandfather was already up. She could hear him making coffee downstairs in the kitchen. Lydie liked the morning routine: those comforting, familiar sounds, the smell of toast, the bowls placed on the table, the coffee machine burbling softly. It felt like normal life, like the lives of other people, like life on TV.

In the bathroom she opened the toiletry bag and spread out her stuff: deodorant, pink razor, various creams in dark glass jars, shea butter shampoo, royal jelly conditioner, make-up remover and cotton-wool balls, toothbrush, hairbands and hairslides, nail files and tweezers, even a coconut candle that she lit to make the room smell nice. She lugged all this stuff around with her every morning. That way, at least, Bruce couldn't stick his nose into her belongings when she wasn't there.

She tuned the dusty old Philips transistor to Fun Radio before turning the heat up as high as it would go. She ran the shower and waited for the mirror to steam up before getting undressed. Since it was Friday, she washed her hair. It always took so long to wash, dry and style that she almost missed her bus, stressing out her grandfather. But what could she do? Her hair had to look good. On the shower's earthenware base, long hairs snaked between her feet. She rolled them up into a ball and threw them into the bin; she had to or the old man would go spare again. What bothered her were the roots. They were getting darker and darker. If she ever stopped being blonde . . . Well, that would pretty much be the end of the world. She felt sad for a while as she held the hairdryer close to her head, then took care of her nails. This was always a moment of precision and reflection. And then her teeth.

As she got dressed, she noticed that – as always – she didn't have any knickers and bras that matched. She did what she could and looked at herself in the mirror for a few seconds. She arched her back, stuck out her tits. She wanted to make them all so hard that they exploded.

Ah, there we go: her grandfather had started moaning. She could hear him downstairs, grumbling as he moved chairs around. She quickly tied back her hair and put on her baggy Complice tracksuit bottoms before hurtling downstairs.

Her grandfather always had RTL on the radio as they ate breakfast, the two of them staring into their bowls.

'I don't suppose you've heard from your brother?'

The old man had asked her this every morning for weeks now. It wasn't even a question really, more an observation. Lydie shook her head.

The old man poured himself some coffee and lit a cigarette. Smelling the smoke, Lydie grimaced. He looked at her without a word. Now and again he took a sip of coffee, then went back to smoking his cigarette. He didn't take his eyes off her. 'You must know where he is, though?'

'No. And I don't give a damn either.'

'Don't talk like that.'

It was true, though. It had been true even before, when he used to take her to school in his car, but it was even truer now that she had to catch the bus with all the others. Yet it wasn't that long ago that they'd had a laugh together, shared some nice moments: Bruce would often come into her room and the two of them would veg out in front of the TV, smoking spliffs. Sprawled on the carpet, they'd have fun criticising the programmes, the presenters' clothes, all the shit they spouted to make themselves seem cool and worth following. That advertising happiness, the bright colours and dazzling lights, those perfect lines, it sucked her in every time. And at the same time she hated those people even more than if they'd done something bad to her personally. The two of them always wound up yelling insults at the television.

Sometimes Bruce would talk about their dad and Lydie didn't like that. She didn't remember him at all and she got annoyed when Bruce started making stuff up and being all mysterious.

Bruce talked about their mother too, but not often. It was a subject that tended to make him angry and sad. Before Bruce had had to go and live in the Centre, when he was thirteen or fourteen, it hadn't been like that, but afterwards their mother had really let herself go. She started talking about 'my cancer' as if it were some beloved pet. And yet she'd been cured! If Bruce spent all his time pumping iron, that was why. He was afraid of getting fat. He needed to sweat out all the poison, all those fears brought on by thoughts of their mother.

Bruce was sulking now. That was him all over. He used to get upset over nothing when they were kids. Like when she'd told him to stop coming into her room at all hours, without knocking, and often half naked, he hadn't talked to her for about two weeks. He also kicked up a fuss because she went out with boys; sometimes he even followed them. So that was why she'd got into the habit of not leaving her things around, and of locking her bedroom. After all, no one had ever told her why Bruce had been expelled from school, but given how uncomfortable they all looked whenever the subject was raised . . .

In fact, he really began to change when he went to work at Velocia. It had gone to his head, being associated with that Martel guy, and he'd got into all sorts of stuff. Lydie preferred it when her brother was a wannabe-Arab, swaggering around in a hoodie and listening to rap, like someone in a film. He'd even called her 'cuz' back then. At least it was funny. Not that their grandfather had thought so. He'd sold Bruce's scooter as punishment. Bruce had pointed two fingers at the old man's head and gone 'boom'. He'd got the truncheon for that.

Now the idiot was like a cross between Tony Montana and Olivier Besancenot, the Communist gangster. That Martel guy was probably just having him on. The worst thing was when he tried to talk politics with their grandfather. You should see the old man's face: pure venom and hate, a sort of twisted pleasure in assuming the worst. Lydie ran straight up to her room whenever that happened.

After eating her toast, Lydie washed the dishes and wiped the plastic tablecloth with a sponge. Her grandfather was listening to the news now. As she was making tea and biscuits for her mother, she heard the RTL jingle and some man saying: 'Good morning, it's seven o'clock . . .' Shit, she was running late. She picked up the tray and rushed upstairs. Cheerful voices from the other side of winter began describing the state of the world while her grandfather lit another cigarette.

In her mother's room, Lydie breathed in the eternal smell of antiseptic and mould. She didn't bother knocking – there was no point. Stunned by her pills and wine, her mother was snoring, like a pig. Lydie went to the window and opened the shutters. The icy wind touched her bare arms and she got goose-bumps.

'Oh, close it quickly!' her mother begged, in a rusty voice.

Lydie waited a few seconds before closing the window.

'Oh, my darling, please . . .' said her mother.

Lydie sat next to her. She turned on the bedside lamp and examined her bandages. They were spotted with yellowish pus stains.

'Leave them,' her mother said. 'They'll be fine like that until tonight.'

'I'd rather change them now.'

'Ah, yes, I forgot . . . It's Friday, isn't it? You have plans for tonight.'

'Don't move.'

Lydie's mother drank too much and her wounds were slow to heal. All along the right side of her body, from her temple to her hip, the skin was soft, a flowering of black, yellow and purple. The flesh was discoloured and swampy, as though something might have been germinating inside it amid the decay. But that something had no form and its state seemed to vary, ebbing and flowing over time. Lydie sometimes had the impression that her mother's burn was another inhabitant of the Farm.

While Lydie changed her bandages, her mother wailed and moaned a little bit. Lydie looked at her watch. She still had to get dressed and the bus would be there at half past seven. Even so, her mother held her arm when she tried to leave. 'You won't be home late, will you?'

'Don't worry.'

'What time will you be home?'

'I don't know, Mum. I'll probably go out with Nadia.'

'You go out too much. Look at your mother – look what happened to me when I went out.'

'Mum.'

'Look.' And her mother tried to sit up to give her daughter a better view.

'It's fine. I'll be home early.'

'Promise?'

'Yes!'

Her mother touched her with her good hand. Her mouth hung open slightly. Lydie, well aware of her mother's talents for melodrama, waited for the end of the scene.

'Nobody will ever love you like your mum does, you know.'

The fat woman with the shaved head began weeping softly. Lydie backed out of the room. Her mother couldn't see her any more. She was wallowing.

In her bedroom, Lydie switched on the TV. A Rihanna video flashed up on the screen. She turned up the volume, did her make-up, got dressed: denim blouse, navy jacket, black slim-fit jeans with pink stitching, black heels. Then her leather jacket with the fur collar. She opened the window to let the morning in. She felt hot, excited. Her face was slightly red. She turned the volume up a bit higher and started to dance. Her hips swung in time to the bassline, her head wobbled on her shoulders, she bit her lips. Oh, yeah, she could feel it, from behind. In the mirror she looked beautiful, happy, kind of slutty, her bubblegum-coloured lips shining. Thousands of miles from the Farm.

'What the hell are you doing?'

Ugh, her grandfather had come all the way upstairs just to tell her to hurry up.

'Coming!'

He kept grumbling for a while, then went downstairs again. And Lydie escaped down the garage ladder as usual, shoes in hand, the handles of her bag gripped between her teeth. Because if the old man got a look at how she was dressed, she'd be royally screwed.

Lydie walked up the central aisle of the bus like a model on a catwalk. Nadia was sitting at the back and a few boys turned and stared as Lydie swayed past. She sat down next to her friend. Her bubblegum bubble popped as she rummaged around in her bag. Nadia watched her.

'So?'

'So it's Friday, baby!'

'Yeah, great.'

'And Gomez—'

'That perv!'

'Stop it,' said Lydie. 'We're going dancing tonight.' She began rolling her hips around, hands in the air, eyes closed.

'Give me a break.'

'Ugh, what is wrong with you?'

Lydie hated it when people killed her mood. It was just her luck to spend most of her time with a girl who was practically a Goth, Docs on her feet, hair shaved on one side, wires trailing from her ears. And you should hear her taste in music! It was all really dark. The only vaguely danceable stuff she liked was Mano Solo. Nadia was never happy. Lydie always had to twist her arm to get her to do anything fun. She was a compulsive liar, and boys hated her. She weighed barely six stone but she would start a fight with any boy in her path at the slightest opportunity. All the same, Lydie liked her. And she was the only other girl in her class. Nadia didn't really have a father either, so that they had that in common.

They sat in silence during the journey. It was still dark outside. The bus whispered with the muffled sound of music leaking from ear buds as the teenagers dozed. Some light started to filter through a gap in the hills. Gradually, the kids started to chat, to laugh. The boys' voices were already harsh-sounding. They talked about mechanics and sport in their strong local accent. The girls gossiped in tight little circles, sharing secrets and bitchy observations. Occasionally you would see hands raised above a headrest as someone stretched. The bus headed down towards the valley, making wide turns through the road's curves, majestic as an elephant, struggling to speed up again after each stop, whining and creaking, its hydraulics emitting long sighs, like a tired old man. Every time the doors opened, a blast of freezing air would travel up the aisle and the teenagers would complain. The driver ignored them.

Nadia and Lydie were the last ones off the bus. They passed clusters of boys standing close together to keep warm and faces turned as they went by. They pretended they hadn't noticed and went straight to the toilets to check their make-up. Lydie reapplied some lip gloss. Her cheeks were bright red, which made her look like a farm girl. She hated that. She powdered them, but it didn't make much difference. They shared a fag, taking a few drags each before tossing the stub into the toilet bowl. The first cigarette of the day always tasted foul, but you had to make a start. As they came out, a young monitor collared them.

'Hey, girls! What were you up to in there?'

'Pulling up my tights,' said Nadia, who was wearing jeans.

'Keep smoking and you'll end up with lung cancer, you know.'

'I know, and I hope I get it soon because I'm sick of seeing your face every bloody morning.'

The monitor stiffened. He grabbed her arm. 'You shouldn't talk to me like that.'

'And you shouldn't go out with students.'

Lydie paid no attention to this exchange. She was preoccupied by something more urgent: a strange gathering in the middle of the playground, a mix of people who usually never went near one another. In general, the playground was organised along fairly rigid social divisions. Each group had its own corner, its own space. The table-football players hung around near the common room; Kamel and his friends buzzed like flies around a rubbish bin; and Riton's gang spent hours spitting on the ground as they leaned against the back wall. Lydie and Nadia's spot was a window ledge. They would sit there together through all the breaks, despising their peers and wishing they lived somewhere else.

So there was something very odd about this gathering, particularly as everyone looked happy and interested, and not in the feverish way that accompanied fights.

Lydie advanced and Nadia quickly joined her. From a distance, they could already hear eager voices, overlapping questions, silences. 'Where are you from?' 'How long are you staying?' 'What's your name?'

'Ah, right,' said Nadia.

'Yep,' Lydie agreed.

It was a newbie.

They soon discovered that he had arrived the day before. The kids who boarded at the school had already met him and the rumours were good. His name was Joe Dekkara, his father was in the army, they were from Tahiti – seriously? – and his father had been transferred to the Vosges, a tough blow for the family who had been through New Caledonia, Nîmes, Corsica, and were now experiencing a real winter for the first time. Joe looked like one of the stars from *Prison Break*, only darker. Because he was mixed. Lydie instantly knew what she'd be devoting her time to for the next couple of months.

The bell rang before Joe had even had a chance to see her. Lydie stayed where she was, as Nadia and the others flooded back into the school. The crowd around Joe drifted away and their eyes finally met. Lydie immediately turned on her heel and practically ran into the corridor. Oh, my God, he was so cute, totally new, and not from around here at all.

And then, as she was going upstairs, a figure appeared before her, muttering hello as the tide of students continued to flow past them. It was that strange kid with long eyelashes again, the one who always looked like he was waiting for someone. Since they'd ended up in the headmaster's office together for smoking behind the pool, he was constantly hanging around her. He'd seemed nice enough at first. He'd taken all the blame himself, sparing them hours of detention. Even so, she had the impression that he was there every time she turned around these days, with his puppy-dog eyes and wagging tail. She said hello, but that was all. She wasn't going to kiss his cheek, especially not now she was in love.

The cafeteria was packed, as ever. Lydie was standing in line with Nadia, holding her empty tray and trying to spot the new boy.

'What a bastard, though!'

'Who?' asked Lydie.

'Gomez!'

'Oh, totally.'

'Well, I don't give a fuck, I'm not going.'

'Yeah, totally,' Lydie repeated, her gaze scanning the tables.

'And I was trying to be cool with him too. You saw that, right?'

'Right.'

That morning, during the technical drawing class, Nadia had left her seat to go and see the teacher at his desk. She wasn't the type to cause a scene, usually, but sometimes boredom and her family problems would get the better of her and indiscipline became her only way of dealing with depression. So, anyway, she got up and walked towards his desk.

'Stay in your seat,' Gomez warned her.

'It's all right, sir, there's just something I need to tell you. Won't take long.'

Laughter and suggestive noises rose from the surrounding desks. Taken aback, Gomez sat up straight. 'Nadia, please go back to your seat. I'll be there in a minute.'

'No need, sir,' she replied, continuing to advance towards him.

'Sit down right now or you'll get a detention.'

Nadia shook her head, looking exasperated, as if she'd seen her little brother trying to shove a cube through a circular hole.

'You don't understand, sir.'

All the students were jabbering, oohing and hammering on their desks now.

'Very well,' said Gomez. 'In that case, the whole class can have a two-hour detention.'

'What?'

'C'mon, sir!'

'Whoa! That's totally unfair!'

Indignation spread through the classroom like wildfire. Twenty-five voices rose in protest and Latif Diop stood up and tried to grab Nadia. He was more than six foot tall and close to fifteen stone.

'Sit down.'

Nadia struggled vainly and some other students got to their feet too, most of them encouraging Latif. Gomez practically leaped over his desk to separate the rhino and the sparrow.

'It's all right, sir,' the boy said, as he dragged Nadia away. 'I've got her in hand.'

The room filled with whistling, and the teacher was striding towards them, but Nadia was riled by Latif's smug words. 'Fuck you.'

She grabbed the boy's sweatshirt and yanked as hard as she could. There was a huge ripping sound and suddenly the young man's dark chest and fat belly burst into view under the bright strip lights. He started insulting Nadia, hitting her over the head. Gomez, in a panic, tried to intervene and got an elbow in the nose for his pains. All around there was chaos: kids standing, yelling, throwing stuff. Just crazy.

In the end, the teacher from the next classroom got involved and it took half an hour to get the situation under control.

Afterwards, Gomez had taken Nadia to the headmaster's office. He'd been in a real state, the idiot, practically on the verge of tears. The headmaster had done his usual good cop/bad cop routine, and then he'd announced his verdict.

'Twenty hours of detention! And you think that son of a bitch Gomez defended me?'

'I know, totally,' said Lydie, taking the dish of burger and mashed potatoes from the hands of the dinner lady.

'*Thank you*,' the dinner lady said in a whining, sarcastic voice, refusing to let go of the plate. She was a thin woman with eyebrows plucked to almost nothing.

'Thank you,' Lydie repeated, forcing a smile.

Nadia refused to eat anything. In protest, apparently. 'It was legitimate self-defence, don't you think?'

'Totally.'

Holding her tray, Lydie looked for somewhere to sit. Where could the new boy be hiding? Oh, God, there he was again, the weird one with the long lashes, staring at her and trying to smile.

'What are you doing?' Nadia asked.

'Nothing. Just looking for somewhere to sit.'

'There are loads of places. Come on, let's sit there. Anyway, I haven't even told you the worst thing yet. That son of a bitch Diop didn't get punished at all! Seriously, it's such a fucking patriarchy, this school.'

They'd just sat down when the new boy appeared at the entrance to the cafeteria. He was surrounded by a whole group of boys tripping over themselves to be nice to him. They were magnetised. Not surprising, really: it wasn't every day that a new guy turned up like that from the other side of the world, wearing those clothes, and with that angelic face. Becoming his friend would be like going on TV or buying the last pair of Vans in the shop. A tall ginger kid rushed over to grab a plate for him and started explaining how the cafeteria worked. The new boy listened, nodded. He seemed a bit embarrassed. Lydie hadn't noticed how short he was, earlier. The other boys were all a head taller than him. But Joe had perfect proportions already, like a man. The boys bustling around him all looked like beanpoles and puppets in comparison. Lydie examined him. He was wearing a hoodie, pale jeans, Caterpillar shoes and a Burberry scarf. It was snowing outside and she could see half-melted snowflakes glistening in his curly hair.

Lydie dropped her fork onto her plate. Suddenly she had no appetite for something as base and material as burger and mashed potatoes. 'That's gross,' she said, frowning.

'No shit,' said Nadia. 'It makes me want to puke.'

'Come on, let's go.'

'What? Hang on, we just got here.'

Lydie headed towards the exit, carrying the tray containing her barely touched meal. Behind her, she hoped Joe was staring. She walked slowly, feigning indifference by gazing vaguely ahead at something in the distance, something really cool that no one else could see.

The other girls in this shitty school called her a whore, but that was just the price she had to pay. Well, that and the kisses she'd rather forget, the wandering hands, the memory of that attic where she'd put her clothes back on while trying not to cry . . . and then all the gossip about her. Oh, well. Ever since she'd turned thirteen she'd been special, advanced for her age. Men took her places in cars, places where minors were not allowed, and paid for her drinks. She hung out with people old enough to have their own apartment or job or at least to be on the dole. Most of them smoked hash and were nice to her. She didn't really get involved in their parties: she remained on the edges and kept her mouth shut; that way, they imagined she was cleverer than she was. She lived the high life, by her own standards. And so she walked out of the cafeteria like a queen, protected by the magic enchantment of sexiness.

But Nadia brought her back down to earth.

'Look, the new kid's over there.'

'What new kid?'

'Ha-ha. Yeah, right.'

She turned around anyway since Nadia insisted. Joe was eating chicken and chips with his fingers, sleeves rolled up. When he noticed that Lydie was looking at him, he dropped the chicken thigh he was holding, clearly vaguely embarrassed. Then he smiled. Everyone in the cafeteria was watching this scene unfold. Lydie felt herself blush and hurried out of the room. She had a mad urge to run and yell.

Outside in the playground, Nadia said: 'Well, well . . .'

'What?'

'Yeah, right. I have a feeling I'm going to be hearing a lot more about the new boy.'

And that was the exact moment when the long-lashed weirdo decided to make his reappearance. It was starting to freak her out, the way he kept popping up in front of her like that.

'Hi.'

'Hi.'

Lydie was in a better mood, so she kissed his cheek this time. So did Nadia. He began to stammer something about that time behind the swimming pool. Lydie half listened, then left him standing there as soon as she could. Curiously, Nadia didn't immediately follow her. She stayed with the weirdo for a while longer, telling him God-knows-what.

'What the hell were you doing?'

'Nothing. He's a nice guy.'

'What?'

Nadia shrugged. 'I think he is.'

'Are you high or what?'

Nadia let it drop and they walked to the common room to buy some Coke and crisps. They were both starving.

During the afternoon break, Lydie decided to stay away, up on the fourth floor. Noses pressed to the window, she and Nadia observed the playground below. There in the corridor they couldn't hear anything but the functional, echoing silence, like in a hospital. Occasionally a banging door or a shout from the ground floor would reverberate up the stairwell, leaving behind a brief, dry echo. From their vantage point, the students in the playground seemed to move with dreamlike slowness, as tiny and insignificant as ants. Watching them like that, Lydie had the feeling that she was looking at a memory.

'Fuck, I feel really depressed,' said Nadia.

'Why?'

'I don't know. I just feel depressed. This fucking school . . .'

'Yeah, totally.'

They fell silent. Lydie took a step back, hands in pockets. She blew bubbles with her gum. Nadia pressed her forehead to the glass and stared out vacantly.

'What can we do tonight?'

'I dunno, we'll see.'

Next to Nadia's half-open mouth, the window steamed up. She sighed, then suddenly straightened and wiped away the condensation with her hand. 'Look!'

'What's up?' Lydie asked.

'The new kid. He's hanging around with those pricks.'

It was true: he was standing with Riton and two of his friends. The three boys touched his shoulder and began waving their arms as they closed around him.

'He's not bad-looking, though,' said Nadia.

'Yeah, he's all right.'

'You really think I'm stupid, don't you? Are you going to go out with him?'

'I don't know.'

Nadia laughed and started breathing on the window. Then, with her fingertip, she drew an enormous dick in the condensation.

'What are you doing?' Lydie gasped, trying to rub out the drawing.

'Leave it alone. You wouldn't understand – it's art.'

Nadia blew again and wrote her friend's name under the erect penis, like a motto on a coat of arms.

'Urrgh, that's gross!' yelled Lydie, finally managing to erase it. The two girls laughed as they pushed and held each other. Then the bell rang.

'Shit, now I'm really depressed.'

'Totally,' agreed Lydie, glancing through the window one more time to see what the new boy was up to.

It looked like he and Riton were best mates.

*   *   *

When school was over, Lydie decided to wait for Riton near his moped, in the bike shed. Nadia didn't really want to hang around, but at the same time she had nothing else to do . . . So she was there too, looking miserable and listening to her music. At last, Riton turned up with two of his friends.

'Hey, girls.'

'Hi.' And, swallowing her pride, she asked: 'What are you doing tonight?'

Riton was the resourceful type. He took matters in hand straight away. Half an hour later, they were sitting at a table in the Alchimiste, the dodgy bar close to the railway station. Riton went to the counter and ordered two shandies and an iced tea. His two friends complained that he hadn't even asked them what they wanted.

'I'm not your mother. Do it yourself.'

So they did.

Riton immediately started chatting up Lydie. When his friends came back with their beers, he even turned his back on them. He talked and talked, all charming and pleased with himself, lacing his words with just the right amount of bullshit.

It was rush-hour in the Alchimiste. Early on Friday evenings, all the school kids went there, filled with hope for the coming night. At that moment, everything still seemed possible. Later, they'd maybe go and eat something at the kebab place next door. They'd arrange to meet up somewhere. Older brothers and cousins would drive over from Épinal, Remiremont, Nancy to pick up the VIPs. Later still, the lucky bastards who were old enough and had rides and the necessary cash would meet up in the local discos. In general, Lydie was part of this select band. Almost without fail, she was to be found every Friday night in Papagayo, the Sphinx, or the Gaulois, in bad company and slightly drunk, looking a lot older than she was in the flickering strobe lights. Not far away, Nadia would usually be standing by the wall, sipping a lukewarm whisky and Coke, and waiting for the night to be over. Above all, she hoped that her friend – flirting in a vest top, hair glued to her temples with sweat – would, this time, manage to avoid getting mixed up in something that ended with a fight in the car park or puking in the back of someone's Peugeot. Lydie danced with her eyes closed as the boys gathered around her. She danced as if she were there alone, hands to the sides of her face, elbows apart. You could see her armpits, sweat dripping between her breasts. The roving spotlights made everyone look the same: big-spending show-offs, hysterical conga dancers, rich kids and Goth sluts, students who'd come on the wrong night and older men with pot bellies bulging expensive shirts. Nadia would end up going home alone while Lydie was taken somewhere. On Monday, they wouldn't talk about it.

Riton was chatting away and Lydie wasn't listening. She was waiting for the new kid to enter the bar. Once he did, she would do her best to ignore him. Then he would come over to her, she would let him do it, and everything would be perfect.

'It's a foam party tonight,' Riton was telling her. 'It's gonna be fucking awesome.'

BRUCE

On Friday morning, Bruce woke with a monumental hangover and it took him almost five minutes to work out where he was: at the flat belonging to the unemployed guy he'd met the night before at the Café de la Poste. He'd slept fully clothed on the sofa-bed, too pissed and tired even to take off his shoes. He stood up, sniffed, and looked around.

At least he knew where the girl was now.

It was pretty dark in the living room but Bruce could tell that the apartment was strangely stylish for an unemployed man who lived alone: coloured curtains over every window, wooden sculptures of parrots or Rodin's *Thinker*, Persian rugs, even a few green plants slowly dying in the corners. The 50-inch plasma TV was lit up with the GTA 3 screen saver. They must have played it before turning in, although Bruce had no memory of that whatsoever. On the coffee-table were an ashtray overflowing with spliff ends, soda cans and Twix wrappers.

Bruce stretched and let out a long, gross-smelling fart. His head felt like a snowball filled with battery acid. He staggered through the apartment, holding onto walls, until he found the bathroom. On the edge of the tub was a bottle of hair conditioner and a pink Bic razor. Clearly, the unemployed guy had been dumped and wasn't over it yet. In the medicine cabinet, he found some paracetamol. He swallowed two pills, then splashed cold water over his face and neck. He blew his nose and spat into the sink. He was starting to feel a little better, so he decided to wake everyone, starting with the flat's owner, because he was starving and he had no intention of making breakfast himself. He was a guest, after all.

The unemployed guy kicked up a bit of a fuss, but in the end he made coffee and got some brioche out of the cupboard. The butcher's boy didn't look too good, though. The other two told him so and he didn't disagree. His face was yellow, and blue under the eyes. He soon had to leave the table so he could lie down again. Not long after that, Bruce and Jobless heard his teeth chattering.

'We're probably going to have to bury him at the bottom of the garden,' Jobless joked.

'I'm going to stay here for a while,' Bruce announced. 'I don't have anywhere else to go.'

He was breathing heavily, avoiding the other man's gaze. He started fumbling around in his jacket and brought out tablets and capsules in various colours and sizes. He lined them up on the table before swallowing them with his coffee.

'What's all that?' Jobless asked.

'Vitamins.'

'Ah . . .' Jobless counted seven pills. 'And, er, how long are you planning to stay?'

'I dunno, we'll see.'

'I'm not sure my girlfriend will be too happy about it.'

'We'll explain it to her. If she comes back.'

Bruce poured more coffee for himself and the unemployed guy. Only then did he dare look up at him. 'I need to make some calls. It'd be good if you could leave me alone for ten, fifteen minutes, okay?'

Jobless scowled at this. He hesitated. But eventually he shrugged and – after picking up his cup and the latest TV guide – locked himself into the bathroom.

Bruce sat on the sofa-bed with the telephone and the directory. It had been a real stroke of luck, bumping into the butcher's boy. The kid had told him everything: the girl running half naked out of the woods, the labour inspector's car accident. It felt a bit like a miracle, because prior to the previous night he hadn't even been close to finding the girl.

He began leafing through the phone directory before realising that he had no idea what he was looking for. He tried to think more clearly. First of all, it would be better not to tell Martel yet. If he screwed this up and didn't get his hands on the whore, Martel would be furious. He might even get violent. Bruce hardly recognised his friend since all this shit with the Benbareks had happened. The best thing would be to find the labour inspector and then the girl. After that . . . Well, he'd see.

He got ready the way his grandfather had taught him. He noted down the names of people to contact, along with his questions, on a sheet of graph paper. He also added a polite greeting at the top of the page, so he wouldn't forget. He memorised what he'd written down, then made his first call – to Locatelli.

Locatelli sounded really happy to hear from him. Bruce guessed that he was bored out of his brains at home. He immediately confirmed that the name of the inspector at Velocia was Kleber. A tough woman. Not bad-looking either . . . if you're into that type. What type? The type that takes no shit, Locatelli said, laughing. In fact, he was surprised that Bruce hadn't seen her at the factory; she'd been there a couple of times since the lay-offs had started.

Bruce listened to him vent for a while. Locatelli had gone off the rails a bit recently, with his wife snuffing it and the factory going tits-up. Better to let him talk. Locatelli gave him all the latest news on the redundancies: tales of blood and thunder, with the inspector and Martel centre-stage. 'You should have seen how that Kleber woman made mincemeat of the managing director! Subodka was out for the count. The head of HR came out of it better, of course. She's a cunning one . . .' Locatelli wouldn't stop talking. 'You see,' he said, for at least the third time, 'we all hated that factory at times, but we miss it now.'

'It's not over yet, though,' said Bruce, trying to be polite. 'You have to keep fighting.'

'Yeah, but it's not the same thing any more. Mangin wants to move south. If the factory doesn't close and they have a voluntary redundancy scheme, he'll take the money and go off to live near Perpignan. He's got family down there.'

'What the hell would he do in Perpignan?'

'Open a pizzeria. There are loads of tourists there. It's not as hard as it looks.'

'Oh, come on, how would Mangin even get down there? The idiot doesn't have a car. He goes to work on a bike!'

Locatelli started laughing. 'You should come and see us. We don't get to see any of you temps now. Seems strange – we'd got used to you being around.'

Bruce made a vague promise before hanging up as soon as he could. The staff workers had spent their time badmouthing the temps while they were there. Now their precious factory was being taken away from them, they'd got all sentimental. Hypocritical bastards.

Next, Bruce called the local garages, trying to work out where the Saab was. It took just a couple of calls to find it. Frowning, Bruce read his notes. 'Yes, hello, sir, I'm sorry to disturb you. I just wanted to know if Mrs Kleber's car is ready.'

'For God's sake!' The garage owner groaned. 'I must have told her a dozen times already. Is your wife taking the piss or what?'

'She's not my wife,' Bruce answered quickly, afraid that the man would keep yelling at him.

'Ah, yeah, she told me she how independent she was! She made that very clear, believe me.'

When the call was over, Bruce googled the inspector's address and number on his phone. She lived in a house halfway between Arches and

Dinozé. The place was clearly visible on Google Maps. From the sky, it looked like an almost perfect square, surrounded by a bit of land and backing onto the forest. There was only one way to get there, a winding road that came off the D157, went past the house, then meandered through fields towards Guménil, Géroménil and a bunch of other crappy little villages. It was seriously remote. Not a soul for miles around, apart from one house quite close to it, more or less the same size, on the same side of the road. It looked like some property developer had planned to build a housing estate there and changed his mind.

Bruce took a few screen shots. He could clearly make out the pale snaking road, the green spread of fields, the two white dots where the inspector and her neighbour lived, and – behind them – the darkness of the forest. He decided to go there that night, to find out what she'd done with the girl.

He spent the day in front of the plasma screen.

After the butcher's boy left, Bruce and Jobless started playing *Call of Duty* while smoking joints. Bruce, who hadn't really played any video games for a few years, was amazed by how good the graphics were, these days. The images and the violence seemed so real, it was incredible. They played for nine hours straight, an entire campaign, from the landing in Sicily to the Eagle's Nest. They took breaks to piss and to stuff themselves with crisps and Coke from Aldi. At one point, Bruce gave the unemployed guy a bit of cash so he could stock up on food. Jobless was pretty pissed off by then and didn't want to leave the flat, but Bruce wouldn't take no for an answer. So the unemployed guy put on his trainers, his Puffa jacket and his baseball cap and went hunting at the local mini-market. An hour later, he came back with his arms full of hot dog buns, cheese and sausages, Doritos and Diet Coke.

'Come on, hurry up and cook, I'm starving,' Bruce said.

'Where are you?'

'Just crossed the Alps. That plane crashing into the church – fucking hell! What time is it?'

'Five,' replied Jobless.

'Cool, I've still got time.'

'What's in that bottle?'

'Just some piss. I couldn't be bothered to go to the toilet.'

'What?'

'Look, stop asking stupid questions and fry those fucking sausages! I'm going to roll a spliff so big you won't even remember your name in a few minutes.'

'Yeah, right, with my hash.'

'Dude, I'm on a sniper mission, just shut the fuck up.'

All day long, the apartment echoed with the sound of machine-gun fire and exploding Panzers. Red-eyed, Bruce and Jobless lay sprawled on the floor, eating like pigs and smoking like chimneys. Occasionally, in the heat of the action, they would start yelling, 'Banzai!' or 'Motherfucker!' and a neighbour would bang on the walls in retaliation. Instantly, the two warriors would freak out. Inside the flat, it was 25 degrees, dimly lit, and they had everything they needed. But outside, there was cold weather, people, and all the shit you were supposed to do to be a normal functioning human being. So, when the neighbour banged on the wall, Bruce paused the game and the room fell silent. He and Jobless stared at each other, hearts pounding, waiting for what would happen next. That was how Jobless came to notice that Bruce had a Dorito stuck to his cheek. He'd been stuffing himself constantly and his T-shirt was covered with crumbs; there was even a bit of dried mustard in one of its creases. From time to time he would wipe his hands on his jeans or the sofa-bed, without paying attention to what he was doing. That Dorito really made the unemployed guy laugh. Bruce didn't find it quite so funny.

Suddenly, it was dark outside. They stopped playing just after eight, before they'd finished the campaign, because they'd run out of time. They felt sick and sticky, bloated and hollow at the same time. Numbed by the images and the food they were digesting, they seemed to be living in slow motion.

'I've got to go,' said Bruce, morosely.

'Go where?'

'Things to do.'

Straight away, Jobless declared: 'I'm not going anywhere.'

The remark irritated Bruce. 'Lend me a clean T-shirt and a tracksuit. I can't go out like this.'

'How do I know you'll even come back?'

Bruce dug into his pockets and took out the keys to his BMW. 'Go downstairs and take my bag out of the car boot.'

'Why can't you go?'

'Just do it. I have to take a shower.'

Jobless stared back at him defiantly, but in the end he did as he'd been told. Just as he was opening the door, Bruce called: 'Hey, by the way, what's your name?'

Bruce listened to the radio as he drove. It was all eighties hits: Jean-Pierre Mader, the Cure, 'Enola Gay'. After an afternoon like that one, he was finding it hard to shake himself out of his torpor. Even with the window cracked open and the cold wind blowing inside, he still felt a bit dazed.

He knew a quiet place – a car park reserved for the staff of an accountancy firm that was always deserted at weekends. He drove there and parked. From that spot, he could watch all the comings and goings around the supermarket fifty yards down the road. For a while he found himself mesmerised by the ballet of headlights and shopping trolleys. He'd turned off the heating to wake himself up. The temperature fell quickly and he had fun watching his breath steam white in front of his face. He let himself shiver like that for ten or fifteen minutes, until his back ached. He was just about to start the engine again when a gang of little kids walked past in front of the BMW, hoodies over heads and skateboards under arms. The first jumped on his board and rolled away. His mates imitated him. The tallest one couldn't have been more than four foot ten. Bruce watched them glide away into the darkness, wheels rattling on the tarmac. Then the first snowflakes landed on the windscreen. The radio was playing 'So Far Away From LA'. His mother liked old songs like that. He remembered when he was little, maybe even before Lydie was born, she used to listen to the radio all the time. She'd always be in the kitchen cooking. Bruce remembered the smell of beef and green beans, the sight of meat in a simmering sauce, the sound of the casserole whistling on Wednesday mornings, when he didn't have school, the RTL jingle on the radio, and his mum singing along. She knew all the songs. Her father was there too, at least as far as he could recall. Every day, after his afternoon snack, he'd do his homework on the plastic table-cloth. And when he'd finished, he'd get a Kinder Egg. His grandfather used to grumble about his mother giving him junk like that just before dinner. There was always a toy inside, usually something pretty crappy. The world of yesteryear went on somewhere inside him, with its rituals, the smell of wellington boots, conkers in the playground, the hum of the extractor fan, the condensation on the windows before lunch, the py-jamas with a sheriff's star on the chest.

'Fuck,' muttered Bruce, turning on the engine.

He began groping around in the ashtray. Amid the cigarette stubs and ash, he found two grams of coke wrapped up in cellophane. He used his social security card to make two neat lines on the back of a Metallica CD. The powder looked pinkish-white against the black plastic. He rolled up a 20-euro note and snorted the coke, one line after another.

He said, 'Aaaaaah!' and blinked, but his heart wasn't really in it.

He waited. Turned up the sound. Started drumming on the steering wheel. Fucking hell, all those morons with their trolleys! His head was dancing on his shoulders and he kept frantically licking his lips. He should never have eaten all that crap. What was the point of eating? This was the best thing: feeling sharp as a razorblade. He looked in his rear-view mirror and ran his hands over his head. Beneath his fingertips, he felt the rasping touch of his shaved scalp. He was ready. Just to make sure, though, he snorted a third line of coke. 'Enjoy The Silence' came on the radio. He felt hard and cold now, like a gravestone. He checked the Colt in the glove compartment, turned on the headlights, shifted into reverse. The BMW drew a wide arc in the thin layer of fresh snow. After double-checking the inspector's address, he set off towards Dinozé.

It was just before ten when he reached his destination. Headlights off, he stopped the car at the entrance to a gravel driveway that led to the inspector's garage. She had a nice house. Bruce pulled a face as he imagined the kind of existence a man could live in a place like that. Bizarrely, the house next door was almost identical. And not a single sign of life in either. Behind the large bay windows, everything was black. They looked like huge, shadowy aquariums, with nervous creatures swimming almost invisibly somewhere in their depths, brushing past each other.

'Fuck,' spat Bruce. 'Don't start this now.'

Earlier, on the road, he'd had a scare. He'd got a call from Martel, but there had been silence at the other end of the line. Maybe because of the snow, or this shitty, empty countryside. The end of the fucking world . . . Think about something else, Bruce. Maybe the girl was there.

Bruce waited for a while. He listened to the night, the wind shaking the car and whistling through the pines behind the house. It had been snowing all the way there, and the BMW's back wheels had skidded out several times. Bruce was so tense that when he tried to put a cigarette between his lips it took a real effort to unclench his jaw. After turning down the music, he dialled the inspector's phone number while continuing to stare at the house. He could almost hear the phone ringing inside. He imagined it. No lights, no people, nothing. The answer machine whirred into life. Bruce hung up and called again. Same thing. The house was empty.

He drove a couple of hundred yards up the road and parked the car. Before getting out, he slid the Colt into his belt. Next, he checked that he had his fags, his phone. He hesitated. Fuck it – he snorted one last line of coke. Then another, because he felt shattered. And because, somewhere deep inside him, his fear of the dark was rearing its ugly head again.

Outside, the snow hit him smack in the face. He pulled his collar tight and set off, back bent against the wind, sniffing constantly. Huge snowflakes stung his cheeks. His boots sank into the snow and he could already feel the damp seeping through the leather. The way back was not going to be easy, especially since the girl would be with him. At least he wouldn't have come all this way for nothing, though.

Just before turning into the driveway to the inspector's house, he changed his mind. First he should make sure that the neighbour wasn't going to cause him any trouble. If he was there, Bruce would explain that his car had broken down a few miles away and that he was freezing. The neighbour would surely offer him a coffee, and Bruce would take care of him. He could figure out the details later. On the letterbox, he read 'Laurent Debef', then went to knock at the door. Here, too, though, there was no answer. Bruce knocked again, then rang the doorbell, leaving his finger pressed to the button for a long time. He heard the irritating *rrriiinnng* sound reverberate through the darkness. After about ten seconds, he took his finger away. Nobody was at home. He could relax.

And yet one thing bothered him. He blew into his frozen hands to warm them up. An unnerving sensation, as if someone were staring at him behind his back.

He turned towards the forest. A wall of dark trees. He shivered. And that silence. Snow changes the sound of silence: it becomes thicker, like a piece of fabric full of folds, and inside those air pockets . . . something it was better not to think about. And the voices rise again.

Bruce spat on the ground and headed towards the inspector's house, slightly spooked now. He found it hard to walk; his legs barely bore his weight. He pulled the Colt out of his belt to calm himself down. That feeling of being spied on intensified. Suddenly, he heard a whisper. Almost nothing. He walked faster. A whisper behind his neck. He started running through the snow as he rummaged in his pockets, searching for his phone. But his hands were frozen and he dropped it on the ground. He had to get down on his knees and search the snow. Come on, come on, hurry up. He wanted to call someone, Martel maybe. After a few seconds he finally found his iPhone but he had no signal. Bruce was all alone. A voice rose louder. The forest, behind the snow, deep in the woods.

All of a sudden, Bruce desperately needed to piss. He stood up and ran to the inspector's house. Turning back the way he'd come, he could see that he'd left a clear line of deep footprints. He couldn't hold it in any longer. Despite the lingering menace, he unzipped his trousers and pissed. A steaming crater appeared between his feet. He was still mid-stream when the voice returned. He hastily zipped himself up and went to the house's northern side, the one facing the forest. There was no snow on the ground underneath the overhang of the roof. The crunching sound made by the frozen grass reassured him. The inspector's house was striking for the austerity of its appearance, the geometric sharpness that clashed with the nature all around. He pressed his face to the bay window, using his free hand as a visor and trying to see inside. The voice whispered again. It sounded clearer this time and Bruce really began to panic.

When he was a teenager in the Centre, where he'd been put after that whole thing happened, the voice would come to him sometimes, in the night. After a while he got so sick of it that he even tried slashing his wrists with a razorblade in the shower. A maintenance worker found him there, passed out under a stream of cold water. Afterwards, the shrink had grilled him for so long that Bruce almost told him everything. But the thought of his grandfather's reaction had been enough for him to keep the voice secret. Besides, it had stopped by then. And it was all the rage in the Centre: kids would slash their wrists over nothing, a confiscated packet of cigarettes, a bigger boy nicking the TV remote. One boy had hanged himself because his Game Boy had been stolen. Bruce hadn't thought about that place in years.

To calm himself, he started to whistle. He put the Colt back into his belt and tried to open the window. It was locked on the inside, of course. He took a step back to think it through. His hands had left two very clear prints on the frosted glass. It was so dark, it seemed possible that those palms belonged to someone else, someone who was waiting for him on the other side. Bruce began to look around for something he could use to lever open or break the window. He found himself facing the forest again. It looked closer now. He moved his hand across his face to wipe away the snowflakes that had landed there. His breathing was uneven. He would have given almost anything to be warm inside somewhere. He thought about past Christmases. Outside the snow fell, even harder than it was tonight, but he was safe inside. In the kitchen, the stove purred like a furnace and gave out so much heat that he could sit and watch cartoons in his swimming trunks. His mother prowled around the house, like a caged lioness, but if he concentrated on the TV screen and the heat from the stove, everything else disappeared. He could almost smell clementines.

MARTEL

Martel opened the door but nobody was there. The doorbell rang again, for the third time. He pressed the light switch in the corridor: nothing happened. The stairwell remained in darkness, and when the doorbell stopped ringing, the darkness seemed to deepen. Martel took his phone from his pocket to provide a little light. Half of his apartment building was occupied by old people locked up in their flats and if he fell downstairs there was very little chance that one of them would risk coming out to help him. He imagined how it would feel to spend a weekend lying on the stairs with a broken leg while a snowstorm howled outside. Just then, his phone started to vibrate. As he checked the caller's number, the screen lit up his face with a bluish glow. It was the Benbareks.

He hesitated and turned towards his apartment door. But he didn't have time to take a single step. A figure appeared out of thin air behind him and shoved him towards the staircase. He felt like he was being sucked forwards, the floor being pulled from under him, and then he was falling head first. He wanted to twist in the air, to break his fall with his hands but he couldn't and he tumbled down the first flight of stairs, his head crashing into the wall at the bottom. But what hurt most was his knee: the kneecap had smashed into one of the metal bars on the banister and the pain was beyond anything he'd ever imagined. He wanted to cry out, but there was no air in his lungs.

Lying on the floor, Martel tried to suck in air like a landed fish, his limbs shaking as his phone continued to vibrate beside him, playing a well-known Bach toccata. The figure came downstairs, a massive torso on slightly bowed legs. Torchlight darted around before coming to rest on Martel's face. He could taste blood on his tongue. He dragged himself along the floor and managed to lean back against the wall, where he started to yell for help before quickly falling silent. This situation was just too ridiculous. The echo of his voice in the stairwell sounded fake. Anyone would have thought it was some kids messing around to annoy the neighbours.

The man with the torch laughed quietly. 'I'd keep my mouth shut if I were you.'

'What the hell do you want?'

Martel brushed his damaged knee with a quivering hand. It was then that he noticed the strange contorted appearance of his index finger. He raised his right hand to the light to get a better view. It looked like an untwisted paperclip. In the bright torchlight he saw drops of blood fall from his fingers to the floor. His head was spinning slightly, but he couldn't feel anything else. He was suddenly very thirsty. Idiotically, he thought about Rita. She was miles away.

'You're all right,' said the man. His voice was gravelly; the voice of someone who smoked two packets of Gitanes per day.

'What do you want?' Martel repeated, trying to suppress the quaver in his own voice.

'You should answer your phone, Mr Martel.'

'Did the Benbareks send you?'

He tried to get up, groaned like a wounded animal, and slumped to the floor again.

'You're in pain,' said the man.

'Fuck, I told them this would all be settled in a few days.'

'Don't waste your breath, mate, I don't even know what you're talking about. I'm just a service provider. I've driven four hundred miles to come and see you. That's quite a trip, you know, particularly as I wasn't expecting this shitty weather.'

And the man held his foot in the air for a moment, letting Bruce observe his Weston loafers. A thin strip of white showed where the snow had bitten into the tan leather.

His attacker sighed, genuinely upset. 'Well, anyway . . . You need to stop playing dead, Mr Martel. You're not a kid any more. So answer your phone if you don't want to get into some serious trouble.'

'We're going to find her,' Martel promised, thinking about that little whore, about Bruce, about the chain of events that had led to this, to his suddenly fucked-up life.

'Ssh, I don't want to hear a word about your little problems. I told you, I'm just a service provider. I pay you a visit, I do what I have to do, and that's it.'

The man explained to him the ins and outs of his business. According to him, there was a lot to be gained from working independently. With globalisation, being self-employed was not like it had been before. Of course, you had to charge as much as you could, but personally he couldn't complain about that. Especially since, after deducting the transportation costs, you were talking about an 80 to 100 per cent gross profit margin.

Martel had no idea what the madman was on about. 'Did the Benbareks send you?' he asked again.

'I have to go now,' said the man. 'I'll leave you the torch. Consider it a gift. But if I can give you one piece of advice? Don't do anything stupid, like trying to get a look at my face. Okay?'

The man put the torch, light-down, on the ground. Martel heard leather soles slapping down three storeys. From his outline, his stride, the weight of his footsteps, that bastard had to weigh close to twenty stone. When he'd walked past, Martel had looked away.

Downstairs, the front door banged shut in a draught of air. Still Martel didn't move. He waited. The sound of a vehicle reversing rapidly in the car park. Martel continued to wait. When he was absolutely sure that the man had gone, he decided to move. But the adrenalin was already ebbing, giving way to pain. His large body shivered compulsively. His nose was running and it took all his self-control not to throw up. Leaning against the wall, he managed to stand up. Bending over on his jelly-like legs, he grabbed the torch with his working hand – the left – and began to search the floor for his phone. It wasn't too badly damaged. Martel slipped it into his pocket and limped back up to his flat.

After locking the door, he collapsed next to his hunting rifle. He was sweating buckets and his teeth were chattering. The pain came in waves. He dialled Bruce's number and for once that idiot answered, but Martel was incapable of saying a word.

'Hello? Is that you?'

Bruce's voice sounded as hollow and mechanical as a robot's. 'Hello? Is that you?'

Martel opened his mouth but no sound came out. His head was spinning. He hung up and tried to support himself against the wall, being careful not to touch anything with his dislocated finger. Only then did he notice that his trousers were soaked with piss.

He dragged himself over to the kitchen and found a pair of scissors, which he used to cut himself out of his rollneck jumper, T-shirt and trousers. He tried to do it quickly, particularly for his piss-stained trousers. But it wasn't easy using his left hand. The scissor blades chewed the fabric. He sniffed, breathed, moaned with pain. He felt hot and cold at the same time and he had the repulsive feeling that his body was betraying him.

He tore the rags off and went to the bathroom. There, he ran the water until it was hot, then splashed it on his face, the back of his neck, before taking another shower. He was careful not to get his injured hand wet. The water ran for a long time. It turned lukewarm and then cold. He just stood there, head lowered. His dick looked tiny from that angle.

After wiping the steam off the mirror, he checked out the damage. His elbows were grazed and there were a few nasty bruises on his back, but his face was in the worst shape. The whole of the right side looked pebble-dashed and there was a deep gash on his forehead, just above his eyebrow. He put his finger to the wound, without really knowing why. It didn't hurt much, but when he saw his finger his stomach immediately heaved and he vomited into the washbasin. He limped to his bed and lay there naked between the sheets, holding his injured hand protectively to his chest. Now and then he would shudder so hard that his body rose off the mattress. His teeth were still chattering and he felt horribly cold. But gradually his temperature rose under the duvet and Martel fell asleep.

Just after eleven, he woke with a start. He was soaked in sweat. The first thing he did was check his phone. Bruce had left several messages on his voicemail, but he didn't feel up to listening to them now. At the same time, though, he knew the situation was urgent. Those Arabs had sent someone to attack him. He had to react. He wrote Bruce a text. No abbreviations: he had to be sure that the moron would understand what he was saying.

We're at war with the Benbareks. I'll call you later.

Martel's brief sleep had given him some strength back. He decided to disinfect his wounds. The index and middle fingers of his right hand were broken, the skin dark blue. He ran cold water over them, which felt good. When he poured disinfectant onto the wounds, though, he almost passed out. He had to cling to the edge of the basin to stop himself falling. His face in the mirror was unrecognisable. His features were blurred, sagging, like the face of some old wino with three-layered bags under his eyes. His own eyes looked like they'd been drawn on his face by someone with Parkinson's: the edges were vague and shaky, while the whites were patchy and far from white, mud-brown in places, fog-grey in others. He seriously wondered if he was about to die right then and there.

He sat on the bathmat and waited for the pain to fade a little. Then he put on underpants and socks and went through to the kitchen, checking on the way that the front door was still securely locked. He was feeling better. He even felt hungry now. The fridge was practically empty: some sardines, a bit of butter, some withered salad leaves, pots of

229

mustard, pickles, mayonnaise, a few beers. He made the best of it, eating the sardines standing up under the strip light, his fingers groping beneath the lid of the tin, which he couldn't manage to open all the way. He drank some water from the tap and decided he needed a pick-me-up. In the freezer compartment he found an almost-empty bottle of Zubrowka. He opened the bottle with his teeth and swallowed a few mouthfuls. The heat rose from his belly and he felt his jaw clench slightly. Bottle in hand, still in socks and underwear, he walked to the living room, where he collapsed onto his chair and lit a cigarette. He stared at his messed-up fingers, sniffed, and did some thinking. From time to time he took a gulp of vodka. The bottle was empty in no time. Little by little, he began to think more clearly.

Those bastards had got him good. The guy in the loafers could easily have killed him. The silence in the apartment was absolute and Martel could hear the tobacco crackling every time he took a drag on his cigarette. Remembering that he'd pissed himself, he pulled a face.

Now he knew for sure that he wasn't going to get out of this situation unscathed, he felt something close to relief. What was the point in hiding, waiting for it all to be over? What did he have to lose, after all? In the darkness, his cigarette end glowed red, lighting up his face. He could see it reflected in the television screen. His fear melted away. He felt like he had before. Before he'd started shuttling back and forth between the factory and the supermarket; before he'd started moaning about taxes and Arabs; before his head was filled with worries about paid holidays and the thirty-five-hour working week. It was crazy, the way he lived, all the anxiety he felt . . . and for what? A job that paid him next to nothing, the Works Council accounts when the factory was about to shut down, all the men who'd elected him and who couldn't do anything but complain and criticise, that little whore who should have died against a tree in the forest. And the Benbareks . . . the fucking Benbareks. He laughed.

After leaving the army, Martel had done quite a bit of travelling. He'd worked as a bouncer in Nigerian casinos, in Italian nightclubs, on the coast. He knew the kind of people who ran those places. In comparison, the Benbareks didn't strike him as all that scary. They were just petty thugs, dangerous but manageable. Then again, it always paid to be suspicious of Arabs.

He came from a family of soldiers. One of his cousins had gone to the Aures mountains in Algeria in 1955 and never come back. His mother had kept a whole collection of *Paris Match* magazines from that period. Oran, Philippeville, Palestro. Old green and yellow covers. A vague feeling that had haunted his childhood. Words that came to him naturally: *bicots, crouilles, bougnoules*, all those terms that people called racist nowadays. In the mountains, the Algerian rebels had murdered entire villages. Men, women, children. They were animals, his mother had said, shaking her head. Then there were all those stories: pregnant women's bellies slashed open; dead young conscripts with their testicles shoved in their mouths, clouds of flies buzzing around them; children thrown into bakery ovens. And after all that, the bastards had shown up in France, to stir their shit over here. All you had to do was watch the news on TV. The prisons were full of them. The Benbareks, the kids in tower blocks, in schools, in local neighbourhoods . . . It was the same old story, forty years on. Compared to the Arabs, the shareholders who were closing the factory were perfect gentlemen.

Before putting on a clean pair of jeans, Martel drank a few mouthfuls of beer to rid himself of the dull taste of cigarettes. He was still hungry. He had the munchies, in fact: he was in the grip of a sort of ugly euphoria. Violence was on his side now.

In his wardrobe he looked for a short-sleeved shirt baggy enough that he could put it on without hurting himself. The only one that worked was navy blue and covered with a yellow orchid motif. Oh, well. Next, he ordered a taxi to take him to the hospital and he put on his leather jacket. His watch told him it was a quarter to midnight. Before leaving, he tied a scarf around his neck that he could use as a sling for his arm, then began searching the apartment. In the box room, behind the vacuum-cleaner bags, he found it at last: an imitation Colt Detective that he'd bought second-hand on eBay. He slipped it into his pocket. A while back, before the bank had cancelled his credit card, he'd bought loads of stuff online. This little gun with its wooden handle and short barrel fired only gas cartridges: it couldn't do any real damage, but the idea of having it in his pocket was comforting. He was getting into character.

When the taxi finally arrived, it was almost half past twelve. It was a white Laguna that kept disappearing in gusts of snow. Martel put his head down and kept his injured hand beneath his jacket as he crossed the small distance separating the apartment building from the waiting vehicle. He sat next to the driver and asked him to go straight to Accident and Emergency.

The man nodded and the taxi set off slowly into the snowstorm. Martel looked at the driver. A small guy with curly hair and olive skin. A *bougnoule* – how fucking ironic! He put his left hand into his pocket and touched the fake Colt. He started to wonder. After fifteen minutes, he broke the silence.

'Stop.'

'What?' the driver asked, glancing anxiously at him.

'Stop over there, outside the station. I need to eat something before I go to hospital.'

The Laguna halted noiselessly in front of a small café run by two Turks. They had the same faces, same moustaches, same bald spots. Probably twins.

Martel got out of the car and ordered a cheeseburger before sitting at a table at the back. The place was shaped like a corridor. The chips were hot and greasy, the burger meat medium-rare. Martel ate quickly, swallowing without chewing, his mind on the taxi's meter, which was still running. The twins watched him. When he'd finished his meal, he glanced outside. The taxi driver was doing a sudoku. He was so short, Martel could barely even see him through the car window. Outside on the street, he knocked on the glass. The driver pressed a button and the window slid down in silence.

'You'll have to deduct the time I spent in the café.'

'What?'

'I'm not going to pay you for the time I spent eating.'

The man stared at him for a moment, then smiled. 'All right.'

'Let's go, then.'

Inside the car, Martel leaned down to the driver, towering over him and articulating slowly as he said: 'You're lucky I'm in a good mood.'

The driver said nothing. He stared straight ahead and waited. He didn't dare start the engine and the windscreen gradually misted over.

'I wouldn't normally share a car with someone like you.'

'I understand,' said the man. He turned the key in the ignition and the engine began to purr. He wasn't surprised: it was too late for that. After midnight, the customers were always drunk or practically fucking in the back seat. The driver thought about his mother, who was waiting for him at home. She didn't speak much French. She slept all day so she'd be awake when he came home from work.

'I'll drive you to the hospital now.'

On the way, they exchanged a few words. Martel explained which route he should take. The Laguna moved very slowly, and after each traffic light they could hear the tyres creaking on the snow before the engine noise covered the night's hushed murmurs.

The driver took him all the way to Accident and Emergency without once getting out of second gear. Before leaving, Martel told him to wait there. The driver took a business card from a box fixed to the dashboard.

'Why don't you just call me when you're ready?'

Martel took the card and read it out loud. 'No,' he said. 'Wait for me here.'

At the reception desk, Martel waved his smashed fingers in front of the fat blonde nurse but it made no difference: she told him he had to take a seat and wait like everybody else. He was edgy, in agony. Even so, he refused to take any painkillers. He was afraid that he would fall asleep, and his night was far from over. He had to call Bruce. The more he thought about it, the surer he felt that he had to take care of the Benbareks. It was the only way. Thankfully, there weren't many people in the waiting room. A mother and her kid. A young guy in an anorak with the hood over his head and a small dog under his chair. A single woman with greasy hair, on crutches. A fat man asleep in a Christmas jumper. Nobody spoke. From time to time, the mother would kiss her son's cheek, and that was the only sound. After a while, Martel started looking for Rita's number on his phone, then changed his mind. At last, after waiting for an hour, it was his turn to see the doctor.

The doctor was a young man in fashionable glasses, already balding. He dealt with the wound above Martel's eyebrow first: three stitches.

'The nurse will bandage you and explain how to keep the wound clean.'

Next, the doctor asked him to undress. He examined him. When he touched his ribs, Martel groaned.

'We'll have to do some X-rays. Of your hand and your chest. We can patch you up for tonight, but it won't be enough.'

Martel was silent as he put his clothes back on.

The doctor said: 'Do you understand what I'm telling you, sir?'

Martel nodded. Things didn't go much better with the nurse, who put his hand into a splint and bandaged it. Standing there stinking of burger grease and alcohol, wearing a Hawaiian shirt in the middle of February, Martel felt like a total idiot. The nurse kept her nose screwed up while she was treating him, then advised him not to drink alcohol with the medicine that the doctor had prescribed for him. Martel said nothing. He put on his jacket and left. The taxi had gone. Martel checked his watch: just after two in the morning. Thankfully it wasn't snowing as hard any more. He lit a cigarette. It was cold, but the wind had died down. He adjusted the bandage around his arm and set off. His silhouette moved away from the halo of fluorescent light and disappeared into darkness. In the thick snow, every footstep made a rustle and then a crunch. He looked back at the trail of deep footprints he'd left behind.

VICTOR TOKAREV

Victor Tokarev sat at the counter of the motorway service station, as he had done every morning for nearly two weeks, and greeted the waitress, a redhead with hazel eyes. The smell of hot coffee filled the room and the waitress came straight over to fill his cup before she took his order – the usual. Victor really needed a coffee. He couldn't have got more than two or three hours' sleep at the most. In any case, he hadn't had a good night's sleep in months. He took a crumpled magazine from the pocket of his beige raincoat, then smoothed down the page that interested him with the flat of his hand. He carried this magazine around with him all the time now. He'd found the article while he was in a dentist's waiting room. The headline had caught his attention and, since then, he'd gone over it every morning, trying to translate the last few sentences whose meaning still escaped him. There was something slightly superstitious about these ritual efforts. Victor had a sense that this article contained within it a truth that might prove the solution to his problems. Yet again, he read the headline:

One paragraph in particular struck him as important.

> *Damien is successful. After graduating with excellent marks from a well-known business school, he has spent the last seven years working for a multinational in the information sector. With a good salary, great prospects, an annual bonus, a family and plenty of friends, Damien would appear to have everything. And yet he isn't happy.*
>
> *'I spend twelve hours a day at work, and for what? We make plans to make plans, without ever knowing where it's leading us or what the point of it all is. We spend so much time writing newsletters that nobody ever reads or creating PowerPoint presentations that don't mean anything. When I talk to my boss about it, he just shrugs. And the harder we work, the more I feel like I'm trapped inside some insane, unstoppable machine.'*

Victor had never identified with those burly Brylcreemed idiots in gang-ster films. This article, on the other hand, had touched a nerve. That young guy trapped in a multinational corporation, that was him. He'd sacrificed everything – his life, his time, his energy – to succeed, to become someone. And yet in the end he slept two hours a night, bit his nails down to the quick and expected the sky to fall in on him every time his phone rang. And all for what? He'd forgotten.

He rubbed his eyes. The fluorescent lighting was killing him. Behind the counter, the girl was waiting for his order to be ready. It was funny the way she acted towards him. Every time he ordered something, she rushed around as if her life depended on it, like a bird making its nest: the same meticulous care, the same hurried zeal. She couldn't be older than seventeen. He guessed this was her first job. At times, Victor had the feeling that she was playing house. He left a five-euro note as his tip every day.

He liked this particular service station. It was the kind of place that had its own regulars, not one of those soulless franchises that tourists visit when they're desperate to use the toilets. The night porter had given him the address. Victor lived in a hotel in Kehl, ten minutes from Strasbourg. Since Radomira had vanished with those two men, he had terminated the tenancy agreements on all the studio apartments. The girls had whined a bit, but he knew it was better to go back to the good old ways. Give 'em enough rope and they would hang themselves – he had the proof of that now. So Victor had come to an arrangement with the hotel owner in Kehl. The five girls came back from Strasbourg in a taxi and slept there for fifty euros per room, while he got his for free. The same thing applied for breakfast at the motorway service station: he'd negotiated a discount. He came here every morning. He saved a lot of money. Except for the tip, but that was different.

When the waitress returned with his sausage, toast and strawberry jam, Victor was busy cleaning his fingernails with a toothpick. He thanked her with a nod and a strand of too-long hair fell over his face. He pushed it back behind his ear before starting to eat. He cut a slice of sausage with his fork, shoved it into his mouth, and took out his notebook.

The previous day, he'd chatted with the waitress. She spoke a little bit of English. Like most French people, she struggled to make the 'th' sound. Victor had asked her if she didn't find the customers too annoying. She'd laughed at that. Oh, no, everybody was very kind, even her boss. She just had to do her job properly. She wasn't especially pretty. Her skin was pale and there were still a few zits around her mouth. When he'd asked her if she had a boyfriend, she'd said, 'Of course,' without thinking. He had a job too, she told Victor – he worked in a garden centre – and the two of them lived with her parents. A good thing they did too, because her father had been out of work for quite a while and the family needed the kids' wages to make ends meet. She sounded proud as she told him all this. She didn't ask Victor a single question. She was fully preoccupied with her own concerns.

Victor felt Ossip's hand on his shoulder and quickly closed his notebook.

'Still counting?'

Victor didn't reply. He put the notebook in his pocket, folded his magazine and – cup in one hand, plate in the other – followed Ossip to a table at the back. Two lorry drivers were eating their breakfast, each of them alone and watching the morning news on TV. A fire-damp explosion in a Chinese mine.

When they were seated, Ossip snapped his fingers to get the waitress's attention. She started to come over, but he made it clear from a distance that he just wanted a coffee. When she continued moving hesitantly towards him, he waved his hand irritably, directing her to hurry up and get his coffee. She blushed bright red, turned on her heels and rushed over to the coffee machine.

Ossip turned his attention to Victor. 'So are you coming tomorrow night?'

'We'll see.'

The young man was amused by this response. Victor had a reputation as a homebody. Unlike the others, he hated poker, hardly ever set foot in a discotheque, and would only ever watch football in his own room. Ossip suddenly looked worried. 'You seem really down.'

'Didn't sleep well.'

'You should take a holiday, relax for a few days.'

Ossip's face immediately regained its cheerful, idiotic expression, as if he'd just cracked the funniest joke of the century.

The previous year, Victor had borrowed quite a lot of money to have a house built in Turkey, by the Black Sea. He'd gone there in the summer to take a look. In fact, all the money had been spent long before and only three walls had been constructed. As for the contractor, he'd vanished. In the premises he'd vacated there was now an electrical-goods shop. The front window was full of washing-machines. Victor had spent his holidays searching for the contractor, in vain. It wasn't just the money: it was a question of principle. Particularly once the others got wind of the story. Ever since, they had teased him constantly about his plans for a second home. Thus far, they had not overstepped the mark. Victor still inspired fear in those around him.

'There were some kids messing around all night at the hotel,' Victor complained. 'I barely slept a wink.'

'Black kids?'

'French kids.'

'Same thing.'

The two men exchanged a smile.

'Arabs,' said Victor. 'They found out the girls were staying at the hotel.'

'That's why they showed up?'

'They were there for a birthday party, as far as I could understand.'

'Were the girls there?'

'Of course not. They were working.'

'So?'

'They rented a room and got wasted most of the night while they waited for the girls to come back. With their fucking music at top volume.'

'Those morons probably never get laid. They do nothing with their days. All they know how to do is spit on the ground and smoke weed.'

Victor nodded.

'So what happened?'

'Nothing. They ended up fighting.'

'And you just let them keep you awake half the night?' Ossip's face was giddy with anticipation.

'There were five or six of them. They were insulting the night porter.'

'Those half-wits could have been armed too. Can you imagine getting shot by one of those virgins?'

'No,' Victor said flatly.

'So what happened? Surely you didn't let those animals loose on the girls.'

'About four in the morning they started yelling and running around like crazy. The night porter told me they'd found blood on the carpet of their room. And those little wankers stole the sheets.'

Ossip looked thoughtful for a few seconds. 'Next time, call me.'

'They won't come back.'

Ossip's face lit up. 'Ah?'

But instead of telling him the story, Victor closed his eyes and sighed.

239

Ossip let it go. He knew Victor was a fairly taciturn guy. His weary, expressionless face was part of his legend. He had an unusual appearance, some strange habits, and a vaguely sleazy air about him, but nobody dared tell him that to his face. Ossip was actually pretty proud of being friends with an old hand like Victor. There were so many stories about him. It was said that he'd thrown some guy into a car crusher. It probably wasn't true, but it gave a sense of his character.

The waitress came over with Ossip's coffee. While she was walking, a few drops spilled into the saucer. She apologised and wiped it off with a paper napkin. Annoyed, Ossip waved his hand dismissively. Victor heard her heels clicking away behind him.

The two men started chatting. Since he handled fairly large sums of money, Ossip was anxious about the economic situation. He spent a ridiculous amount of time in his car, listening to the radio, so it wasn't unusual to hear him say stuff like: 'China's monetary policy is an aberration' or 'Obama's stimulus package is insufficient'. This was all the more surprising since his French was awful. Each time, Victor would just nod, trying to block out the metallic din Ossip made by rattling his chain bracelet and the oversized steel band of his Breitling.

After a while, the small-talk ended and Ossip said: 'So?'

'Six thousand,' said Victor.

'You're short.'

'I know.'

'You're getting yourself into a complicated situation, Victor.'

'I know.'

'Give it to me anyway.'

Victor put a locker key on the table. It was attached to a plastic bracelet stamped with the number 559. Every Thursday evening, Victor went to the municipal swimming pool and deposited the money that Ossip would collect on Friday. This had been Ossip's idea: he went swimming every morning.

'All right, you know how it works,' the young man said.

Yes, Victor knew. The figures in his notebook were like a line of ants, keeping a precise count of his debt. He had to pay Ossip 10,000 euros a week. That was just how it was. An old debt that went back to his arrival here, when he'd had to buy his first girls. Other debts had been incurred later, notably for the house by the Black Sea. Every Friday, Ossip came to pick up his 10,000 – the debt plus interest. That figure also included a sort of tax, to be on good terms with the ones back home. Whenever Victor couldn't pay the full amount, the difference was added to his debt. So, by paying only 6,000 euros he was getting a further 4,000 euros into debt, at the same interest: 10 per cent per week. His payments had been short for several weeks now. On the graph paper of his notebook, his ruin was multiplied, crossed out and recalculated a dozen times a day.

When business was going well, those weekly payments were merely a formality. In the past, Victor had sometimes paid several weeks in advance because he knew he'd be out of town for a while. He would also sometimes lend money to others who were not in a position to repay their own debt. Victor had enough, so he helped them out – at an interest rate of 30 or 40 per cent. The poor bastards thought they had less to fear from Victor than from their primary creditors. And then one day, usually quite early in the morning, Victor would drop by and the poor bastards would understand. He'd bled quite a few dry like that, taking everything from them, sometimes more. Each time, Victor had found himself wondering how those cretins could have got into such deep shit in the first place.

Things had started going wrong at the radiologist's office. For some time, Victor had been finding it hard to get around. He would walk for maybe five minutes and then he'd have to stop and get his breath back. He'd gone to see a GP, who'd prescribed him painkillers, but nothing that really helped. After that, he'd gone to see a gypsy in his caravan, a guy who was supposed to have the gift of healing. He hadn't done any good, but neither had the physio he went to see, while the osteopath was the same shit only more expensive. His hips were still practically paralysed and sometimes it felt like rusty nails were being hammered into his spine. In the end, a radiologist had diagnosed spurs on his vertebrae. In the long term, that could cause the spinal canal to shrink. 'Meaning what?' Victor had asked. The radiologist had looked genuinely sorry as he replied that he could not rule out total paralysis, the rest of his life spent in a wheel-chair. In the meantime, they had to try every possible treatment.

Lost in his thoughts, Victor popped a cigarette between his lips. He was about to light it, then changed his mind. He'd been smoking like a chimney since he was a kid and he couldn't get used to all these restric-tions. He put the cigarette on the table and began listening, groggily, to what Ossip was saying. Apparently, this idiot was telling Victor about his car. Victor could go back to worrying himself sick in peace.

The treatments were insanely expensive. While that was happening, the girls were taking it easy in their studio flats. It was a good thing Jimmy Comore was there to keep an eye on them or the little sluts might have started working for themselves. Anyway, the whole thing was a pile of shit: his medical expenses had grown and grown, he'd had trouble making his debt repayments, and then the youngest girl had disappeared. Some cock-and-bull story. Two men had come along at dawn and kidnapped her in a burgundy Peugeot 605, a car that didn't even exist any more. Thankfully, Jade had recognised one of them – a bodybuilder with an American first name. The kind of little thug who made his living dealing coke cut with baby laxative until he came up with a better idea. The better idea was generally his last. Just some young guy who pumped iron, dealt drugs and thought he was tough. As a Photofit picture, it didn't help him much. All the same, Jimmy Comore had followed his trail. He'd found the whole family living in an old farmhouse about sixty miles from the border. Jimmy watched them for a while. He saw the bodybuilder, but there was no sign of the girl. He knew he had to be careful. You never knew what you were getting into, with those mountain people.

Victor was so absorbed in these thoughts that at first he didn't under-stand what Ossip was proposing. So he just waited, without saying a word.

'You can think about it if you want,' said Ossip.

And as Victor still didn't say anything, Ossip added: 'I can give you a friend's price. Let's say twenty-five per cent. With forty or fifty thousand you'd be afloat again, and afterwards the two of us could come to an arrangement.'

Victor was starting to understand. 'And why would I want your money?'

'They're getting worried back home. With the banks crashing, they want to bring as much cash back as they can.'

'What have the banks got to do with it?'

'Doesn't matter. Point is, you'd be better off dealing with me, so you're clean with them.'

Victor nodded earnestly, then stopped rolling his cigarette around on the table, picked it up and lit it. Almost immediately, the two lorry drivers started kicking up a fuss. They didn't see why he could get away with it when it was against the law. Enraged, the two men looked at each other, then glared at Victor, who continued smoking as though he hadn't noticed anything. As for Ossip, he was ecstatic. Just as a precaution, he put the locker key into his pocket and his Breitling flat on the table, in case there was a punch-up. The waitress decided to visit the bathroom. The skinnier of the two lorry drivers stood up first, thinking that would be enough.

'Hey!' he said.

Victor calmly picked up his cup and swallowed a mouthful of coffee, not even glancing at the man. Then he gave an amused look at Ossip. 'You remember the first time we met each other?'

'Of course,' replied Ossip, suddenly wary.

'You knew your place back then.'

Ossip let it slide. He regretted offering to help this old fart. He wasn't afraid of violence, particularly not with lorry drivers. On the other hand, he'd never really understood what lay behind Tokarev's big liquid eyes. And then there were all the stories. He wiped his forehead and dried his hand on his trousers. He tried to smile. The other man – the lorry driver with a fat belly – stood up too and went over to join his skinny friend. The two men were hatching plans together, furious yet hesitant. The sound from the TV went up a notch. An advert.

'And now,' Victor went on, 'you want to lend me money.'

'As a favour.'

'As a favour,' Victor repeated.

He took his time peeling a strand of tobacco from the end of his tongue, then turned towards the two lorry drivers. They tensed. Victor looked back at Ossip. He was very pale. For several minutes, he'd felt as if someone was plunging a cruciform screwdriver between two of his vertebrae. He thought about the codeine pills in his pocket, but he couldn't take them in front of Ossip. He kept smoking as calmly as possible.

'You know why they're not coming any closer?' he said, gesturing at the two men with his chin.

'Because they're scared.'

It was true: the fat driver had decided to sit down again, leaving the other high and dry. His gaze kept alternating between the TV screen and Victor. In the end, he concentrated on the screen.

'They're wary because they don't know me. They don't know what I'm capable of.'

Ossip nodded in agreement.

'That makes them superior to you,' explained Victor, crushing his cigarette stub against his plate, next to the sausage he'd barely touched. 'You think you know me. You think you know what I'm capable of.'

'Victor, it's nothing to get worked up about. I was just offering to help you.'

'Shut your mouth.' Victor was speaking very quietly now. He was in a lot of pain. 'The only person in this room with any intelligence at all is that waitress, who went to hide in the bathroom. You know why?'

Ossip shook his head. One day, he promised himself, he would shoot this old bastard in the head.

'Because she's minding her own business.'

Ossip glanced over Victor's shoulder. The girl still hadn't come back. He hated women like that, at ease in their boring lives, content with their fate, cheerful and hard-working. 'Stupid bitch,' Ossip muttered.

'No, Ossip, you're the stupid one,' Victor replied coldly.

'Watch your mouth.'

'Try lighting a cigarette.'

'What?'

'You'll see. Try it. Those two guys will be over here in seconds. Because they know what you are. They know what you're capable of.'

Ossip wriggled nervously on the red imitation-leather banquette. His packet of Marlboro was on the table, next to his keys. He hesitated.

'Go on. Try it. They know you. They know the kind of man you are. Most importantly, they know you deserve it.'

A brief smile flickered on the young man's lips. He glanced at the two lorry drivers, who'd finished eating. The one with the belly was picking his teeth, a hand wedged under his belt. The other one was typing something into his phone. Expressions of concentration and amusement kept appearing on his face.

Finally, Ossip shook his head and stood up. He tried to pass himself off as a good sport, leaving Victor to his eccentricities. Victor paid the bill and left a fifteen-euro tip. Then he followed Ossip to his car. They exchanged a few more words as Ossip sat behind the steering wheel. One arm leaning on the car's roof, Victor murmured: 'Don't worry about me, Ossip. I'd hate for you to be anxious.'

Ossip shrugged. 'Why would I worry about you, Tokarev?'

He pronounced Victor's surname disdainfully, as if it were some ridiculous or faintly disgusting object.

Ossip's face disappeared behind the electric window and he drove out of the car park and onto the nearby slip road. The big wheels of his Mercedes SL 600 left spatters of water on the ground of the damp car park.

Victor found his pills and swallowed two. His raincoat flapped in the icy east wind. He went back to his own car. He drove straight to his hotel; he needed to lie down for a while. All the way there, he had to grip the steering wheel tightly to stop his hands trembling.

Even so, he slowed down as he reached the site of the accident. There were now only two cones, a police car and some sawdust on the ground. On the way to the service station, he'd seen vans, ambulances, and a fireman in a helmet standing on top of the wreck, cutting open the roof with an angle grinder, sparks flying. It had been dawn and the few cars had been moving slowly as a policeman in a phosphorescent vest directed traffic with the aid of a luminous stick. Victor had recognised the Passat in which the Arab kids had left the hotel. None of them had got laid, in the end.

Jimmy Comore was waiting for him outside the hotel, sitting on the bonnet of his BMW. They went up to Victor's room together. Victor explained that they'd have to watch out for Ossip now. Jimmy undressed, appearing to pay no attention to what Victor was saying, then got into bed. His skin was dark between the white sheets and he fell asleep immediately. Victor took some more codeine and sat down with a book, an old Stephen King novel he'd found in another room a few weeks before. The story of a dog possessed by the devil. Fuck, if only he'd had an animal like that, he could have made a fortune back home. Two or three fights and his debts would be nothing but a distant memory.

An hour later, Jimmy woke up and stretched. His nudity didn't bother Victor, but he put on a pair of underpants before sitting up.

'The Vosges people,' Jimmy said. 'I'll take care of them tonight.'

'Good.'

'We can think about Ossip after that.'

'You want to eat something?'

'No, I'm just going to grab a Coke.'

'All right. Watch out for those hicks. You never know what to expect with people like that.'

Jimmy nodded. He was a man who rarely smiled, but he smiled just then. And the codeine was starting to work at last.

JORDAN LOCATELLI

After the trouble with Riton in the shed, Jordan found his father asleep in front of the TV, mouth open, a blanket across his chest. On the living-room coffee-table, there was an empty glass and an empty can of Kronenbourg. Jordan checked the level of the Picon bottle in the cupboard. He'd been making marks on the glass for some time now.

Jordan couldn't wait for all this to be over. The factory would close, that was obvious: it was what factories did. His father belonged to a generation that still couldn't accept that kind of thing.

Still wasted, Jordan found himself mesmerised by the images on the TV screen. A man in wellies was walking through a destroyed forest. Trunks lay on the ground, their massive roots in the air. The man's dog ran ahead of him, zigzagging from side to side, climbing on top of a trunk to wait for its master, nose in the air. Jordan wondered if all of this – the factory, his father asleep on the sofa, the spliff he'd shared with Riton, the images on the television – was nothing but a dream. Maybe he was just rushing around in someone else's imagination. Maybe everything he thought of as reality was just a fleeting thought in some strange, infinite mind. And maybe his own thoughts created worlds of their own, where factories closed, where fathers and sons tried to get by. Where mothers died before their time.

Better just to forget it all. He started clearing the coffee-table. He always ended up having these Russian-doll thoughts whenever he was high. In general, he enjoyed it. But this time, Riton had messed up his good mood with that stuff about the disco. He felt trapped inside something dark and vaguely depressing, like one of those old episodes of *The Twilight Zone*.

Lydie.

He went back to the kitchen and gulped down Coke. The bubbles went up to his eyes, stung his nose. It felt good. There wasn't much to eat. When his mother was alive, she used to plan the menu for the whole week; she'd go to the supermarket every Wednesday afternoon with her shopping list and everything was perfectly organised. As a kid, Jordan would go with her, sitting on the little folding seat in the trolley. If he was good, he'd be given a pack of strawberry Hollywood gum when they got to the till. Later, when he was older, he didn't bother going with her. Even so, she kept buying him those packs of chewing gum. He gave up strawberry in favour of menthol. Occasionally, to annoy him, she'd buy him the old pink Hollywoods. In her mind, Jordan was still her baby.

No matter how hard he tried, his father had never managed to stock their home with enough food. He always had to go back to the supermarket on Saturday evening or eat noodles three nights running. For a while now, he and Jordan had mostly been eating ham sandwiches or own-brand frozen ready-meals.

The food shortage really became a problem when you had the munchies. Jordan opened the cupboards and drawers and the door of the fridge two or three times each, just to be sure. Whenever he smoked hash, it was always the same: he ended up cleaning out the entire kitchen. After rummaging around, he managed to find some frozen lasagnes in the freezer compartment. Fifteen minutes in the microwave. While he waited, he ate some Laughing Cow cheese triangles and the last remaining peanuts, which had gone a bit rancid. The taste of the salt was delicious. He wanted to make it last longer. Jordan took the peanut packet out of the bin, licked his fingertip and stuck it inside, to get the last little bits, the salty dust at the bottom. The lasagnes would be ready soon. He set the table and went back to the living room to wake his father.

His father always seemed to be asleep, these days. He'd lost quite a lot of weight recently. Quite a lot of hair too. He was really starting to look like an old man. And yet his father wasn't even fifty yet. Jordan looked at him for a moment before covering his shoulders with the blanket. His father loved lasagne – he'd be happy. Anyway, Jordan was sure that the smell would be enough to wake him.

'Oh, you're back.'

Jordan was flicking through the TV guide. He looked up and saw his father standing in the doorway. He'd already eaten. He felt full. He felt good.

'You looked knackered, so I decided to let you sleep.'

His father collapsed dejectedly onto a chair. Jordan noticed the bitter lines at the corners of his mouth. When the old man spoke, he sounded groggy and dry-mouthed. 'Give me something to drink, will you?'

Jordan stood up. 'I'll warm up your lasagne.'

His father grimaced as he drank a glass of water, then hoovered up the steaming lasagne. He stuffed forkful after forkful into his mouth, head down, in silence. At last, he looked up and said, 'So how was school?'

'Wonderful.'

The old man glanced at him. 'I hope you're doing your work.'

'Don't worry about it.' Jordan got up to pour himself another glass of Coke.

'You shouldn't drink so much of that crap. You'll end up with a stomach like a sieve.'

'You should take it easy too,' muttered his son.

Another silence. Jordan was used to dinners like this. The old man was just waiting for an opportunity to pick a fight. It was always the same old song. Even back when his mother was alive, it had been like this. There was never any lack of reasons. His colleagues' jibes; the temps making more money than him after two weeks at the factory; the overtime that always went to the same arse-lickers. Not to mention the drive home, the obligatory shower, the rush not to miss the news, before falling asleep in front of the weather forecast . . . and then the whole thing would start again. In general, this routine suffering was not enough to put him in a rage. That required something else, a catalyst. It might be an unexpectedly high electricity bill (he was always switching off lights that his son had left on), or a Green Party candidate appearing on TV, or a news report about a school kids beating up teachers in Seine-Saint-Denis. Jordan and his mother knew him well and had developed little tricks to avoid a spat. His mother even managed to see the funny side. She would mimic him or roll her eyes behind his back. But now she wasn't there, things had changed. It wasn't really anger any more, more like hate.

When he'd finished the lasagne, the old man collared Jordan. 'Are we out of bread?'

'Oh, yeah, I forgot.'

'How am I supposed to clean my plate without bread?'

'Shall I warm up something else?'

'Forget it.'

He tried to scrape the sauce off his plate with his fork, then gave up and used a finger instead. He stuck it into his mouth and left it there for a second. There was now a perfectly white line at the bottom of his plate. The father turned to look at his son. Jordan, still slightly wasted, tried to avoid his gaze.

'I'm going to sell the car.'

He said this in an insulting tone. Jordan didn't react.

'The R8, I mean. I'm going to sell it.'

'Why?'

'We need the money, that's why.'

'It's not even finished.'

'At this rate, it never will be. And you obviously don't give a fuck about it, so why not get rid of it?'

'You shouldn't do that. I'll give you a hand with it, I promise.'

His father laughed sarcastically. 'You and your friends,' he said, shaking his head.

Jordan stood up and made to leave the room.

'Come back here a minute.'

'What?'

'You really think I'm an idiot, don't you?'

'What do you mean?'

It was getting serious now. Jordan recognised that expression – the gaping mouth, the puzzled frown, the hint of despair – and feared that the old man was about to start crying.

'You have no respect for anything. You're just like all those other little shits, insulting their teachers.'

His father raised two fingers to his lips. His fake smile had vanished. 'What did you think? That I wouldn't notice?'

Of course. The car. The other night, when he'd come home, the Yamaha had fallen against it.

'You think it's normal?' his father asked, in a high-pitched voice.

For the old man, this wasn't just a manner of speaking. He really believed there was something unnatural in the way Jordan was acting. Something sickening.

'I'm sorry,' Jordan muttered.

Maybe it wouldn't have been so bad if his father had stood up then and given him a good hiding. But he didn't. He just sat there and put his head into his hands.

'I want you to go.'

'What?'

'Go away. Get out of here.'

He didn't move, so his father said quietly: 'Please go away.'

It was the politeness that really hurt him.

Jordan retreated and left the kitchen. He was holding back his tears. He hated the old man. He grabbed his anorak and his helmet and ran downstairs to the garage. The R8 was there, his bike next to it. He straddled it, kickstarted the engine, and roared away from the house without bothering to close the garage door behind him. First, second, third . . . the 125's engine popped and whined like a chainsaw, its metallic rage spreading for miles around. He drove like that for 150 feet then the back wheel skidded out. The bike seemed to hesitate before crashing in slow motion into the snow. Gradually becoming aware of what had just happened, Jordan got to his feet, dusted himself off, and took one last look at the house. In the neighbourhood, nothing had moved; all was quiet. His jeans were drenched now and he was starting to get cold. Oh, fuck it, who cared? He got back on the bike and set off in the direction of Épinal.

Third time was a charm. Then again, there weren't exactly hundreds of open bars around here, particularly in the middle of winter. Shivering with cold, Jordan had gone to the Commerce and then to the Wellington before riding the wrong way up rue des États-Unis and parking outside the Rivoli. Some teenagers were smoking outside, huddled together under the green neon sign. Among them were some kids he'd gone to school with when he was younger. Jordan blanked them, just as they blanked him. Those wankers went to a better school now.

Inside, they were playing a song by Red Hot at deafening volume; you had to shout to make yourself heard. Jordan glanced at his watch. It was just after ten and quite a lot of young lads who had to be home by midnight were already pretty pissed. He could see them staggering back and forth between the tables and the bar. The floor was sticky. Some girls were queuing up outside the toilets. A guy with dreadlocks stood on a chair and yelled as he made the sign of the horns with his hand. The owner made as if to come out from behind the bar and the guy quickly got down from the chair.

Jordan pushed his way through the crowd while unzipping his anorak. In the tangled mass of bodies, certain faces struck him as familiar. There were lots of pretty girls. A man carrying several glasses bumped into him, but Jordan was the one who apologised. He felt completely muddled. There he was, red-nosed and depressed, while everyone around him was busy flirting, laughing and getting drunk.

At a table at the back, he recognised Lucas, who signalled to the others. Riton and Samir turned to face him. Even Boris was there. They didn't look very happy. Jordan moved towards them. On the way, he spotted Lydie. She was leaning on the bar, standing next to an older guy – Riton's cousin, Martial. They were waiting to be served and Lydie was chattering away like a sparrow, shaking her head to make her hair fly around her face. She saw Jordan and let out a cry of surprise before rushing over in his direction. It was crazy – Jordan felt like he'd woken up in the middle of a fantasy film. She'd changed too. She was wearing a very low-cut vest top, low-rise jeans and square-heeled boots. A few beads of sweat glistened between her breasts. Her hair was wet at the temples and her cheeks were scarlet.

'Whoaaa, I'm so happy you're here!' she said, squeezing him tight.

He got a whiff of her scent: sweet and a little spicy. He was blushing.

'You haven't seen Joe, have you?' she asked, still hugging him. 'Do you want a drink?'

She turned to a waitress and ordered two shots of 'Petit René', a local speciality that consisted of eau-de-vie mixed with coffee liqueur. The waitress insisted on taking the money then and there, but Lydie had no cash so Jordan paid. A man in his fifties standing at the bar asked if someone would buy him a drink occasionally too. He was wearing a hat and his fingers were covered with large rings. Jordan recognised him; he'd seen him hanging around plenty of times before. He always wore black, and cowboy boots. Apparently he'd been the singer in a pretty successful band, back in the 1980s. Jordan had also heard that the man had taken loads of drugs. Anyway, he'd never learned to drive: an oddity in a place like that. So he walked everywhere, or caught a taxi when he was too smashed. You could often see his long, dark, stoop-shouldered figure roaming the pavements. And there was always a new generation of teenagers who would take him seriously, listen to his stories: opening for the legendary Daniel Balavoine; spending a thousand euros on a pair of leather trousers; downing bottles of Jack Daniel's with his rock-star mates. Jordan bought him a drink.

'Fuck, I'm really pissed,' said Lydie, bursting into laughter. Then, pressing her breasts against Jordan again: 'Do you know where the new kid is?'

'So what are you doing here?' Riton had come over and grabbed Jordan by the shoulder. 'Your dad let you go out? Fucking hell, what a night, eh?'

Jordan was totally disoriented. Usually, all it took was a glimpse of Lydie's freckles and he'd be practically fainting. So now, with her tits touching his arm, her joy at seeing him and her scent in his nostrils, he didn't know where he was. He took another sniff. There was her perfume, which reminded him of candy floss, and behind it, an earthier, spicier, more intimate smell: Lydie's sweat. He could have wept.

Riton led them to his table and sat between them. Lucas came back from the bathroom and started grumbling that they'd taken his seat. Nobody paid any attention to him. Bundled up in his Quechua jacket, Boris was playing with his Samsung, while Samir stared at girls, still on the lookout for his soul-mate. Nadia, who had been smoking outside, came over to join them, hands in pockets. Her face was white, her pale lips almost invisible as she swayed towards them. She smiled at Jordan before heading to the Ladies. The others watched her go past. There was still a queue outside the toilets so Nadia leaned against the wall and waited her turn. Just above her head, a speaker blasted out the latest Britney Spears hit. She closed her eyes.

'She's fucking wasted,' said Riton.

'Don't worry about her,' Lydie told him.

They had a few more beers. Jordan didn't feel too good. His head was heavy, his eyelids drooping. Riton, on the other hand, was on top form, babbling non-stop into Lydie's ear as she began checking her watch more and more frequently. At the bar, Riton's cousin was chatting up a flat-nosed blonde.

'We won't have enough space in the car if he carries on like that,' Riton said.

After a while, he put his arm around Lydie, on the back of her chair. She advised him to get his filthy paws off her. An hour went by. Jordan recognised Beck, Kylie Minogue, Daft Punk, the Pixies. Nadia finally returned from the bathroom, looking very grey.

'You look like death warmed up,' Riton said.

'Shut it.'

Her forehead was dripping sweat, but she could walk straight.

Lydie was openly yawning now. Riton offered to buy her another drink, even a gin fizz, but she said no. Martial was now getting off with the flat-nosed blonde. The others watched them snogging at the bar. Eventually, the bar owner told them to cool it – this wasn't their private fuckpad. Jordan pretended to be into the music by nodding. DJ Shadow, Justice, Blondie, Gnarls Barkley. It was cool.

Samir and Lucas left first to play pinball at the bar next door, a sleazy place for pool aficionados called the Madison. Nadia had already suggested they should leave about three or four times. When she started on the subject again, Riton told her to stop being such a pain in the arse. She was so tired, she didn't even react. Boris's phone buzzed in his pocket and, after checking it, he abruptly cleared off.

'Must be his mum.' Riton laughed.

Everyone was bored out of their brains. In the end, Jordan couldn't stand it any longer. 'All right, I'm off. See you!'

'Yeah, let's go.'

Nadia stood up, too, and stared at Lydie, hoping her friend would finally come along. Lydie hesitated, then got up in turn. Riton tried to grab her arm.

'Hang on! The night's still young . . .'

If Riton had got down on all fours and started eating dogfood, Nadia couldn't have looked at him with any more contempt. As for Lydie, she'd put on her sweater and was now wrapping her long scarf around her neck. After a moment of pure panic, Riton got up and stood in front of her.

'Come on, we should go to the Sphinx. Trust me, it'll be brilliant!'

'Yeah, well, I trusted you when you said the new kid would be coming too. Anyway, I'm shattered. Bye.'

With perfect timing, Johnny Cash was singing 'Hurt'.

Riton, losing his cool, grabbed hold of Lydie's wrist. Nadia, meanwhile, had come around the table and was pulling Jordan by his sleeve.

'Let's go. We can wait for them outside.'

She was looking better now. She had very wide dark eyes. Jordan had never noticed before. She took his hand. Her skin was soft. He let her lead him away.

Lydie watched them leave while Riton continued talking up the Sphinx like a market-stall holder. She felt totally depressed. Nothing had happened. She was going home. Outside, Nadia and the guy with the long lashes were waiting in the falling snow, shoulder to shoulder. Her throat tightened. She freed herself from Riton's grip and ran outside to join her friend. It was just gone eleven. Maybe the night wasn't over, after all.

RITA

'No way, Greg. She's coming home with us.'

'Ever heard of something called freedom of choice?'

'Oh, give it a rest. Are you really going to start quoting the Declaration of the Rights of Man just so you can screw this young girl? Hey, hey, hey! You're staying here!'

Rita caught Victoria by the arm as she was trying to hide behind Gregory. 'I warned you before about this. I told you not to try anything. Come on, that's enough now, we're going.'

Rita turned to her mother to kiss her goodnight, without letting go of Victoria's arm.

'Bye, darling,' said her mother.

'Bye, Nena. I'll call you soon.' Then, turning back to her brother, Rita forced herself to smile at him. 'Don't fret – you'll see your girlfriend again. All right, bye now.'

She kissed Gregory on both cheeks, but he barely noticed. He was staring at Victoria. The girl's chin started to quiver. Rita sighed. This bullshit was really starting to get on her nerves. She'd supported this girl single-handedly for weeks, running the risk of trouble with the police, and the little idiot had fallen in love with the first man she saw. Their farewell scene dragged on for about ten minutes as the snow continued to fall heavily. In the end, she let Victoria hug her brother goodbye. They looked like a pair of lovelorn teenagers parting ways on a station platform after a holiday romance. They had the same bewildered look, the same ridiculous sincerity; the same total indifference to the rest of the world, as well. It hurt to admit it, but they did look cute together. Later, when she got home, maybe she'd send Martel a quick text.

'Come on, we're not going to stay here all night.'

Greg held Victoria's arms and pushed her gently away, while nodding reassuringly. The girl imitated him. She tried to smile. Rita sensed it wouldn't be long before she was sobbing her heart out.

'Well, I'm going anyway,' said Rita's mother. 'I'm done in.'

'Drive carefully, Nena.'

'Don't worry, it's not far. But you should watch out. The radio said there was going to be a storm tonight.'

'I think it's already started,' Laurent pointed out.

'It'll be worse than this,' said Greg. 'A blizzard, apparently.'

Around them, heavy snowflakes whirled in gusts of wind. The lights from the Capri seemed suddenly distant, their surroundings all covered by the same turbulent dark matter.

Laurent and Rita's mother were the last ones to say goodbye, the old lady draping an arm affectionately around her almost-son-in-law's back. It was funny seeing them like that now, when they'd been at each other's throats for years. In reality, Nena had only started considering Laurent a member of the family once his relationship with Rita was on its last legs. They even phoned each other sometimes to chat, Rita knew. Her mother was convinced that they would end up together again. Age would bring them to their senses, she believed: nobody wanted to die alone.

Victoria did not stop staring at Gregory until he'd disappeared inside Nena's Renault 4. The old lady honked her horn twice in farewell.

Laurent and Rita waved. Victoria wedged herself between them, holding tight to their arms.

'Don't worry, my lovely,' said Rita, lighting one last cigarette. 'We'll find a solution.'

They walked in a line to the Mercedes. Behind them, the Renault's taillights vanished into darkness. The tyres had left two thin furrows in the snow, like a sledge.

'An evening with your brother is never dull, is it?' said Laurent, sitting behind the wheel.

'No. But I think I could have done without that one.'

'Maybe it's not such a bad thing, though. The little bird's ready to fly the nest now.'

Laurent had raised his eyebrows to point out Victoria in the rear-view mirror.

'Hmm, I'm not sure about that. Let's see how she behaves with the cops tomorrow.'

The heavy Mercedes manoeuvred out of the car park, splashing the night with its xenon lights. Rita dropped her cigarette stub out of the half-open window and turned up the heat. They drove out of the car park, leaving behind tyre tracks three times as wide as the Renault's. Laurent turned on the radio. Sardou was singing 'Dans Les Villes De Grande Solitude'.

'Oh, great, this miserable prat is just what we need,' said Rita, unzipping her parka.

She couldn't wait to get home.

BRUCE

'Come on, boy, come over here.'

The dog, docile, followed Bruce, leaving bloody paw prints behind it.

'Good dog! Come on, boy.'

Bruce opened the kitchen door and the dog went past him, wagging its tail. Then it stood still, tongue lolling and eyes wide with affection.

'What a good dog!'

Bruce was thrilled. He almost felt convinced that the animal had saved his life. In any case, the hysterical fear that had gripped him earlier had now completely gone. He started rummaging through cupboards. No sign of any bandages or disinfectant. Meanwhile, the dog was shuffling around, leaving traces of blood all over the floor.

'Don't move, boy. I'll take care of you.'

Bruce paused to pet the animal and to reflect for a moment.

When he'd first heard the pitter-patter of claws on the bay window behind him, he'd almost fainted. Turning around, he'd found himself face to face with this enormous, warm, hairy creature. He could have wept with relief at seeing that big old family pet through the window, partly because it seemed happy to see him, too, and partly because it was very obviously a living, physical being. Bruce and the animal had immediately become friends, despite being separated by a pane of glass. The forest could swarm menacingly all it liked: these two had each other.

'Yeah, you stay there, boy,' said Bruce, walking away. 'I'll find something to make you better.' And as the mastiff showed signs of following him again, Bruce spoke more loudly while pointing at the floor. 'Stay! All right, now be a good boy and don't move.'

The animal stared at him sadly as it lay down and nuzzled its nose between its front paws.

'Good dog! Don't move now. Stay. I'll be back soon.'

Bruce closed the kitchen door behind him and started searching the rest of the house. It wouldn't be easy to find anything in this place – it was huge.

When it came to entering the premises, Bruce hadn't messed around. He'd ferreted around the garden until he found a flower box under a layer of snow. Made of solid granite, it must have weighed close to eighty pounds. Bruce had raised it above his head before throwing it through the window. To his surprise, the glass hadn't shattered as in a movie. The flower box had just bounced back, leaving a small star-shaped hole at the point of impact. Bruce had used the Colt as a hammer while the dog, understanding what the visitor was up to, had begun running around excitedly in the shards of broken glass. Bruce had quickly made a hole the size of a 45 rpm single and put his arm through it, all the way up to his shoulder. In that way, he'd managed to reach the handle of the French windows and the glass door had slid open, releasing a blast of warm air into his face, along with the house's pleasant, familiar smells: wood, tobacco, a woman's perfume. And the smell of the dog too. Straight away, the mastiff had rubbed its nose into Bruce's groin and he'd defended his privates while giggling. Then he'd knelt down to pat and stroke the dog from head to tail. After a while, he'd felt the animal resting its head on his shoulder.

That was when he'd noticed the bloody paw prints on the floor. The dog must have hurt itself running around on the broken glass. Just to be sure, Bruce had trapped the animal under his arm and examined it. Its right hind paw was quite badly wounded, the pads cut open. When he'd pressed down on the wound to work out how deep it was, the dog had whined. Bruce had felt like such a bastard: this was all his fault. Now, he needed to find something to treat the poor beast.

Without really knowing why, Bruce began by heading upstairs. In the inspector's bedroom, he lifted up the duvet, opened cupboards and drawers. In many ways, her wardrobe wasn't much different from a man's. He wished he could find some photographs to get an idea of what she looked like. Her underwear wasn't very sexy either. He rummaged through her knickers, just for fun. He picked up a pair and held them to his nose. They smelt of washing powder. He emptied all the drawers out onto the floor. A box of Lindt chocolates went flying.

'Let's find out what this bitch is up to . . .'

Bruce knelt down. He discovered letters, some old postcards, Post-it notes with messages scrawled on them, a few love notes. Some of the letters – from a certain Laurent – were written in pencil. There were several sophisticated-looking, old-fashioned greetings cards from Nara, in Japan. Bruce opened various envelopes and read them diagonally. There were birth announcements, letters from an Aunt Nine who always wished her niece well and hoped she was in good health before ending with a curt, reproachful line asking why she never came to see her. There were some drawings by a kid named Léo, with coloured stickers around his name. Bruce even found an old cinema ticket. On the front, he read *Le Grand Bleu*, and on the back there was a telephone number. Other than that, there was just a bunch of stupid knick-knacks: some sugared almonds in fancy lace packaging, a beer mat with a bull's head on it, some Arab coins, some letters written on yellowed graph paper that all began 'Dear Sponsor' and were postmarked Madagascar.

Bruce thought about this for a moment. He wondered. Then he tore up everything he could find. He did this carefully and it took quite a long time, but it seemed important to do it properly.

It was in the bathroom, under the sink, that he finally unearthed some disinfectant and cotton pads. He felt weirdly upset without understanding why. After all, what did he care? He looked at himself in the mirror for a moment. He thought about his mother, about the Farm. He picked up a bottle of Cartier perfume from the glass shelf, took the stopper out, and poured the contents down the drain. He did the same thing with the toothpaste, then opened a pot of anti-ageing cream and smeared it across the mirror. He hoped it was one of those madly expensive creams. He'd just started smashing up the medicine cabinet when his phone buzzed.

It was a text from Martel. He felt suddenly flushed, as though he'd been caught red-handed. The message was simultaneously clear yet extremely vague.

We're at war with the Benbareks. I'll call you later.

What was that supposed to mean? He reread it again and again until the words lost all sense. Martel had tried to call him earlier too. Bruce closed his eyes and tried to concentrate.

When they'd got involved with the Benbareks, Bruce had thought he was finally going through the looking-glass, entering the world of serious business. In Nancy, those guys ran the show. They wielded influence as far away as Strasbourg. He would see them in the evenings sometimes, blowing massive wads of cash without a second thought; they didn't even seem to be enjoying themselves. He'd spotted them at the Arquebuse, buying bottles of Cristal for blondes in high heels, girls with no bras and faces like ice picks. He remembered seeing the shortest Benbarek reaching into his inside jacket pocket for his Visa card and revealing the red silk lining. It was like catching a glimpse of paradise, behind the scenes, a world where fucks were dirty but the sheets always clean. The blaze of the silk in the darkness, all that comfort, that excess.

He'd heard a story about them too. A kid from Haut-du-Lièvre had gone to study in Egypt and returned three years later to be a preacher in his housing estate. He was a small guy who looked like the television comic Jamel Debbouze: the same sparkling eyes, the same girly lashes. In fact, he was pretty funny too, and he'd caused a real stir with his caftan and his red Pumas. Some local television journalists had gone to interview him, to witness the phenomenon for themselves. Who was this guy persuading young people to read the Qur'an with a wit sharp enough to deserve his own late-night TV show? A perfect amalgam of Islam and Western pop culture, he was a breath of fresh air.

The Benbareks did not share this high opinion of the young preacher. He was becoming too influential: teenagers in Haut-Dul were starting to talk about morals, to say no to drugs and all that crap. So the Benbareks took out their wallets and paid for a handful of poor old people to go on a pilgrimage. These old people were immigrants from the 1970s whose only wish was to visit Mecca before they kicked the bucket. The trainers-wearing imam had complained, but what could he say really? It was all for a good cause. That was how the Benbareks had got into the do-gooding business. A bus tour to the seaside for some kids who'd never left their village before; three bottles of Banga and some packets of crisps for the local festival; some new speakers for the prayer room; a flat-screen TV for the preacher's mother . . . It was nothing, really: they were just being good neighbours. And then one day the preacher found himself behind the wheel of a brand-new Peugeot 307 HDi. After that, everybody knew it was settled: things could go back to normal.

Deep down, what worried Bruce was that the Benbareks had told Victor Tokarev about him. That bastard was Russian or Bulgarian or something. He'd fought in Afghanistan. Or was it Chechnya? Some war-torn shithole like that. Apparently he had a particularly nasty habit. He wasn't the sort of gangster who was content to make you suffer – he went after your family too. Bruce thought about his grandfather then and it made him laugh.

The dog sat obediently as Bruce disinfected his wounds. When he'd finished, the dog sighed, then licked his hands and face.

After that, Bruce felt suddenly unsure what he was doing there. The girl was nowhere to be seen and he felt a bit remorseful about going through the inspector's drawers and ripping up her letters. He felt confused, uneasy. Sweaty hands stuffed into pockets, he began pacing from room to room, looking through windows, waiting impatiently. The mastiff followed him, its claws click-click-clicking on the tiles. Occasionally Bruce would check that his Colt was still tucked into his belt, at his back. He talked to himself, insults and prayers. *Come on, hurry up. She'd better be here.* He was tempted to clear off, but where would he go? Better just to wait for the inspector to come home. And hope that the girl was with her.

Outside, the snow had already covered the tracks left by his car. Everything looked brand new. He was getting hungry, so he looked in the fridge. After drinking an Actimel yoghurt, he made himself a ham sandwich. It tasted faintly of cardboard. He ate two mouthfuls then gave the rest to the dog. To ward off loneliness, he listened to the radio, the volume turned down low. Jazz music. He tried to find a better station, but it was all shit. His boredom intensified. In the end, he found the woman's bar – inside the oven, bizarrely. He went back into the living room with a bottle of 10-year-old Bushmills and a Spongebob glass. The bottle was almost empty. He finished it in front of the TV. Soon he felt nervous, excited, sad. A quick line of coke probably wouldn't do him any harm. He was just feeling a bit down. A combination of tiredness, not having a home, all his worries. The dog was sitting next to him, staring up with glassy, gentle eyes.

'What's up, boy? Didn't get enough to eat?'

The animal stood up and rested its head on Bruce's knees. He stroked it. There was a rugby match on TV, the radio murmuring from the room next door, the dog's warmth pressed against him. His throat tightened. Outside, the sound of a car engine.

In an instant, Bruce jumped up, turned off the television, radio and lights, and stood waiting next to a window. The dog stayed close to him, circling his legs.

'Ssh. Sit. Stay!'

When the animal wouldn't calm down, Bruce gave it a whack. It whined and ran into the kitchen.

A Mercedes came to a halt outside the neighbour's house. A woman emerged first, from the passenger-side door, then the driver got out too. They talked for a few seconds before the back door opened and a third passenger appeared. It was the girl. Bruce's heart started hammering. He grabbed the Colt.

A few goodnight kisses and the man went into the house next door while the woman and the girl came towards Bruce. The girl hung back, a few paces behind. Bruce regretted hitting the dog. He slid the breech back, sending a bullet into the chamber of the barrel. Just then he realised that his nose was bleeding. The idea was a turn-on.

JORDAN LOCATELLI

'Just so you know, kids, we'll be closing in half an hour.'

Jordan and the girls nodded politely and the manageress went back to her crossword as they sat down. With her blue rinse and string of pearls, she looked more suited to running a jeweller's or a pottery shop than this old bar. The floor was tiled, the counter orange and the barstools wooden. In the window, the name Café du Marché was displayed in the same sort of type usually reserved for butchers' shops. Jordan, Lydie and Nadia had just entered in single file, Lydie leading the other two. The light was yellow, the drinks cheap, and some 1970s ballad was playing on the radio. Nobody was there, apart from one young guy in a denim jacket and a baseball cap, who was sitting at the bar with a *croque-monsieur* and a glass of red. When Jordan and the girls entered the café, he looked over his shoulder to make sure they hadn't left the door open. As they walked past, he discreetly checked out the girls. The three of them found a table at the back, near the door to the toilets. Lydie spoke first.

'What are we doing here? This place is fucking dead.'

'You're the one who kept going on about how cold you were,' Nadia replied.

Jordan didn't get involved. He didn't really understand what was happening. The girls had been at each other's throats ever since they'd left the Rivoli. They wanted to go home, they wanted to go out, Lydie accused her friend of screwing up the whole evening, Nadia claimed the opposite was true, and round and round it went. This had been going on for at least an hour now.

For his part, Jordan was just trying to find a way to make it last a little longer.

At one point, as they were walking down rue des États-Unis towards the city centre, Nadia had taken his arm; it was snowing and she felt cold. Straight away, Lydie did the same. Jordan had found it hard to conceal his joy. That morning, Lydie had barely even said hello to him. Anyway, Nadia was really cool. He'd always assumed she was just some stupid Goth, a man-hater who spent her time wallowing in misery and listening to sad songs. But she wasn't like that at all. She was actually pretty clever and he felt at ease with her. This was a good thing, as it would probably help his chances with Lydie. But first things first: keep the night going. After that, boredom and alcohol could do the rest. The essential thing was not to let this opportunity slip away.

'So what are we gonna do?' Lydie asked again.

'How should I know?'

'We should just go dancing, like I keep telling you.'

'Go dancing where?'

'I dunno. The Sphinx.'

'Yeah, right. All three of us on his bike.'

'I could take one of you there and then come back to get the other one.'

'Forget it. We'll just freeze our tits off for nothing.'

'God, you're so depressing . . .'

On Monday they'd see one another again at school and he'd be back to square one. Jordan kept thinking. There had to be a way to avoid that.

A whiff of jasmine brought them back to their surroundings. The owner was standing next to them, waiting to take their order. She smiled patiently, like a priest, her face lit from within. All three of them still had their jackets on. They were sitting there, shoulders hunched, red-nosed, hands in pockets. They looked at each other questioningly.

'A coffee, please,' said Nadia.

'And three glasses of water,' added Jordan, wiping his nose with his sleeve.

'Will that be all?'

Jordan nodded and the woman turned on her heels. She hadn't sighed or anything. They felt like they'd found themselves in a refuge. Someone to look after them. It was nice. The guy in the cap and the denim jacket, thinking that the roar of the coffee machine would drown out his voice, muttered: 'You've got some real big-spenders there, Marie-Jo.'

His glass was almost empty. The manageress filled it. 'You can talk. How many times did you and your friends order glasses of water?'

The three teenagers heard all of this and felt embarrassed. All the same, they were starting to warm up, even if not yet quite enough to dare take off their jackets. They looked at each other. Lydie's eyes widened. 'So, what, we're just going to stay here?' Nadia was sulking and Jordan couldn't think of much to say. Lydie shrugged. The guy at the bar swung around on his stool and stared at them with a sarcastic little smile. Lydie was the only one not to look away.

'It's true, though. It is bloody boring here,' the man admitted, before going back to his sandwich.

The manageress brought over their drinks. Just then, a taxi parked outside the café.

'Ah! It's your chauffeur, madame,' the guy at the bar announced ironically.

The manageress ignored this and went back behind the counter. She smiled as a man walked in.

He had dark brown curly hair and wore a rust-coloured duffel coat. His face looked gentle, despite the sharpness of his features and the thickness of his beard. He rubbed his hands together and nodded at all the other customers, bowing slightly for each of the ladies.

'How's business?' asked the man at the bar, shaking the newcomer's hand.

'So-so,' replied the dark-haired man, leaning over the bar to kiss the manageress's cheeks. She held his shoulder affectionately. 'Nobody goes out in weather like this. Except a few lunatics.'

And the man winked at the three teenagers.

'I'll be closing in half an hour,' the manageress warned him, checking the time on the clock behind her.

'I just want a quick coffee to warm myself up,' he said in his foreign accent, before rubbing his hands again.

'Good idea,' said the manageress.

There was something radiant yet slightly sad about the woman. Jordan watched her. He felt compelled to watch people wherever he was – on the street, on the bus, in the school corridors. Maybe, in reality, he was the one who felt sad.

Nadia put her hand on his face to turn it towards her and said: 'Come on, stop staring at them like that.'

Her hand was soft and very cold. Jordan barely felt it, but for a few seconds he just sat there in a daze. Unsure what to do in response, he sniffed loudly and lifted his glass of water to his lips. The adults were talking in low voices now. Lydie was making some calculations.

'Well, we can't stay here all night.'

'That's true,' Jordan said.

'Besides, they close in five minutes.'

'We could go to my place,' said Lydie. 'If we go through the garage, my grandfather won't see anything. I've done it loads of times.'

'What about your mother?' Nadia asked. 'Will she go mental again?'

'Don't worry about it. I'm telling you, she won't hear a thing.'

'We could try it,' Jordan suggested.

'Oh, right, yeah, course *you* want to go,' said Nadia, annoyed. 'And how do we get there?'

'I could make two trips.'

'Course you could. You could shoot two bullets in your head, too, if one wasn't enough.'

'Fucking hell, we've got to do something.'

'We could go to the hotel.'

'With what cash? We just bought one coffee for three of us, in case you forgot.'

'Yeah, and going to the hotel is kind of a weird plan anyway.'

They were silent for a moment. Their silence drew the attention of the manageress and the two other customers.

'Those kids . . .' said the man in the baseball cap.

'Well, it's not much fun for youngsters around here,' the taxi driver pointed out.

'I always found something to do, when I was their age,' said the manageress.

'Yeah, like getting water from the well or putting oil in the lamps,' said the guy in the cap, laughing.

The manageress whipped him across the shoulder with her tea-towel while the taxi driver shook his head.

But the three teenagers remained where they were, motionless and bored out of their brains. The night was screwed. Tomorrow, they'd be back to square one. A terrible old 1980s synth hit came on the radio.

The three of them stood outside the bar's glass door. They'd just left and now they were shivering. Light fell slantwise from a nearby streetlamp and an icy wind swept through the street behind the market. They hopped about, sniffing, bumping shoulders without even realising.

'So is that it?'

'Yep.'

'Fuck, I don't believe this.'

'I know.'

'Fucking hell.'

'What a downer.'

'Can't wait till I'm eighteen. I'll be out of this place first chance I get.'

They were killing time. They had to stay out a bit longer. Avoid tomorrow.

'I can't go home anyway,' said Jordan.

'Why not?'

'I had a big row with my dad.'

'Ah, that doesn't mean anything.'

'Yeah, it does. This time, it really does.'

'Maybe you could come to my place,' Nadia suggested.

'What?' said Lydie.

'My mum's working tonight.'

'Why didn't you say that before?'

'Well, she's not all that keen on me bringing people home.'

'Oh, really?'

'But, you know, if he's out on the street, it's not the same thing, is it?'

'Oh, yeah, that's true. I'm sure your mum'll be dead happy that you're taking a boy back home while she's out at work.'

'You can come too. But you'll both have to clear off early tomorrow morning before she gets home.'

'What time does she get home?'

'I don't know exactly. Her shift ends at six, normally. But then she has to drive back.'

'That could work,' said Jordan. 'We could enjoy the rest of the night together, and then we'll get out of your hair.'

Lydie stared at him contemptuously. 'Calm down. We don't even have a ride there.'

Jordan turned towards the café, where the last two customers were helping the manageress put chairs on tables. 'Maybe we could ask the cab driver. He doesn't look too busy.'

The two girls followed his gaze.

'But we don't have any money.'

'We could negotiate something.'

'Go on, then, negotiate.'

'Yeah, we don't even know that guy.'

'Well, we have to get home somehow,' said Jordan, becoming irritated. 'And the simplest way would be to ask the cab driver, and tomorrow morning I'll take Lydie home on my bike.'

The girls hesitated. The taxi driver had gone back to the bar. His duffel coat was neatly folded on top of a barstool. His shoulders were surprisingly broad. He was wearing a strange grey sweater with red edging. He turned to the man in the cap. When he wasn't smiling, he looked totally different: less harmless, more handsome, and – in a way – more disturbing. His eyes were extraordinarily dark. You could see them shining, even from a distance.

'Well, I'm not going in there.'

'Me neither.'

'All right. I'll go, then.'

'Those kids don't seem to want to leave.'

The taxi driver nodded, without bothering to turn around. He could see their silhouettes in the mirror facing him. The manageress picked up his empty cup. Her pale hand came into contact with the man's very dark hand. They both acted as if nothing had happened.

The driver went into the café every night, more or less, for one coffee just before closing. There usually weren't many people in there, just the manageress, the guy in the baseball cap, one or two regulars who always sat in the same places. The man in the cap liked to tease him. But that didn't matter. Not so long ago, he'd led a different life. But here, his diplomas were worthless. The taxi driver had almost forgotten the civil engineering school, the meetings in cellars, the posters hot off the press, the smell of the ink and the glue, the evening light, the doors always open, the scents of eucalyptus and charcoal, the endless discussions with his comrades from the union. When they'd arrested his mother, he hadn't hesitated. He'd ditched everything, even Sarah. He hardly ever thought about it. Except when he smelt certain odours, even if they didn't have any real connection to his homeland. He would smell them at the hairdresser's or in the garage where he left his cab. Sometimes, too, he would glimpse a face in profile, a woman's hair, and his guts would tighten. On the other hand, places and names were gradually being erased, and it was better that way.

Later, he would go home to see his mother. Her legs had become very swollen recently. She didn't complain. Patiently, swallowing her pain, she talked about the weather.

The manageress had finished tidying up and was now standing beside him. She put a hand on his shoulder. She smiled at the young man in the cap.

'All right, gentlemen, it's time.'

'I don't know if they're going to let us leave,' said the young guy, gesturing with his chin at the door.

The three teenagers had been standing there for more than ten minutes, like a litter of puppies waiting for their mother.

'What do they want?'

'Why not go and ask them?'

'Maybe they're waiting for the taxi,' the driver mused.

'You're kidding! They just ordered one coffee and three glasses of water.'

'They don't seem like bad kids anyway,' said the driver, putting on his coat.

'Yeah, they're just bored shitless,' agreed the guy in the cap.

'So what do you reckon they want?'

'They probably want to go dancing,' the driver said. 'It's that time of night. Lots of customers ask me to take them to nightclubs after the bars have closed.'

The two groups watched each other through the glass door, like fish and humans at an aquarium.

'Look, here they come.'

Jordan had just opened the door. He was careful to close it behind him before starting to speak.

'Evening.'

'We're closed, young man.'

'I know.' He lowered his head to avoid the three pairs of eyes staring curiously at him. 'We were wondering if you could . . . I mean, well, we wanted to know how much it would cost to take us to a house near Charmes.'

'That depends,' said the driver, leaving his barstool.

'It's my friends. They have to get home.'

'Do you have any money?'

'We've got about ten euros.'

'That won't get you far,' said the man in the cap.

The manageress smiled at Jordan's awkwardness. She could see the girls outside, waiting wide-eyed for the outcome of these last-ditch negotiations.

'Come on, let's go,' the driver said, heading towards the exit and slapping Jordan on the arm as he went past.

'I'll follow you on my bike,' Jordan explained.

'That's fine,' the driver said. Then, turning to the manageress: 'Just put the coffee on my tab.'

The manageress and the man in the cap couldn't help laughing when they saw the girls' reaction to the good news. The three teenagers followed the taxi driver, all of them disappearing into the darkness.

'All right,' said the manageress, pointedly looking at her watch.

'Yeah,' said the man, paying his bill. 'Oh, let me pay for his coffee too.'

'Thank you,' she said, putting the money into the till.

'Can't wait for my nice warm bed,' the man said, stretching his back.

The manageress walked him to the door, where they kissed each other goodbye. Then the man in the cap walked towards the Saint-Maurice church. The manageress was closing the metal shutters when her phone, which she'd left next to the coffee machine, made a chiming noise. He must have sent her a text, as he did every evening. He'd be back again tomorrow for a coffee, to warm himself up.

RITA

The alarm clock wakes her too early: five thirty in the morning. Rita had deliberately gone to bed early the previous night. March is almost over. Time to move up a gear.

She stands in the kitchen in an extra-large T-shirt and white cotton knickers. Behind her, Blondie pouts scornfully. The entire room is bathed in the soft, early-morning light as Rita slowly drinks a glass of orange juice. She tiptoes around on the icy tiles, her long legs tensed. From behind, she still looks like a teenager, except perhaps for the sort of creamy, alluring softness at the tops of her thighs, just below the fold of her buttocks.

From the room next door, she can hear the clicking sound that her dog always makes as it moves about, its metal chain collar knocking against its chest. The animal paces around the entire house, as it does every morning. This is its ritual, as soon as its mistress is out of bed. Its short, thick tail bangs against the wall as it goes. A reassuring sound.

Rita is sleepy, her eyes sticky with tiredness. All she wants is to go back to bed. Maybe it's time to stop this nonsense. The sun is rising already, casting sharp golden shapes on the floor. Outside, the grass is white and wreaths of mist are lazily uncoiling and dispersing. Rita checks the time on the microwave clock and makes up her mind.

By the front door, she puts on her leggings, her trainers, her Lycra gloves and a fleece. She takes the Walkman from her right-hand pocket and presses the ear buds into her ears. The mastiff stands there watching her, hoping as always that she's about to take it for a walk.

In the doorway, the light slaps her in the face and she feels like she's zipped open the winter. She stretches. She hasn't done this for months. Her knees crack as she does a few squats. She beats her arms like wings and blows her white breath into the radiant morning. She can feel the cold in her mouth, in her nostrils, all the way down to her belly. She shivers, her face drenched with sunlight, her eyes dazzled by the immaculate blue sky. There was a freeze last night and she can smell the cold now. The scent of her childhood. The cold of spring. She sets off as the first bars of 'Johnny And Mary' beat in her eardrums. She runs in time with the music. Her feet hit the tarmac as she moves, calm and straight-backed, hands covered by the sleeves of her fleece.

She runs in the middle of the road, the blue and black pine trees forming a guard of honour above her. The tarmac stretches out far ahead and she watches her shoes as they eat it up. She doesn't feel strong, though. She can feel the judder of each stride in her knees. Her thighs are heavy, her buttocks cumbersome. Her tensed stomach muscles ache. She still feels sleepy.

Rita has been doing this for almost twenty years now: as soon as the first glimmers of spring appear, she runs along this B-road, making amends for all that alcohol, those cigarettes, the dark moods. Running washes it all away.

Ten minutes pass, then twenty. Sunlight spills through the trees. The road slides like a treadmill under Rita's regular stride. She frees her hands from her sleeves, unhunches her shoulders. Starts to breathe more freely. Regrets fill her mind. This life she's leading: she has to change it. She stands up tall, perpendicular to the road, tracing a perfectly straight, smooth line, her progress mechanical, her long legs like the hands of a compass, so still and composed that it's hard to tell now if she is advancing or the road is retreating.

After twenty-five minutes, the road slopes upward, though she can't feel it any more. The village appears in the distance: fifteen houses scattered either side of the street. Here she makes a U-turn. The smell of cold fades, giving way to the forest's damp fragrance: humus, pine sap, the waterlogged rot of the black earth, a swarming, shadowy smell.

The smell that had tightened her throat when she came back from Montpellier.

She was twenty years old at the time, returning from the South with her tail between her legs. She'd left home in a rage: her parents were idiots, she was going to live her life as a free woman. She and her law lecturer had gone off together without really thinking things through. They could see the road through the floor of the Peugeot 104. Rita drove while her teacher talked. That guy always had something to say. It was Rita who'd wanted to leave. Montpellier? Why not? her lecturer had said. He had some friends down there – a nice, environmentally aware gay couple, who'd tried to start a publishing house and had ended up running a restaurant. It was the first time Rita had met activists who also liked a laugh. The men at college took themselves so seriously: chain-smoking, shirts unbuttoned, born too late and nostalgic for the glories of '68. They wanted to overturn everything, but they'd rather die than let a girl talk.

The two gays in question were called Bernard and Bernard, so it was a good thing that they had a sense of humour. They argued constantly, but other than that they were great fun to be around. Rita had kept up a correspondence with them for a long time afterward.

The people her lecturer knew belonged to a completely different world. Almost all of them had holiday homes, which was convenient. Ramatuelle, Nice, Antibes, Menton. They talked about housing prices and the Programme Commun while drinking rosé in the shade of pergolas. They used big words and thought about their holidays. The lecturer had a habit of departing their houses early in the morning, leaving behind a brief, friendly note explaining that he hadn't had time to clean up. This made him laugh, but Rita didn't find it so funny. One morning, he left her a brief, friendly note and their affair was over. It had lasted only a summer.

It was autumn when she got home. She remembers the smell of the earth and the rain; she remembers the early cold. She came back tanned and depressed. Her parents lectured her a bit, but not too much, and she started college again, though not for long. Soon after this, her father became ill and she regretted all those problems that had seemed insurmountable at the time: boyfriends he'd disapproved of, exams she'd failed, holidays ruined by rain or lack of money. When she saw her father asleep in bed, his soaked hair on the pillow, his lips drawn back revealing inexplicably long teeth, she understood that real life had begun. And that it probably wouldn't be much fun.

Now the pain becomes a background, a test of will. Rita thinks she could run for ever. Tomorrow, her legs and glutes will ache and her knees will creak, but for now she makes the law and her body obeys. She listens to Depeche Mode and feels like a church, a stadium, full of a rising roar.

Soon the slope flattens out and she enters the town. She sees drops of dew on the seats of parked tractors and combine harvesters. Outside the windows of farmhouses, the flowerpots are empty. All the shutters are open: the only people who live here are old, early to bed, early to rise. A voice calls from a first-floor window.

'Hey there!' shouts a tiny old man, his scrawny neck poking out of a checked shirt.

He raises his bowl of coffee to Rita's health. Rita waves.

'Go on, keep going, you can do it!' The old man chuckles.

He's there almost every morning and he always says the same stuff, like he's lining the route of the Tour de France again, egging on the riders. Rita's happy to see him. You never know, after all. It's been a long winter.

She rounds the fountain. Now she has to go back: the gentle slope up out of town and then the steep hillside. A sort of deep intoxication slowly overwhelms her. This is the best part, when tiredness starts to list its conquests, when Rita gives herself up to something vast and harrowing. Her throat tightens. She sees things far in the distance, from above, like a bird of prey. She can't hold her body straight any more. Now her stride becomes everything. She has to keep it up, to be hard on the pain.

Because Rita does not belong to the winning side. She knows this and no longer feels sad about it. When she was younger, at law school, she would feel humiliated by the sight of those girls in duffel coats, those elegant Frenchwomen with their proprietary airs and their perfect manners, as if they knew in advance that everything would be fine. Rita could only dream of apartments with moulding, of comforts she could justify to herself. Perhaps her anger was born back then, a fit of temper becoming a philosophy. Today, she knows she will never belong to that world of easy options and allusive violence. Her mother always worked, and she was earning less by the end than she did at the beginning. As for her father, he spent his life in grain silos and ended up in an iron lung – a common fate for those who spend thirty years breathing in grain dust. Whether she likes it or not, Rita belongs to this world where people die at work. She sees these people who keep their mouths shut, take Fate's blows, scrimp and save, and almost never complain. Just as long as they could end their days at home, the walls around them like a summary of their pain: thirty years of debt, followed by death. No matter what she does, this is her life.

Rita is not especially proud of this. She doesn't go around thinking that her family are the salt of the earth or anything like that. The good people are also bastards like you and me; that's just how it is. You could hardly even say they have mitigating circumstances, like the poor, the sick and the old, when they're stupid or evil. Nena comes from a Spanish republican family, so she doesn't speak ill of foreigners. But she could. That's the kind of thing that happens when you belong to Rita's world. Families who squabble as much as they love one another; parents who bitch about the boss but still turn up to work with a temperature of 102 degrees, who would never see a shrink but have nothing against healers, who talk about classical music and buy books at France Loisir. They get divorced like the others now, vote less and less, and imagine that they represent the norm, the average person.

Rita eats up the slope. She's breathing fast. Everything hurts and it feels fantastic. She seeks help from her Walkman. Kim Wilde comes on and the world is filled with a painful clarity. She can't keep going. She speeds up.

But Rita's race – those stubborn, troubled people who moan constantly about immigrants and taxes and speed limits, about transit camps and technocrats, about the cost of living and how crap everything is on TV, about snow in winter and heatwaves in summer – this race of hers won't let her go. And Rita climbs, the bit between her teeth, her back soaked with sweat, her hair unwashed, the stench of body odour and alcohol hovering around her like a halo. Her body still obeys her. She keeps going. At last, she sees the house. Once again, she's proved that she can live.

So she goes inside, taking off her clothes and dropping them onto the floor as she staggers to the bathroom and slumps beneath the handle of the shower. The water pours down on her, hot and heavy. She washes herself, her hands caressing her well-preserved curves. Her body is hard. She feels the pain quivering under the surface of the skin, like a small animal's speeding heart. She can still run. She has warded off her father's fate. She promises herself not to drink tonight. She feels like having sex. Soon, winter will be over.

RITA

It was a long drive and nobody in the car moved a muscle or spoke a word. Victoria because she was asleep, Rita and Laurent because they knew that in this weather – when it was snowing this hard – prudence was not enough. You needed something else. Reverence, perhaps. Certainly humility. They stared straight ahead at the road until it hurt.

When they got home, they caught their breath and Rita wanted Laurent to come and have a coffee at her house, to stick around for a while. It was nice, in fact, having him close like this. Of course she could manage on her own – she knew how to change a tyre or use a drill – but, still, Laurent was there. Then she saw the look on Victoria's face and she decided to drop the idea.

'Good night.'

'Yep, sleep well.'

'I'm knackered. She can sulk all she likes, I'm going straight to bed.'

* * *

When she opened the door, Rita whistled the same two notes she always whistled to call the dog. Usually, Baccala would immediately come charging at her legs and almost knock her to the ground. But not tonight. She whistled again, before turning and yelling at Victoria, who was dragging her feet several yards behind.

'Come on, hurry up! It's freezing!'

The inspector had a strange, nagging feeling, the kind you get when you leave your apartment and you feel certain you've forgotten something. She was groping for the light switch when she felt a draught of cold air brush past her neck. A draught coming from inside the house.

'Shit, the window,' she muttered.

Victoria finally arrived and Rita moved out of the way to let her past.

It was weird, though. Surely she hadn't gone out and left a window open – not in this weather. At last her fingers found the light switch and a hand grabbed her wrist. She yelled, 'Hey!' and in the blink of an eye she was on all fours in the middle of the living room. The door slammed violently behind her. She wanted to turn around. Light burst from various angles, flooding the entire room with its bright yellow glow. A monstrous man was standing in front of her.

'What the hell are you doing here? Where's the dog?'

'Shut your mouth.'

Victoria dropped her purse on the floor, her face deformed by fear. And then her eyes turned glassy and she wasn't there any more.

'Where's my fucking dog?'

'Lower your fucking voice!'

The man took two steps forward and slapped her as hard as he could. It made a sound like a whip crack and Rita fell back, dazed. The man stood over her, legs apart. In his left hand, he held a gun. Rita tried to get up but her head dropped back onto the carpet. The taste of blood in her mouth. She heard the dog scratching behind the kitchen door.

'What did you do to my dog?'

The man stepped over her and opened the kitchen door. The dog rushed to its mistress, whining and slobbering. In an instant Rita saw that one of its paws was thickly wrapped in bandages.

'What did you do to it?' she demanded.

'I bandaged it up.'

Rita nuzzled her head against the animal, cuddling it until the man pointed the gun at them. The inspector found herself staring directly into the mouth of the barrel, a perfectly circular well, black and indifferent. The gun's design gave her an impression of extreme speed.

'I'm going to spell things out for you,' announced the man, who kept sniffing as he spoke. 'If the girl tries to escape, I'll kill you. If you try to escape, I'll kill you. If you manage to get away, I'll go next door and kill your neighbour. Got it?'

Rita nodded. She stared at the man below the Colt's barrel. There was something familiar about that face of his, the forehead pockmarked with acne. When he stopped speaking his mouth hung slightly open and he looked like a grouper. She was almost sure she'd seen him somewhere before.

In the meantime, the man had shoved Victoria onto the sofa.

'You – stay there and don't move.'

The poor guy seemed completely out of it and there was a waxiness to his skin that made him look vaguely aquatic, like a drowned man. From this moment, Rita thought, every second is going to matter for the girl's future. She took a deep breath and tried to think clearly.

'Do you want money?'

'No. Well, yeah . . . Oh, just shut up.'

The big man was standing by the front door now, glancing through the high window. His gun was still aimed at Rita. That small black mouth with its look of false promise.

'We're going to wait for your neighbour to hit the sack. Everyone is going to stay calm. After that . . . we'll see.'

Rita kept petting the mastiff, then picked up its swaddled paw to get a better look.

'It cut itself by walking on glass,' the man hurried to explain. 'But I bandaged its paw.'

Since he seemed to be waiting anxiously for her response, Rita thanked him.

He shrugged. 'No problem.'

The first step was over. Now came the hardest part: the waiting.

'It's a nice dog. Maybe a bit too nice . . .'

The smile on the man's face was like the smile on the face of a rich man as he holds a door open for an old lady.

The minutes passed, slow as a glacier. From time to time, the intruder would take a look outside. He was nervous and silent, except for the constant sniffing. Victoria appeared paralysed by fear. Rita could see patches of damp sweat on her temples and her upper lips. Maybe she had a fever. In any case, that sort of reaction was not a good sign.

Rita had taken refuge at the bottom of the stairs where she was patting the dog, which had wedged itself between her knees.

She had to think. Keep calm and think. At the same time, what most surprised her was how little panic she felt. She was in a sort of resigned stupor, as if the worst had already happened. In fact, her overriding emotion was disgust. Watching that huge moron pacing around her house, she felt more or less the same way Steve McQueen feels in *Papillon* when he finds himself trapped on the leper island and the chief leper tells him that they sometimes bring in leper whores. An unimaginable revulsion.

'There's no point waiting, you know.'

'Shut up.'

'How long are you planning to wait?'

'That's for me to know. Now shut your mouth.'

'He's an insomniac.'

'What?' The man turned to glare at her.

'My neighbour. He stays up all night, drawing in his studio or watching TV. He doesn't sleep.'

The man's face relaxed. 'Ah . . .'

'What are you planning to do? Wait until morning? Anyway, if he hears a gunshot, he'll call the cops in a heartbeat.'

'We'll see. Now shut up.'

Rita obeyed. She could feel tiredness rise up the back of her neck, weigh down her eyelids. It occurred to her that this guy wasn't exactly the sharpest knife in the drawer, and that gave her a chance. As in a chess game, she tried to plot her strategy several moves ahead: what she was going to say, how he would respond, how she could manipulate him. But her thoughts weakened before they were strong enough to stand on their own; her memory stumbled and she started to yawn. Finally, after about half an hour, the man spoke again.

'So, what, this wanker never sleeps at all?'

'That's what I was trying to explain.'

'Fuck.'

Silence again. Soon, a strange sound came from the sofa; a high-pitched, intermittent sound. The dog's ears pricked up.

'What's she doing?'

'Sounds like she's grinding her teeth.'

'Tell her to stop it now.'

Rita crept over to the sofa, the man following her with his gun.

'I think she's asleep,' said Rita.

'You're kidding! How is that possible?'

'I dunno. Maybe this is how she reacts to stress.'

'Fantastic.'

Rita stroked the back of her hand across Victoria's cheek, but the girl did not react.

'So?' the man asked, annoyed.

'What do you mean?'

'I mean what the fuck are we going to do?'

'Surely you don't think I'm going to help you . . .'

He strode across the room and pointed the pistol at her skull. The feel of the metal was almost unbearably cold and solid against her skin.

'Wake her.'

'She's in shock. There's nothing I can do.'

'Listen carefully, you old bitch, because I'm not going to repeat this. Whatever happens, I'm leaving with that whore. If you don't help me, if you piss me off . . .'

He flipped his gun sideways, the way black guys do in American films, and started fake-shooting the whole room. He really did look like some overgrown kid with a sugar rush. He'd lost Rita at 'old bitch'. She stared defiantly at him.

'You stupid prick . . . What are you going to do? Shoot me? I can smell the booze on your breath. I saw your fingerprints on the bottle, the glass – all over the house, in fact. Haven't you ever watched *CSI: Miami*?'

'What?'

He let the hand holding the gun drop beside his thigh and stared daggers at her. Rita didn't look away. It was like one of those staring contests at school. In the end, he smiled. Rita had no time to savour her victory. Her head was filled with bees and then with black space and she fell back onto the floor, unconscious. Bruce had pistol-whipped the side of her head. He wished he'd broken the snobbish bitch's fucking neck. He felt better now.

Yes, he felt happy in fact. He was finally starting to relax.

PIERRE DURUY

Jimmy Comore had found the old man doing sudokus in his kitchen. The transistor radio was playing some west-coast jazz song that neither of them knew. Pierre Duruy had come across it by chance as he was twiddling the tuner. He'd sat there, lost in the staticky trumpet sound, pencil in hand, in the dim light, frowning with concentration through the pair of glasses perched at the end of his nose. He hadn't seen it coming.

Jimmy had come through the woods. He'd circled the house before going through the garage, the door of which was never closed. In the days before, he'd noticed the girl sneaking in and out that way. He'd been watching the Duruy family for almost a week now, and he was used to their ways. From the garage, he climbed the ladder to the first floor, a penlight between his teeth, a Glock in his belt. His mobile had started to buzz but Jimmy hadn't even blinked. He knew it was Victor – he'd deal with it later. Jimmy had given quite a lot of thought to the Ossip situation that day. He wasn't worried about it. It was more like a weight on his mind. Yet another problem to solve. He'd do what he needed to do later.

That day, after leaving the hotel where Victor and the girls were staying, he'd spent most of his time at a pool hall in the centre of Strasbourg,
spending almost fifty euros in two-euro coins on a rally-car game that he
knew by heart. He kept driving along the same tracks, the same circuits.
Each time, he became a little more perfect. After a while it didn't even
feel like he was driving and his mind was free. That was when he did his
best thinking. He reflected that killing Ossip did not pose a problem.
Afterward, however, he would have to deal with the others. They all
thought they were warlords but they acted like farm-boys. Of course
Jimmy could kill them all, but others would appear in their places. It was
like trying to stop the sea.

Maybe he should just get rid of Victor instead. That would be quicker.

In any case, he needed to start by finding Victoria and either regaining possession of her or making an example of her. Nothing had gone
right since the kidnapping.

Before heading to the Duruy farm, Jimmy had gone for a Big Mac
with fries and a Sprite. Then he'd asked the guy behind the counter to fill
his Thermos with black coffee. After that, he'd gone to the Farm. In the
first days of his stakeout, he'd been freezing, so then he'd bought the
necessary equipment: snow boots, dry suit, even a waterproof sleeping
bag.

Next, he'd waited a couple of hours, leaning against a pine tree, in
the damp silence of the woods. He thought about old Duruy. The countryside was full of would-be gangsters, spotty kids who sold a bit of hash
and imagined they were running cartels. Jimmy had done some digging,
though, and he knew that old Duruy was a different breed altogether.
Like Jimmy, he'd gone to war, made quite a lot of money, been in business
with serious people. Jimmy had spotted him on several occasions. The
old man hardly ever left the house but from time to time he would nip
outside for some fresh air, wearing wellies and smoking a cigarillo, the
end glowing red in the evening wind. He would take a few steps, cough
and hawk up phlegm, look around the junk-strewn land, then go back
inside. Pierre Duruy was a shadow of his former self, but Jimmy knew he
had to be careful all the same.

When Jimmy finally appeared in the kitchen, Glock in hand, the old man barely blinked. He just removed the burned-out cigarillo stub from between his lips and said: 'Are you a friend of Bruce?'

Jimmy didn't answer. He sat facing the old man and placed his gun flat on the plastic tablecloth.

Pierre Duruy turned down the volume on the radio. 'You're here because of Bruce, right?'

Jimmy nodded. He seemed distracted. His eyes roamed the room, surprised that anyone could live like that. The old man pushed a box of cigarillos towards him but Jimmy shook his head.

'Bruce isn't here. He doesn't live here any more.'

'I know. What about the girl?'

'What girl?'

Jimmy's handsome face froze. He'd been hoping that the old man would spare him this kind of run-around.

Duruy shrugged, then admitted the truth. 'She's not here either. There's nobody here.'

'Where did she go?'

'I don't know. I was the one who set her free. Bruce had nothing to do with that.'

'Okay.'

The young man seemed to prefer it that way. Duruy admired his calmness, the impassivity of his face. Oddly, he was tempted to put his hands on that dark face. Maybe it was the scar on his head. Pierre felt an instinctive desire to run his fingers along it, to feel its contours, to find out whether it was soft or hard. You have some strange ideas, he told himself, rubbing his hands to rid himself of them. His skin made a sound like parchment.

'I need to know where the girl is,' the young man said.

'I can't help you, son. She left.'

Jimmy licked his lips. His tongue was surprisingly pink against the darkness of his skin. 'I can't just leave like that,' he said apologetically.

Pierre avoided looking at the Glock on the tablecloth. As soon as the young man had entered the kitchen, he'd understood. He'd seen the way he handled his gun, the discretion, the experience. A few years before, Pierre might have tried knocking the table over, but he knew there was no point now. The young man himself looked like a weapon. And yet Pierre couldn't help liking him. There was something familiar about him.

'Did she leave a long time ago?'

'Yes.'

'And you let her go?'

Pierre shrugged again.

'You need to tell me where your grandson is now.'

'I can't.'

After a moment's hesitation, Jimmy acknowledged that he understood.

He still wasn't showing any impatience. The only time he'd shown any hint of aggression had been when Pierre had pretended not to understand. Everything was all right now. The young man smiled and the old man returned that smile. They felt like two travellers far from home who'd bumped into each other on a railway station platform. There was nothing else, there was only them. They recognised each other.

'Would you like a drink?' Pierre asked.

'All right. Something hot.'

'I'll make us some tea.'

Pierre put a pan of water to boil.

'It's quiet here,' Jimmy observed.

Soon the water started to bubble. Pierre got out two cups, added teabags and sugar without asking the young man if he wanted any, and poured the tea

'What are you planning to do?' the old man asked, sitting down again.

The young man, who had lifted the cup to his lips, did not have time to reply before the phone started ringing. At this time of day, Pierre knew it could be only one person: his friend the gendarme. He'd given him the Saab's registration number after the accident because he wanted to know the identity of the woman who'd picked up the girl. Since then, he hadn't heard back. The timing wasn't ideal. The old man didn't want to answer the call. If he found out the woman's name, he might be tempted to give it to the young man, to save himself, to shift the blame. Cowardice is a temptation. He preferred not to put himself in the way of temptation.

Jimmy gave him no choice. He picked up the Glock and gestured with his chin at the telephone, which was on the wall near the door. It rang twice more before Pierre picked up the receiver. He took so long to get there that he was almost surprised to hear a voice at the other end. Maybe he'd been expecting it to be the young man himself.

'Hello? . . . No, I was in the cellar . . . No, no, that's all right, I was expecting your call . . . Yes, thank you.'

Pierre opened a dresser drawer and took out a pencil and notebook. Jimmy watched him.

'Yes, I'm ready.'

As he noted down the name, he repeated each letter out loud and said, 'Uh-huh . . . Uh-huh . . .' At the end of the call, he thanked the other person again, then said reassuringly: 'Yes, yes, everything's fine, there's nothing to worry about. Just a minor accident, nothing serious.' At last he brought the conversation to an end: 'Yes, that's right. Talk to you soon.' And then, holding the notebook, he sat back down and carefully tore out the page containing Rita's name and number. He folded it twice and slipped it into his shirt pocket.

'Who was that?' asked the young man.

'Nobody. Just a friend.'

Jimmy smiled, as if the old man was pushing his luck.

'All right . . .'

Jimmy liked it here. The warmth from the purring stove, the silence for miles around, the feeling of being cocooned . . . A cat slid between his legs and curled up near the stove. Jimmy almost felt like chatting for a while, asking the old man a few questions. But then he heard a muffled sound from upstairs, like something moving. The two men looked up. Jimmy held the Glock across the table, the barrel pressing against the old man's chest. The old man took a tight grip on the gun. His hand didn't tremble. The tea was cold. The cat ran away and Jimmy squeezed the trigger. The sound of the gunshot lit up the room. The wall behind

Pierre's head splattered with blood and bits of bone and lung. The old man died with his eyes open, his chin falling onto his chest. There was a fist-sized hole in his back where the bullet had exited his body.

A woman started yelling upstairs. She wasn't yelling with fear, though, just complaining about the racket they were making. Jimmy grimaced. He didn't feel like walking around this weird old draughty house. But he knew he had to. Maybe Victoria was here after all. So, back to the wall, gun in hand, he crept upstairs. The old man's blood was all over the Glock, his hand, his forearm. He could feel it warm and thick on his skin. The voice continued moaning and accusing, a woman's voice, nagging and unpleasant. Suddenly there was another voice, young, probably the Duruy girl's. She was very close. She must have just got home.

Jimmy decided to get out of there. He hurried back downstairs. As he passed the kitchen he saw that the old man had fallen off his chair. Jimmy took the time to put him back in place. He'd shot him in the heart, through the pocket where the old man had put that slip of paper a few seconds earlier.

JORDAN LOCATELLI

Lydie and Nadia got into the taxi, leaving enough space between them for a third person even though Jordan had decided to follow them on his bike. The driver asked them if they still wanted to go to Charmes but got no response. The silence in the back seat was even frostier than the weather outside. All the same, he set off slowly, watching the two of them in his rear-view mirror.

They had no manners. Here he was, doing them a favour, and they couldn't even be bothered to reply to him. Through the back window he saw the motorbike's single light swell and shrink. The kid was doing his best to stay close to the taxi, but it wasn't easy with all that snow.

The driver put the radio on, turned up the heat, and headed towards Charmes. That was where Motorbike Boy had told him to go, after all. What did it matter, anyway? He almost regretted his decision to help them now. He should have gone back to the city centre to find some real clients. Although the pickings were slim at that time of night. Drunk men, sexually frustrated because they hadn't pulled; small groups of tipsy girls laughing too loudly; a couple, quickly formed amid the racket of a bar, who would have to untangle their misunderstandings between the sheets on Saturday morning. But he was used to all those idiots, and at least they paid full fare.

He glanced into the mirror again. Each girl was staring out of her own side window, as if mesmerised by the passing landscape. The dark-haired girl had sharp features, slightly blurred by fatigue. In profile, she looked a bit like those women from the north of Italy: beak nose and full, dark lips. The blonde was the exact opposite: a round, radiant face, a button nose so tiny it looked almost silly, tangled hair, and two little folds in her neck like a toddler. The driver didn't like the way they were behaving, of course, but their youthfulness was appealing. He had his old mother, the pains of exile, the price of petrol, unhinged customers, like the one he'd taken to the hospital earlier that night ... and then, suddenly, the strange little miracle of a teenage girl. A teenage girl was such a simple design: a quick, freehand sketch, no crossings-out, no shading. Whenever the driver saw them – walking the pavements, riding bicycles in summer, wherever – he was always slightly taken aback. It was like the world was always starting again. With their too-long hair, their phoney dramas, the boots they'd been eyeing up for the past two weeks, without which life wouldn't be worth living, with all their wonderful razzmatazz, teenage girls had the power to make him feel better, and a bit worse too, since he would never again be that stupid, wide-awake kid on his bike, whose figure he could see pulsating in the rear window as he moved closer or fell further behind.

'Well, you got what you wanted anyway,' muttered the blonde, who was definitely not thinking she had her whole life ahead of her.

'What?' snapped the brunette, swivelling to face her. 'What are you on about?'

'I know what you're up to.'

'What are you talking about?'

'Yeah, right,' said the blonde, with a knowing laugh.

'Where do you get off being jealous? You've been blanking him for months.'

'So?'

'Anyway, I don't give a toss about that guy.'

'That's not the problem.'

'What is your problem, then?'

'The problem is that you follow me around like a little dog and I'm starting to get sick of it.'

'Are you high or what?'

The brunette seemed genuinely shocked. The other one was staring contemptuously at her, as if she were a stain on a brand-new pair of jeans. Suddenly the driver didn't know what to do with himself. He lowered his head. All those touching thoughts he'd been having about the miraculous nature of teenage girls were forgotten.

'Stop here.'

'What?' the driver asked.

'Stop,' hissed the blonde. 'We're not far from my place now. He can give me a ride.'

As the driver was struggling to understand what she was saying, the blonde girl half opened the door.

The driver slammed on the brakes and the boy on the bike almost crashed into the taxi. The bike stalled. The blonde got out of the car and ran towards him. The driver and the brunette watched this unfold in silence, like spectators in a cinema. Outside, the night was frozen and soundless. They could see the white vapour pouring from the girl's mouth as she hurriedly said something. The brunette stared at the two of them, her dark eyes like mountain lakes. When she saw the boy nod, she turned and told the driver to set off.

'Are you sure?'

The words emerged from her throat with difficulty: 'Please. I have to go home.'

The driver saw the blonde girl hop on the back of the motorbike. She wasn't wearing gloves or a helmet. She put her hands under the boy's anorak to keep them warm. The taxi driver stepped on the accelerator and drove the other girl home. She wasn't crying, but she might as well have been.

RITA

When Rita regained consciousness, she thought she just had a massive hangover. She was lying on the sofa, her head was a mess, and her eyes were puffy. There was a taste of lead and blood in her mouth. It was only when she felt her jeans sliding down her thighs that she realised something was off.

She opened her eyes and blinked in the dazzle. Suburban trains were speeding from one side of her head to the other. The spotty guy was pulling her jeans down, his tongue sticking out of his mouth as he frowned with concentration. Rita tried to free herself but her jeans were round her ankles now and when she pushed off the armrest all she managed to do was fall off the sofa onto the carpet. The bodybuilder watched as she tried to crawl away, her thighs naked. That bastard was enjoying the view.

'Hang on a second,' he said, sounding surprised.

He stepped over her and stood in the way, then dangled a set of keys in front of her face.

'You're wasting your time. All the doors are locked.'

Rita tried to retreat towards the French windows.

'Give up, will you? You pissed yourself. I was just trying to take off your jeans.'

Rita checked. Her jeans were dry, and so were her knickers. And yet he'd sounded perfectly sincere when he told her that.

'I'm not going to hurt you. Just stay calm and nothing bad will happen.'

She wondered how long she'd been unconscious. She looked at the digital clock on the DVD player. It was gone midnight. She couldn't have lost more than half an hour. And she still had her jeans; she pulled them back up while she had the chance. He couldn't have done much, could he? But, fuck, how could she be sure? She shuddered. And what about Victoria?

'Where is she?' Rita demanded, trying to stand up.

No sooner was she upright, though, than dizziness made her wobble pathetically.

'Don't worry about her,' the man replied. 'I locked her into the bathroom. Nothing can happen to her.'

'What do you mean? Why the bathroom? What the hell's she doing in the bathroom? There isn't even a lock on the door.'

'I don't know,' he said impatiently. 'She was acting weird. She was starting to creep me out.'

'What?'

'She was talking in her sleep. I didn't want to have to deal with that. I tied her up with the belt from your dressing-gown, so she can't get away. Same with the dog.'

It was true: Rita could see the poor mastiff tied up under the staircase, its mouth taped shut. It was whining half-heartedly. Rubbing her temples, Rita found a scab of dried blood in her hair. Her head was spinning and she felt nauseous. She just had to hope that it was nothing too serious.

The man started laughing. 'You should see yourself!' he said, pointing to his own face, from ear to chin. 'Your face is all the colours of the rainbow. It's pretty cool.'

'I'm so glad you like it.'

'Don't complain – you left me no choice. Try anything else and see what you get.'

Rita looked down. There was something odd and disturbing about the way the guy behaved: the childlike aspect, the lies, the mood swings. How was she supposed to act with someone so unstable? He was standing next to the window again, watching the house next door.

'Doesn't your twat of a neighbour ever sleep?'

'I told you. He sometimes stays up all night.'

'What's his fucking problem?'

'What do you expect me to say? We all have reasons not to sleep.'

He turned and stared at her, trying to work out what she meant by that. Rita felt really unwell.

'I need an aspirin and I need to put something on the wound.'

'Stay where you are. I told you, the bathroom's occupied.'

'I have some paracetamol in the drawer of my bedside table.'

'What – you've got a blocked nose now?'

He barked this, but his anger seemed to die out as quickly as it had flared up. In fact, he suddenly looked quite pleased with himself. 'All right, then. I'll go with you. We should get some rest anyway.'

Rita preferred not to wonder what he meant by this. She needed to buy some thinking time. The man grabbed the Colt again and waved it at her, signalling that she should walk ahead of him. Rita hesitated. She'd just thought of something: the clay-pigeon-shooting rifle. It was under the sofa.

'Come on, get a move on!'

He walked straight at her. She had no choice but to obey. As she went upstairs she could hear him sniffing just behind her. She speeded up, taking the steps two by two despite the pneumatic drill inside her head. Upstairs, her visitor stopped in front of a rattan flowerpot that contained a dying rubber plant. He pulled out the carbon stake and started waving it around like a riding crop, whipping the air with it a few times before pretending to hit Rita. She turned to face him, teeth gritted. 'Don't you dare hit me.'

He struck her on the hips. The pain sprang up in one precise spot before spreading through her body, like a wave, and bringing tears to her eyes.

'Now hurry up, you're starting to get on my nerves.'

Inside the bedroom Rita found her letters torn to pieces on the floor. She knelt down and gathered a few scattered scraps.

'I'm warning you, don't give me a hard time about this.' He whipped the air with his stick again, delighted by the sound it made. 'Come on, let's go!'

Rita stood up without a word and reached the bedside table where she kept her medicine.

'You'd better change while we're here.'

She pretended not to have heard him.

'Change your clothes. I can smell the piss from here.'

To swallow the pills, she drank a mouthful of water from the bottle that she always kept beside her bed. The bodybuilder collapsed onto the duvet, very close to her, and bounced happily on the mattress. From that distance she could see the reflection of the bedside lamp on his head, his skin shining like a slice of vacuum-packed ham. He poked her in the ribs with his stick.

'Jeans, knickers, socks. Change 'em all.'

'I don't need to change.'

'Fucking change!'

He poked her harder and Rita took a step back. Before she could move out of reach he whipped her left thigh with the plant stake. Rita gasped. She felt a jet of acid reflux at the base of her throat.

'Your underwear must be soaked. Come on, no need to be prudish. I've got a little sister, I've seen it all before.'

After uttering these words he looked briefly dumbstruck. He tried to whip her again but she was too far away now and the stake whistled through the empty air.

'Come on, get on with it. We're not going to spend the whole night here!'

Rita didn't move. The intruder's appearance had changed. His face was very pale and his eyes were blank, like a fish's eyes. Rita found no hope in those eyes.

She turned away from him and undid her zip before taking off her boots, then she pulled down her jeans, exposing her knickers and her thighs. She tried to control the trembling in her limbs. She had to concentrate. Focus on breathing. Inhale, exhale. She had to think. He wasn't thinking. He was just behind her. Fish eyes.

She took off her sweater now, to delay the moment when she'd have to remove her underwear. What did she have in her favour? For a start it was two against one, although Victoria was tied up and probably about as threatening as a cooked prawn at this point. There was also the rifle. That was a big plus. Then there was the fact that this moron had been drinking or taking drugs. Beyond the house, Laurent could be an ally, of course. Although not much of an ally given that he generally fell asleep as soon as his head touched the pillow and he'd probably been snoring for the last hour at least. The thing about leaving the lights on all night was just a trick to deter burglars. After watching too many true-crime TV shows, her ex had become as cautious as an old lady. That was why he'd been so determined to install an alarm system in her house. 'I'd rather be kidnapped by hordes of Gypsies,' Rita had told him, a joke that left a bitter aftertaste as she thought about it now.

Overall, the rifle seemed like the simplest and most effective solution. She just had to get back to the living room.

She took off her T-shirt and then she paused, eyes riveted to the floor, as during a school medical visit. Inside her mind she was simulating her escape: what she would do, the exact sequence of movements and spaces. Did she dare? Three strides to reach the door. He'd have time to shoot her before she got out of the room. Deep down, though, she didn't think he'd be capable of that. But he could certainly hurt her. Her body was shaking uncontrollably.

'Now your knickers.'

She didn't react. Behind her, the bed base had started squeaking regularly. Rita was still staring at the carpet. She hadn't taken off her socks yet. They would offer her another brief reprieve, she thought, as in a game of strip poker.

'Come on, get 'em off!'

She felt shivers all the way up her thighs. He put the sole of his Timberland boot on her bottom and gave her a shove. The humiliation made her blush.

'Hurry up! What's the big deal anyway?'

'Go fuck yourself.'

She hissed the words between her teeth, almost inaudibly. She heard him moving around on the bed. Then there was a whistling sound instantly followed by searing pain. Sweat poured down her face and she almost fell to her knees. He'd whipped her with the stake on the fleshy part of her thigh. Her lips were trembling now and her throat was so tight that she knew she wouldn't be able to hold back the tears for long. Under the sofa, she reminded herself, the rifle is loaded. And a good thing, too, because I'm not just going to threaten him with it. As soon as I have it in my hands, I'm pressing the trigger. And I hope it blows that piece of shit in half.

This idea comforted her as she slid her knickers down her legs. She had goose-bumps running from her inner thighs up to her lower back. A sensation of cold, as if death had just moved between her legs.

'Stop,' the man ordered her.

And she had to stay like that, her ankles shackled by the underwear. Leaning forward, fully exposed, she could feel the man's fish eyes on her. He was practically body-searching her with those eyes. At last she cracked, kicking away her knickers and quickly grabbing another pair from among the pile that he'd dumped out of the drawer. She put them on as fast as she could, contorting her body and rolling the cotton over her skin. The whole exhibition hadn't lasted more than thirty seconds but she was left with the impression that he'd opened her up like a pomegranate.

'You've got nice legs for a woman your age.'

She heard him get off the bed and she turned around to see what he was up to. He was already very close. And the wall was right behind her: there was no escaping him.

'I'd like to see if the rest is up to the same standard.'

He was speaking playfully now, as if she'd just invited him up for one last drink after a particularly enjoyable third date.

'It's funny how slow you are. Why do I have to repeat everything ten times?'

As a kid, Rita had spent her holidays in the countryside: her parents rented some outbuildings at a farm in the Lot. The owner had two abominable red spaniels. She must have been six or seven years old when those two dogs tried to attack her for the first time, strangling themselves as they tried to strain beyond the lengths of their chains. After that she'd used various detours and tricks to avoid them during their stay at the farm. The owner had explained to her that it was her fear that encouraged them to attack. Back then, Rita had not known what to do with this information. But she had not forgotten it, and she tried to use it to her advantage now, relaxing the grip of the claws of terror so that she could speak with authority.

'It's over.'

Make-up and sweat were mixed up on her face now, forming a strange landscape, like an oil spill on a sea of milk. Her feverish red eyes were floating on this surface. The man reached out his hand to touch her face, to wipe away the dribble of mascara beneath her eye. Rita turned her face away.

'We've got time, you know.'

'It's over. You can do what you want – it's over now.'

He pressed her against the wall, tapping her thigh with his carbon stake. Beyond a certain level, fear became a hazy sensation, a sort of weightlessness.

'You should leave now. You still can. Just go downstairs and out of the door.'

He slid two fingers inside the collar of her T-shirt, stretching it to gauge its elasticity.

'I want you to show me everything.'

But just as he was about to tear off her clothes, he was surprised by the sound of a chain coming from the stairs. A sort of swinging, clinking sound. In the blink of an eye, he shoved Rita deeper into the room, dropped his stick and aimed the Colt at the door. He was breathing hard. It was his turn to sweat bullets.

The dog appeared in the doorway. It was limping. It still had bits of tape stuck to its mouth – remnants of the gag it had bitten through. The cloth leash hung from its collar, still drenched with drool. It had chewed through that too. After finding the two humans in the room, the dog sat down and dutifully barked twice.

'Fucking hell, that stupid dog! I almost shat myself.'

Baccala didn't usually come upstairs – partly because the bedroom was off limits, but mostly because he preferred not to expend any effort at all unless it would lead to being fed. Some overpowering instinct must have provoked him to climb the stairs on his three working legs.

Rita clapped her hands and the dog waddled over to her. She began rubbing and scratching it affectionately.

'That's a good dog, that is,' said the man, clearly touched. He moved closer to cuddle the animal.

Rita could feel the thick steel chain of the dog's collar beneath her fingertips. Without thinking, she searched for the clasp. The man knelt down next to the dog, stroking it with his free hand. Several times, his hand brushed Rita's. She found the fastener. She was trembling uncontrollably.

'What's the matter with you? Calm down, for God's sake.'

By the time he understood, it was too late. The chain slid across the black fur. He tried to grab hold of it but Rita smashed the steel collar violently into his face. Eyes wide, he brought a hand to his lips and the blood spurted between his fingers. Rita took a step back and hit him again, harder this time. Bruce yelled as he curled up on the floor and she whipped him again, with all her strength. After a few seconds the inspector jumped onto the bed, trying to reach the door, but the man was on his feet again in a flash and he managed to grab her ankle. Rita stretched out lengthways but he'd let go of her now. Turning, she saw him holding his face in both hands as if afraid that it might pour through his fingers. The blood was falling in thick heavy drops onto the carpet.

'You bitch,' the man shouted. 'You fucked up my eye!'

Rita thought about running downstairs now but decided to take advantage of his shock. Standing firm, she started whipping him with the chain as hard as she could, raining blows down on his head and the hands he was using to shield himself. The chain whistled above his head before landing with a repulsive, fleshy crack. Soon the man began to beg her but she kept going until the walls of the room were splattered with red stripes. Rita's face was painted for war.

Then she ran into the corridor. She was thinking about the rifle. The staircase was just there, at the end of the corridor. On the way she opened the bathroom door to check. Victoria sat tied up on the floor, completely naked. She was swaying back and forth and she didn't even notice Rita.

'Hey! Sweetie, look at me,' said Rita.

The girl kept swaying.

'Shit.'

She thought about untying her but the bodybuilder had left the room now. Rita could hear him spitting, groaning, bellowing in the corridor. She just had time to glimpse him before she hurtled downstairs. The features of his face had been obliterated. He was drowning in blood. Wounds like lips were open on top of his head. And then there was that bone-white eye.

'Bitch!' the man yelled, reaching out with one hand.

Rita's socks skidded on the oak stairs and she fell onto her elbows, rolling head over heels before coming to a halt, her body lying motionless across the steps. She could hear the man's breathing getting closer. Or maybe it was the dog. She wasn't in pain but she couldn't move. From where she lay she could see one corner of the sofa. The rifle.

She felt warm drops landing on her. He was right there.

JORDAN LOCATELLI

Jordan didn't hesitate for a second when she told him to leave his bike. He abandoned it next to a tree in the middle of the woods. He padlocked it, but he might just as easily have forgotten. His time had come at last and he no longer cared about material things.

'Follow me.'

He followed her. Lydie walked fast despite her high heels. He offered to carry her, since it was snowing.

'Don't worry, it's not far.' She took his hand but it was more to hurry him up than anything else.

As soon as Lydie had got out of the taxi, he'd done everything she wanted. It was a shame in a way because he almost wondered if he preferred her friend. She lingered in his thoughts now. It was strange: before tonight Nadia had been one of those girls who, for Jordan, didn't even count. The annoying ones, the boring ones, the ones who already look like tired mothers, the studious ones, the ugly ones. He'd never imagined going to the cinema with a girl like that – what would have been the point? Except that now, running behind Lydie through a forest of fifty-foot pines, he couldn't stop thinking about her. Nadia. He wished he could chat with her, touch her hair. She had a mouth like Vienna bread. And she was really nice. His heart felt like it was beating the wrong way.

And now they had to go to the Duruys' house. Lydie's grandfather wasn't exactly easy-going, but it was her brother who worried Jordan. Bruce Duruy had gone to their school a few years earlier, leaving behind mixed memories to say the least. Nobody really knew what had happened – something bad involving a teacher – but anyway he'd been expelled and had ended up in a place for special cases. It was probably no big deal: the school was full of social misfits. But Bruce did come back occasionally, whether to give his sister a ride home or because he was going out with some fifteen-year-old girl, easier prey than women his own age. In any case, everybody tried to avoid him, with his weirdly small pupils and his monstrous shoulders. Jordan could do without bumping into him at two in the morning.

Lydie went inside first and he waited for her signal before joining her two minutes later, going through the garage. She held the door open for him and he went past without touching her, on tiptoe. She left him in the dark for a moment. With the cold and the fear, he felt a sudden need to piss. He didn't dare use the light on his phone. He just had to deal with the darkness, the sound of the wind, the smell of diesel and damp cement. At one point he had the impression that a shadow had passed behind him and he shivered. He thought about Lydie, about her breasts. He was going to spend the night at her house. It wasn't the most reassuring thought he'd ever had.

Ten minutes ticked by, very slowly. In that brief eternity his brain came up with all sorts of paranoid ideas. Finally a square of light appeared above his head, then Lydie's shadow, and he climbed a shaky ladder to join her.

'Ssh,' she said, closing the trapdoor. 'I'll take you to my room. But you've got to be totally silent.'

She turned off the light and held his hand. He had to follow her now. And he did, through long, damp, pitch-black corridors. Downstairs he could hear voices – a group of people, or maybe just a television. Jordan put all his trust in Lydie. Her hands were tiny. After a while she stopped moving and he felt her fingers digging into his palms. They stood completely still. Maybe someone was about to find them. Jordan's imagination was running wild. Soon beams of light showed the outline of a closed door. The night was fading.

'We're nearly there,' she whispered, her body close to his. 'Just don't make a sound.'

They took a few further steps across the freezing, creaking house. And suddenly there was a huge bang, from God knew where, followed by a booming echo. The noise was so loud it almost hurt. Lydie stopped dead and Jordan bumped into her.

They were motionless for a moment, face to face. Jordan could feel her heart hammering against his chest. He put his nostrils close to Lydie's hair. It smelt of outdoors, of mammals. They stood there together in silence. In suspense. Nothing happened. The silence was vast, an underwater silence. Jordan felt her round bottom against him. It was softer than he'd expected. She started rolling her hips against his crotch, or maybe it was imagination. He was frightened and his dick was hard. Lydie's breathing seemed to change. She took his right hand and placed it on her belly. He closed his eyes and nuzzled his face into her neck. His hand moved under her sweater and he felt her skin, the shape of her navel, the soft hair beneath it.

A woman's voice began to shriek, very close.

'It's okay, it's just my mother,' Lydie whispered. 'Follow me.'

Jordan had recoiled at the sound but Lydie held his wrist and pulled him towards a half-open door dimly illuminated by the bluish light of a TV screen.

'This is it, this is my room.'

The woman's voice kept moaning. She sounded like a child playing with a toy aeroplane, the engine whining louder and then quieter as it came closer and flew away in never-ending loops. Lydie sat him down behind her bed and they had a whispered conversation.

'What was that noise?'

'I don't know. My grandfather shoots stuff for fun sometimes.'

'In the house?'

'No. I don't know.'

'And your mother?'

'Stop freaking out. I told you it's fine.'

Jordan froze, vaguely offended.

'She's always whining but she never gets out of bed. And my grandfather hardly ever comes upstairs. Stay here, okay?'

'Where are you going?'

'I'll be back in a minute.'

He looked around at her bedroom. He'd thought she was cold and distant but her room was smothered under the weight of cuddly toys, posters and all sorts of girly crap. Just before she closed the door she winked at him. He smiled. She was pretty great, wasn't she?

He tried to overhear the conversation between Lydie and her mother. The mother's voice was a plaintive murmur, her daughter's responses higher-pitched, annoyed. The mother went wah-wah-wah and the daughter ssh-ssh-ssh. It went on like that for a while. He almost forgot the huge bang they'd heard earlier, this mess of a house. But, shit, if the grandfather was shooting his gun inside, that wasn't a good sign. At last it sounded like Lydie had won the argument. A door clicked shut. It was over.

But Lydie didn't come back straight away. Jordan didn't know what to do. He felt uneasy, afraid that at any moment he'd be discovered by someone from this crackpot family. Without really knowing why, he found himself under the bed. The carpet was disgusting, the springs of the old bed base thick with dust. All the same he felt comforted, just as he used to when he was a little kid and he'd lie in ambush under his own bed, with a rifle, a flask of strawberry cordial and a pair of plastic binoculars so he could spy on the enemy. It was warm under the bed. He could hear water running through the pipes. Lydie must be taking a shower or having a pee. He heard a toilet flush, confirming his theory. All the same he thought he'd look like a bit of an idiot if Lydie came in and found him hiding there. He crawled out and found that his black sweatshirt was now covered with dust. Just then, Lydie came into the room.

'Psst.'

Jordan's head emerged from behind the bed. She smiled.

'It's okay now.'

'So what was that noise earlier?'

'Who cares?'

She'd changed her clothes too. She was wearing a pair of velour jogging bottoms and a white cami. Plus slippers. She was going to bed – these were her pyjamas. And he was here. Whoa . . .

She walked towards him, smelling of mint and coconut. She was holding a bottle of water that she put on the windowsill before sitting cross-legged on the floor. The light from the TV screen flickered on her round shoulders.

'We've got Coke, too, but my grandfather's in the kitchen and I don't want him to have a go at me.'

'He's not asleep yet?' Jordan looked at his watch and saw that it was nearly half past two.

'Old people don't sleep much anyway, but since he discovered sudoku he basically never goes to bed.'

Jordan tried to pay attention to what she was saying – in other words, not to dive head first into her cleavage – but he'd noticed from the sway of her tits when she walked across the room that she wasn't wearing a bra. This thought was like a bit of sticking plaster at the end of his finger.

'Are you sure you don't mind me sleeping here?'

'Nah, it'll be fine. They'll never know.'

'Do you do this a lot?'

He immediately regretted asking this question. Lydie acted as if she hadn't heard it. She had a jewellery box in her lap and she was methodically emptying it.

'My mother had a go at me for about ten minutes just now. If it's not one thing, it's another – school, going out at night, what I eat, everything. It's like she can't go a day without driving me mad. God, I can't wait to get out of this shithole.'

'She won't come in, will she?'

'You've asked me that about ten times already. I told you, it's fine.'

'Okay, cool.'

She looked at him. Jordan was trying to find an expression that went with the idea of being cool. Lydie smiled. He was sort of cute in fact. He wouldn't be much use if she wanted someone to beat up one of her exes or carry her on his back but he wasn't bad-looking, at least not in this light. Or maybe she was just tired . . . And he was taking his time, which was pretty rare. A shy boy, with long lashes. There were worse things in life.

In the jewellery box, beneath the compartments filled with fake pearls and cheap rings, she opened a false bottom where she'd hidden her rolling papers and a thumb-sized piece of hash.

'Have you got a fag?'

Since the episode in the headmaster's office, Jordan had been practising his smoking skills. He handed her a Chesterfield and she started mixing the hash with tobacco.

'Here,' she said, pushing the jewellery box towards him with the unrolled spliff on top. 'You can roll it – I'm no good at that.'

Jordan did his best but he was all thumbs. In the end Lydie took the spliff back from him and began to roll it herself. The images on the TV screen bathed everything in a soft, flickering light. As she leaned over, fully focused on the task in hand, Jordan stared down her low-cut top. He could see all the way to her belly button. Lydie caught him looking and sat up. It was almost worse when she did that.

'Here you go,' she said, handing him the two-paper spliff she'd constructed.

They opened the window to smoke. The wind blew into the small, overheated bedroom, billowing the smoke from the joint and the incense paper that was burning in the ashtray. Lydie had put her anorak on and she held it tightly closed around her neck to keep herself warm. They were sitting on the windowsill, facing each other. Lydie slid her feet under Jordan's bum.

They didn't say much while they smoked.

Jordan really wanted to see her naked. He was trying to come up with an idea to get her out of her pyjamas.

BRUCE

'Yeah, it's me.'

'For God's sake, what's the matter with you? You're calling me now? Have you seen what time it is?'

'I had a problem.'

'The girl?'

'Yeah, there was a problem.'

'Did you find her?'

Bruce's voice breaks. It's hard not to cry at this precise moment. Bruce is sitting in the snow. His face is gaunt. He's cleaned himself up but there are still traces of blood under his nails, around his ears, stuck to his hair. His eye really hurts. Something that isn't blood is trickling from it and he can no longer close the lid over the swollen, milky eyeball that bulges out of the socket and looks vaguely like a hard-boiled egg. He saw it earlier, in the bathroom mirror.

'You found her,' says Martel's voice, on the phone.

'Yeah,' says Bruce.

He's only half lying.

'Where is she?'

'Over there.'

'Give it a rest with your fucking riddles, will you?' Martel says impatiently. 'Just tell me what happened.'

'I found her, like you asked me to.'

'Where? Where is she?'

'I bumped into this kid on Thursday night. He told me what happened. The whore got away in a car.'

'What car? What are you talking about?'

'The Saab. The one in the accident . . .'

Bruce has started crying softly now and it's a relief. He's going to tell the whole story and finally someone will take care of him.

Martel says nothing. He doesn't understand. He fears the worst. He's right to fear the worst.

'The problem is the old woman,' Bruce spits bitterly. 'And I wrecked my car too.'

This is what upsets him most, in fact. Earlier, he touched his eye with the fingers of one hand. The sensation was indescribable. It wasn't really painful, but feeling that smooth, warm egg bulging out of his head like that . . . He still isn't over it.

Martel forces himself to think clearly. In three or four hours the sun will rise and he has the feeling that another life will begin, not a better one by the sound of it. Tonight, certain things to which he thought he could cling have disappeared. He's surprised by how little all this bothers him. He's naked in bed, leaning on one elbow, his other arm in a sling. He looks at the numbers on the radio alarm clock: 03:47, it says, though he knows it's slightly fast. Maybe in the end it never really mattered that much, this whole life that he'd patiently built around him. The idea is almost funny. Unfortunately, Bruce is preventing him from enjoying these moments of newness, of take-off. When his phone rang he was sleeping deeply, more deeply than he'd slept for months. Not only that: he was dreaming.

After an effort of concentration, he tries to get things straight.

'Where are you?'

'Not far from Dinozé, I reckon. I don't know what to do.'

'So you crashed the car?'

'Yeah.'

'Are you injured?'

'Yeah.'

'Okay, okay, stop crying. I'll call for an ambulance.'

'No. You should come and get me yourself.'

'Why? What's up? Give me some details.'

Bruce wants to please. Deep down, this is all he ever wanted to do – to please Martel. But he can't gather his thoughts. He stands up and walks back towards the car, hoping this will relieve the numbness in his legs. Anyway, it's probably not a good idea to leave the girl all alone like that.

'It's the girl. I managed to get her back, but we had an accident. I had to walk about half an hour to find a signal on my phone.'

'How is she?'

Bruce sighs and looks up at the sky. 'I don't know really. Not great.'

'But what happened to you?'

'It was that old bitch.'

'Concentrate.'

'The inspector.'

'What – the cops?'

'No. That woman who came to the factory. The labour inspector.'

Martel sits up in bed. Sweat starts to run down his forehead and his chest.

'That bitch practically took my eye out.'

'But what happened? Tell me what happened!' Martel stands up and tries to put on his jeans. Not easy with the phone pressed to his ear and one arm in a sling. He wants to stay calm, not to yell at Bruce, who seems completely out of it. The curtains are open and a glimmer of light seeps into his room. He goes to look outside. A thick layer of snow has simplified everything.

'Listen, you need to pull yourself together. It'll be all right. Just tell me what the inspector wanted.'

'Don't worry about that,' Bruce reassures him. 'I took care of her.'

Martel holds his breath. He's not even dressed yet and his shirt is already soaked with sweat. His legs are still numb from walking. He came home from the hospital on foot. It was a long walk.

'Tell me what you did,' he demands. 'I want to know exactly what you did to her.'

'Martel, you have to get over here. Everything is not okay. We had a crash. The Beemer's a write-off and the girl . . . I don't know. You have to come. Seriously. You have to come here now.'

Martel tries to think. 'Did anyone see you? Have you asked for help?'

'There's nobody around, with all this snow.'

'But the inspector – what happened? I have to know.'

The line goes dead. Martel tries calling back five or six times, but there's nothing.

Walking back towards the car, Bruce has lost the signal again. He's all alone. He thinks about the situation. Either he walks away again to try to call Martel back or he returns to the car and the girl and hopes that Martel got the message, that he'll come and pick him up. Unable to decide, he stares at his phone screen, hoping for a signal, or at the sky, hoping that Fate will intervene. He holds his hand in the air, trying to capture that capricious, volatile signal, which he imagines fluttering through the air, like a butterfly, just out of reach. Bruce waves his arm then suddenly pulls it down. When he hiccuped just now, his mouth filled with blood. He spits on the snow and wipes his mouth with the back of his hand. The accident happened in slow motion. He can see it again now. He can feel that skidding sensation, the loss of control.

He sets off again, limping through the thick snow towards the car. From time to time he blows into his hands to warm them up. His ribs and legs ache. Yet it wasn't much of a collision really – he was driving pretty slowly. To give himself courage he whistles something cheerful and well-known. A Julien Clerc song. 'Never tell anyone I said that/Or Melissa will kill me.' He passes remote houses with hostile faces. The pines are dark and stars prick the vast empty sky. There's nobody around to see him or hear him so in the end he does it. He says: 'Please, God, please, I'm begging you . . .'

Soon after this he finds the BMW where he left it, which comes as a relief despite everything. It's stuck in a ditch, the drive wheels in the air. They kept spinning for a while after the impact, even though the engine stalled instantly. He feels sick about it. He was being careful too. If only she'd kept calm . . . He glances inside. The girl isn't there. She's vanished again.

'Oh, for God's sake, for God's sake . . .'

Bruce doesn't understand. She was naked except for a raincoat he wrapped round her shoulders as they were leaving the house. He looks around and quickly finds footprints in the snow. He could go after her, but he's had it up to here with that girl. And he's so tired. Besides, he quite likes the idea of her freezing to death alone in the forest. If that happened, it'd be like she never got away from him. Just then he glimpses his reflection in a car window and immediately turns away, with a shudder. That eye – like a peeled lychee stuck to his face. He hesitates, then – to reassure himself that things are not as bad as they seem – he looks again. Oh, fuck. Obviously he's not going to search for her. It's too late, too cold. He's going to lose his eye, he feels sure of it. He sits behind the steering wheel and pours himself one last line of coke. After all, why should he give a fuck now?

JORDAN LOCATELLI

Jordan and Lydie sat cross-legged on the floor, both hidden behind the bed. They felt good – tired, of course, but in a nice way. Lydie's hash had intensified the gravity in the room. The feeling of heaviness was slowly dissipating now. They'd talked loads too. Lydie had told him some secrets. It was funny that a girl like her could be so unsure of herself. And, honestly, the other girls were such bitches.

The only light came from the small TV set: R&B videos showing hot girls wiggling their butts against obese thugs or guys with six-packs. At the bottom of the screen was the mute symbol.

Jordan had been talking non-stop for quite a while now. He was afraid of silence, afraid she would say, 'Okay, let's just get some sleep.' All the same he kept wondering if he should kiss her or what. He'd begun by telling her some really personal stuff, to show her he was sensitive and all that. Lydie didn't look too impressed, though. On the other hand, as soon as he'd started slagging off Riton, she'd perked up. Jordan had taken advantage of this to badmouth everyone he could think of: Riton, the

319

school headmaster, Justin Bieber, the police, guys who drive flash cars, Riton again, oh, and not forgetting Sarkozy, and then his father, because all fathers were bastards but his was one of the worst. And the proof of it was that the old man spent his time saying bad things about everything and everyone.

His dad complained about the Right and the Left, about immigrants and the bourgeoisie, about Americans, Jews, Arabs, bosses, lazy young people, rising prices, falling wages, tasteless vegetables, the expense of organic food, taxes on diesel and atmospheric pollution, sanctimonious bobos and shady dole-ites, socialists who want to take everything away from you and capitalists who won't let you have anything they own, Wall Street and Al-Qaeda, the decline of France and the rise of the French stock exchange, council tax and the Social Security deficit, the TV licence fee and the national debt.

Lydie was being patient but Jordan knew he was pushing it. If he started going on about his dad's R8 he'd probably end up sleeping on the floor. Plus, while he'd managed to avoid any embarrassing silences, he hadn't really got any closer to the moment when he might get to see her naked.

'Yeah, so my father reckons that the world is fucked now,' Jordan concluded. 'What he really needs is a time machine.'

'Yeah, totally. My grandfather's the same.'

'Oh, yeah?'

'Yeah. They used to live in Algeria. He never talks about it but it's like it's always there.'

'Yeah, I know what you mean.'

'The worst thing is that he can't even imagine our generation might be okay. He doesn't give us a chance.'

'Right, totally.'

Jordan didn't have enough words to express how much he agreed with her.

'It's my mother who gets the worst of it, I reckon.' Lydie felt cold all of a sudden. She picked up a Miss Sixty sweatshirt from the back of a chair and draped it round her shoulders.

'And your father?' Jordan asked.

Lydie didn't answer. She was pulling threads from the carpet.

'My mother died,' said Jordan. 'About a year ago.'

The words just came out. Three words that he'd never spoken aloud before. My mother died. He felt stupid saying it like that.

'Is that true?'

'Yeah.'

'Fuck, that must be horrible.'

She didn't sound particularly sorry for him. Her intonation suggested curiosity more than anything, and maybe a bit of anxiety.

'Yeah,' Jordan admitted. 'So, you know, even if my father can be a bit of an idiot . . . I'm all he's got really.'

'Yeah, it's the same with my mother.'

Probably better to stop there. Because when Monday came there'd be school and friends and they might regret these confessions. He'd heard about that stuff plenty of times before: drunk guys who gave away their secrets or girls who said more than they should have done one night on a camping trip. Those poor bastards had woken up the next day with three school terms of shame to look forward to.

A long silence opened up between Jordan and Lydie. They both desperately needed to sleep, but at the same time they couldn't go to bed. And they couldn't smoke another spliff either or they wouldn't be capable of doing anything afterwards, plus they'd have dry mouths. They'd already been eating breath mints for the last hour. They didn't know what else to say, and their patience was wearing thin. Lydie, who'd been looking at him strangely for a while now, abruptly stood up. Beneath the fabric of her jogging bottoms, Jordan could see the exact outline of her knickers. His heart speeded up. Lydie spent a few seconds digging around at the bottom of her wardrobe, then came back and sat down holding a biscuit tin.

'Your face really reminds me of someone, you know. I'm sure we were in primary school together.'

'Well, yeah,' said Jordan, slightly annoyed. 'Don't you remember?'

'Not at all. It's really weird.'

She started going through the photographs inside the tin. Class pictures, photo-booth shots with friends, family stuff with faded colours: old stones, pale palm trees, piss-yellow dust.

'What's that?'

'Nothing. Just my mother's things from Algeria.'

'Can I see?'

'No, it's boring. Hang on, look at this . . .'

'Jesus!'

They laughed. There were two rows of little kids, like Playmobil figures, dressed in 1990s clothes: stonewashed jeans, multicoloured sweaters, enormous trainers. And Lydie in her balaclava.

'Ha, you've got to be kidding! A balaclava?'

'Stop! My mother made me wear it. All my family really freak out about the cold.'

'Yeah, but you must have been *really* warm in that!'

They started naming all the other kids together. They were sitting closer now, skin brushing skin. Soon they started messing around. Maybe she pinched him first. Neither of them can remember. At one point, Jordan grabbed the end of her sock and pulled. Lydie's bare foot appeared. Jordan touched it; the urge was overwhelming. The TV went off. Jordan could feel Lydie's body heat very close to him. Her hair on his cheek. He was surprised by the soft touch of her mouth. It was like fresh sheets in bed, like a mix of whipped cream and the soft fur of peach skin. It was totally unexpected and really cool.

She suddenly disentangled herself and he heard her crawling away. It was hot in her bedroom and getting hotter all the time.

'Hey, what're you doing?'

Little by little, the faint light from the sky outside was making certain shapes visible. Jordan began to locate objects, pieces of furniture, a silhouette.

'Psst,' said Lydie.

He crawled towards her but she wasn't where he expected to find her. In fact she was already standing next to the window. How did she get there? He watched her dark outline, backlit by the window. She drew the curtains. Now it was really dark.

'Hang on, I can't see anything.'

Jordan was starting to feel ridiculously happy and when he heard her giggling nearby he could feel fireworks going off in his chest. He crawled fast across the floor to catch her, but he couldn't see a thing and ended up banging his head on a corner of the bed.

'Sssh,' Lydie said mockingly. 'You'll wake up the whole house.'

'Fuck, if I get hold of you . . .'

He listened, then rushed at her. He thought he'd got her this time but was left clutching at air. She pinched his thigh.

'Ow!'

'Ssh.'

Hysterical laughter began to simmer inside them. They moved around quickly and found loads of opportunities to touch, squeeze, stroke each other. He felt a breast in his hand, then a slap on his wrist. But she didn't say anything and they kept on wrestling. She was breathing hard and he could smell her scent everywhere he went. He reached out a hand and realised that she'd taken off her jogging bottoms. She shushed him again and his fingers moved to her inner thigh. They kissed. She touched his dick.

Lydie struggled away again, playing with him, biting and pinching. But Jordan wasn't worried any more, and every time he found her on the floor he got his reward. After a while she climbed onto the bed and pulled him by the hand. He remembered to take his socks off first. Their fingers intertwined. Their kisses grew harder, as if they wanted kissing to be dirty, to hurt, to be *more* . . . Then the house creaked. Jordan shivered and freed himself from Lydie.

'Wait,' she said. 'Don't move.'

He was on top of her, her legs wrapped around him.

Another creak. It sounded like it was coming from the stairs.

'What's going on?'

'My grandfather never comes upstairs. It's just the house making noises.'

Jordan felt her tongue on his neck. He was braced on his elbows, his crotch pressed against Lydie's. She began rubbing herself against him, against his dick. He leaned his face close to hers and her hot, wet tongue flickered between his lips. He was hard. He started moving his hips around too. Then he knelt down to take off his sweatshirt and T-shirt, and Lydie unfastened his belt.

'Come on.'

She lifted up the duvet so they could get underneath. She touched his chest, he stroked her hair, her neck, her ribs. He held her hips. She was caressing his cock now and their mouths were locked together.

Lydie's hand on my cock. She was wanking him off and Jordan couldn't believe it. It was almost weird still to exist at all, simply to breathe, to be there, stupidly.

He hitched up her cami and rubbed his face against her breasts. He was surprised by how round and firm they were. He'd expected them to be softer. They were almost too rubbery. He couldn't see them.

'I want to see your tits.'

'Shut up.'

They were licking each other now. Jordan's face moved down towards Lydie's knickers. She arched her back. He felt the fabric under his lips, and under the fabric the wiry hairs. He started gently rubbing her with his nose, his mouth, his fingers. Lydie's breathing grew faster. For the first time Jordan didn't feel like she could make him do anything she wanted, that she belonged to some superior species, that she reigned over him like the queen over the worker ants. He was taking the lead now. He peeled back the fabric and slid his tongue inside. Her pussy was complicated, hot, with a captivating taste. He licked it and she tensed. At one point she pulled his hair so hard his eyes watered. He kept licking her until he felt like he'd done it enough, that he'd done his duty. Then he wiped his nose and mouth on the sheet and crawled back up her while she contorted her body to get her knickers off. Lydie's hand slipped between their bodies to grab his dick. She squeezed it tight and wanked him while guiding it towards her. Their faces were close but they weren't kissing any more. It was going to happen. At last. He wouldn't be a . . . Weirdly he thought about his mother. Oh, there it was. His cock was inside Lydie's cunt. It was impossible. It was happening. He was fucking Lydie.

'Oh, fuck me, fuck me,' she said, like a girl in a film.

He started thrusting in and out quickly. He wasn't too sure what he was feeling. He was trying to do a good job. Drops of sweat fell from his forehead onto Lydie's breasts. He heard a noise from outside, or maybe below. A chair falling, perhaps, or her grandfather coming upstairs.

'Forget it.' Lydie groaned.

She was short of breath.

'Not so fast,' she told him.

She moaned and said some surprising words. Jordan would never have guessed that girls might like that stuff too. In his mind, they only did it because they had to, as a sort of favour to men, who were the ones with needs, a monopoly on filth. Now Lydie was sweating, breathing heavily, and she was saying, 'Your cock . . . Your dick.' She was wet and nasty. He could feel her hands on his buttocks, pushing him every few seconds to get the rhythm right. She was a sex-hungry fucking machine, as curious and desperate as he was. He just wished he could see her. He held her hips, moved his face down, bit her tits. She freed herself and Jordan whispered: 'We could have used a condom.'

'Do you have any?'

'No.'

She got out of bed and turned on the TV, which filled the room with a bluish light. At last he could see her naked, her buttocks spread as she crouched in front of a chest of drawers. In the bottom drawer she found some condoms and came back towards him. Her belly was slightly rounded. He lay on his back and waited. She took his cock and slid the condom over it. She was dextrous and beautiful. He couldn't take his eyes off her. When she leaned down, her breasts pointed towards the mattress. She held his dick vertical and straddled him, then squatted lower and swallowed him slowly inside her pussy, face hidden by her hair.

They fucked like that for a while. She didn't speak until the moment when she asked him to take her from behind. Then, with her head in her arms, she started to moan really loudly, to tell him stuff. His crotch slapped against Lydie's fat buttocks, making the flesh shake like crazy. He grabbed her by the hips and at one point he even dared pull her hair, bringing her face up to his as he upped the pace. It was coming. At the same time he was starting to feel tired and almost lonely. The image of his erection going into Lydie's pussy was less new now. She used her free hand to caress him, her face buried in her elbow.

'Go on. Go on.'

Her voice sounded almost hostile. He felt something accelerating inside her. She was regaining control. He let her do it as he continued ramming himself into her. Afterwards she fell to the side, hair tangled and skin slick with sweat. In that light, her breasts, her ribcage, her belly, her pubic hair all looked incredible. He watched her, unsure what to do.

A few seconds later, when she'd got her breath back, she sat up and pulled off the condom. She spat on her hand and rubbed the saliva on his dick, then licked it a little bit before starting to wank him off slowly, from base to head. She sat on the bed, back to the wall, legs spread, shining and solid, and she stared into his eyes. He was close. She kept wanking him, even more slowly, and it was almost painful. The semen spurted out and fell on the bed between them. She held his cock in both hands and rubbed her thumbs over the rim of his glans. He felt like he was going to die there and then and that maybe it wouldn't be such a bad thing.

After that, they both went to the bathroom, sat on the floor and ate some biscuits, then gave each other head again, in the incalculable night, lying on the carpet with its oppressive smell of old dust. She was subtle and she was in charge, but Jordan was the first one to fall asleep. He was happy, he thought. At the same time, he couldn't wait to leave, to see how it felt to live in the world outside after he'd done all that stuff.

Overall, it had been a pretty amazing night.

Except for Nadia. That was a shame.

MARTEL

Swedish cars have a good reputation. The Italians not so much, and with the French it depends, but you can really count on the Swedes.

It was about four thirty in the morning and Martel felt happy to be driving a Volvo rather than a Fiat or whatever. The wind had died down and it wasn't snowing any more, but the road was still barely driveable. The car advanced slowly and Martel sometimes had the impression that it was actually at a standstill while someone was making the landscape move past the windows, that ink-black sky and the downy white earth.

As he left the car park he'd used his left hand to shift into second gear and after that he hadn't touched the gearstick again. His right hand was resting in his lap, wounded and bluish. Now and then he would stick a cigarette between lips as dry as emery cloth and let it burn down as he took the occasional drag. Concentrating on the road, his eyes narrowed to slits.

He'd cracked open the window despite the cold, to keep himself awake. His back and his collarbone hurt and he felt tired and old. In his head, he went over the events of the past few weeks. The kidnapping, the fall downstairs, the Benbareks parked by the motorway, his date with the inspector. That had been only a matter of hours ago. Long before the end of the world.

'I took care of her,' Bruce had said. What did that mean? Martel's phone sat silent in the passenger seat. There was no signal around here, though; Bruce hadn't called.

Martel didn't bother stopping at red lights. He just pressed down the clutch pedal before continuing at the same slow, stubborn speed. If he got stuck in the snow, there was a good chance he'd never get going again. He'd been driving like this for at least an hour now, driving through the night.

One thing was sure: he didn't have to worry about the police. They wouldn't venture out in weather like this. Snow encouraged disorder. You could see it every time it snowed, how their entire society went into a spin. The arteries that led to the cities became blocked; blood clots obstructed the motorways, frightening the police commissioners and throwing reporters into warlike postures. On the TV news they would stand, scarf around neck, talking about the suburbs of Paris like they were Vietnam or Beirut, describing the hundred-mile traffic jams, the ghettoes like tinderboxes, five thousand years of civilisation stuck in slush and what was the government doing?

In the Vosges, of course, they were used to it. Even so, the cops preferred to stay at home until the roads had been salted, the snow shovelled away.

Martel wedged the steering wheel between his thighs to find a news station on the radio. The presenter was describing blocked roads and predicting an improvement tomorrow. He sounded enthusiastic: after all, snow was beautiful. Shame we didn't get any at Christmas. All the same, Météo France was advising people to stay home. Since Martel was now not far from Dinozé, he changed to a local station and found out that the storm was about to start again. He glanced at his petrol gauge. The tank was three-quarters empty. Still, it should be enough to get him there and back again. Unless he got stuck, obviously. In any case, there was no point in turning back now. He kept twisting the dial on the radio until he found some music: 'Blue Hotel' by Chris Isaak.

Don't worry about that. I took care of her.

When Martel saw the BMW poking out of the ditch, he lifted his foot from the accelerator and parked the Volvo sideways across the road. Before getting out, he slid his injured hand into the Velpeau sling that dangled from his shoulder. He turned off the engine but left the head-lights on. Outside the snow creaked under his weight and a shadow stretched out in front of him, like the line around a dead body. Martel examined the tracks in the snow left by Bruce's car. Bruce had been lucky: on the other side of the road there was a ravine over a hundred feet deep, the ground spiked with pine trees. He moved closer on tiptoe, as though afraid of waking someone, and immediately spotted Bruce's silhouette behind the steering wheel. Fearful of slipping and hurting himself again, Martel sat down and slid into the ditch on his bottom. His jeans got wet and he felt the cold rising up his back to his neck. Inside the wrecked car, Bruce appeared to be drowsing, his head thrown back against his shoulder. The back of the car was in tatters and the axles were broken. The windows, on the other hand, had withstood the collision. Martel knocked on the passenger-side window. Bruce's face was concealed behind a thin layer of condensation.

'Hey!' Martel shouted. He shook the door handle but nothing happened.

He banged his fist harder on the glass. There was a movement inside and Bruce wiped the mist off the inside of the window. Martel recoiled and almost fell over.

'Shit! What the fuck is that?'

Bruce's face was pressed against the glass. He was smiling. Martel retched. That smile, so close to that ovoid milky eyeball, was truly disgusting.

Bruce tried to shoulder open the door. Martel pulled at the handle. In the end, unable to budge it an inch, Martel signalled him to lower the window.

'Hey,' said Bruce, when the glass no longer separated them.

'Fucking hell, what happened to you?'

Bruce raised his hand as if to touch his eye but stopped before he made contact. He was still smiling piteously. 'It was that old bitch.'

'The inspector?'

'Yeah. She gave me a hard time.'

'What happened? Where is she?'

'Up there,' Bruce said, gesturing up the road with his head.

'Let's get you out of there.'

'I got the girl.'

'Where is she?'

'I did some investigating and I managed to find her.'

'Where? What happened?'

Bruce signalled for a cigarette. Martel handed him one. The lighter flame was reflected for an instant in his porcelain-coloured eye.

'Fuck, you're a mess. What about the inspector?'

'I know I shouldn't have called you back. I had everything in hand but then, I don't know, it all went pear-shaped.'

'Try to focus. Look at me.'

Bruce's head was swaying. 'God, I'm shattered,' he muttered. 'I've never felt this tired in my life.'

The cigarette dropped from his mouth and rolled across his knees before landing on the floor. Bruce made no attempt to pick it up. He started coughing. Martel noticed that his sweatshirt was soaked with blood.

'Come on, Bruce, don't fall asleep . . . Hey!'

Martel pinched his neck and he groaned.

'The girl! What happened to the girl?'

'I'm sorry, I don't know, I . . .'

Bruce was struggling to keep his eyes open and kept jerking his head back to stop himself nodding off.

'I think I broke something,' he whined, clumsily patting his stomach.

'The girl, Bruce.'

'I think I'm going to die.'

'No, you're not,' Martel replied impatiently. 'Look at me, you need to concentrate.'

At that precise moment, he felt a snowflake land on his right cheek. He looked up at the sky. Deep in the darkness, the snow had started falling again.

'You have to concentrate. You have to think. We're in a rush here. Just tell me where the girl is.'

'I don't know, I swear.'

A few seconds passed in the vast snowy silence. Bruce's chin had fallen onto his chest. His head swung lazily from side to side.

Martel sighed. He was weighing the odds. He saw the inspector's face again. He put his arm through the open window and searched Bruce. He found his iPhone and checked his call and search history. He recognised Rita's address. Bruce didn't have a signal, but Martel, whose phone used Orange, did. So he called the inspector's number with his own phone. No answer. Next, he called for an ambulance. He told the man who answered that there'd been an accident not far for Dinozé and the man asked him if it was serious.

'I'm not sure.'

'Because it's started snowing again and it won't be easy to get there,' the man explained. 'I need to know if it's a real emergency. Have you thrown up? Are you in pain?'

Martel looked at Bruce, who'd fallen asleep. He glanced around. Whiteness all the way to the horizon; sparse, heavy snowflakes; the yellow beam from the headlights lighting up the swirling snow. He took his time.

'Actually, I think it's okay. I can wait awhile.'

'Okay,' said the man, sounding relieved. 'We get so many accidents when the weather's like this. We have to prioritise.'

'Should I call the police?'

'You could. Actually, yeah, go ahead. But they probably won't be able to get there any time soon either.'

'Okay.'

'Keep warm and try not to fall asleep. We'll send someone as soon as we can. You think you'll be okay for an hour or so?'

'Yeah. Thanks.'

Martel hung up, then put the iPhone back into Bruce's pocket. Using his handkerchief, he wiped the blood from Bruce's lips. Then he spotted the Colt in the passenger seat. He tried again to open the door, but it seemed to be welded shut. He stretched in with one arm to grab the gun but couldn't reach. So he put his head through the open window and had to twist his body sideways before he could catch hold of it. He was careful not to look at Bruce while he was doing this. Even so he caught a brief glimpse of his eye and the hairs stood up on the back of his neck.

Before abandoning Bruce, Martel turned on the radio then rolled the window up as high as he could. The snow was still falling softly. It was probably his imagination but the whole time that he was desperately struggling to climb out of the ditch, Martel had the feeling that Bruce was watching him. An old Kiss song echoed faintly from the crashed car.

The first thing he saw when he arrived at Rita's house was the light blazing from the windows of the house next door. It wasn't even five in the morning. A witness would be a pain in the arse. At the same time, he had to move quickly. He wondered what state Rita would be in when he found her. He remembered that night, a few weeks earlier, when he'd driven her home because her old Saab wouldn't start. He parked at a distance and ran towards the house. The snow was falling hard now and Martel breathed in the familiar smell. Soon the wind would start to howl and he wouldn't be able to see more than ten feet in front of him.

Before entering Rita's house, he estimated the distance to the neighbour's place. The Colt was in his hand. It had been a long time since he'd held a weapon of this calibre. He straightened his arm and let the memories rise through his body: the delicious solidity of the metal, that blast of air at his shoulder. He couldn't help smiling, despite the situation. This was way better than his flare pistol. There was no need to worry about the neighbour now.

The front door to the inspector's house was wide open. Inside it was dark and full of cold draughts. He found the light switch and the room appeared before him. Lamps lying on the floor, the coffee-table knocked over, burn marks on the sofa. There was a broken rifle lying further off and he thought the burn marks might be traces of gunshots. A large dog trotted over to him. It was limping. Unthinkingly Martel patted its head as he took stock of the damage. Almost immediately the animal turned around and limped back to a dark corner under the spiral staircase. Martel followed it and found the inspector, lying unconscious face down on the tiles, wearing knickers and a T-shirt that had been hitched up under her arms. He knelt down and crawled under the steps where she'd taken refuge. He placed two fingers on her jugular: a regular pulse. He pulled her T-shirt down. He was trembling and his lips uttered silent words without him being aware of them. He held her shoulders then bent down to whisper into her ear.

'Rita? Can you hear me?'

He leaned closer, only an inch or two from her ear, and repeated the same words. She didn't move.

He carefully turned her onto her back.

'Oh, Christ,' he gasped.

Her lips were split, her eyelids puffy, and there was dried blood under her nose, which looked like it had moved sideways across her face. He barely even recognised her. There was a huge bump on her forehead, and a yellow, purple and green bruise ran all the way from her right cheek to the back of her neck.

'The bastards,' he muttered, without really knowing whom he had in mind.

He picked her up and held her to him. She was cold and he began to rock her, kissing her forehead, her cheeks, her mouth, the dark swellings of her eyelids. She grimaced with pain then. Under those smooth purple lids her eyes were like the eyes of a deep-sea creature, some repulsive prehistoric fish that should never see the light of day. They were so tumid that she couldn't open them.

'Don't worry,' said Martel, teeth gritted. 'Everything's okay now, I'm going to get you out of here.'

Recognising his voice, she tried to turn away.

333

'Just relax, you'll be fine. I'm going to take you to hospital.'

She tried to say something and her mouth half opened, but instantly she brought her hands up to hide it and tears escaped from between her lashes. Martel had already seen it, though – the black hole between her lips. That stupid bastard had knocked out all her front teeth.

'Ssh,' he said, gently kissing her forehead. 'Just relax. Don't worry, we're leaving now. They're going to take good care of you.'

He lifted her up as if she weighed nothing and walked towards the door. She desperately tried to turn her face away, finally finding refuge in Martel's neck.

Outside the wind was howling. Martel did his best to shield her from the cold as he carried her to the Volvo, the dog following close behind. Martel laid the inspector down on the back seat, covering her with his leather jacket, then let the animal into the passenger seat.

Driving past the house, he saw that he'd forgotten to close the door behind him. In the warm light that spilled from the living room through the doorway, snowflakes danced in wild gusts of wind. Martel drove slowly as he contemplated this strange spectacle. He had the impression that he was abandoning the house, beginning an exodus, leaving the light behind for a long time.

Beside him the big dog sat, tongue lolling, and kept looking through the windscreen at the road ahead and then behind, checking that his mistress was still there. Martel was finding it hard to see where he was going. The landscape was flat, white and featureless. He tried to find landmarks, the shape of a hill, some trees, anything to help him work out where the road ended.

He'd been driving for about fifteen minutes, face pressed to the windscreen, when sky and earth seemed to become one. He had to stop for a moment, letting the engine tick over. The dog turned in a circle twice before settling down and waiting for whatever would happen next. The petrol gauge had barely changed since he'd left Bruce behind. He hoped there would be enough; under normal circumstances, it would be fine. Behind him, the inspector had stopped moving. He leaned across to her, checking that she was covered up and taking the Colt out of his jacket pocket. Martel and the dog stared out at the nothingness in front of them. The storm bumped the car, pressed hard against the windows, held them tight in its sharp, deafening fist. The Volvo swayed from side to side as the radio quietly played 'I Forgot To Forget Her'.

Suddenly Martel shivered and the dog barked.

They'd both seen the same thing. A silhouette, a shadow, something had crossed their field of vision. It was there, somewhere, behind the curtain of snow.

After a moment's hesitation, Martel got out of the car, just to make sure. He started moving forward, shielding his face with one forearm and holding the Colt in his other hand. He was wearing only a shirt on top and he soon began shaking all over. He ran forward, calling out. He still thought he could see something, a presence. Maybe the girl, but how could he be sure? He could barely even open his eyes. He yelled into the storm: 'Hey! Hello?'

But the storm swept away his words. He couldn't see anything and all he could hear was the wind. He was so cold now that he couldn't feel his hands or feet. He turned around to check on the car. All he could see was the distant halo of the headlights, like the light a TV set emits just after it's been turned off. After another brief hesitation he moved forward a little further and found some footprints on the ground, already being erased by the snow. The shape of bare feet. He rushed back to the car.

PART THREE

But we are not wise at all, we believe in books, in children,
we live as if the world was not even going to end.

PAUL NIZAN,
The Conspiracy

THE FACTORY

In the factory courtyard, where the first rays of spring sunlight were fall-ing, they stood side by side, squinting in the morning dazzle, as surprised and anxious as if the police were hammering at the door. A wave had swept them up and deposited them on this shore. But they knew the worst was still to come.

The machines had been sold. For the past few weeks, there had been only the staff representatives coming here to negotiate the final details of the severance scheme. Before that, they'd organised strikes, obstructed the delivery of raw materials, sabotaged production and even come close to imprisoning the CEO in his own office. As time went on, Martel had distanced himself from what was happening, which was fine with the others because towards the end he was starting to frighten them.

It was all over now. The pressure had dropped. They had agreed the criteria for redundancy, the support schemes; a redeployment committee would be appointed; a handful of older workers had taken early retirement. The youngest had chosen voluntary redundancy and the 3,000-euro pay-off that came with it, with 1,000 euros for each year that they'd worked at the factory. Soon the first dismissal letters would be sent. And even though they'd long been expected, they would come as a shock. In recent weeks, the men had been holding their breath every time they looked through their mail. As for the temps, they had nothing to worry about: they'd be assigned to different positions, where they would have to learn new habits, make new friends. They would not receive any compensation. Everyone considered this normal. Even so, they'd been invited that day in late April.

Before gathering in the courtyard, the men had taken one last look around the buildings, hollow and echoing now, cleaner than they'd ever been before. They'd walked in groups of two or three, looking sad, but there was something funny about it all the same. Old Cunin reminisced; that was his job now. And, for once, people actually listened a bit. Always the same old stories of crushed hands, severed fingers, men's lives destroyed in return for the minimum wage. The epic saga of the working man, the bosses trembling before the masses as they rose up in revolt. Old Cunin had been a Communist. He didn't boast about it so much any more, even if he still claimed to be proud of it. The younger ones no longer believed any of that stuff. They'd seen too many Soviets getting blown up on TV by MacGyver and Rambo. Having said that, some had changed their minds over the past few months, even some of the temps, because through solidarity they had at least managed to delay the inevitable and to be given a few extra euros before they were kicked out of the door. Capital had won in the end; hardly a surprise to old Cunin. What grieved him most was not being able to pass on the torch. Martel wasn't a believer, and the others would lose touch with one another. The great battle would end with a whimper.

At the corners of the buildings, tiny flowers were growing through cracks in the tarmac. There weren't enough work boots to trample them down now, so this was their time. Velocia would have to spend more than fifty thousand euros to decontaminate the site. Men had worked there for a hundred years and the earth had been nourished with nothing more than their sweat. The workers were happy about the decontamination costs because their old bosses would take a hit, and also because it meant the men had left their mark there; their presence couldn't be erased so easily.

Mrs Meyer, the head of HR, had watched them wander across the factory floor. Little surly ones, tall fat ones, skinny tireless Arabs, red-faced supervisors, anxious ones still wearing their overalls, the last skilled workers in the world. They all looked so timid now, unsure what to say or do. Once the machines had gone, their jobs vanished, they were left in a strange land where they would have to learn new balances of power, new habits, new ways of being. In this new land, long friendships were cut short, ancient hatreds neutralised. The men were left naked. Like ducks caught out by the first frost, their pond suddenly covered with ice, they were touchingly clumsy.

A makeshift stage had been built in the main courtyard from breeze blocks and a few planks of plywood. It was very obviously a rickety, temporary structure. To one side a trestle table contained a few bottles of cheap wine, fruit juice and Coke, bowls of crisps and peanuts, some sand-wiches. There was only a small supply of alcohol, out of fear that the men might get too rowdy. A couple of wives were helping to organise things, but most of the workers had turned up without their better halves; this wasn't a joyous occasion, after all. And, deep down, maybe they hoped things would get out of hand. Not that it seemed very likely: the manage-ment had arranged this send-off at the last minute, surprising everyone by scheduling it in the middle of the week – a Tuesday.

'What about the inspector? Hasn't anyone seen her?'
Locatelli was talking to Martel, who seemed miles away.
'She had an accident. The night of the storm.'
'Oh, no. She seemed like a nice person.'
'She's not dead, just had an accident.'
'Yeah, yeah, of course.'

*   *   *

Subodka parked his Audi and Mrs Meyer immediately set off to meet him. They exchanged a few words in the almost empty car park, looking furtive as everyone stared at them. All the same, they had to get it over with. The men watched as they hesitated before walking the fifty yards that separated them from the little get-together they'd organised. They were obviously wondering how to behave: should they smile or look grave? In the end they divided up their roles, the head of HR adopting a sorrowful expression while the CEO grinned awkwardly, an expression that made him vaguely resemble a stingray.

'They found him in his car, stiff as a board.'

'Who?'

'The big one.'

'Oh, yeah?'

'Hadn't you heard?'

'No.'

'You knew him pretty well, though, didn't you? The bodybuilder, remember?'

'Yeah, yeah, I know who you mean,' said Martel, looking increasingly irritated.

The CEO and the head of HR did the rounds. Some of the men – the hardliners, like Denis Demange with his big bulldog face – refused to shake their hands. Others, such as the company accountant and the administration staff – middle-aged women all dressed in their Sunday best – kissed them on both cheeks, looking contrite and understanding. Nobody dared be cheerful.

'Yeah. Apparently he was drugged up to his eyeballs.'

'How would anyone know that?'

'It said so in the paper. There were a couple of crashes that night. My brother-in-law was stuck on the motorway between Nancy and Charmes for about five hours.'

'They hadn't salted the roads.'

'Yeah, you're not kidding.' Locatelli laughed. 'Lazy wankers.'

The CEO went up first, in shirtsleeves. He looked uneasy as he stood on the wobbly stage. Smiling around at the assembled faces, he bent his short legs several times to make sure that the planks were not about to give way beneath his weight, then invited Mrs Meyer to join him. She was wearing a Japanese-style sleeveless blouse, fitted grey slacks, almost invisible earrings and a leather watch strap that went twice around her wrist.

'Hello, everyone.'

Subodka was smiling his 'trust-me' smile, the one that said, 'Okay, I'm not going to lie to you . . .'

'First of all, I'm happy to be here, and to see you all. Some of you may not believe that, but it's true.'

Mrs Meyer was standing on tiptoe, frowning with concentration. When she looked up, it was to nod at a familiar face: yes, we need to meet up afterwards, I have some papers for you to sign. She looked beautiful. None of the men had a wife like her, with her slim arms, her tasteful outfits, the vague enigmatic scent she always wore, and that unchanging hairstyle. Seeing her like that, they knew that there really was still a civilised world out there. They just weren't part of it.

Subodka was a different type altogether. He was from the I-got-my-hands-dirty-and-pulled-myself-up-by-my-bootstraps school. He saw nothing wrong with buying fifty-euro boots or Yves Dorsey shirts and he wore his phone on his belt. He could hold his ale pretty well and laugh at the same stuff that the workers laughed at. All the same, nobody was fooled. That man counted more quickly than a calculator and spent his holidays in Scotland playing golf, fishing, and drinking twenty-five-year-old whisky with his friends from engineering school.

'I always believed that your problems were mine, and vice versa. The more senior among you will remember the troubles we had in 'ninety-five and how we got through them. This is not one of those short-term companies that live or die by the stock exchange, and I've been here long enough for you to know that.'

Locatelli had lowered his voice and, standing just behind Martel, he was still grumbling. Martel could smell the alcohol on his breath but he wasn't listening to what he said any more than he was listening to the CEO. The day before, he'd been to visit the inspector, just before she was discharged from hospital. Since then, all of this had struck him as completely meaningless. Locatelli put a hand on his shoulder, dragging him from his thoughts.

'It's a bargain at that price.'

'What is? What are you talking about?'

'The Gordini. Five thousand euros is all I'm asking.'

'What the hell would I do with your Gordini?'

'Or maybe you know someone else who'd be interested.'

'In tandem with your representatives we've done everything we can to make sure everyone is compensated. I understand that there will be anger and frustration. But you read the papers, the same as me. The firm's sales are down forty per cent in the last quarter. A business is like a living organism. It's born, it grows, and in the end it dies.'

He searched for signs of agreement in the faces below. Most were content to let him flounder. Others admitted that, yeah, all things considered, that did seem to be the case, the way things were at the moment. Martel touched the Colt through the fabric of his jacket. He didn't care about any of this crap now. He'd made his decision. His focus was elsewhere.

'Anyway, I want you to know that Mrs Meyer and I will be here till the end. I'll visit once a month to check what's happening with the redeployment. Mrs Meyer will be here every Wednesday. I think you've received notice of your compensation. You also know what you'll be getting from your health and disability insurance.'

'I'll give you all my mobile number,' the head of HR added. 'That'll make it easier to get hold of me.'

She lowered her head like a *pietà*. It was clear that she was deeply saddened by this whole scenario.

'We are responsible and we will bear our responsibilities until the end,' Subodka proclaimed, nodding earnestly. 'You know you can count on us.'

Nothing. Usually, when the CEO spoke, his final words were delivered in a tone that invited applause or at least a few murmurs of agreement. Here, there was only an embarrassing silence. The men weren't embarrassed by it, though, only Subodka.

'Does anyone have any questions or remarks?' Mrs Meyer asked.

'What will happen to you two?' someone called.

The CEO and the head of HR exchanged a glance. After a brief hesitation, she answered: 'We don't know yet.'

'We'll remain at the company's disposal,' said the CEO.

'So you'll keep your jobs, in other words.'

'We're not in the same situation as you. As employees, we do what we're told.'

Nobody rose to the bait. This mess had been going on for three months now; they'd had plenty of time to get everything off their chests. The time for rows and reproaches was over. It was spring. The bracing air, the birds singing, that razor-sharp light.

'All right,' concluded the CEO. 'Well, despite everything, we do have some good news to celebrate. Is he here?'

Martel felt his phone buzz inside his jeans pocket. Here we go. He put it to his ear and made his way through the crowd to find a quiet corner. Several of the men patted him encouragingly on the back as he passed them. He reached Hall One, the bigger of the two halls, the one directly opposite the stage.

'Come on, where is he?' the CEO was asking.

'He's being shy.' One of the men laughed.

'Go on!' someone else said.

'There he is!'

'Mr Hirsch, please?'

When the head of HR called his name, he appeared, climbing onto the stage as some smartarses in the crowd sang 'The Final Countdown'. The atmosphere had changed completely now. There was laughter in the air. The CEO and the head of HR warmly shook hands with the man and positioned him between them, facing his former colleagues. The time had come.

'As you all know, Mr Hirsch is now entitled to his pension. How long have you worked with us, Roland?'

'Forty-four years,' the man said.

'You've worked here all that time?' the CEO asked, surprised. Mr Hirsch put his hand to his ear and the CEO said in a louder voice: 'You've worked here forty-four years?'

'And my father before me,' the man replied.

'Well, it doesn't look like it did you any harm,' said Subodka, poking the old man's shoulders.

A dubious frown appeared on the man's red face and his friends in the crowd all laughed.

'I mean, you look like you're in good health.'

'Works keeps you fit,' the man admitted, deadpan.

'Yeah, hello?'

From where he stood, Martel could see Mr Hirsch. Balding and sly-looking, he was an old hand, worn out but still standing after all those years. At least he ought to be able to enjoy his retirement. His father had sent him to the factory when he was thirteen – that was the normal age back then – and he'd swept the floors for a while before being put on the assembly line. Later he'd done a bit of welding, before ending up a super-visor. He and his wife had bought a small flat on the third floor of a new apartment building, the kind of place where teenagers did wheelies on their bikes outside after school. What a career he'd had, old Hirsch. His parents had worked like dogs and gone to war. His daughters had failed their exams, signed on the dole, and been through a succession of temporary jobs. Roland Hirsch had been lucky. He wasn't a brilliant man or a bad man, just an average man who'd kept putting one foot in front of the other, trusting that things would improve and that, like him, everyone could hope for a better life if they just put a shift in.

'The money, Martel,' said the voice on the telephone. 'You need to give us back the money now.'

'I know,' Martel replied.

If he looked even taller than usual, that was because he'd lost quite a lot of weight recently. Some of the men called him King Kong now because he walked around with his arms dangling, head tilted forward, wild-eyed, more likely to grunt than talk. Behind him, the empty warehouse was full of echoes and draughts. Soon kids would come to throw stones at the windows. Rain would mix with the dust. One day, they would send in the bulldozers and the factory would be replaced by houses or a brand-new shopping centre where people could buy Chinese clothes, crappy furniture and vegetarian burgers.

'You'll see me soon,' said Martel. 'I've got the money and you'll see me soon, don't worry about that.'

'Anyway,' said the head of HR, in a firm tone, since some of the men were getting a little unruly, 'we noticed that poor Mr Hirsch had been forgotten when the work prizes were handed out. So we wanted to remedy that, didn't we, Mr Hirsch?'

The old man nodded, docile as a child, then rubbed his thumb and index finger together to indicate what he hoped to gain from this award.

'Ah, yes, that's true, there is also a cheque,' Mrs Meyer said, laughing. 'But let's start at the beginning, shall we?'

A blue velvet case was brought over and she took from it a medal on a ribbon, which she hung around the old man's neck. Then, holding him by the shoulders, she kissed him on both cheeks.

'Now, if you'd like to say a few words, Mr Hirsch,' she said, inviting his colleagues to applaud.

'I'll meet you at three o'clock behind the Vallar sawmill depots, in Ramber. Both of you should be there.'

'You really think we're going to turn up in the middle of fucking nowhere just because you tell us to?'

'I'll be there with the money. Don't be late.'

'You make us laugh, Martel.'

'Oh, I don't have much to say,' Hirsch lied. In fact he never wasted an opportunity to share his opinions, which were always vehement. He liked to keep abreast of current affairs.

The men yelled encouragement, some chanting, 'Speech! Speech!'

He stepped to the front of the stage and cleared his throat. He was wearing the same blue overalls he'd always worn and some rubber-soled shoes that were supposed to act as shock-absorbers and spare him the chronic headaches that were the bane of his life.

'All right, that's enough,' he said, silencing his over-enthusiastic friends. 'I'll do it, since you ask. So . . . Well, first of all I'd like to thank management. For a change.'

The workers' laughter mingled with the embarrassment of the managers.

'In the end, I worked about forty years and I just wanted to say that on the whole it went pretty well. Kids these days don't want to get their hands dirty. They all think they're stars or something and they'd rather annoy us with their scooters than do an honest day's work.'

The men, who knew what Hirsch was alluding to, laughed again.

'I don't want to get all political, but in my opinion you have to work first and then you can be a pain in the arse afterwards. Work makes the man. Anyway, time for a few drinks . . .'

'The old git,' sighed one of the temps.

'He's not wrong,' the CEO said, looking moved.

'Drinks! Drinks! Drinks!' chorused a group of men, as they headed towards the trestle table.

Martel heard nothing of this from where he was standing, but the spry figure of that little old man, a wage-earner for almost half a century, inspired in him a pinch of respect and a large dose of melancholy. The ancient dodo was taking its bow, blissfully unaware that it was more or less the last of its kind.

The management had been thinking small, but the workers had other ideas. They went to their cars, opened the boots and took out a barbecue set, merguez sausages, pork ribs, chipolatas, and six-packs of Kronenbourg. The embers glowed and they began drinking and playing football. One team went topless while the other kept their shirts on.

When it came time to eat, they separated into groups – the young ones, the old ones, the administrative staff in their own little corner. The accountant must have slipped away when no one was looking. The CEO and the head of HR did the rounds of them all, attentive and encouraging. They understood, they knew, they were hopeful. The men sensed their discomfort and almost began to feel sorry for them.

Under the effects of the alcohol, the groups began to mingle.

'Have some merguez,' Atmen said.

'Why not? No point standing on ceremony given where we are now,' replied old Léon Michel.

'You're right – we're all in the same boat.'

'Have some pork rib then.'

'Oh, I wouldn't go that far!'

'See? Solidarity won't work with the Arabs.'

'It's the same thing with the full-timers and the temps. Sure, we're all in the same boat, but when it comes to handing out lifebelts it's every man for himself.'

'I reckon we did the best we could, though.'

'Anyway, the managers are almost worse off in my opinion. You're not in charge of anything any more. You just do what you're told.'

'That's true.'

'Yeah, that's true, that is.'

'It's the Americans who are in charge.'

'Or the Chinese.'

'Well, one thing's sure: nobody in France is in charge of anything.'

'Come on, let's not talk bloody politics!'

'Eat some merguez, then,' repeated Atmen.

They'd known it was coming for a long time. The faces on the TV had told them: they wouldn't all get the chop straight away but they would all be affected. Now it was their turn. It was still strange, though. How was it possible to end like this, stunned and half drunk in the factory court-yard? Their jobs taken away and given to other men: Chinese, Indians, Romanians, Tunisians, an enormous, invading wave of immigrants. They were all lazy buggers, though. You could tell from the way they acted in school – at Seine-Saint-Denis, on TV, everywhere. It was totally mind-boggling. But those people – dark-skinned, slant-eyed Polish plumbers, whatever – all had one thing that the French didn't: they were cheap.

Unless it was all the fault of the others: the ones in charge. You didn't see them very often – only at elections would some of them deign to visit the Vosges. That was your chance to tell them about all the shit in your life. The little things – problems with the roads, with the neighbours, your cousin's college course, your gran's pension. They barely even listened, just nodded in agreement. As soon as the camera wasn't on them, though, it was another story altogether. They vanished into thin air, went back to their mansions to organise macro-economic strategies. And in the corner of the local café you talked to your mates about last night's match and how the economy seemed to be getting ever more micro.

One day all of this would be brought to light. And then, maybe, there'd be war.

In the meantime, however annoyed you got, you still had to live. Count your pennies when you went to the supermarket, put off buying the plasma TV screen you'd promised yourself, forget about going on holiday to Saint-Malo, explain to the kids once again that those big-name brands were just a load of crap. So much to look forward to . . .

'What's up? You're not drinking?'

'No,' said Martel. 'I have a meeting.'

'Oh, yeah, where?'

'For work?' one of the men asked anxiously.

'No, it's a family thing.'

'Ah.'

'So when will we see you again?'

'It's over.'

'What do you mean?'

'Look around, mate. It's over.'

Amid the golden sunlight, in the quivering rebirth of April, four men looked around while Martel stood motionless at their centre. They stared incredulously at the walls around them, feeling suddenly sober. Their world had been stolen from them. One of them swore.

The CEO and the head of HR anxiously observed this group of rebels. It would be an understatement to say that those five men had made them suffer. At certain points, the management had been genuinely frightened. Martel and his friends were no Einsteins. They'd ended up at the factory because there wasn't anything else. Fate had made them employees, stuck in a job that gave them no pleasure, complaining constantly about their conditions. But now it had been taken away from them, they found themselves with nothing, deprived of their masters and their enemies. Violence became a possibility.

In the meantime they would stagnate in their pitiful apartments, marginalised in their suburbs. They would be poor and their children even poorer. Maybe they would become the very people they'd once despised: vagrants, workshy idlers, drug addicts, profiteers, mixing with Gypsies, Arabs, Blacks, the lowest of the low, until they were all one muddy uniform mass, the underclass.

Once there had been such a thing as the working class. They could bear witness to that. If anyone ever asked.

'Right. Bye, then.'

'Yeah.'

'Goodbye.'

The cold, reserved handshakes, eyes averted. The management making one last effort.

'I think we did the best we could.'

'I'm sure you'll find a solution. You're still young.'

'Yeah, right.'

The men share a few cursory hugs.

'All right, that's enough, we're not queer.'

'Ha-ha.'

'Right, then.'

'Well, see you later.'

'Yep.'

'Fuck, this is weird.'

'Yeah . . .'

'When you think about everything we went through here . . .'

'Hey, look who it is.'

'Are you leaving, Mr Martel?'

'I have to go.'

'We did a good job, I think.'

Martel's massive fist closes around Mrs Meyer's tiny hand. They look into each other's eyes for a moment, their faces blank, both of them aware that they will never meet again.

'You really looked after your colleagues' interests. I think you can be proud of what you achieved.'

'If you say so.'

The head of HR flashed him a perfect smile. His sarcasm was like rainwater on Gore-Tex. These people had a nerve, she thought. The company had signed some large cheques for them when really it wasn't obliged to do so. For five or six years this factory had produced nothing but debts. Of course the human aspect had to be taken into account. The mayor, the prefect and the chairman of the local council had got on their soapboxes too. Anyway, it was all done and dusted now. She could finally turn her attention to matters that actually interested her: internal promotions, training schemes, career advice, upskilling, employment planning, recruitment strategies, anticipating needs, proactive sourcing policies, facilitating synergies, sharing good practices. She was going to optimise, prioritise, galvanise, empower, implement, outsource, benchmark. For now, though, she just had to smile politely.

'I'm sure you'll all bounce back stronger than ever. People these days often have four or five careers.'

'That's the problem.'

'Come on, you can't say that.'

'Yes. Yes, we can.'

'Where did Martel go?'

'I don't know.'

'Looks like he cleared off.'

Patrick Locatelli ran to the factory gates where the workers had hung funeral wreaths and a banner. He went out onto the street. In the distance, a figure was slowly shrinking. The words on the banner declared: 'Velocia dug our graves.'

Martel sneezed three times.

He walked calmly down the street towards his car.

He sniffed and thought how much he hated spring.

Later he would meet up with the Benbareks, who wanted their money back.

After that, nothing would matter much.

It was all the Benbareks' fault.

In fact, everything was the Arabs' fault when you thought about it.

RITA

It's still early in the morning when the Saab stops outside La Lanterne, a café where a handful of construction workers are drinking coffee before going to work. Rita finds a seat at the bar and orders a black coffee. The men look at her without saying anything. She can smell them from several yards away: mint shower gel and yesterday's stale clothes.

The woman who serves her has large bags under her eyes. Beneath the layers of fat and tiredness, you can still glimpse the girl she used to be.

'Here you go,' she says, with a welcoming smile.

Then she turns back to the TV. The presenter looks a bit rough too. The woman who runs the bar swirls ice cubes around a large glass of Orangina. She has nicely manicured hands and a hint of cleavage. Other than that she looks like an undercooked semolina pudding.

Rita sips her coffee in silence. She watches the bar owner, the TV, the sleepy-eyed men. Some are already joking, others not in the mood. The youngest ones are the quietest; they look like they've just been given some bad news. When a short guy asks for a glass of brandy, his friends all laugh and playfully shove him before heading for the exit. The bar owner calls, 'See you tomorrow,' without taking her eyes away from the TV screen. Rita pays for her coffee and the woman says: 'You don't look too good.'

Rita nods.

'Long night?'

Rita says yes and searches her pockets before putting a piece of paper on the counter. There's a girl's face drawn on it. The portrait vaguely resembles that actress – what was her name again? The one from *Last Tango in Paris* . . .

'Do you recognise this girl?'

The fat woman takes a closer a look and does a sort of little fart with her mouth. Nope, not at all. 'You don't have a photograph?'

Rita smiles and shakes her head.

'Because all those girls look more or less the same to me.'

'Do you know anyone who might be able to help me?'

'Ask around. You're from one of those charities, are you? Trying to help get them off the streets?'

'Something like that, yeah.'

Rita puts the drawing back into her pocket and finishes her coffee while the fat woman explains that nothing's like it used to be although, when you think about it, things have always been like this. When she was a girl, you never used to see foreigners around. Well, maybe a few Black women, one or two Poles, but not like it is now. Looking pensive, she wonders if the country is going to the dogs. On the TV, it's time for the morning news: a suit and tie, a war, a primary school, some cows, the Chinese. 'It's all about them now,' the bar owner notes, without any real anger. Could be worse . . .

Rita doesn't argue. She leaves with a grudging 'Thank you.' Outside the sun is higher in the sky and the air has started to warm up. She takes off her jacket, stretches. Time to go home now. She gets back behind the wheel. The bar owner, who's come outside to smoke a Vogue, gives a brief wave.

The pavements are still deserted and Kim Wilde's 'Cambodia' is playing on the radio. Rita comes to Strasbourg like this as often as she can, whenever she has time. She walks around, asks questions. Sometimes she wears a miniskirt. To start with, the girls would tell her to piss off if she didn't want her throat slashed. She shows them her crumpled drawing that doesn't even look that much like Victoria. They all think she must be a bit crazy. Sometimes she'll buy a drink for a girl who resembles the one she lost. Once, a man asked her to go up to his apartment. She followed him, just to see. He wasn't especially good-looking or especially ugly. She remembers that he spoke with a lisp, which made him seem harmless. In the end, though, she had to tell him to fuck off.

The light turns green and she slowly sets off. The Saab becomes a black stripe against the unlit shop windows. One morning like this, around dawn, she thought she saw Martel. Impossible, of course. She's going home now. She needs to get some sleep. Tomorrow's Monday, lots of work to do. There was an accident in the paper mill. Some guy was almost killed. Everyone feels bad about it. She turns up the volume. She's not sad. She keeps going.

NICOLAS MATHIEU

And Their Children After Them
Winner of the Prix Goncourt

'An exceptional portrait of youth, ennui and class divide'
John Boyne, *Irish Times*

'A lyrical, almost-Lawrentian saga of left-behind France'
Boyd Tonkin, *Spectator* Books of the Year

August 1992. Fourteen-year-old Anthony and his cousin
decide to steal a canoe to fight their all-consuming boredom
on a lazy summer afternoon. Their simple act of defiance will
lead to Anthony's first love and his first *real* summer – that
one summer that comes to define everything that follows.

Over four sultry summers in the 1990s, Anthony and
his friends grow up in a gritty France trapped between
nostalgia and decline, decency and rage, desperate to
escape their small town, the scarred countryside and grey
council estates, in search of a more hopeful future.

'Masterly'
Times Literary Supplement

'An elegiac anthem'
Financial Times

SCEPTRE

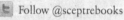
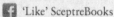
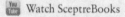